BITTER HONEY

BITTER HONEY

Lọlá Ákínmádé

HEAD of ZEUS

An Apollo Book

First published in the United Kingdom in 2025 by Head of Zeus,
part of Bloomsbury Publishing Plc

9 7 5 3 1 2 4 6 8

A catalogue record for this book is available from the British Library.

ISBN (HB): 9781804548172; ISBN (XTPB): 9781804548189
ISBN (E): 9781804548158

Cover design: Leah Jacobs-Gordon

Typeset by Siliconchips Services Ltd UK

Printed and bound in Great Britain by
CPI Group (UK) Ltd, Croydon, CR0 4YY

FSC
www.fsc.org

MIX
Paper | Supporting
responsible forestry
FSC® C013604

Bloomsbury Publishing Plc
50 Bedford Square, London, WC1B 3DP, UK
Bloomsbury Publishing Ireland Limited,
29 Earlsfort Terrace, Dublin 2, D02 AY28, Ireland

HEAD OF ZEUS LTD
5–8 Hardwick Street
London, EC1R 4RG

To find out more about our authors and books
visit www.headofzeus.com

For product safety related questions contact productsafety@bloomsbury.com

"The deepest well can also be drained."

Swedish proverb

"Because people use usable things."

Ida Sonko

For those who have never known rest,
may the soft life find you soon.

This book discusses issues of abandonment, infidelity, mental abuse, and nationalism.
It also depicts drug use.

PART ONE

ONE

TINA, 2006

She wonders how the sizzling-hot iron would feel against her eyes.

Would it first peel off the skin surrounding them? Would her irises melt into something viscous like honey and her pupils into black tar?

Tina absorbs her reflection in the vanity mirror, which is outlined with bulbous spotlights. The sharp shrill of her phone interrupts the macabre thoughts swirling around in her mind.

"*Grattis på din födelsedag,*" that familiar voice croons over her tiny flip phone. *Happy birthday.*

"*Hej, Mamma,*" Tina says, her nerves settling a little. "*Tusen tack.*" *Thousand thanks.*

"How does it feel to be twenty?" her mother Nancy asks, her tone more jovial than normal.

"No different." Tina adjusts the phone as a makeup artist dabs her bottom lip with neon-pink gloss.

"I can't wait to see you win tonight."

"I'm so nervous right now," Tina says. *Not like me,* she thinks as she banks her head to the left for rouge blush.

"You made it this far. Your nerves will settle, my dear."

3

"God, I hope so," Tina chuckles. "Look, please no *Nancy time*, okay? Tobias will pick you up at three. *Älska dig.*" *Love you.*

Tina hangs up. Picking Nancy up at three means she'll be ready by five. Even after twenty years of living here, her mother still refuses to bend to time.

"*Drottning,*"—*queen*—the makeup artist flatters after applying rose-gold glitter across her eyebrows. Tina assesses herself in the mirror. Dark eyeliner drawn into a cat-eye look framing honey-colored eyes, making them more piercing. Her reddish-brown tresses have been flat-ironed silky-straight. The artist has touched up her freckles, darkening the larger ones for effect.

Sweden's sweetheart. Pop sensation. Musical prodigy. ABBA's legacy rolled up into a single girl. The kind of accolades the national headlines have been sharing the last two years since she was discovered at a singing competition.

Tina sits cross-legged in black fishnets beneath denim shorts so skimpy they often invoke the sign of the cross. She's wearing a matching denim vest, unbuttoned with nothing else underneath. On the surface she sits a queen atop her stool, but beneath the glitter and nets, Tina's nerves are raw. The biggest night of her career thus far. A chance to win Sweden's beloved Melodifestivalen music competition, on her birthday no less, and potentially represent the country at the Eurovision Song Contest in May.

The song that got her here: an original Tina Wikström titled "Honey."

Two short verses and a sparse melodic refrain sung over and over until tears fall, taking black mascara with them. A part of her performance on stage, yet a glimpse of her pain off-stage inspired by eyes she'd inherited from a man she never knew. A man who never wanted to know her. A man who ran off to Gambia, leaving Tobias, a toddler, and her, a baby, behind.

Honey lies, honey dies, honey cries like the sun…

Honey mine, thine alone, rip this comb from my eyes…

She won a *Grammis*—the Swedish equivalent of a Grammy—for the song last February.

Tina mouths a few lyrics to calm her nerves. Stage rehearsals in an hour. Her dressing room is already drowning in a sea of birthday flowers. The largest is a statement bouquet from her Sebastian. She pulls a yellow gerbera daisy from his bunch and lifts it to her nose for a sniff. She knows he'll be there later tonight, cheering alongside a few of his mates from the national football team, signing autographs in between.

She reaches to put the flower back in place when she hears a light rap on her door. Her assistant Lotta pokes her head in with a look of resignation. Tina's heart skips.

"What's wrong?" Tina asks. The last thing she needs right now is that look Lotta is giving her.

"I'm sorry," Lotta begins to draft an apology. "I told him this was your night, but I couldn't stop him."

"Stop who?"

Lotta visibly swallows. "He—he says he's your father. He's got VIP access backstage. I checked his pass."

Tina freezes, her nails digging into her armrest. "What?" The words barely leave her.

Lotta falls silent. She lets the door open to reveal the man behind her, and Tina peers into eyes matching hers for the first time in her life.

Her breath catches.

"I told him not to," Lotta continues in her defense.

The man steps around her assistant and into the room. Tina's lips tighten as her amber glare blazes past Lotta to fully take him in. She watches emotions play across his face, his lips trembling, his brows arched upward. All that fiery hair. The cause of her pain, the taunts of *fire crotch* throughout high school. *It couldn't be, could it?*

"Tina," he starts to say, taking a step forward, a bouquet of lavender-colored lilies in hand.

Tina presses her lips tightly as tears begin to pool. No, her father was dead. Her father is dead. Uncle Leif and her mother had told them so. All these years. He can't be the man standing in front of her with matching freckles, honey-colored gaze, copper-hued hair. A middle-aged male version of herself.

Tina slowly rises to her feet, anger swiftly replacing her initial shock, her bedazzled nails sinking deeper into her armrest.

"Who are you?" she asks, her gaze cutting through him. "Who the fuck are you?"

She sees tears well up behind his eyes. He gasps audibly, his mouth hanging open before introducing himself.

Lars.

"Seeing you in person"—his voice shaky—"feels so unreal. How much you look like me." He starts to sob. "I wanted so much to be there for you, but she made me promise," he cries on, his hands death-gripping his flowers. "She made me promise never to contact you."

"Who?"

"Frida," the man says. He gasps once more and places a

hand over his mouth to compose himself before continuing. "Frida made me promise."

"Who the hell is Frida?" Tina demands.

They lock eyes before he exhales. "My wife."

The room descends into silence so heavy Tina feels her ears pop.

"All these years," the man croaks through his tears, "I've dreamed of meeting you. I've loved you and your brother from…"

"My father is dead," Tina snaps. "He died in Gambia." Her voice cracks. "He died in…"

"Nancy had to tell you that," he says. "To protect you from what I couldn't give you and Tobias." He pauses. "H-how is Nancy?"

Her mother and brother's names sound foul on the stranger's tongue.

"How dare you?" Tina whispers. "How dare you?"

"Please, Tina," he cries. "I just want to give these to you," he holds the bouquet of lilies forward, "to celebrate you. To let you know just how proud I am of you." His voice catches. "I know that song is about me."

"*Vad i helveete?!*" she curses. *What in the hell?!* "Get out of here." Tina's tone deepens. "Get the fuck out of here."

"I know your song is about me," he continues.

"You're so selfish," Tina cries. "So selfish," she chokes on her sobs, "on my biggest night."

"Tina…" Lotta chimes in.

"Fuck you too, Lotta." Tina points a gemstoned fingernail at her. "Get out of here. Both of you."

Once Lotta and the stranger leave, Tina falls back into her chair and ruins her mascara.

She misses her stage rehearsal, and finally emerges from her room disheveled, refusing any touch-ups. She walks slowly onto the stage to a cheering crowd which simmers down once her full look is projected onto screens across Globen arena. Tina stands while the entire arena waits with bated breath. Black mascara tracks already run down her face; her eyes are rimmed red.

She motions with a splayed hand to her band and backup dancers. Stop, that hand says. Only me, that hand says. She begins to sing a cappella. No backup vocals or dancing. No strumming. No drumming. The words pour out of her. Tina singing those words to *that man* somewhere in the audience.

Your honey is poison.

I don't want your honey.

She croons those last two lines, her voice trembling, to utter silence from an audience of over ten thousand souls.

There are a few seconds of quiet before Globen arena erupts in fiery cheers like a volcano.

Way past midnight.

Tina leans her chin on her arms folded across the edge of the indoor swimming pool. She had requested solitude from the hotel, who opened it up especially for her as a hearty congratulations. Beyond the occasional drip and gurgle of water, Tina rests silently in the pool with her thoughts, hoping the champagne wears off.

In the end it had been unanimous. Tina will be representing Sweden in Athens at Eurovision. She'd won their hearts with what everyone assumed had been her act, her audacious performance. Not the frightened little girl who had glimpsed a man claiming to be her dad for the first time since birth. She lays her head on her arms along the edge, her hair now plastered like mud down her back. By daybreak, it will spring back into bouncy coils.

She lets out air, collecting her thoughts. She hadn't even had enough time to fully take him in, in the flesh, before screaming at him to leave. What she'd seen was enough. Relatively tall and lean. Well kept for his age, clearly in his mid-sixties. Clean-shaven. Wrinkles fanning from the corners of his eagle eyes—her eyes. It was clear she was his. *Is his.* There may have been a few brushes of gray right above his ears, but there was no mistaking that mane. Her mamma always called it "terracotta-blood." Gambian soil bleeding red after rain.

One half of the double doors to the pool area creaks open. Tina recognizes that form.

Sebastian. Sebbe. Her *Seb.* He gingerly pads into the hall and assesses her from a distance.

"Who let you in?" Her voice carries over the length of the pool to him.

"Whoever knows you need me right now," he answers. She curses Lotta under her breath.

Sebastian strolls up to the edge, wearing white boxer briefs. She chuckles at his attire. He dives in and glides under the surface until he pops up right in front of her. He brushes his wet hair with a palm off his face as he peers down at her through piercing eyes.

"You've been watching too many movies with that lame move," she smirks.

He smiles and traps her between his arms as he rests his hands on either side of her along the edge.

9

"Is it working?" he whispers.

She holds his gaze. He leans in, brushing his lips featherlight over hers. She receives his caress, then presses her head against his chest. He lets her silently draw whatever she needs from him before mouthing the words, "I'm so sorry, *älskling*. Lotta told me."

Tina bursts into tears. "I hate him. I hate him so much."

Sebastian strokes her hair, soothing her as water ripples around them.

"Does Tobbe know?" he asks. Her older brother, Tobias. The only other person who will loathe Lars Wikström more than she does, once he finds out.

"I don't know," Tina mumbles before looking up into his eyes. "I want to forget him," she murmurs against his lips. Her hands roam underwater. He groans against her mouth. "Make me feel better, Seb."

"Tina," he says, drawing out her name, low and heady. "Are you sure?" He backs her against the edge with his weight. "*Älskling?*"

Tears film her eyes, drowning them, making them glow like quartz in that low-lit swimming hall.

She traces his lower lip with her thumb before whispering her permission.

TWO

NANCY, 1978

She feels the dampness of sweat beneath her two jackets. Her irrational attire was stoked by Aunty Yaya's pre-trip warning over the phone. *It's like entering deep freezer here*, she'd punctuated in broken English. Nancy is sure she is over-bundled.

"*Nancy!*" A bellow cuts through the low humdrum. Besides the shuffling of feet and dragging of wheels, the Arrivals section at Stockholm Arlanda Airport exudes solemn reverence reminiscent of a wake, rather than joyful reunions.

Aunty Yaya. Her *binki*. Her father's sister.

Nancy swivels toward the sound. She is immediately wrapped in a tight embrace.

"My dear Nancy." Aunty Yaya's mittened hands move to cup her face. "Look at you! Looking like a boy!" One hand sweeps over Nancy's buzz cut.

Nancy grins, flashing their family inheritance—that gap between their front teeth passed on through generations.

"You're looking more and more like my brother every day." Yaya's hand moves to her chin, giving it a quick flick. "Your first time on a plane," she beams at her. "*Kori tana te?*" *Hope you're fine?*

"I have no words, Aunty," Nancy giggles before launching into her arms again. Those giggles die into an awkward chuckle before they're replaced by sobs as her grip on Yaya tightens.

"*Kana dewuŋ.*" A warm mitten moves over her back, soothing her, overheating her beneath the jackets. *Don't worry.* "It's okay, your aunty is here."

A few minutes later, Nancy pushes a cart bearing three leather suitcases behind Yaya, who scurries ahead, giving Nancy time to size her up. A long russet-brown calf-length coat, thick mittens with only the outline of thumbs, a round white-and-taupe fur hat, hips wider than the last time she saw her in Banjul.

Aunty Yaya had come home two years prior to introduce the family to the man who now pops out of a wood-paneled rectangular-looking station wagon as they approach, a wide smile etched across his round face.

Mr. Benke. Benke Larsson. Her white uncle.

That first meeting would go down in Ndow family history. Yaya pulling a ruddy-faced dashiki-wearing man with pink cheeks and the brightest green eyes into the parlor where Nancy's father, Omar, was tucking into his fish *benachin*.

Her parents froze for a full minute after Aunty Yaya introduced him, then her *baabaa* uttered, "*Mune mu ñiŋ ti?!*"
What is this?!

Even for her father, a Muslim who had gone against tradition and married her mother from the Aku tribe of Christians, bringing Benke into the family was too much. Nancy had followed her mother into her faith, while Lamin remained Muslim like their father.

"Is that Nancy?!" Benke guffaws, rounding the car and pulling her into a crushing hug. Then he holds her at arm's length to properly assess her. She gives him a weak smile. "Yes, it's you!" he exclaims. "You cut your hair?"

"*Benke, hjälp henne!*" Yaya motions for him to help with her bags. Benke grabs them, loads two into the trunk, and heaves one onto the roof before tying it down with cables.

Soon, they're hurtling down the highway, Nancy's face pressed against the frigid window. Rolling hills lightly dusted with snow like the powdered sugar her mother always sprinkled specially on her own *pankeet*—beignets. She'd done her homework. Frost, snow, ice, winter, Scandinavia. Cars whizz by. Hers and Yaya's are the only dark faces, kilometer after kilometer.

Benke and Yaya are deep in conversation. Swedish. Since receiving the news of her scholarship three months ago and once her mother's screams of elation had died down, Nancy had rushed over to the National Library in Banjul to find any book she could about her new home. There were two children's books: the first was *Pippi Långstrump*, about a girl with impossibly red hair that resembles a cross between terracotta and blood. That hair color was not conceivable on a living human being, Nancy decided. Dots splashed across her cheeks and nose. *Freckles.*

The second children's book featured a brown bear wearing blue. *Bamse.* He grows stronger whenever he eats honey. This she deduced, since both books were in Swedish.

The third book she found was an English-to-Swedish dictionary.

All three "borrowed" books now lie in her soft tan portmanteau sitting on the fur-lined backseat of the station wagon next to her. Her presence is forgotten as Benke and Yaya continue their chat. She reaches for the box; pops open its latch and pulls out her dictionary.

She fingers its well-worn pages. The first few hold basic conversational phrases—*My name is. How are you. I am fine.*—before delving into the alphabets.

She has been memorizing those phrases for months. So, when Benke and Yaya fall silent at her next words—*Vart ska vi? Where are we going?*—it's a reticence filled with pride.

Where is Benke's apartment in a neighborhood called Odenplan, he explains. An apartment that once belonged to his grandfather and was passed down, otherwise he would never be able to afford it on his bank clerk's salary.

Nancy steps in with trepidation. Low light, heavy furniture, the likes of which she'd seen at the National Museum back home. Chandelier with glittering crystals; she isn't sure if they are real or not. She doesn't want to touch anything and instantly feels out of place. She notices that Yaya pads around her own house with trepidation too, and Nancy wonders if her aunt has fully processed this new life.

"There is your room." Yaya points down the hall and Nancy follows her finger to the right. "Clean up and come join us in the kitchen. Benke is making food. You'll find towels." With that, the massive apartment swallows Yaya up.

It takes Nancy five minutes to figure out how to balance both hot and cold water from the shower. Pride keeps her fiddling with those knobs. Back home, one full kettle of hot water was poured into a pail with four times the quantity of that kettle in cold water. Perfect balance every single time.

Nancy sponges her buzz cut with a lavender-scented bar of soap. She'd done her homework. She wasn't sure about salons or hairdressers in this land, where people simply shake their hair and go. She figured cutting her hair would give her at least six months to figure out her regular beauty routines. She moves the sponge over perky breasts and a flat stomach, over the shimmering dark cocoa skin she nourishes daily with pure shea butter. She feels that familiar shudder as emotions bubble to the surface. Her plump lips crumble as tears flood her eyes.

At twenty years old, she has never been more scared in her life. Not even when she was shipped off to boarding school in Kwantu village at ten years old. Not even when robbers stormed their property once Benke had left, asking for whatever gifts the white man had brought for the family. Not even when her older brother Lamin caught yellow fever, and they were on the verge of losing him.

Nancy sobs as she wipes off foam, and yelps when the shower grows too hot.

Right now, she stands in an unfamiliar lavender-infused bubble thousands of kilometers away from home.

And all she wants is her mother.

THREE

TINA, 2006

Five ten a.m.

Tina lies under a heavy white plush duvet at the hotel on the dark March morning post-Melodifestivalen win. After an hour in the pool with Sebastian making her feel better as requested, they came back to her room to finish off.

She gazes at him from under her covers as he pulls sweatpants from a large duffel bag emblazoned with the Swedish flag on both sides and slips them on. He's sitting on the edge of the bed, tying the laces of his sneakers. She catches the muscles in his toned back straining as he works and resists the urge to kiss down its groove. He seems ridiculously perfect.

Heartthrob athlete. Part-time underwear model. Her high school sweetheart. *Snygg Sebbe*, as his fans love to chant.

Five years in, they remain inseparable.

He was born in the northern suburb of Täby often associated with wealth but ended up in Norsborg—where she was born and still shares an apartment with both her mamma and brother. An eleventh-floor perch in a sand-toned apartment block in their complex of similarly colored blocks. A government-assigned space part of the *Miljonprogrammet*, the social democrats' ambition of building a million living quarters to provide affordable public housing.

Sebastian's family had netted one of those apartments too. She'd wondered how this golden boy had ended up in her hood—if his parents had been trying to save money, or if they simply had no choice. He stuck out like a chunk of potato in a bowl of kidney beans.

The first time she laid eyes on him as a teenager was when she found him cowering in a corner, both eyes swollen shut behind bruises, with a bloodied lip and the skittishness of a frightened kitten.

Those well-meaning apartments have segregated the city more and more with each passing decade.

Seb turns to take her in, his bright eyes twinkling in the lowlight.

"*Du är så jävla vacker*," he whispers, his gaze roaming her face before traveling down her exposed torso. *You're so fucking beautiful.*

She chuckles at his compliment, her head propped up on her palm. "Admiring your work in my afterglow?"

"*Fan*," he curses softly, then leans in for a kiss. "I wish I didn't have to go to practice." He traces his tongue over her lower lip.

"You have a World Cup to win," she teases against his mouth. He tugs her toward him with another kiss, his right hand beginning to roam.

"Promise you'll be there? In Germany?" He pulls back to peer at her and morphs into his teenage version with that look. A boy looking for validation in her gaze.

Tina responds with a possessive kiss. He takes over and shifts his weight. She playfully pushes him aside.

"I don't want Lagerbäck calling me up because you're late for practice," she scolds, thinking of his coach. Seb lets out an exaggerated sigh and launches off the bed. He pulls on a jersey then settles strands of whipped-butter-colored hair back in place.

"I'm a spare," he says, lifting the duffel bag onto his shoulder. "I'm not Freddie or Henke. Definitely not Zlatan," he adds under his breath.

"But you're on the team." Tina holds his gaze. "You're not a spare, you're a star."

She catches his nostrils flaring as he presses his lips together. A shy gesture of pride.

He bends low to seal a kiss on her forehead and pushes a few curls, still slightly damp from the pool and their sweat, behind her ear. "*Lycka till idag, älskling,*" he mutters before leaving her room.

Good luck today, darling.

Once he leaves, Tina grabs a pillow and screams into it.

It will start all over again today. A makeup artist will arrive to spruce her up before she appears on a morning show at national TV station SVT to discuss her win at Melodifestivalen. Then a series of press interviews for major newspapers *Dagens Nyheter, Svenska Dagbladet, Expressen,* another press conference at Kulturhuset for both domestic and foreign journalists, including the BBC, radio shows including P4, and two more evening shows.

She knew her life was going to change when she won the televised talent show that launched her onto Melodifestivalen's stage. She hadn't realized how immediate it was going to be. Little blond girls giggled shyly, their faces flushing red whenever she walked down Stockholm's streets. Little brown girls took more brazen steps forward to ask for selfies, all wide-toothed grins, seeing their older selves reflected in her.

Her assistant had arranged a dinner reservation later, so she could meet with her mother and brother to tell them about the man who showed up because he was feeling guilty. *Lars Wikström.*

By the time Lotta arrives with a makeup artist in tow, concerned Tina refused to open her door for room service breakfast, they find her with a puffy face and red-rimmed eyes.

Grattis Tina! Grattis! Snyggt jobbat! Stjärna!
Congratulations Tina! Congrats! Well done! Star!

Those words, yelled by strangers from other tables, form a tunnel around Tina as she makes her way toward the back corner of Brasserie Riche in Stockholm's glitzy Östermalm district. Her table is out of earshot. Enough privacy, as requested.

"I could have cooked rice at home," are Nancy's first words upon Tina's approach. Nancy casually glances around the eatery, her eyes washing over each group of diners, all white. She pats her thick, short Afro before turning back to her daughter. Tobias chuckles, showing the small gap between his front teeth he inherited from Nancy, his grin narrowing his eyes into slits like their mother's. Low-cropped reddish-brown hair, freckled face, dark-brown eyes. Three years older than Tina. A head turner.

Nancy's brows crumble when Tina peels off her sunglasses. "*Gumman?*"—*Sweetie?*—"What's wrong?"

Tobias is instantly on his feet, pulling Tina into his broad swimmer's chest, embracing her. Tina bursts into tears and Nancy pushes onto her feet as well to stroke her back in comfort. The waiter, standing close by with a white napkin draped across an arm, takes a few steps back to give them some privacy.

When Tina pulls out of Tobias's hug, he cups her face between his wide palms, locks eyes.

"Tina? Är allt okej? Är det Seb?" he prods.

She shakes her head, glancing around, self-conscious.

"Please let's sit before they think we're causing a scene," Tina says, pulling away from him and grabbing a chair.

"What's wrong?" Nancy's voice takes on a reprimanding tone. "What is all this drama about?"

"Mamma?!" Tobias starts. Nancy dismisses him with a flick of her hand.

"He came to see me," Tina says after gathering her breath.

"Who?" Nancy asks.

"Him." Tina lets the word settle as she glares at her mother. *Liar.* If their relationship was already fraught before, knowing that Nancy has been lying all these years threatens to sever it altogether.

Nancy's nostrils flare as Tina reads her face, realization settling in.

Tina continues, "A man who looked just like me." She pauses for effect. "Hmm, Mamma?"

"Your father." Nancy finally understands, her eyebrows arching upward.

Tina turns to see Tobias's face as he leans back into his chair at their mother's words, his forehead crumpled with emotion.

"Don't call him that," Tina hisses at Nancy. "Don't you dare call that stranger that. He died in Gambia. You told us he died there."

She watches her normally calm mother shift uncomfortably in her seat, while throwing a quick glance over her shoulder. Tina turns to Tobias, who seems frozen at the revelation.

Nancy swivels back to her daughter. "When? Did he come to your hotel? What did he want?" The words pour out breathlessly.

"What?!" Tobias's first words since the news. "What are you talking about, Mamma?"

"Before the show," Tina says. "Before my performance. He said he was proud of me and wanted to come support me."

"Wait, wait, Mamma?" Tobias interjects. "Pappa is alive?"

Nancy reaches for a brioche bun instead of answering.

"So, it was real?" Tobias says to Tina. "Your tears, your look on stage?"

Tina nods. Nancy tears a piece of bread and pops it into her mouth.

"Mamma?" Tobias waits for an answer.

She addresses Tina instead. "What did he want? Why is he reaching out now?" Nancy nonchalantly picks at her bread, not looking at either of them.

Tina's heart sinks, her mother confirming what she'd already suspected the minute she'd looked into the man's eyes. Once he'd left her dressing room, she had pulled out her laptop to search for him via Yahoo. *Lars "Lasse" Wikström*. A semi-famous artist known for his suggestive paintings. Living publicly right under their noses for close to two decades.

My father is dead.

When Tina doesn't answer, Nancy asks again, "What did he want from you?" This time there's an edge to her voice.

Tina stares at her mother as tears drown her eyes, silently accusing Nancy.

Liar.

"Don't you get it?" Tobias turns to Nancy, exasperated. "Tina is a star. He wants to claim her now. *Jäveln!*" *The bastard.* "Get a restraining order against him."

"So, Frida is dead, then?" Nancy drops, a hint of humor to her tone.

Tina and Tobias pivot sharply toward her. Tina hardens at the name *Frida.* All slivers of doubt evaporate.

"A married man, Mamma? Don't you dare make excuses for him and yourself." Tina grits the words between clenched teeth, finding her voice. "Why did you lie to us?"

"I know, I know." Nancy shrugs her shoulders. "But you know, she told him never to contact us. Never to contact you."

"He's a grown man!" Tobias seethes. "He could have taken responsibility if he wanted to."

Tina recognizes her own anger and sadness in her brother, a confluence of emotions. "So, Pappa was alive all these years?"

Nancy exhales audibly. She gathers herself. "He abandoned us. He had to make a choice." She pauses for effect. "So, he chose his wife and children."

"Why didn't he choose us?" Tobias chimes in.

"It's not that easy, my dear," Nancy explains. "You know

your father's people. They don't like to stand out. You're outcast from society the minute you make the slightest mistake."

"We're mistakes?" Tina's voice bristles.

Nancy holds her gaze. "No, my dear. You are my blessings. What Lars and I had was a mistake. We should never have crossed that line."

"So loving an African woman was wrong? A mistake?" Tina's voice is sharp.

Nancy sighs. "Loving a woman who isn't your wife is wrong," she explains. "Frida tried to save their marriage, his career, his image. I don't blame her."

"At what cost?" Tobias spits. "Robbing him of his relationship with us? Why did you tell us he was dead?"

"It's complicated. He didn't love her," Nancy explains. "He never did." Tina notices her mother evading the question, a tactic she has often used over the years.

"Why marry someone you don't love?!" Tobias asks, his eyebrows now dipping inwards, rage finally winning the battle within him.

"My dear Tobias," Nancy turns to him with shimmering eyes, "his parents were tired of him jumping around Gambia in the name of research. They wanted him back home on Swedish soil." She pauses. "With a Swedish girl."

"So, what? They forced him to marry Frida?" Tina jumps in. "Why are you still absolving him of any responsibility?"

Nancy pulls a face, clearly tired of their interrogation.

"He looked so much older than you when I saw him," Tina adds.

She catches her mother's wince. Nancy takes a bite of bread, chews to her children's silence, then continues.

"He was my professor," Nancy confesses.

"What?" they gasp in unison.

"Twenty years older than me—but did not look his age." Nancy bites off more bread. "All that Pippi Longstocking hair and freckles"—she chews—"and Bamse honey eyes," she chuckles beneath her breath. Then her gaze turns to Tina. Nancy's eyes roam her features, her face. Tina watches her mother purse her lips before turning back to her bread.

"What the fuck are you talking about, Mamma?" Tina exclaims.

"Don't use that tone with me," Nancy reprimands sternly. "The world is easier for you now. You can do and say whatever you want. Things were tougher back then."

"Spare me." Tobias reaches for his own brioche bun and tears it apart. He grabs soft brown butter and starts spreading it aggressively.

"You don't understand," Nancy starts. "Once is a mistake." She pauses, then looks at Tina. "Twice means love." She exhales audibly. "That is too much for any wife to bear."

"Then why did you do it?" Tobias drops his bun and glares at his mother. "Why did you carry on for so long with that man?"

"If I hadn't, you wouldn't have been born." Nancy's voice breaks with emotion.

"Bullshit." It's Tina this time around. "Maybe Tobias was a mistake. But I was a choice. You knew exactly what you were doing and what would happen. You liar!"

The tension around their table is palpable. Tina notices Nancy twisting her lips, probably trying to prevent tears. It hadn't been her intention to upset her. It must feel raw for Nancy too.

"If he didn't want to choose us, I had to kill his memories," Nancy starts. "I never knew he was married with children until I had Tobias." Her voice breaks but she holds her composure. "He promised me he was divorcing Frida and that they were already separated," she says, before turning to Tina. "Then we had you."

"So, we have older half-siblings somewhere?" Tobias's tone is low and terse. "The real Wikströms?" He pauses. "And you never got tired of lying to us all these years? You and Uncle Leif?"

Tina processes her brother's words. Older siblings? More sisters or brothers, maybe both, somewhere? All living in the same country, probably unaware of each other?

"Did you bring me here to accuse me?" Nancy raises her voice. "*Ehn?* I could have stayed at home and cooked in my own house. But you bring me here to embarrass me in a fancy place."

"*Sluta, Mamma.*" Tina urges her to stop.

"You think this was my wish for you? To not have a father all these years?"

"You could have picked an available father." Tobias laughs scornfully.

"The heart wants what it wants, or else it does not care," Nancy says. "Emily Dickinson. American poet."

"Really, Mamma? You're quoting poetry now?" Tina hisses.

Nancy repeats those words again. "The heart wants what

it wants, or else it does not care." She holds Tina's gaze. "You of all people should understand that."

"Are we at this again? Talking about Seb?" Tina lets out a strained laugh. "I know you've never liked him." She points to her brother. "Never mind that Tobbe only dates white girls."

"It's none of my business." Nancy nonchalantly reaches for another bun. "You picked him out of all the available boys."

"Of all the available boys?" Tina parrots her. "You mean of all the available Black and Brown boys? And why are you not asking about Tobbe's girlfriend? Fucking double standards."

Nancy shrugs her shoulders and takes a bite of buttered bread. "You children are watching too much American TV with all that foul language." She frowns at Tina. "That boy is going to derail you from your dreams," she adds.

"Derail me?" Tina furrows her brows at her mother. "Now you're just projecting."

"Mamma, you are the queen of deflection," Tobias chimes in. "Now we're talking about Seb while you continue to protect that *jäveln*."

"That's enough." Nancy's voice comes on hard. "Stop calling your father a bastard."

"He is not my father," Tobias yells, his fist hitting the table so hard it sends cutlery shifting in disarray. Chatter from nearby tables sinks at his outburst.

This must be why Lars reached out to her first, not Tobias. He probably thought she, as a woman, would be easier to prey on emotionally. She was probably the easiest and, quite frankly, weakest link in their tight-knit trio. Lars

Wikström must have known that reaching out to Tobias would land him in a coffin. And he clearly doesn't have the audacity to reach out to the woman he didn't choose. Is Tina really that weak? she wonders. Is that what people see when they interact with her or see her face projected across screens? Is she easy to sway because she has one unsteady foot each in both worlds—black and white—rather than two firm feet?

"He stayed away because he loved you," Nancy continues, breaking her thoughts. "When you were younger, he sent money to take care of you. Of us."

"Money is not love," Tobias fumes. "Sending money to take care of your children is the bare minimum." Tobias turns to Tina. "What did he want from you?"

"He just said he was proud of me and that he knows my song was about him," she sighs.

"Oh, a narcissist too," Tobias adds, tossing his napkin onto the table.

An unfamiliar voice breaks their conversation. All three turn to find their waiter stepping out of the shadows.

"M-may I take your order?" he asks after clearing his throat.

FOUR

NANCY, 1979

Pippi's terracotta-blood hair. Dots in a darker shade splashed across his face. Eyes the color of Bamse's honey behind large frames. In living flesh, scribbling words on a chalkboard in front of her anthropology class, one of the courses she needs for her degree. The class of eighteen students listens as chalk screeches across that board for what feels like a full minute.

She'd assumed those colors were reserved for children's fantasy books.

Nancy arrived at the tail end of 1978 in the throes of winter, to start at Stockholm University come January. International relations with a minor in political science. Her *baabaa*, Omar, had shrugged his shoulders at her choice, since he wasn't the one paying for it. Fatou, her *naa*, had simply expressed her desire to see her only daughter on the path to becoming Gambia's first female president someday. As for her only sibling, her older brother, Lamin, they haven't spoken since she received that letter from Sweden. She wonders how long it takes jealousy to leave one's system.

Lars "Lasse" Wikström, Socialantropologi.

The bespectacled children's book protagonist stops scribbling and swivels back to face his class. She takes in his attire. A thick beige sweater that covers his neck, wraps his tall lean frame, and falls past his hip. Mahogany-brown trousers which flare out at his ankles and look corduroy in texture.

She's craning to assess his well-worn fawn leather boots when the perfect pronunciation of her name startles her.

"Ndow? Nancy?"

Seventeen pairs of eyes from fellow students pivot toward her, pinning her in place. None look like hers. A few people use the opportunity to scan her once more. Her close-cropped hair, her dark skin, her modest sweater dress with boots she borrowed from Yaya.

"You must be one of mine," he sing-songs in English with a distinct melodic lilt, before clearing his throat, his cheeks flushing pink. "I mean, my mentees from Gambia." He pauses for effect. "*Naka nga deff?*" *How are you?* he asks her in Wolof, a grin surfacing, clearly trying to impress her.

Nancy remains quiet. He presses on. "This class will be conducted in Swedish, but the university has made extra provisions for foreign students who might need special assistance while they learn Swedish to keep up with coursework." Nancy listens, peering at him. "My anthropology expertise and research cover the Gambia and Senegal. So, I have you and one other student, Malik from *Satey Ba*."

That grin reappears on his face; he's seeking validation of his knowledge of her land. Nancy ignores it. *Satey Ba*. Their local nickname for one of Gambia's largest cities, Brikama. Clearly Professor Lasse has done his research. She's seen his type crisscrossing Banjul in *too-short* shorts, rubber flip-flops and flowing long hair, learning all they wanted, flashing those grins at local women, returning home as experts on her country, while leaving their spawn behind.

So, she isn't easily impressed.

"Please stay behind for a few minutes so I can explain more, okay?"

She nods at him, then murmurs, *"Tana te"* in Mandinka, her own tongue, in response to his first question. *I'm fine.* Professor Wikström pauses, probably trying to decipher her words.

"Okej, välkomna allihopa!" *Okay, welcome everyone!*

With those words and a clap, he begins to lecture in unintelligible Swedish. It's the longest forty-five minutes of her life.

She'll catch up someday, Nancy knows she will. She's been registered for intensive Swedish classes alongside her core courses. But this buoyant feeling, this moorlessness. It's disorienting. She feels disembodied in this place where she can count fellow Africans she has seen so far on one hand and the melodic lilt swirling around her feels like drowning in deep water.

So, once Lars waves his hand in dismissal, she quickly pops open her portmanteau, shoves her books and pencils into it, and rushes to her feet. At close range, she sees him more clearly, though his coloring isn't any less jarring to her. Slight wrinkles at the corners of his eyes intimate that he's older than she initially estimated, his freckles maintaining his youthful appearance.

"Nancy." Lars's grin reappears as he settles his hands on his hips, stretching to his full height. To any observer, they probably looked like the number eighteen, standing next to each other. "I'm sure that lecture went over your head, but don't worry. On Fridays, I will be doing a high-level weekly summary in English for both you and Malik." His tone is jovial, light, fatherly.

"Thank you," she says weakly. His gaze holds hers as he smiles, and she banks her head away awkwardly.

"They only use their eyes to communicate," Yaya had said during an impromptu cultural lesson over the dill-baked salmon and potatoes Benke had cooked for them. "No hands or arms. Their bodies stand stiff. So, keep looking straight into their eyes, even if it makes you uncomfortable." Yaya had mimed, with two fingers pointing toward her own eyes, before spearing salmon with her fork.

Nancy turns her eyes back to Lars. His hands leave his hips as if unsure what to do with them.

"Okay," he finds his voice. "Come back here on Friday at ten for our English summary." One hand moves to readjust his wide-framed, maroon-tinted glasses. "As your mentor as well as your professor, my job is to help you integrate. Help you understand the culture, so..." He pauses. "I'm here whenever you need me, okay?" He claps his hands.

She nods before turning to leave.

"*N be i je la sambiŋ.*" His next words stop her in her tracks. Fluent Mandinka. She spins back around, her eyes widening, taking all of him in. He repeats those words with a grin of pride etched across his face.

See you soon.

Later that evening, Nancy pushes diced potatoes, tiny bits of beef, and onions around her plate, the antique-looking dining room cloaked in silence, Benke watching as she barely eats.

"You don't like it?" he asks, his fork midway to his mouth.

He's still dressed in his work clothes. Short-sleeved lightly checkered shirt and a tight burgundy tie loosely hanging around his neck. "It's called *pytt-i-panna. Small pieces in a pan*." He chuckles at the translation. "Not very creative," he adds. "Do you have something similar in Gambia?"

She shakes her head, answering both his questions at once.

It's past ten and Yaya isn't home yet. Since moving to stay with Yaya and Benke a month ago, Nancy quickly realized there's daily toil behind her *binki*'s roar of positivity. Her facade carried itself flawlessly all the way to Banjul via letters and occasional phone calls. Yaya was probably working harder than she needed to as *hemtjänst*—home service for the elderly, injured and disabled.

Benke's modest bank clerk's salary was enough for them, Yaya had told her. After all, they had zero rent or mortgages to pay for Benke's heirloom apartment. Like her mother, Fatou (who subsisted on her father's professor salary so she could run the household), Yaya didn't need to work, but she wanted to.

"There are different kinds of privilege in this world," Yaya had proclaimed over a dinner of tasteless baked cod cooked by Benke. "The privilege of a man who cooks for his wife and the privilege of a wife who doesn't need to work but wants to. Especially when that husband is old like mine." She added her signature chuckle, a tongue-protruding, deep roar that always caught its audience by surprise. At sixty-five, Benke was fifteen years Yaya's senior.

"How was school?" Benke tries switching topics, his face flushing with color.

Nancy shrugs. "It was challenging. I didn't understand

a word of what my professor said." Lars flashes across her mind. "But I think he speaks both Wolof and Mandinka. His pronunciations were quite good."

"Really?" Benke says. She reads what looks like genuine shock, maybe envy, in his eyes.

Nancy nods. "He teaches anthropology. His research work was on Gambia. He has been assigned as my mentor."

"Really?" Benke asks again, and this time his voice dips. Nancy glares at Benke, who still can't speak a lick of her language.

It took Yaya four years to get comfortably fluent in Swedish. "You're smarter than me," she once said. "You'll learn it in one year."

"Yes," Nancy says before turning back to pushing her *pytt-i-panna* around and descending into silence once more.

Ten minutes later, they both hear the keys turning the lock. Yaya shuffles in, her shoulders slumped. She sheds her layers of warm clothing, hangs them where they need to go, and saunters toward the dining hall where Benke and Nancy sit.

Benke asks her something in Swedish, the cadence indicating concern about her day. She pulls out a chair, hefts herself onto it, audibly sighing.

"One of my clients died today," she says. "And she has no family, no children, no one we could call on her behalf." She stares off into the distance, her eyes focusing nowhere in particular. Lost in her thoughts. Then she swivels sharply toward her husband.

"Benke, I want children."

Benke's fork falls out his hand and hits his plate, the clanking sound vibrating through the wide room.

"Yaya," he starts. "We have children. *Bonus barn.*" He mentions two names—children from his previous marriage. This is the first time Nancy has heard those names. Their photos don't grace Yaya and Benke's walls or shelves. They never mention those names inside this apartment.

Nancy never even knew Benke had children.

"Your children don't like me. Their African stepmother!" Yaya spits back with an edge to her voice. "I want my own children."

"You're fifty," Benke tries to reason with her.

"I serve a God of miracles," she insists. "I want children."

FIVE

TINA, 2006

Rule number one of newfound celebrity: *Don't you as much as whisper about private issues in public*— especially not where waiters lurk in shadows, because the morning after Tina's heated dinner with her family, the tabloid *Expressen* ran a dramatic headline:

Drama på Riche. Stjärna Tina i tårar.

Drama at Riche. Star Tina in tears.

The article goes on to detail, almost play by play, what had happened at their dinner table.

The "*scandalous affair*" between an African woman and her professor-turned-artist, Lars "Lasse" Wikström.

The martyr wife "*Frida*" who tried to save her marriage and hold her family together.

The African "*refugee*" who must have tricked him into bearing Swedish children. Is Tina even truly Swedish?

The song "Honey" is about him.

He has never seen his children.

They even drag Sebastian's name into the piece; heartthrob "*Snygg Sebbe*" still isn't good enough for Tina.

"Everything we discussed," Tina's voice cracks. "Every single thing."

Tobias races his fingers across his forehead, trying to think.

"What are we going to do now?" He isn't asking so much as wondering aloud how they'll navigate their new reality, Tina is sure of it.

And her dear Seb? She has been fiercely protecting their love since she found him beaten up as a teenager, but the media have now dragged him into her messy battle too.

"I told you I should have cooked at home," is all Nancy says, her eyes never leaving her toes, which she is nonchalantly painting on the coffee table.

Tina's assistant, who she now designates the bearer of bad news, had rushed over to their apartment that morning with a copy of the newspaper. Well, Nancy's apartment in Norsborg.

Tina flips through the pages of the paper. An eight-page spread had been created out of nothing, speculating on who Tina's real father was.

"*Your father is dead!*" Tina remembers Nancy screaming those words at her one Christmas when she was six years old. She'd been watching a festive show, longingly poring over dads shoveling snow and setting up lights. Uncle Leif had traveled somewhere to spend Christmas with someone else. Up until then, Uncle Leif had never missed Christmas with them. She had asked her mother when her own father was going to come back from Gambia.

In hindsight, she now realizes Nancy never delivered information with warmth or understanding. *Your father is dead.*

Tina flips to a page that stuns her into silence. A double-page spread. On the left, her full mugshot. On the right, the full mug of the man that had come to see her in her dressing room. The large title, spanning both pages in Swedish, read, "*The musician and her muse.*" Reminiscent of a human anatomy book pointing out limbs, there were pull quotes and lines connecting their features, the curve of their noses, the freckles fanning across their cheeks and the bridges of their noses, the similar outline of their lips. Tina's are much fuller.

Though the article is speculative, her resemblance to the renowned oil painter is undeniable. No DNA tests are needed to prove their connection; her mother had already confirmed it over dinner at Riche.

"What the fuck?" Tina mutters before ripping both pages out and starting to shred them. Tobias lurches for the pages before she turns them into confetti. He straightens out Lars's crumpled face, scans the text, his features hardening.

"Lasse Wikström," Tobias reads out loud. "The artist." He turns to Nancy. "The artist? The millionaire artist?" Nancy shrugs her shoulders and continues to silently paint her nails.

Tina thinks about their last name. *Wikström.* "Was *Farbror* Leif his brother?" she asks.

Nancy looks up, her eyes intense. "Let your uncle rest in peace."

Tobias curses and throws the creased page to the ground. He growls in frustration.

Tina picks up the piece and stares into Lars's eyes once more. She'd heard of the artist but never followed his work. She'd never cared to investigate him herself. Yes, he was also red-haired and had the same last name, but there were dozens of men named "Lars Wikström" in Sweden and, as her mother had said, her own father was long dead.

Maybe it had been clear as day and she hadn't wanted to look into him, because knowing he was out there on an international stage, but not wanting to see her and Tobias, would have been too much for her heart to take.

New emotions begin to swirl within her, and they border on loathing.

Hard pounding on the door causes Nancy to yelp. "Who wants to break down my door?!" she yells.

Lotta rushes to open it, and Seb enters the room.

"Ah, Snygg Sebbe," Tobias greets him, his tone flat. "So, you've heard? *Sweden's hottest player still isn't spicy enough for Miss Tina.*"

Sebastian hisses at him before beelining for Tina, pulling her into a hug. "*Älskling.*"

"I'm gonna sue Riche and that waiter," she growls into his hug. "I'm gonna sue."

"But you know you can't prove it was the waiter," Seb says.

She pushes out of his embrace. "Aren't you supposed to make me feel better? *Gud!*"

"Sorry," he apologizes. "I don't know what to say."

"This is a complete shitshow." Tina runs fingers through her straightened hair. "Now I'm no longer trustworthy." For a Swede, she knows a lack of trust is the hardest weight to bear. The most damning part is the revelation that Tina Wikström's father isn't dead as she'd previously said in interviews. Unbeknown to her, the name written on her birth certificate is Leif Wikström; a man they had called

Farbror Leif—Uncle—while growing up. Nancy had finally confessed this to them over *that* dinner.

They hear someone singing. *"Praising the Lord... always..."* The three of them turn to stare at Nancy, who is now humming a tune as she continues painting her nails.

SIX

NANCY, 1979

Nancy observes him from the slightly ajar door of the classroom. Her fellow countryman.

He waits with muscular arms folded across his chest, leaning back in his chair, a resting resignation etched across his face. He sports a three-inch Afro and his skin is smooth.

She pushes the door open, and his gaze moves toward her. He gets to his feet. *A gentleman too*, Nancy notes. She does a quick scan. Tall, sturdy, two shades darker than she is, easy on the eyes.

"Nancy? *Naka suba si! Sama tur Malik la*," he reels off in Wolof. *Good morning. My name is Malik*. "I hope you speak Wolof too. Professor Lasse told me all about you," he continues breathlessly.

She wonders aloud what her professor could have told Malik about her, since she has only met him once. "That you're Mandinka," he responds. Malik's eyes sweep her length, over her maroon turtleneck flared dress, settling back on her low-cropped hair. "My hair *cannot* be longer than yours," he adds jovially.

She flashes her gap-toothed smile, and he returns a blindingly white one. "*Enchanté*," she responds. She settles into the chair next to him under his gaze. Once she's seated, her portmanteau resting by her feet, he slides back onto his own chair.

"So, what brings you to Sweden?" he asks.

"A scholarship. International relations with a minor in political science."

"So, you want to be a diplomat?" He chuckles.

"My *naa* thinks *Madame President* will suit me better," she retorts, her voice light.

"Trust me, the life of a diplomat is overrated. That's why I'm here."

"Really?" she prods while adjusting in her seat.

"My father is the ambassador." He puffs his chest outward. "I'm studying economics. Not planning to follow in his footsteps."

"So, you've lived all over the world?" Nancy asks in awe. Her first time on a plane had been to Stockholm on a returning Vingresor chartered flight that had already dropped off Swedes in the Gambia for winter.

"London, Paris, Cairo," he rattles off. "My favorite was London. Have you been anywhere else?"

"My life isn't as exciting as yours," she says.

"Says who?" He flashes that blinding grin. "Tell me."

"Only Banjul," she shares. "I haven't even been to Brikama. *Satey Ba.*"

"Ahh," Malik launches into faux drama. "Then I have so much to teach you."

"Who says I want to learn from you?"

He chuckles. "Nancy, Nancy, Nancy." She loves the sound of her name on his lips. "So, how is your family?"

"They're fine, thank you. One older brother. *Baabaa* is a professor and *Naa* a homemaker. And you?"

"Too many siblings to count." Malik's laugh booms, filling up the small room. "At least two or three in every city we were stationed. My mother quit her nursing job to travel with my father."

"And your full siblings?"

"Two younger sisters in boarding school in Switzerland. I know. Don't judge me. That's the life of us diplomats."

Nancy studies him. A wealthy African man flippant about his lot in life. He's wearing a wrinkle-free black long-sleeved shirt tucked into chestnut-brown corduroy pants and darker brown boots. On his wrist glitters a gold watch and around his neck there's a thin gold necklace.

She takes in his musky, spicy scent. Malik looks and smells like money. The kind of man Fatou prays every day for her daughter to land; one who will take care of her financially. Fatou also prays for Nancy's future run of independence as Madame President, so Nancy isn't sure which prayer to take seriously.

"How long have you lived here?" she asks him, his charm reeling her in with every passing second.

"Long enough to sample its goods," his eyes twinkle. "If you know what I mean." He winks. Nancy understands his insinuation, though she has no experience in that area. Fatou always bobbed and weaved around the topic, before leaving her with the parting words, *You'll get pregnant if you look at a man!*

"If you drink milk every day, and then one day a tall glass of cold dark *julbrew* arrives, you're eager for a sip," he says.

"Is that right?"

"Would I lie to you?"

"You already have," she giggles.

Malik's brow wrinkles. "Already? How did I lie to you?"

"You're already following in your father's diplomatic footsteps." She winks at him. She watches his features soften; warmth rapidly rising.

"Nancy, Nancy, Nancy," he starts.

"What?" She shrugs her shoulders.

"How many times did I call your name?"

"Not enough," she flirts back.

His laugh booms once more, enveloping her. She already knows that she wants to hear that roar every day. A kindred spirit in lightness of being.

Someone clears their throat. Nancy and Malik both swivel to find Lars leaning against the wall, arms folded across his chest. Nancy isn't sure how long he's been leaning there, listening to their flirty banter.

"So good to meet you, my sister," Malik whispers as Lars slowly pads toward them.

"Don't call me that," she whispers back.

"Let's have lunch together after, *my friend*," he replies, a glint in his eye.

"I see you two have already met," Lars says in Wolof, his voice sharper than when she'd met him in class. They both quiet down as he positions himself in front of Malik, his hands at his hips. "Malik moves fast." He switches to English.

Malik chuckles. "I can't help my charm."

"Sure you can." Lars's voice remains firm. "My class isn't a pick-up spot."

"Well, Nancy is my—"

"Shall we begin?" he cuts Malik off, glaring at Nancy. She

wonders if he's having a rough day. It's Friday morning—maybe he's tired after a long week of lectures?

"Why do we do what we do?" Lars begins. "How do we organize our societies? What are the stories waiting to be told that we have yet to tell?" He turns to Nancy. "What do we want to say to each other?" She shifts in her seat. "Those are the questions I ask as a social anthropologist. How we live and how we make our lives make sense. I study culture. I study humans. My main expertise is teaching international relations."

"So, Gambia was your laboratory?" Malik sniggers. Nancy places a hand over her mouth to stifle a giggle. Lars responds with a slight smile that lifts a corner of his mouth, his freckles transforming it into a boyish grin.

"Correction. I fell in love with Gambia," he said. "Since my twenties, I have spent long stretches of time in Senegal, Guinea, Gambia," he continues. "I did my PhD work on Gambia and focused on learning Wolof"—he flashes her another quick look—"and Mandinka."

"Since your twenties?" Malik questions.

"Yes," Lars beams. "I lived in Gambia for many years."

"How old are you now?" Nancy's curiosity surfaces. She sees color rise in his cheeks.

"Sorry?" Lars asks. She's sure he heard her the first time.

"How old are you?" she repeats.

"Forty-one," he responds.

"Old enough to be your father, Nancy," Malik laughs. "Am I right, Professor?"

Lars doesn't seem amused. His nostrils are flaring, his mouth a firm line. "Shall we continue?"

Twenty years older. He could have fooled her. Only three years younger than her own father.

Fifty minutes later, Lars shuts his textbook. Malik is taking human geography and Nancy social anthropology. Lars's English summaries will be a half-and-half venture for both of them. As their mentor, he'll be supporting their integration with extracurricular activities.

"Now you're up to speed with this week's lectures. How about we go *fika*?" Lars offers. "We could all go grab some coffee and buns together. Then I can answer any cultural questions you have." He turns to Nancy. "What do you say?"

"Sorry, I'm already joining Malik for lunch," she says.

Nancy watches his eagle eyes dim before he turns to Malik. "You do move fast, don't you?"

Malik chuckles, but Nancy notices the air shift, getting denser by the second. Malik's laughter seems to infuriate their professor. She hushes him.

"Maybe next week?" Nancy offers as consolation. "Then I can bring any questions I have?"

"Sure," Lars says. "We can take *fika* in my department." He turns to Malik. "You're welcome to join us if you'd like."

"Nah, I'll leave you two to it." Malik starts gathering his supplies. "I'm already learning about the culture in... different ways," he gives Nancy a wink. She rolls her eyes at him, a grin on her lips.

"Very well." Lars claps once. A move fast becoming his signature, Nancy notices. "Class is dismissed."

SEVEN

TINA, 2006

Med Gud skall jag kämpa för hem och för härd
för Sverige, den kära fosterjorden.
Jag byter Dig ej, mot allt i en värld
Nej, jag vill leva jag vill dö i Norden.

The stadium is silent as Tina croons in her sultry alto to a sea of margarine-yellow jerseys. She's standing in the middle of Friends Arena. To her left is a long line of Swedish football players, hands held behind their backs, heads high.

With God I shall fight for home and for hearth,
for Sweden, the beloved mother soil.
Exchange you, I won't for anything in this world
No, I want to live, I want to die in the North.

She belts the final verse of the Swedish national anthem, and the stadium erupts into cheers. She'd been invited to perform at an international friendly—an exhibition game— to get the team geared up for the World Cup in Germany in a few months. After all, no one was hotter now, fresh off her win to represent Sweden next month in Athens.

That article followed her across the airwaves. Radio

shows dissected the affair. Alongside segments on NASA crafts entering orbit, Chile's first female president and the launch of Twitter, news channels ran the story, the side-by-side mugshots of Tina and Lars plastered on TV.

The two stars are leading double lives, according to the media, and they discuss all the innocents caught in the crossfire—especially Lars's wife, Frida, who, according to the outlets, has stood by his side for decades. Scandal always follows celebrity and reconnecting with family isn't uncommon, but Tina's "case" is extra-special, the media keeps stressing.

Everyone knows why.

The addition of older siblings, Lars's estranged twin sons—strangers she never knew existed. They're prominent members of a right-wing political party, the most vocal voices against immigration. And they now have half-siblings with African blood.

"Thank you, Tina Wikström," the announcer says, "for singing the words we can always trust as a nation." She holds her wide smile in place, her insides churning. The crowd's cheers continue.

Then she hears it. Additional chanting once the crowd settles down. *Åk hem nu! Åk hem nu!* A group of ten or so protesters suddenly rush from the corner of the stadium toward where she stands. All she can see from that distance are bald heads and a few flowing blond locks wearing dark outfits. They're intercepted by security before they get close enough.

Åk hem nu! Åk hem nu!
Go back home now!

Home? Tina freezes. She just belted the anthem at home...

for her home. The announcer gets back on the speakers to apologize for the disruption. "They haven't scored yet. There's still time to protest," he jokes, trying to rev up the crowd into joviality once more.

But their chants, like claws, have already broken her skin.

Tina begins to panic, her chest heaving. Her eyes search for Seb, and he meets her terrified gaze. *I've got you,* his smile says, but he doesn't make his way toward her.

Tina frowns. Seb always rushes over. Always scans her face for the slightest sign of discomfort, sadness, anxiety. Always pulls her into a crushing hug to reassure her of his eternal loyalty. Always crafts a bubble of isolation around them whenever he kisses her in public. As if no one else exists, matters. Now he only cocks his lips at her from afar while nationalists picket the game against her.

Tina bites her lip and turns to leave the field. As she walks back toward the locker rooms, head down, she feels the light brush of his fingers on hers. She turns at his touch, only to stare at his back as he jogs over to his team's half. It seems the headlines are claiming his love too.

By the time Tina lands in Athens in May to represent Sweden at Eurovision, the scandal has followed her there too.

EIGHT

NANCY, 1979

They spend three full hours at lunch, and both miss their afternoon classes.

"Do you like ABBA?" Malik asks as they stroll toward the bus stop.

"Who doesn't?!"

Nancy starts miming "Dancing Queen" and side-stepping to the beat she mouths as they walk.

"Well, my sources tell me they might be making a sneak appearance at Alexandra's Night Club in town this weekend," Malik says. "Maybe even a photo shoot for their new album, 'Voulez-Vous.'" He flashes her a quick grin, lowering his voice. "I have connections."

Nancy stops dance-walking and turns to Malik. He pauses as well, clearly unsure of what she wants to say to him.

"You're such a mystery, Malik," she says, her voice low.

"On the contrary, my dear, I'm quite an open book." He takes her hand. "You don't have to flip the pages." His eyes hook hers. "I'll read the words out to you myself."

Nancy feels her cheeks heating up. "Malik…"

"I'd like to get to know you, Nancy," he says, his deep tone turning serious. "Will you come to the club with me this weekend?"

She holds his gaze, cocks the corner of her lips. "Do I have a choice in the matter?"

"Always." He smiles, gives her hand a gentle squeeze.

The next night, Nancy can barely hear Malik over pounding music as she sips a crimson-colored cocktail under the flashing strobes.

"What did you say?" she yells at him as she glances around at the heady mix of souls. They're all different shades, all gyrating in a technicolored paradise. Malik grabs her by the elbow and moves her further away from the DJ spinning disco.

"I said, can you imagine?" Malik screams into her ear. She leans back. "A Caribbean man opened this club. The first disco in the entire country." He takes a sip of his drink, pauses for effect before pressing on. "Trinidad. In this land." He sucks in air. "Talk about a true utopia."

"I believe it," Nancy laughs before taking another sip of cocktail. "Look at us. Me on a scholarship. You with VIP access to get us in."

His grin is a shy mixture of pride and humility. He assesses her over the rim of his beer. She turns away, pretending to be interested in the other gyrating patrons of the nightclub.

"So, where's the ABBA you promised me?" She turns back to Malik. He chuckles at her, his eyes roaming over her outfit: a dark-purple halter top baring her midriff, hip-hugging maroon velvet pants, golden loops dangling from her ears. His eyes don't make it past her hips.

"So beautiful." He mouths the words at her with a smile. She smacks his shoulder in jest.

"Okay, let's play *Spot the King!* instead." Malik cackles before chugging, then setting down his empty glass. He motions to the bartender for a refill before scanning the room.

Nancy slaps his shoulder once more. "Stop it."

"What? You know he comes here often. Maybe in the back room? Should we go look?" Malik says, eyes twinkling.

A refilled tumbler slides toward him. He catches it. "So," Malik starts, "what do you think about our professor?"

About to take a sip herself, Nancy stops, her glass midair. "Professor Lasse?"

"Who else?" He laughs weakly.

"I don't know...what about him?"

"Don't you think it's odd? A white man fluent in both Wolof and Mandinka? Who knows more about our country than both of us?"

Nancy ponders his words. Why was Lars Wikström so fascinated by her country? Enough to research it for his PhD. Enough to learn two indigenous languages.

"I don't know, maybe he really developed a connection to Gambia?"

Malik laughs, drinks some more. "You think his kind come to Africa without an ulterior motive? Have you forgotten your history lessons already, Nancy?"

"Well, I don't know him so I can't answer," she says, defensive. She doesn't need Malik questioning her intelligence.

"If you ask me, I think he likes to play dress-up."

"Good thing I didn't ask you."

He ignores her tone. "I think he likes to try on other people's cultures for size. Out of vanity. I don't trust him."

"All this after one class together?" Nancy scoffs. "You're not serious."

"I see it in his eyes," Malik adds. "The way he looks at me." He mimes, with two fingers pointing toward his own eyes.

"The way he looks at you?" Nancy smiles while parroting him. "What do you see?"

"Irritation. He looks at me like he wishes he didn't have to talk to me."

"Are you sure?"

"Trust me."

Silence envelops them. Nancy shifts. She feels the weight of his conflicting emotions. How can a man who supposedly loves everything Malik represents also regard him with disdain, as Malik claims?

"How does he look at me then?" Nancy eyes him over the rim of her glass. "Hmm?"

Malik holds her gaze, lowers his head, and laughs before scanning the crowd once more. "So, where's the king?"

They leave Alexandra's past midnight.

Malik hails her a taxi, squeezes her tightly in their goodbye hug, and watches as the taxi shuttles her off.

I see it in his eyes. The way he looks at me.

Malik's words ring in her mind in the weeks that follow. They continue as she sits in the communal kitchen area of

Lars's anthropology department for the *fika* she promised to have with him.

She waits, her hands folded in her lap, behind a rectangular table. Other professors dart in and out, greeting her cheerfully as they grab mugs and nip homemade cookies from a plastic container someone brought in. They're all sporting at least one item—scarf, beads, earrings, shirts—from whichever country or culture they did their research on.

Except Lars. He isn't wearing Gambia on his body. He has yet to wear any items from her land. She requested tea so he's standing next to the boiling kettle, occasionally glancing over at her and smiling awkwardly, until steam rises.

"There." He brings her a floral-pattern mug with the scent of rooibos wafting from it. "I picked this flavor for you since it's African." He sets the light-red liquid down in front of her.

"I was looking forward to Asian green tea," she jokes.

"Oh, I'm sorry. I should have asked. Can I get you green instead?" He's panicking, backing away.

"No, it's okay, thank you." She cradles the mug and lifts it to her lips. Scalding.

Lars settles across from her with his own mug of coffee. Several seconds of dense silence passes between them.

"So, how are you liking Sweden? Adjusting?" Lars asks, fiddling with his glasses.

"I like it," Nancy says. "Very different from Banjul, that's for sure."

"I know," he chuckles, "I know Banjul very well." He lifts his coffee to his lips, his eyes still on her.

"I don't doubt that," she laughs. "I'm just curious—why?"

"Why what?"

Nancy detects a tinge of defense. "Why Banjul? Why Gambia? Of all the countries you could have picked."

Lars sets down his mug, laughs. "Let's just say Gambia chose me."

Nancy eyes him suspiciously. "How so?" She assesses him over her rim this time around.

"It's a long, boring story." He shrugs before lifting his mug back to his mouth.

Nancy notices color rising in his cheeks. "I've got time," she says.

Lars takes off his glasses, holds her gaze. She can't read him, but she knows she must maintain eye contact. Yaya has coached her. This is how the Swedes communicate.

He breaks their standoff and turns back to his coffee. "After my first degree, I traveled around West Africa on my motorcycle. I was young, wild... free." He lingers on the last word.

"Two years," he continues before she can ask. "Two years. I traversed the region from Mali down to Sierra Leone. But Gambia." He pauses. "Gambia stole my heart. So, I decided I wanted to come back and study everything I could about it."

"Even Wolof and Mandinka?" Nancy asks.

"Especially Wolof and Mandinka." He smiles, the corners of his eyes crinkling. "You need to be able to speak the language of the place that stole your heart. Otherwise, how can you fully understand your love?"

Is he a poet? Nancy wonders.

"So, why did you come back?" She notices him shift in his seat.

"Why did *you* choose Sweden? Of all the countries?" he retorts. His freckles make him seem more boyish without his glasses on. Maybe even *pleasant*, she admits to herself.

"I live with my aunt and her white husband," Nancy explains. "I chose a place where I already knew someone. I could never move to a place with no one to receive me."

Lars sharply sucks in air—the quintessential way of agreeing in Swedish—before lifting and splaying his left palm toward her.

She examines it. What does he want her to see? The absence of a ring? A lifelong bachelor?

"Long-time divorced," he says before she asks. "No kids either." He drops his hand and sighs.

"I'm sorry. Did you want kids?"

"I thought this *fika* was going to be about cinnamon buns, Midsummer, and Swedish culture," he responds, his guard up again.

"Sorry..." Nancy begins. She reflects that he was the one who'd taken their chat down this personal route in the first place.

Lars picks up his glasses and slips them back on. "So, what would you like to know about my culture? It's only fair, since I've learned all about yours." Lars grins, but the smile doesn't reach his eyes.

Was this what Malik had been talking about—this smugness? Beyond his position of authority as her professor, the air between them feels heavier.

Nancy doesn't answer. He presses on. "Have you made

friends yet? Besides the obvious one we both know?" She knows he means Malik.

Nancy bristles at his tone, then smiles. "I'm working on it."

"Well, I want you to know that I'm also a resource and safe space for you. You know, as you navigate this new culture, which can be weird sometimes." He sounds unsure. "I mean... I know how hard it can be to make Swedish friends right away, so I want you to know that you can always count on me."

Nancy nods at his offer. She's sure he is completely harmless, nothing to worry about, yet she feels unsettled as he peers down at her.

"Thank you," she finally says. "That's very kind of you."

"Kind? You think that's kind?" His tone dips curiously.

When Nancy doesn't answer, Lars claps once, ending their *fika*.

"So," he says, "shall we do this again, same time next week?"

NINE

TINA, 2006

Tina sits in the back of a black luxury sedan as the chauffeur, wearing a pilot's hat, shuttles her from Athens International Airport to her five-star hotel reserved for musical acts. She's wearing midnight-black sunglasses, channeling superstar energy while hiding red-rimmed eyes. She thinks about the picketers from the football match. What would they have done if security guards hadn't broken their stride? She could feel their anger, even from that distance. They didn't want her singing their anthem.

Her national anthem.

Growing up, sure she'd had the occasional kid asking her where she was *really* from. Despite being more white-passing than Tobias, she still had to explain her lineage to complete strangers. But no one had ever told her to go back to where she came from. Go back home. Home to where? Africa? Go back to a continent she's never visited simply because her mother is Gambian?

The press has been excavating her life like an archaeological dig. Not many twenty-year-olds face national scandals. She isn't sure she has the emotional capacity to deal with the headlines which are now pelting her like raindrops.

She wishes she had Seb by her side to help her weather this storm, but the World Cup kicks off in a month. He needs to be at camp and in top form. Tina had simply kissed him when he left, saying she understood and didn't need an explanation, but he promised to fly in to join her in time for the semifinals.

The look that Seb had given her from a distance, though. She has mulled it over daily since the match.

Lotta sits beside her in the sedan, taking Seb's place. Lotta seems to have been put within her orbit to sabotage her mental health, because once again she's solemnly handing Tina another piece of bad news.

This time, it's a joint statement by Lars's estranged sons— the scandal has clearly reached their ears, and they weren't too pleased with Tina flying off to Athens to represent Sweden at Eurovision.

We're concerned about the allegations which
have been presented in the aftermath of
Ms. Wikström's Melodifestivalen win.
And we are even more concerned about
the fact that her birth certificate information is false.
How can we prove she is Swedish if the man listed as
her father may not be correct?
We must question if Ms. Wikström is fit to represent our
great nation.
We are investigating. In the meantime, we have
presented our concerns to the organizers
of Melodifestivalen to see if runner-up Anikka Berg
can represent our country instead while these
investigations are underway.

*As for any alleged familial connections to Ms. Wikström,
we will be making no further comment.*

Next to the statement is a picture of the twins, Ludvig and Lukas. They are standing shoulder to shoulder, one hand each tucked in a trouser pocket. They're looking straight into the camera.

Tina growls in frustration after reading their statement. She pitches sharply toward Lotta, her golden eyes now drowning behind tears.

"Why do you keep bringing me bad news?" The petite blond presses her lips together and holds Tina's gaze. "Do you vote for them or what?!"

In the past two years, Tina has gone from working at fast-food chain MAX to earn summer cash to getting a record deal, belting her lungs out in front of millions of people and having an assistant. A freaking personal assistant, sent from the record label to coordinate her schedule.

It must be irritating for Lotta, Tina concludes. Having to be an assistant to someone fifteen years younger, who was very recently flipping burgers.

After gingerly pulling the newspaper out from Tina's tight grip, Lotta presents a small envelope. A name, Lars Wikström, is printed in the top-right corner.

Lotta clears her throat. "He dropped this off with me yesterday."

Tina sniffs and wipes her wet nose with the back of her hand before snatching the letter from Lotta. She tears open the envelope, ripping part of the note in her violence.

"My dear Tina," Lars writes. "I'm so sorry. I simply wanted to be there for you. I didn't want to..."

Tina crumples the paper and tosses it toward the dashboard. It hits the driver's shoulder and Lotta swiftly apologizes on her behalf. He lifts his hat in a gesture of understanding, his eyes still on the road.

Silence envelopes their sedan once more, Tina's anger palpable and dense. His audacity, to think he means anything to her. First, his appearance causes a scandal that is burying her career with every news headline it generates. And second, his sons are coming after her like hound dogs. And now he's trying to gain access to her by writing personal letters. She will show him she isn't weak. That she isn't afraid of his sons, and that he will never be her father.

Lotta pulls out a folder and rattles information off a printed schedule to temper the atmosphere:

Makeup at 4pm
Rehearsals at 6pm
Press conference at 7pm

Two days later, one of Tina's producers, Pelle, stands in front of her, his face a block of red fury, his hair a frizzy blond Afro. "This is ridiculous," he mutters under his breath, his calm tone masking his anger. "You can't do this."

Tina sits in a makeup artist's chair in her assigned green room at Olympic Indoor Arena. She stares straight ahead, looking at her reflection in the mirror as the makeup artist dabs blush across her cheekbones.

Pelle presses on. "We've already flown the dancers in. The band is ready. What is this, Tina?"

"I want to perform it the way I did at Mello?." She pauses to assess the blush. "The way I won." She had already threatened to pull out of the competition if he didn't allow her to perform her artistic rendition.

"*Herregud!*" *Oh my God!* Pelle is exasperated. "This is fucking Eurovision. Home of sequins and tambourines. That emo shit won't work. Not here."

"That's why we need to sing it this way. Something different. Something fresh. I could try with tears again."

Maybe the audience will understand what she's trying to say if she sings it that way. Maybe they'll see that she's just a lost girl thrust into a body she still hasn't fully owned. It's a gamble worth taking, she thinks.

"That was different," Pelle tries to reason with her. "That felt different. It was spontaneous and unexpected. Something that happens once. You can't recreate it on demand."

The makeup artist applies neon-pink lip gloss to complete her signature look for the performance. Tina pushes strands of hair behind each ear and rises to her feet. She adjusts her cheeky denim shorts. Beneath them, black fishnets. She's wearing the matching vest, braless and unbuttoned, her breasts small and perky, taped to the insides for a touch of modesty.

"Have faith," she smiles.

"It's too risky," he protests. "You're under contract and now you're going against my directions once again."

She holds his gaze. "But we're allowed to make last-minute modifications. It's going to work."

The exasperated producer storms right up to her, inches from her face, staring her down.

"This is the problem with your generation; you think

you know everything. So entitled. My kids are older than you, you little brat! There are hundreds of girls who would gladly take your place." Spittle flies from his mouth. "A dark cloud is already gathering over your head back home, Tina. Don't let it rain."

Tina continues holding his gaze, her mind churning, holding every unspeakable thing she wants to hurl in his face. Instead, she turns on her heel and glides out of the dressing room.

"You're making a mistake," he yells after her. She responds with the hard slam of the door. Waiting outside the room stands a tall, lanky dark-haired man, one of the festival ushers, kitted up in headphones and a walkie-talkie.

"Ms. Wikström is on her way to rehearsals," he mutters in accented English into the receiver. He turns to Tina, his eyes darting over his shoulder to glance her way as they walk. "Welcome to Athens," he continues, beaming. "We love Sweden."

Tina offers a weak smile, still rattled by her encounter with her producer, who had made her feel like a petulant child. Emotions are cresting like waves within her, unmooring her. She's been suddenly thrust into the limelight, reckoning with a ghost of a father, about to go onto the world's largest singing stage.

Her original folk-pop hit, "Honey," with its light springiness and choreographed dancers wiggling in slow motion like earthworms, is going to be replaced by an emo ballad. Same lyrics, direr performance. Tina is betting on her vulnerability creating a connection with the glittering audience. When she'd performed at Melodifestivalen back home, the Swedish audience had been stunned into silence at first, confused, processing what was going on. Then they'd enveloped her with applause and showered her with adoration, and she felt pure love wash over her.

Now, standing on the stage here in Athens, getting ready to practice, her dancers staring blankly at her from the sidelines with arms folded across their chests, Tina swallows, unsure.

She takes in a few deep breaths, closes her eyes, and starts. Her singing voice is deep and sultry, a smooth alto that makes her seem much older than her twenty years. She holds her fist to chest, trying to force out tears.

Halfway through, she hears an audible yawn and stops. Her eyes bolt open. She flashes the dancer in question a death glare. In response, he pumps his shoulder in a "What?!" gesture.

"From the top, please." The festival producer's voice comes over the speakers. This time, her nerves are raw, and she shifts on unsteady feet. She feels it deep down. This is what she needs to do.

Tina restarts. Three minutes later, Lotta is the only one clapping.

"Thank you, Sweden," a voice comes over the speaker. "Up next is Finland, please get the stage ready for Lordi."

SEVEN P.M. THAT EVENING

Her rehearsal for the semifinals has left her feeling insecure. The only thing she can keep down all day is an apple and seltzer water. After wrapping a royal-blue brocade robe over her barely-there performance outfit, she struts nervously over to the grand hall set up for the press conference. She sets herself behind the long, white-linened rectangular table. Switzerland's entry, a bleached blond, flashes her an uncomfortably wide smile as she takes the mic, and Tina knows she's equally nervous.

Tina leans back in her chair, arms folded across her chest, side-eying Switzerland as the blond yodels for effect. The press room bursts into applause and the woman gives a mock bow, that Cheshire-cat grin still on her face.

"Ms. Wikström," they now move on to Tina and she readjusts, sitting taller.

Several journalists start talking all at once.

How are you feeling?

What is it like to represent Sweden?

What inspired your hit?

We hear you have something up your sleeve. Can you tell us?

Were you a model before becoming a singer?

Is it true you're a bastard?

At that last question, the room gasps in unison. Dozens of eyes turn to its source. A bespectacled middle-aged white man. A journalist from Sweden, he'd clearly chosen that word for effect.

Tina focuses on him. "Excuse me?"

The man clears his throat, less confident now that all eyes are on him.

"There is a petition in Sweden led by the Wikström brothers to replace you with the runner-up because the authorities can't prove you are Swedish." He waves his own copy of the newspaper statement she read a few days ago.

"You mean a petition started by Nazis?" she asks him tersely. "What is your question?"

"We have obtained a copy of your birth records. Allegedly, the man listed is not your father," he says, his voice cracking. He is a weak interrogator. "There are no adoption records either. To be recognized as Swedish, one of your parents must be a Swede born in Sweden. Your mother is from Africa."

"Gambia," Tina adds.

"So, if you can't prove who your real father is and your birth records are false, are you fit to represent us?"

"My father is dead," Tina retorts. The words spill out of her before she realizes she's opened yet another can of worms. Based on what they've read in the news this week, Europe now knows her father is alive and is most likely Lars.

"What connection do you have to artist Lars Wikström?" He adjusts his glasses, looks down at the newspaper once more. "You are his spitting image. Except"—he pauses, unsure of himself—"you know… Brown."

"Are we here to talk about rumors or my music?"

The man chuckles. "They go hand in hand, and this is the biggest—"

"What is your question?" This time, it's the Greek moderator jumping in to move the press conference along.

"Sorry. My question, Ms. Wikström, is: Do you feel qualified to represent Sweden?"

Tina peers at him. She flashes the yodeling Swiss contestant a quick glare, and then turns back to the journalist.

"More than you'll ever be in this lifetime," she retorts. "Because I'm a walking, breathing representation of our modern values." Her golden eagle eyes pin him to his seat. "You're its archaic history."

The room erupts into applause, her words finally giving them room to react, as if they were collectively holding their breath underwater.

The moderator futilely tries moving on as more hands shoot up into the air. "Ms. Wikström is taking no further questions."

Tina gets to her feet, pulls her brocade robe tighter, and spins on her heels.

Later that night, Tina unlocks her hotel room door to find Seb inside. As promised. She notes his wheat-colored stubble, the bags under his bright eyes.

"Seb?"

"Lotta gave me a key," he says, his eyes taking her in, tired.

"Looks like Lagerbäck has been working you guys like crazy." She smiles weakly and shuts the door, then slinks into the room. Seb remains silent, watching her, something clearly weighing on his mind.

Tina pauses in her tracks. "What's wrong?" she asks. She sees his jaw tense as he swallows, eyes locked on hers.

"I read their statement," Seb says.

Tina sneers. "And? Why should it matter? They're fucking lunatics."

"They're your brothers," he says. "They're senior

members of that party." He takes an audible breath. "I'm scared for you," he adds.

"Is that why you hesitated?"

"Hesitated? What do you mean?"

"On the field. When those protesters came running toward me."

"*Älskling...*" Seb starts to say.

"Were you ashamed of me? Hmm?" She sees his eyebrows wiggle in confusion, not sure of which emotion to settle on.

"What do you mean?"

"You know what I mean."

"T*iii*na," he says, drawing out her name. "Come on, I couldn't leave the lineup. I couldn't leave the team."

"While lunatics were rushing at your girlfriend?" she fumes. "Even when they were going to hurt me?"

"I panicked, babe. I didn't know what to do."

"You can't be serious,"

His face tells her otherwise. He reaches a hand to her. "Forgive me? Please? I panicked."

Tina hesitates before stepping in closer, grabbing his hand. He continues, "I watched your press conference." His nostrils flare. "Are you ready? For all this?"

"Stop it," she snaps. "I'm not a child."

Tina grabs the back of his head, pitching his face upward. She peers down at him for a few seconds before pressing her lips softly against his. Seb's right hand moves up to cup her face, his mouth opening to taste more of her.

"Seb..." His tongue darts in, cutting off his name, as he pulls her down to straddle him. "Seb," she whispers against his exploring mouth, "tell me what's wrong."

He doesn't answer. His hands run along the sides of

both her fishnet thighs, disappearing under her denim shorts, heating up her skin. She hums against his mouth, savoring his touch.

"*Så jävla vacker*," he mumbles in response, one hand working its way beneath her open braless vest to cup her.

She remembers their first kiss as teenagers. Awkward, sloppy, Seb trembling against her. He'd been worried about what she thought of him. One of a handful of white boys in her predominantly Brown neighborhood. She could have had anyone.

Years later, now in their early twenties, he's still as awkward. Staring at her, still unable to believe that she chose him. That she let him near her. Every time they make love. *So fucking beautiful.* Despite having the societal moniker "*Snygg Sebbe*"—*Heartthrob Seb*—he still needs to be told he's enough. And now he's afraid for her, as if those racist assholes can take her away from him. She senses this.

"I'm yours," she whispers, her lips brushing his pale skin lightly. "Always."

He shuts his eyes at her caress, a low groan escaping him. "I worry about you, my love," he says.

She moves back to his lips, smiles against them.

"You don't have to worry about me, Seb. I can take care of myself. I'm not going anywhere."

TEN

NANCY, 1979

Lars watches her as she bites into the neon-green and chocolate oblong-shaped delicacy. A rush of sugar hits her. *Too sweet.*

"Do you like it?" Lars takes off his glasses mid-question and rests them on the table.

"What's it called again?" She wrinkles her nose and holds it in the air.

"*Dammsugare.* Vacuum cleaner. Because it looks like one."

She purses her lips. "And why do you like it again?"

Lars laughs. He reaches for her *dammsugare*, his fingers lightly brushing hers as he takes it from her. He bites into it, his eyes on her as he chews slowly.

Nancy turns away, looks around, feigns interest in the only other guests—a couple, she deduces, based on how they're holding hands—in the dimly lit space. They're sitting on taupe-colored armchairs in a small six-table café tucked in a backstreet on the bohemian island of Södermalm, once a nineteenth-century slum neighborhood.

Lars had insisted on bringing her here. Now she knows why. Dark, dim, private.

"Hmm, so good," Lars murmurs before licking his fingers and cradling his coffee once more. "So how many other *fikabröd* have you tried since you've been here? Besides cinnamon buns?"

"Probably too many," Nancy says. "I'm beginning to like cardamom buns."

He nods. "My favorite. I could eat them every single day."

"How do you stay so skinny?"

"You think I'm skinny?" he asks. She shrugs in response. He continues, "Well, I cycle when I can. Run too."

Silence wraps them up once more. "So," Lars says, breaking it. "Have our summary sessions been helpful for you... and Malik?"

Tina smiles at the mention of Malik's name. She looks forward to her Fridays with Malik under Lars's tutelage. Afterward she and Malik grab lunch together. Each week their fingers had inched closer across the table; now, they eat lunch with fingers tightly intertwined.

She updates him, play by play, on her *fika* sessions with their professor which Malik had opted out of. She feels she needs to, to reassure Malik that she has eyes for no one but him. She acts as a buffer between their professor's irritation and Malik's laissez-faire behavior around Lars. They often pass each other looks during Lars's lectures. Malik blows her air kisses, and she struggles to stifle her giggles.

She notices the grin drop off Lars's face, his look now more intense as he peers at her.

"Yes, thank you. Those summaries are saving our lives in your class," she adds.

"That's good to hear. The way you two carry on in class, I wasn't too sure." His tone is dry.

"You're grading our assignments, aren't you? If I wasn't paying attention in class, you'd know."

He smirks into his coffee before taking another sip. "So, same time next week?"

Nancy reluctantly agrees to another dry, formal *fika* with Lars.

The rest of the semester crawls along that spring.

"What's so funny?" Lars asks, stopping mid-lecture. The room dips into silence so heavy Nancy finds it difficult to breathe. "Malik? Can you please tell me what's so funny?"

Normally boisterous Malik quiets down, his dark eyes peering back at Lars.

"Tell me. What is so *jävla* funny?" Lars presses as he slowly moves closer to Malik, his gaze sharp, focused. Nancy notices Malik frowning at that Swedish word, *jävla*. She feels for her dictionary and quickly flips through, looking for the word's meaning in English. *Fucking*.

Lars stops in front of Malik's desk and glares at the younger man. Nancy, who is sitting next to Malik, notices the laser focus in Lars's eyes. His black pupils seem to be disappearing, gold expanding.

"I apologize," Malik says a moment later, his gaze never leaving Lars's face. "It won't happen again."

"It better not. If it does, you will feel it."

"That sounds like a threat, Professor," Malik chuckles, a lightness to his tone. "We diplomats don't condone threats. We don't negotiate with terrorists, either."

Lars's nostrils flare. He turns to Nancy, and she sees his

black pupils slowly growing once more as he stares at her. A few seconds later, Lars walks back to his own desk, packs up his teaching materials and exits the classroom.

When they get their midterm report from Lars, it's clear Malik needs to study more and hold her hand less.

Since Yaya mentioned wanting kids that one evening, she hasn't brought it back up. It had been a random fit of madness, Benke had told Nancy later. She wonders how long her aunty had been having these "random fits" before she moved to live with her.

She barely sees Yaya. When Nancy wakes up for school in the mornings, her aunt is still fast asleep, recharging from her night shift visiting the elderly and disabled across Stockholm.

"You should come with me one night," Yaya had casually dropped one weekend. "Maybe I can get you a part-time job here. You can make some extra money so my brother doesn't have to keep sending money every couple of months. Things are getting tight back home. Something is brewing." That was all Yaya had said, but Nancy knew there was more to it.

Now, at the end of her first full semester, summer is on the horizon, offering glorious days ahead. Her first summer in Sweden, and she plans to explore with Malik on her arm. Yaya and Benke know nothing about him yet, and she wants to keep it that way. After all, he is the Gambian ambassador's son: everyone wants to grow their connections.

APRIL 30, 1979

"Valborgsmässoafton—or Valborg—was named after Saint Valborg, who was a missionary in Germany in the eighth century," Lars explains as they trudge uphill toward Skansen. He's wearing a tan-colored trench coat and a matching fedora under his black umbrella. "Though its roots are historically pagan, from when people believed lighting fires would ward off evil spirits, now we use it to welcome spring."

Rain pours out of dark clouds above. Monochrome umbrellas dot the landscape, with an occasional red or striped one breaking up the sparse but steady flow of people heading in the same direction. The streets seem barren. Besides the occasional car or bus whizzing by, Nancy hears raindrops hitting the large maroon umbrella Malik holds over her, and soggy booted feet stamping by in a hurry.

Lars was explaining to them that during Valborg, bonfires are lit all over Sweden, local celebrities give longwinded speeches to acknowledge spring, sweet-sounding choruses permeate the air, and people dance till midnight. They'd crossed Djurgårdsbrons—Djurgård's Bridge— with its panoramic views of Stockholm's harbor and posh Östermalm district and were now making their way up to the world's oldest open-air museum and zoo, Skansen.

Professor Wikström has been keeping his promise to help her and Malik integrate—though she suspects Malik's cultural education is only happening because of her role as "teacher's pet."

Malik had called her "teacher's pet" one Friday during

their customary lunch date. She had bristled at his words, which to her mind inferred the relationship was reciprocal, that she was enjoying Lars's attention too.

"You have a whole embassy. I have only Yaya," Nancy had explained. "That's why he's trying to be a good friend."

"A good friend?" Malik had asked. "Really? After a few *fika* meetings?"

"Yes, Malik. After a few meetings. He's harmless."

"A white man who speaks both Wolof and Mandinka seems harmless to you?"

They had left the conversation there.

Once inside Skansen, Nancy, Malik and Lars trek up steep hills and gravitate toward the sound of melodious, angelic music wafting through the thick air. The hymn-like choruses, Lars explains, are actually "spring songs" welcoming the sun.

Within minutes, the wet crowd grows to a couple of hundred people. Resolve unwavering, they seek solace under umbrellas. Standing patiently and watching the choir, they sing along under their breath, low and muffled.

Malik wraps an arm around her beneath their umbrella, pulling her closer to him. Lars, who is taller, stands behind the couple, giving them a better view of the bonfire as patrons are packed shoulder to shoulder. The bonfire grows. Faces hidden beneath umbrellas are lit up, and they stare, mesmerized by the leaping flames. Almost trance-like, the crowd soaks up the heat from the bonfire.

Thousands of tiny hot embers float into the sky like secret wishes. Nancy closes her eyes, makes one of her own. Then she turns to Malik and presses a chaste kiss against his lips.

His arm around her tightens. She rests her head against his chest, absorbing his heat.

The rain that is lightly pelting the crowd goes unnoticed. Mouths hang open, eyes angled toward the sky as the dark indigo night lights up with a warm glow. Like rays of the morning sun slipping through curtains and splaying across sheets and faces, the bonfire seems to be jolting Stockholm back to life.

Nancy remembers Lars is there too and turns back to look at him. He stands stoically beneath his umbrella, flames reflecting off his glasses, his eyes and the fire now one merged entity. He cocks the corner of his mouth at her in a half smile.

He leans forward. "Are you enjoying the heat?"

"It's quite something. Thank you for bringing us here."

"Of course." He smiles, lingering, observing her beneath the night's glow. "Of course," he repeats.

With his umbrella open above him, embers and sparks floating around him, he gazes at Nancy intensely, causing her to shift on her feet. Malik's notices, and looks over his shoulder at Lars, the two of them in a silent standoff. Lars's grin has vanished, and he adjusts his glasses, resettles them on the bridge of his nose. With his arm still around Nancy, Malik pulls her in for a kiss in front of their professor. This time it's not chaste.

The crowd finally thins out. A hundred or so still surround the bonfire, basking in its warmth and hoarding enough heat to last them a few more days.

★

By June, Malik's results have not improved—a warning, perhaps, after his territorial display during Valborg. Nancy resolves to do everything she can to help Malik, even if that means embracing her role as teacher's pet.

At their last summary lecture, Lars seems to be in a bright mood.

"So, do you both have summer plans?" he asks as he closes his folder, then sits his long, lean form on the edge of his desk.

"Well," Malik starts, glancing at Nancy. "We plan on traveling around Sweden."

"That sounds like a wonderful plan," Lars says, his voice lighter than usual. "Why not come to my cabin next weekend? For a pre-Midsummer *fika*? It's not too far from here."

"Your cabin?" Nancy asks. She turns to Malik. They exchange looks.

"Yes, I've got a small one on Vaxholm. You both can take the ferry over. It's a beautiful ride through the archipelago."

"But what about your family?" Malik asks. Nancy realizes she never told Malik about her conversation with Lars, when he'd talked about being single. She notices Lars tense up at the mention of family.

"Well," he clears his throat, "my ex-wife and I have been divorced for years now."

"Sorry to hear that," Malik says, offering sympathies. "And children?"

Lars peers at him for a long time before shaking his head, and turning back to Nancy.

"So? What do you say?" he asks.

"We'd love to," she beams, answering for both her and Malik.

★

Their professor hadn't been lying. The ferry ride from Strömkajen in the center of town to Vaxholm is scenic. They pass lush Djurgården island; excited screams coming from Gröna lund amusement park; dozens of minute islands peppered with tiny Falu-red cottages—she'd learned about that color in school—and skerries.

Nancy's wearing a white summer terry romper with large black polka dots, her hair now a two-inch Afro. Malik's Afro is larger. He's in a loose-fitting floral-pattern short-sleeved shirt and tight shorts. They look great together. The breeze whips their clothes while they stand out on deck, and Nancy leans in to steal a few chaste kisses. Malik returns her shy pecks, letting her lead and take what she wants.

Lars had given them directions from the pier through the woods to his cabin. When he meets them at his door, he has morphed into a stranger—a handsome one at that, dare she say. His hair is wet, brushed off his face and slicked back so it looks like clay mud plastered down. His glasses are gone, and his amber eyes pick up the summer sun, shining bright. He's barefoot, and wearing a loose white shirt, rolled up to the elbows, and cargo shorts—more casual than she's seen him before.

As they step into Lars's petite summer cabin, Nancy is transported back to the continent. Artifacts, rugs, carvings, paintings grace every wall, floor and corner of Lars's cottage.

"Professor Lasse." Malik freezes by the door, his eyes sweeping the place, taking in Lars's shrine to his own motherland. He looks at Nancy, communicating wordlessly, before turning back to Lars. "Either you have an obsession with my country or you're looting our treasures," he jokes.

Lars laughs, but Nancy notices it is strained. Nancy knows what Malik is thinking. No one comes to the continent without an ulterior motive. Witnessing Lars's lair proves his point.

"All in the name of research," Lars attempts to lighten the mood. "Come this way."

He leads them to an outdoor patio a few steps from the water. Bending over the table, arranging flowers, is another middle-aged white man in short, tight-fitting striped gym shorts and a fuchsia pink vest. His hair is a mass of wispy ginger curls, and when he turns toward the guests, Nancy sees he is sporting a matching red mustache. He straightens up and takes off his sunglasses.

"My God, you are a vision. He won't stop gushing about you," the man says to Nancy in accented English, his walnut-brown eyes lighting up, his shoulders relaxing.

Lars clears his throat. "Leif, this is Nancy and her *boyfriend*, Malik," he stresses. He turns back to her. "My older brother, Leif."

"So pleased to meet you." Nancy steps toward the man and up on her toes to give him a peck on each cheek. He smells nice—sweet. His gaze turns to Malik, roams his features. He stretches out a hand to Malik. "*Enchanté*."

Soon Lars is running in and out with dishes—deviled eggs, meatballs, five flavors of home-pickled herring—while Leif smokes in the fresh summer breeze, legs crossed, eyes behind tinted sunglasses, listening to Malik's many stories about the life of a diplomat.

Nancy leans back in her deck chair, soaking it all up.

This time last year, she was still in Banjul, still figuring out what she wanted out of life. Now she's here in Stockholm's archipelago with her formidable boyfriend. His easy humor and shiny dark eyes have Leif giggling, and she's near bursting with pride as she listens to Malik's eloquent voice. The secret wish that she'd made at Valborg had been for God to give her a sign that Malik was "the one" her mother had subconsciously conjured up through her prayers.

She feels heat on her skin. She turns. Lars's eyes are on her. He holds her gaze intensely before his eyes slowly make their way down her sleeveless shoulder. He lingers over her curves before deliberately bringing his attention back up. His eyes are now darker, those pupils larger.

"Really?!" Leif's voice cuts through their moment. Malik turns toward them as well.

"What did I miss?" Lars asks before putting a bottle of Carlsberg to his lips.

Malik jumps in. "Oh, I was just asking your brother about your divorce."

A signal she can't quite read passes between the brothers. With his hard gaze back on Leif's once more, she reads what seems like fear in the older man's face.

"Right! Right!" Leif places a hand on his forehead. "Of course. Exactly what he said."

Malik furrows his eyebrows with amusement. "Okay?"

"Leif wants me to get back with my ex-wife," Lars says, his voice low, cool. "We've been divorced for years now." He turns back to Nancy.

"Our parents, *God bless their souls in hell*"—Leif makes a quick sign of the cross over his chest—"summoned Lars back from Gambia immediately. Told him to stop playing around and get settled." He lifts his glass of elderflower juice for a sip. "So, he was forced to marry her. A woman who shared their leanings and"—he coughs a bit—"ideologies. Now they're divorced. See?" He splays his right hand out dramatically.

"I'd rather not talk about her on this lovely day," Lars says, glaring at his brother. "Nancy, come with me. I'd like to show you something special."

"Only Nancy? Can I come too?" Malik laughs.

Lars gives him a wry smile and leads Nancy by the elbow back into the house. Her interest is piqued.

The cottage is relatively modest for a summer home. One bedroom, two floors, a basement that leads out toward the pier where a rowboat is docked. Lars pushes the door open to the dark basement and flips on the single bulb dangling there. She sees several canvases. Most are blank white, but some have finished artwork. Oil paintings, it seems, lush and richly layered. She makes out the outlines of thatch-roofed huts, of silhouettes standing in long fishing canoes, markets bustling with people with trays of fruits on their heads. All of the figures have brown skin. Clearly inspired by his time in West Africa.

"Are you an artist?" Nancy asks, walking up to one of the canvases.

"I wouldn't call myself that yet," he says. "They're terrible." She turns to look at him. Color rises in his cheeks.

"You're an incredible painter. These are really lovely,'" she says, turning back to his work. "Are you painting a series?" She hears him moving closer. Feels his body heat behind her. She dares not turn around.

"I was, but I've lost my inspiration. Nothing is coming

to me anymore. I need a new muse," he says breathlessly. "And I think I may have just found it." She turns toward him, his face inches from hers. "I want *you* to be my muse, Nancy." He's standing much closer than she'd like. At this proximity, she fully appreciates their height difference, her head grazing his chin.

"I have a boyfriend, Professor."

"Oh! Not like that... no... it would be totally innocent," Lars says, flustered. "I just want to paint you. Take photos of you and then practice painting from those. You would inspire me, Nancy." He rakes fingers through his hair, avoiding her gaze.

Nancy feels emotions coursing through her: discomfort that this authority figure wants more of her; flattered that he thinks she will reawaken his artistry. Flustered, she changes the subject.

"Are you exhibiting these somewhere?"

"They are not worthy of exhibition yet," he says, his eyes roaming over his art. "They're not right. I want to work on an abstract series of the human form."

Nancy swallows. Is he asking her what she's thinking?

"I can't pose naked for you," she says quietly.

"Oh, God! No! I would never ask that!" Lars's face is now bright red with horror. "That would be entirely inappropriate. I would never ask such a thing. I just want to get the African curves right. The Afro. The mouth." His eyes settle on her plump lips. They linger there for a second or two.

Nancy wants to keep him at bay. "Well, I think you're very talented, Professor."

She sees a smile of defeat on his lips. She may be

inexperienced, but she knows that look. One she'd been batting off whenever she rode buses or the *tunnelbana*. There weren't many faces like hers milling around town, so she remained a curious novelty everyone wanted to gawk at.

"Thank you." He smiles at her, a grin that takes years off him. He moves over to a shelf, grabs something off it. A Kodak camera. "Can I?" He lifts the camera in question. "My first attempt to get my inspiration back?"

She holds his look for a while before nodding. He directs her to stand close to one of the high basement windows, so daylight floods her face. He turns into a photo shoot director, telling her where to place her hands, how to look up at the light, how to elongate her neck, how to look at him over her bare shoulder, how to...

"Like this?" she says, facing him, her hands stretched over her head, so she is backlit, becoming a dark silhouette against the light. She sees his Adam's apple jump in his neck as he swallows. The sunlight coming from behind her form dances across his eyes. They shimmer like gold.

"Yeah, just like that," he whispers as he moves closer.

She puts her arms down and wraps them across her chest protectively.

"Nancy?" Malik's voice from above startles her. He's calling down from the open basement door. "Are you all right?" She hears pounding feet coming down the stairs and she moves toward the sounds.

"I'm fine, come down." She meets him at the foot of the stairs. "Our professor is a man of many talents. Look at his secret paintings."

When Malik strides into full view, Nancy sees the look in Lars's eyes. Jealousy and resentment.

And in that moment, Nancy knows she must protect her Malik at all costs.

ELEVEN

TINA, 2006

It's the semifinals of Eurovision.

They will determine who will perform in the finals on Saturday.

"And we have a special guest in the audience!"

The camera pans to Seb, sitting off-stage in Sweden's designated booth alongside Tina's producer. The crowd screams when they see his clean-cut face on the screens, livestreaming to millions around the world. He's wearing a light royal-blue dress shirt, his butter-blond hair slicked off his face: a physical manifestation of the Swedish flag. Color rushes into his cheeks. He smiles, gives a shy wave.

Tina chuckles from the back room as she watches him on screen, waiting for her turn on stage. Right before, the Finns had presented a demonic-looking rock group wearing monster outfits and chanting "Hallelujah" that had driven the crowd wild. It warranted a call from Nancy, praying over the phone and verbally covering her daughter with the blood of Christ.

"It's the Swedish Heartthrob," the announcer continues. "Or, as they call him in his country, *Snygg Sebbe*." Screams fill the arena. Seb plants his face in his palm.

Tina has promised to join him in Germany for the World

Cup as soon as this is over. She needs to take a much-needed break from this cotton-candy life she's been violently thrust into.

There are a few more performances—a Turkish group wearing capes, reminiscent of fruit bats, a twirling duo from Romania, a hip-gyrating saxophonist from Moldova—before Sweden.

"From the legends of Eurovision, Sweden, comes this year's entry, twenty-year-old Tina Wikström," he announces. "She is a vision, isn't she?"

The crowd wails. She pushes strands of straightened auburn hair behind her ears. The lights dim. Tina breathes slowly, attempting to calm her nerves as she struts toward the stage. Wild cheering welcomes her as a single spotlight illuminates the stage. The noise disappears, leaving pin-drop silence.

Tina takes a beat before she starts. You can never fully be ready, she knows this, but she feels that glimmer of doubt creeping in again now. This is the most-watched singing show on Earth. She craves Nancy's boisterous laugh telling her that *All will be well, my dear*. She wants to nuzzle into Tobias's broad chest, his arms wrapped around her. She wants to stare into Seb's bright eyes, see his eyes crinkle with love.

Tina places a manicured hand to her chest, closes her eyes, and belts out "Honey" as a low a cappella ballad, her voice deeper than usual, her alto echoing in the silent arena.

When she finishes three minutes later, the crowd isn't sure if she's done or about to sing another verse. Two awkward seconds tick by before trickles of applause fill the silence, gradually building into a roaring wave.

"*Tack så mycket*, Tina," the announcer says. "Thank you, Sweden!"

The lights dim and Tina shuffles off stage toward the dressing room.

"You were great," Lotta says, rushing after her. "You really were."

Tina keeps walking without saying a word, her heart beating rapidly. She pulls off her shoes mid-stride and continues in fish-netted feet.

"Can I get you anything? Some water?" Lotta scurries behind her.

"I just need air."

"I'll get Seb for you."

Tina stops dead in her tracks and pivots to face Lotta, her eyes burrowing into her assistant.

"I said, *I just need air.*" Tina's voice starts to crack.

Lotta peers at her. "Well, he always makes you feel better, so I figured..."

"You figured I have no agency without him?"

"I figured you shouldn't be alone right now." Lotta holds her gaze. "This is a lot even for me to process and I'm not the one on stage," she continues. "You've got to be kinder to yourself, Tina. You became a star overnight."

Tina absorbs her words. "Thank you," she says quietly. She turns on her heels and rushes off to her dressing room.

"You were incredible. Sit, let me touch you up before the announcements," her makeup artist says.

Tina plants her tired body into the chair and peers at her reflection in the mirror. *She is a vision, isn't she?*

Then she lunges for her phone and, within seconds, has her mamma on the line.

"My baby," Nancy screeches back over the receiver. "I'm so proud of you."

"I wish you and Tobbe were here," Tina sniffs.

"We're there in spirit, my dear. You know your brother needs to work."

"What about you? You said you were going to come!"

"I said I would try."

"You never try, Mamma. You never try for me! You never missed any of Tobias's swim meets."

There is a long silence on the phone before Nancy answers. "I didn't want *that* scandal to follow me if I came," she starts. "I am glad you don't have to see the news here."

"Why do you care what people think? You're my mom!"

"It's easy for you to talk like that, my dear." Nancy sounds too calm for Tina's liking.

"I need you here," Tina cries into the phone. "I need you."

"Tina, act like a big girl, okay? When I was your age, I moved to Sweden without my mother. With nobody." Tina has heard this story a million times.

"What does that have to do with this? I'm singing in front of millions!"

"You've done it before, and you'll do it again," Nancy retorts. "I would only have brought a dark cloud with me."

"Where is your faith? Hmm?"

"Tina, Tina, Tina. If you knew what they're saying about your mother, you would want me to go into hiding, trust me."

Tina takes her words in. She thinks about what the media storm has already brought. The Wikström twins and their campaign. Her disastrous press conference. The petition demanding that she be replaced at Eurovision, even though she's already here, representing her country. The last thing she needs is them plastering Nancy's face on the screens, her mother having to dodge vitriol simply because she is sitting next to her in Athens.

Her mother, who Tina always thought was unflappable, is now cowering in fear, and all because of her. Nancy doesn't want the brewing storm to rain on her daughter. She's acting as an umbrella, trying to protect her from the gale. *At least she's trying this time.*

"I wish I could be there," Nancy says, breaking the silence.

"I just want you with me. I miss you," Tina responds, her voice soft.

"I know, my dear. All will be well."

Tina disconnects the call and leans back into her chair, grateful for a moment of peace. Her eyes land on a bouquet of dahlias colored a dusty blush cream, a handwritten note tucked into the bouquet. The flowers had magically appeared while she'd been on the phone to Nancy.

"Special delivery," the makeup artist says, beaming. She had placed them right on the table while Tina was distracted. Tina reaches for the note card.

Kära Tina,
Jag är stolt över dig
Lars

A low gasp escapes her at those words—*I'm proud of you.* She crumples the note and tosses it across the room. The makeup artist clears her throat, then gets to work, adding missing glitter back onto Tina's face, dabbing her oily shine off, and retouching her lips with color.

They both hear the tentative knock on the door.

"Come in," the makeup artist yells back.

"Tina." Seb pokes his head around the door. "It's time."

Fuck, Tina mutters to herself as she assesses the glittery fake nail she's accidentally bitten off. She tosses it to the floor, a bundle of nerves as she sits in Sweden's VIP booth in clear view of the cheering audience.

Lights, camera, action.

Seb is running a soothing palm up and down her back as they wait for the announcement. The ghoulish-looking rockers from Finland have already sailed through to the finals with their hair-raising chant.

He leans in close. "Breathe," Seb whispers, trying to calm her nerves. "They love this drama…" She shuts her eyes, absorbing his words. Of course. The most melodramatic stage on Earth.

It's now down to Malta and Sweden. One will advance and the other will be on the next plane home. The energy in the arena is so dense she could cut through it with a knife. The two presenters, one in a sparkly blush-pink gala gown and the other in a sharp navy-blue tuxedo, rile the crowd, manufacturing suspense.

"And the final spot goes to…" The male host grins widely before putting his fingers through the envelope and pulling out the result. He stares for an extra second, his face not dropping its grin. He must be excellent at poker, she thinks, as a nervous distraction.

"MALTA!" he screams.

Tina feels Seb's roaming palm on her back stop. Her eyes

jerk open. She turns toward him and sees every unspeakable thought flash through his baby-blue eyes. The one emotion she feels in that moment is terror.

A deep collective gasp fills the arena at the host's announcement before applause rings out once more. The clapping fades into sounds of rushing blood in her ears. Tina sits, frozen solid, staring at the acrylic nail on the floor.

For the first time in Sweden's history, they don't advance to the Eurovision finals. Her chin begins to quiver. No, she can't cry now. Not in front of the millions of people watching across the globe. She feels her heart pounding, trying to burst through her ribcage. Faces flash across her mind. Her producer, the picketers rushing toward her, the Wikström twins, Tobias frowning, Nancy laughing.

She's torn away from these terrifying thoughts by Seb, who is now peering at her, his palms cupping her face. She sees his mouth moving but can't comprehend his words. She'd gambled and lost spectacularly.

"I can't breathe," she hears her own voice. "I can't breathe."

"*Älskling.*" Seb's voice grows clearer. "*Älskling. Andas! Andas!*" Darling, breathe! Breathe!

"I can't..." The words catch on her breath. "I can't..."

Seb pulls her to his chest, tightens his hug around her. Tina buries her face in him as he strokes her hair. With her face hidden from view, she feels herself shuddering in his embrace, tears still refusing to fall. No one understood what she was trying to say with her performance, through those lyrics. No one had seen the frightened little girl who simply wanted the world to understand her, to give her space to fumble her way along, to fully wear her mixed skin. She thinks of the days to come with horror. Will she still be loved? Will she even have a home to return to?

The picketers' words resurface in her mind. *Åk hem nu! Go back home now!*

Tina suspects that this is the beginning of the end. Her worst fears are confirmed the following morning when all media hell breaks loose.

TWELVE

NANCY, 1979

Her first summer in Stockholm was decadently delicious.

Long walks in parks with Malik, licking ice cream cones and subsequently the sweet residue off each other's fingers. Cycling after him as he played tour guide around town. Finally going to events at the embassy. Several more put on by the Gambian-Swedish Association as his date. Meeting his friends and being welcomed into their circle. Meeting his father, a shorter, stockier version of Malik, and his two stunning younger sisters, fresh from their Swiss boarding school summer break.

Yaya worked almost every evening, taking a break only on Sundays and Mondays. Still, she and Benke made sure they found time to help Nancy celebrate her first Midsummer. Wearing a wreath of wildflowers on her short Afro and soaking up the festive atmosphere, Nancy realized she was slowly falling in love with her new home.

Once school resumes that September, she is thrust back into the stressful situation that began in Lars's Vaxholm cottage. After she'd left his basement, Malik had asked her if she was okay. He must have sensed the unspoken in that dark space. She'd simply nodded in response.

Months off in the sun have been good to Lars's skin.

He's several shades darker, his copperish hair now sporting bleached tangerine-colored highlights. He still reserves his look of disdain for Malik, though.

"I think Professor Lasse hates me, Madame President," Malik casually drops one Friday in October as they cradle mugs of hot chocolate at an outdoor café on Södermalm. *Madame President.* Nancy reflects on the nickname. Her scary audacious path, if God wills it. When she had told Malik about her mother's wish for her to become president, she'd expected him to cackle. His look had turned serious as he urged her to really try. That her dreams aren't outlandish. Could she really become Gambia's first female head of state if she worked toward it?

"Why are you saying that? I don't think he hates you," Nancy says. She blows her foam of cream before taking a sip.

"Everything I do, everything I say, seems to irritate him." Malik reaches for his cardamom bun. "It's like he can't stand to look at me, and I've done absolutely nothing wrong." He takes a bite. "He can't bear to give me a top grade—he's deliberately undermining my diplomatic dreams."

Malik's smart. He knows that Lars is punishing him because of his relationship with Nancy. Lars seems to crave her, and it's inappropriate. But at the same time, he *is* growing on her. He's been going out of his way to be kind to her, to be a friend she can count on if needed. He's organized *fika* meetings, experienced Valborg with them, and invited them to his cottage. And he softens slightly with each interaction.

She feels herself becoming more attracted to him as they continue meeting for *fika* in his department, talking about

Swedish politics and which bun—cinnamon or cardamon—
is clearly the superior choice.

New feelings begin to surface within Nancy. She doesn't
need to feel guilty yet—it's just a harmless crush. It's a rite
of passage in college. A crush on your professor—but she
does know she needs to protect Malik. Each grade he gets
from Lars is bad, but he can't prove his grades are lower
than he deserves, because with each marked assignment
comes a lengthy explanation from their professor as to why
Malik's answers aren't nuanced enough, insightful enough,
elevated enough.

"You, on the other hand, are his pet," Malik says. "I
guess I need to work on my curves."

"If I wasn't his pet, you would have failed by now,"
Nancy giggles. "He probably feels threatened by you. Do
you know how handsome you are?!"

"No, tell me." His beautiful smile surfaces. "Why is he
threatened by me?"

"I'm not indulging your ego." She smiles into her drink.
He reaches over to stroke her thigh gently. She meets his
eyes. They haven't crossed that line yet. In due time.

"I've been thinking about his brother, Leif." She tries
changing the topic. "They seemed tense around each other."

"That brother is definitely hiding some secrets."

"Secrets?"

"The way he was looking at me," Malik said. "I think
Mr. Leif likes him some chocolate too... of the male
variety." Malik laughs. "But," he lifts a finger into the air
dramatically, "I don't think they've talked about it. Both of
them were estranged from their parents—Professor Lasse

for gallivanting around Gambia, and Mr. Leif for liking who he's not supposed to like, if you know what I mean."

"Well, I like Mr. Leif," Nancy says, sipping more hot chocolate. "I like his energy. Professor gave me Leif's phone number, so I can have a chat with him," she adds. "I'm sure he knows the most fashionable places to be in this town. I'm thinking of giving him a call. Maybe meeting up with him."

"Are you looking for gossip?"

"No, I'm looking for more friends here in case you decide to leave me," she laughs.

"If you go after Leif, you know you'll be barking up the wrong tree, right?"

"Can't women and men be friends without it being sexual?"

"Are you sure you're from Gambia?!" Malik jokes, taking another sip.

When she gets home that evening, the atmosphere is heavy. Benke and Yaya are sitting on the sofa, forlorn looks on their faces.

"Is everything okay?" Nancy asks upon entering. "Has something happened back home?"

"Come and sit." Yaya pats the spot next to her on the couch. Nancy hangs her coat, kicks off her boots, and sits next to her aunt. Once she's settled, Yaya continues, "My brother is sick. I spoke to him and Fatou today."

Nancy's parents. The last time she'd checked in was a month ago—she'd been so wrapped up in Malik and Sweden that she'd completely lost track of time.

"*Baabaa?*" Nancy tries to calm her rapidly racing heart. "Is he okay?"

"The doctors are not sure," Yaya says, her eyes serious as she studies Nancy. "They are currently running tests, and they will know more by next week."

"What happened?" Nancy's eyes fill with tears.

"He was first complaining of shortness of breath. Then he became dizzy and fainted." Yaya glares at her. "This is my younger brother. If he is sick like this, what do I do at my old age?"

"You're not old, Aunty," Nancy says, switching to comforting her aunt instead. "Fifty is nothing."

"I'm turning fifty-one soon," Yaya starts to cry. "Time has left me. You see, this is why I want my own children," she exclaims. "I want my own."

"Yaya." Benke jumps in, grabbing her hand, which she bunches into a fist. "Let's stop talking about this. Is it your job that is making you so stressed? Maybe it's time to find something else?"

"No!" Yaya is belligerent. She rises to her feet, starts pacing the room. "I'm tired of seeing people die left and right. No one to care for them."

"What happened today?" Benke is on his feet, trying to console her.

Yaya stops moving and buries her face in his shoulder, sobbing. He strokes a palm up her back to soothe her.

These outbursts seem to be coming on more often. Every time a patient in her care passes away, Yaya unravels. It is not so much the fact of dying that seems to bother her, which Yaya knows is inevitable, a fact of life. It is the conditions in which she finds people afterward. Many without close family to come check up on them. Some who've been living in isolation for years. No real friends. Seeing your wards die alone is hard to comprehend. Seeing their memories trivialized in the aftermath, with no friends or family to care for them, is traumatizing.

Nancy knows Yaya fears her own future in Sweden. After all, Benke is fifteen years her senior. What will become of Yaya when he passes? She could move back home, but she's lived overseas for so long that she's more Swedish than Gambian at this point.

And Nancy knows Yaya is coming around to this fact. The day she moved abroad was the day she decided to be less Gambian so she could be more Swedish. The thought scares Nancy. Has she been living in a bubble with Malik, not wanting the pressure of choosing a side?

Yaya had told her time and time again that the only way her life was going to be smooth in this country was to drop everything that made her feel different. Quickly assimilate, she said, and you'll navigate this new life with ease.

Now Nancy isn't sure Yaya believes her own words.

Yaya is suddenly tugging at her shirt, breaking her thoughts. "Help me, Nancy." She isn't sure she heard those words clearly. Maybe her mind conjured them up.

"Help me, Nancy," Yaya repeats, turning to her with tears in her eyes. "Maybe you can help me? Help us?"

Nancy freezes, her mouth hanging open as she sits on the couch. Her gaze moves from a disheveled Yaya to Benke, whose pupils are now pinheads of pure terror.

"What are you saying, Yaya?" Benke finds his voice. "This is crazy. Don't say such unspeakable things out loud."

"Why not?" Yaya looks crazed. "You are not related. She is young. She can help us."

"*Yaya.*" It's the first time she's ever heard Benke raise his voice. His face is bright red, a potent mixture of rage, restraint, and embarrassment. He turns to Nancy. "I'm so sorry, she's not thinking straight. She's not thinking. Forgive her. Please forgive her."

Yaya is clearly teetering on the edge of something—depression? Something darker? Nancy slowly rises and backs away from the couple.

"Nancy? Nancy, please," Benke yells after her as she rushes back toward the door to grab her coat, her purse. "Please wait." He reaches for her bicep. She recoils sharply as if he's burned her. "Please forgive your aunt. She's struggling..."

Nancy can't look at him. She bundles herself up, fumbles to open the door, and bolts out.

She walks, then jogs toward the bus stop. Tears pool in her eyes. She needs to get out of there. She thinks about Yaya as she jogs—the desperation in her voice, her tone, her carriage, had been so intense it suffocated Nancy. Was this country driving her aunt mad? How could she suggest such an abominable act otherwise? Nancy suddenly feels exposed, unsafe. The only person she wants right now is Malik.

She suddenly realizes that, in the midst of Yaya's breakdown, her father's illness had been completely forgotten. She finds a phone booth next to the bus stop, pops several coins in, and dials, her finger winding.

Fatou picks up on the third ring. The connection is patchy.

"*Naa*," Nancy cries into the receiver she cradles with both hands. "What happened to *Baabaa*? What's going on?"

"We didn't want to scare you, my dear," she says. "Your father is resting now."

"Is it his heart? Is he going to be okay?" Nancy asks, her heart beating wildly.

"Yes, he will be," Fatou assures her. Her voice helps to soothe Nancy's nerves.

"I'm so scared," Nancy cries. "I wish I had called you sooner."

"Don't worry, dear. The doctors are conducting more tests, but we have faith, Nancy. We serve a God of miracles."

Hearing those words, Nancy holds the receiver away from her ear. They're the same words Yaya had once spoken to her, and her aunt and the unthinkable request are now back on her mind.

Bringing herself back to the conversation, Nancy asks, "How is Lamin? Is he there? Can I speak to him?"

"Hold on," Fatou says. Over the receiver, she hears voices, one gruffer than the other. A terse exchange follows, then her mother comes back on. "He's not at home."

Nancy takes a moment to absorb her brother's rejection. Even in a family emergency, he wants nothing to do with her. She feels her heart pounding faster. What had she done wrong besides getting the scholarship he wanted? Must men always be the center of everything? Her mother's life revolves around her father, catering to his needs, feeding him three meals every day, getting his bath ready, his clothes ironed, his exterior shined. Were her own dreams similarly supposed to slot around Lamin's? Knowing he's there and doesn't want to hear her voice forces tears down her cheeks and tracks down her heart.

She exchanges a few more words with Fatou before hanging up and continuing her race through Stockholm. She hops on a bus that takes her out to the affluent suburb of Danderyd, where a few embassies and consulates are quietly tucked away. She glances down at her wristwatch. Ten twenty-four on a Friday night. Malik is probably in town partying with his friends from school or the Gambian-Swedish Association, but she tries the door anyway.

The security guard buzzes her in, and Malik shows up at the door wearing flannel pajamas.

"Nancy, what's wrong?" His voice is low with concern.

"I—I—" She starts to tremble. "I can't go home this weekend. I need somewhere to stay."

"Why? Did something happen?"

She launches into his unprepared arms. He wraps them around her, pulling her tighter into their embrace. Nancy turns her face toward his, leans in for a kiss. She loves the taste of his ample lips on hers.

This kiss feels different—it tells Malik all he needs to know. He pulls back and leads her by the hand through the nineteenth-century villa-turned-embassy. They slowly make their way to the living quarters, to his own modest section of the property. His balcony door is open, overlooking an inlet of the Baltic Sea. She hears waves gently lapping in the distance. She steps out into the dark night, takes a deep breath, savors the crisp Nordic air.

He wraps his arms around her from behind and rests his chin on her shoulder as they both gaze into the night. He plants a kiss on her shoulder. Then another. He tugs her with a slow, seductive kiss. She murmurs against it.

He breaks off. "I'll be right back."

Nancy turns back to the view, arms wrapped around herself, thinking about her Valborg wish, when embers had floated into the dark sky. This is the sign she wished for. The ease and comfort she always feels in his arms, nothing forced.

"Are you sure about this?" His voice quietly floats over her. She turns to him. His pajama top is off. Her eyes race down the chiseled grooves of his chest and stomach. They make their way back to his dark eyes. Her normally boisterous Malik has no more words for her as he silently takes her in.

"Yes," she murmurs. "I want you, Malik. I want this."

Nancy steps up to him, runs her fingers through his Afro, pulls him down to taste his lips. He hungrily takes over. She obliges. She loves the feel of his touch, as his large arms roam her back and travel down to cup her backside. She gasps. He stops.

"Are you okay?" he asks against her lips. "You know you can tell me to stop whenever you want, and I will."

"I know," she whispers. "It's just that"—she stops for air—"this is new. I've never done it before."

The room grows silent. She sees Malik's features soften as he processes her words.

"Oh, Nancy," he gasps her name against her neck. "I swear to you. I won't hurt you."

"Promise?" she asks softly, her arms wrapped around his neck.

He nods against her cheek. "I promise you, Nancy. I'll take care of you. I'm yours. *Always.*"

THIRTEEN

TINA, 2006

"From Sizzling Fest to Royal Snoozefest."
"Playing Russian Roulette with Swedish Dice."
"Wikström's Honey Leaves Bitter Taste."
"History Made. Sweden's Own Waterloo."
"The Dancing Queen has Fallen Off Stage."
"Overnight Star. Overnight Shame."
"A complete joke and national disgrace."

The last line is from her half-brothers, the Wikström twins, who have now launched an inquiry into the validity of Tina's representation. The headlines grow worse with each passing hour. Her loss makes CNN breaking news, it's that historically significant for the country. Back home, every single news outlet and morning paper has her face plastered across its screens and pages.

And her disdain for Lars deepens with each new headline.

"I mean… is she even allowed to do that?" an exasperated anchor said during a live taping of a morning show on SVT, Swedish National Television. "People are blaming Wikström's childlike arrogance for this unfortunate moment," they continued in Swedish.

Eurovision experts were called onto the show to dissect

performance rules and question if Tina had already inadvertently disqualified herself when she adapted her song from its folk-pop rhythm to the "snoozefest" of an emo ballad.

In Athens, Tina sits on her hotel bed, wide-eyed, a plush blanket wrapped around her. Her normally straightened hair is now regaining its curls, and her face is makeup-free. Her reddish-brown freckles are her only adornment. She still hasn't shed a tear. They refuse to fall. Her mind hasn't caught up with what's waiting for her back home. Her dreadful semifinal performance was three days ago, and yesterday the Finnish rockers went on to win the entire damn thing with their hell chorus. Even at that news, Tina's tears hadn't followed—she had simply screamed into a pillow.

Nancy had cried on the phone, citing the work of the devil and his lies. Tobias had promised to take the next flight out to come be with her. She stopped him. No, she'd be back in a few days. Seb was here with her. They didn't need to worry about her. She was a big girl.

Now she feels like a petulant child as Pelle, her producer from the record label, paces her room, his face the pink grapefruit color of fury.

"You arrogant little bitch," he curses at her as he paces. "Look at the mess you've made."

"That's enough!" Seb, who'd been leaning against the wall, jumps in. "That's enough. Don't talk to her like that."

"Don't you have a game to play for us?" Pelle turns his rage to Seb. "*Eller hur?*" He matches Seb's intense gaze. "Go to Germany and be useful!"

Seb shoves him in the chest. Pelle stumbles a few feet before collecting himself. He dusts Seb's imaginary handprint off his chest.

"Now you want to go to jail over *her?*" Pelle turns back to Tina, who is staring straight at the Persian rug strewn across the floor. "You had one job, Tina. One job. And you blew it. For what? To prove to the world that you have complete control over yourself, and everyone else be damned?"

When Tina doesn't answer, Pelle growls in frustration. "It's over, Tina. You are finished. The label has already pulled their contract," he informs her. "And her too." He points to Lotta. "Gone. Finished. Get yourself home."

With that, Pelle barrels out of her room, leaving Lotta behind. The assistant steps forward tentatively, unsure.

"I'm so sorry," she says. "You were really good. I think everyone was just surprised, that's all."

"*Tack så mycket,*" Seb says, thanking her on Tina's behalf. "She needs her space."

Lotta nods back, her eyes washing over Tina, who is bundled up like a child waiting for chicken noodle soup. "This came for you." Lotta is holding a black card.

Tina remembers Lars's note and flowers. How "proud" he said he was of her. Now when there's a sign of him, all she sees are omens. Luckily, Seb intercepts the latest omen before Tina has a chance to rip it out of Lotta's fingers and shred it.

"I'm sorry," Lotta adds. Tina twists her lips and nods quickly, still in shock. Lotta turns on her heels to leave. Tina calls her name softly, and Lotta spins to look back at Tina, a mess on her bed.

"Thank you. I'm sorry if I…" she falters, "was ever rude to you." She sees Lotta press her thin lips tightly together, before giving Tina a quick nod and walking out of the door.

Seb walks over with the card in hand and plonks himself down next to Tina. He kisses her, throws an arm over her shoulders, and pulls her close. She rests her head on his shoulder, pulling the blanket tighter.

"How are you feeling?" he whispers into her hair.

"Just open the damn card," she replies.

With his free hand, Seb examines the card and its embossed lettering. ONYX. Frowning, he flips open the card, scanning its content.

"ONYX," he reads aloud. "Does it sound familiar?"

"ONYX?" She scrunches her nose, thinking. "What else does it say?"

"It's an invitation," Seb says as he scans the card. "Dinner tomorrow."

Tina pulls out of his hug and peeks over his shoulder, reading the contents. "Darryl Walker." She reads the signature. "Who is this?"

"I don't know." Seb flips the card, looking for more clues. "I guess we need to google him."

And when they do, they decide to accept his invitation.

The next evening, they find themselves in Athens's Metaxourgeio neighborhood, a haven for visual and performing artists. They'll be dining at a newly opened contemporary Greek restaurant located in a renovated neoclassical mansion.

Tina hides behind sunglasses, a scarf wrapped around her head and shoulders. Everyone knows who she is. The Swedish honey turned sour.

"Ms. Wikström?" The maître d' greets her with a slight head nod. "Mr. Walker is expecting you. I see you've brought a guest with you…. Mr.?" He turns to Seb.

"Mr. Ljungberg," Seb adds.

The maître d' scribbles something down before tapping his pen. "Right this way," he says, smiling.

On their approach, Darryl rises to his feet. He's wearing a crisp white shirt that beautifully contrasts with his chestnut-brown skin, Tina notices. He's clean-shaven, with a fade buzz cut, one pierced ear with a diamond stud. His bright ad-worthy smile reels them in.

She pulls off her sunglasses, her scarf still shielding her as her eyes roam Darryl's face, processing him. He looks relatively young to have all those hotshot music producer credentials that had flashed across the screen when they'd googled him—early thirties, perhaps. Voted one of *Rolling Stone*'s rising stars. A genius when it comes to picking the next superstars. His latest find was a Barbadian pop star who is now enthralling the world with powder-soft vocals that blend pop and rap.

"Tina," he says, arms spread open to receive her like a long-lost friend. He doesn't go in for the hug, though. "You're even more exquisite in person." He reaches out a hand to her, his American accent sailing through the space between them. "Thank you for coming," he says, his warm brown eyes squinting in a smile.

Tina cocks her mouth to the side in a shy gesture. "Thank you for the invite."

"And I see you brought your bodyguard with you." He laughs, stretching out his hand to shake Seb's.

"I'm her—"

"I know who you are," Darryl cuts him off, his eyes holding Seb's. "This conversation might bore you."

"You don't have to worry," Seb says in shaky English, his confidence wavering. "I like music."

Darryl gives him a wry smile and gestures for them to take their seats. He clicks a finger to summon a waiter, whispers an order and then turns back to his guests.

"So," he links his fingers, resting his hands on the pristine, cream-colored tablecloth, "how are you feeling?" His voice dips with concern.

Tina holds his gaze. "Take a wild guess."

He studies her face, lips pursed. "I'm sorry."

"Shit happens." She shrugs, pulling off the silk scarf. She's wearing her curls in two French braids.

"Their loss. That's why I'm here." Darryl pauses for effect. "You were incredible on stage, Tina. That voice," he continues, playing with the rings on his fingers. She notices his heavy titanium watch. "You're a fucking star and they couldn't even see it."

Tina gasps at his bluntness. She tries to respond, but an unintelligible croak escapes from her instead.

Darryl continues. "Standing there with only the spotlight. No backup vocals. No band. Nothing. Just you and that voice." He's animated now. "When I saw you, I said, that's a girl that takes chances. That girl is brave. She is fire." He mimes flames with one hand. "In front of millions, you said, *I am enough. Deal with it.*" He pauses to suck in air. "And you belted those lyrics."

Tina feels heat on her back. Seb's hand. She turns to see him beaming awkwardly at her, pride in his expression.

"I'm a music producer," Darryl says. "But you already knew that, because you're sitting across from me." The waiter materializes; he's holding three wide-brimmed cocktails filled with flaming red liquid on a tray. Darryl reaches for his, waits till both Tina and Seb have theirs in hand too. He gives a small toast. "To the Swedish Siren," he says.

"Swedish Siren?" Tina asks.

"You know it," Darryl says over his glass. "I come to Eurovision every year to find the freshest, hottest new act. And Tina…" He stops, a smile across his face. "Your sultry voice. Deep, intense, wise beyond your years. That voice was made for lovemaking." Seb clears his throat dramatically. Tina laughs.

"Do you always lay it on this thick?" Tina asks, color rushing to her cheeks. This is the first time she has felt like herself in weeks.

"Only on those who leave me flustered," Darryl responds, taking another sip. "You're already a star, but I'm going to make you the motherfucking sun."

Seb shifts uncomfortably in his seat. "We haven't even ordered dinner yet," Tina says, a feeble attempt to lighten the mood.

"I know what I want, Tina." Darryl's voice is serious now. "ONYX wants to sign you. Right now." He holds her gaze while reaching into the breast pocket of his crisp white shirt. He pulls out a card with words scribbled on it and places it in front of Tina. She notices the two large rings on his index and little fingers.

"What is this?" She picks up the card, flips it, and reads. A number. Multiple zeros. Her breath catches at the sum.

"I'm serious." He pulls his menu closer and scans its contents. "ONYX is serious. We want to make you the Swedish Siren. I've seen lots of acts. Very few are raw talents like you. You weren't just singing on stage, Tina. You were telling a story. It wasn't about the song. You were telling the world to stop and listen to your pain, your anguish." He takes a deep breath. "I want to know that story."

"Darryl," she says. She loves the way his name sounds on her tongue. Melodic. "This is all so flattering, but I need time to think. I haven't even been back to Sweden yet. There's a shitstorm waiting there for me."

"I'll make that shitstorm rain roses instead, Tina," he says. "We can make it all go away."

"Thank you…" And at that, Tina breaks down. For the first time since she led Sweden into this Eurovision disaster, she sobs. Embarrassed by her outburst, she tries to contain her tears. After all, she's sitting at a fancy restaurant with patrons who were already craning their necks the second she whipped off her scarf, vying for a good look at the "siren." She realizes Darryl's words offered her relief and release. She isn't a fraud; she'd taken a risk as an artist. Tina is settling into this. She feels like she'd aged several years since the day Lars showed up in her dressing room, and she wanted the world to witness the pain behind her music. Behind the vision they saw on stage, and the skin she was still trying to wear with pride because it didn't belong to one culture or the other.

Tina had morphed from performer into storyteller in front of that crowd. And Darryl was promising to make the rest of the world see it too.

FOURTEEN

NANCY, 1979

Nancy spends the weekend holed up with Malik while he licks every inch of her. By Monday, she decides she's going to move in with her boyfriend.

They haven't spoken about it again since her aunt's breakdown that evening. It seems Yaya doesn't even recall uttering those horrible words; it's as if she'd been pulled into a dark vortex, where her thoughts and words were an intertwined mess. Benke remembers, though. The man who normally maintains prolonged eye contact can no longer meet her gaze.

Did her aunt *really* want her to sleep with a man forty-five years her senior to give her a child? Does desperation turn people mad? Or was this country so open and free that anything was permissible when it came to intimate topics? These questions swim round Nancy's mind as she heads to their apartment to gather her things.

Yaya is clearly feeling apologetic. She promises to help Nancy find a job.

"Once a position opens up at *hemtjänst*, I will let you know," Yaya says while she watches Nancy collect her belongings.

"The same job that is turning you into a madwoman?" Nancy spits back. "Over my dead body!"

She hands her aunt a number where she can be reached. Yaya scans the hastily scribbled numbers before turning back to her niece.

"What is this? Who is this?" Yaya's tone is low and heavy.

"The Gambian ambassador's son." Nancy thrusts her chest out like a peacock before turning her back and slamming the door.

By the time she makes it back to Malik's, he has news for her.

"Without proper security clearance, the embassy doesn't want you officially staying on the premises," he says, sighing. "Too much intimate access to whatever secure communications come through the pipeline." He studies her face before cupping it between his palms. "So, I've agreed to move out of the residence." His eyes twinkle.

The embassy promises to find the couple a new place after the holidays and "unofficially" lets her stay with him in the interim because, according to the ambassador, she makes his son happy.

Nancy hides behind a clothing rack of dress shirts as she observes Leif interacting with a customer. His wide smile, hearty laugh and soft gestures as he hands the shopper, an older woman wearing a floral church hat, a shopping bag. She's at NK, or Nordiska Kompaniet, the iconic department store right on Hamngatan in the middle of town. She had finally gathered the courage to reach out to him. Leif had been ecstatic, inviting her to meet him for lunch.

Once the customer leaves, she emerges from her hiding place, and Leif spots her.

"Nancy!" He waves frantically before calming himself down. "Come," he motions her over, "give me a minute to clock out and we'll grab lunch downstairs."

They settle on *räksmörgåsar*—shrimp sandwiches— in a café brimming with lunch guests and store staff. She watches Leif as he daintily cuts into his open-faced sandwich loaded with pink baby shrimp. He looks dapper in a gray suit with a handkerchief tucked in his breast pocket. He's wearing brown-tinted glasses and his copper hair, a shade or two darker than his younger brother's, is brushed off his face.

"I was quite surprised to get your call," he says before taking a bite.

"I liked chatting with you at Professor Lars's cottage and wanted to get to know you better."

"Professor Lars." Leif chuckles. "I still can't see him as anything but my obnoxious little brother."

"Obnoxious? As in rascally? I would never have imagined him a rascal. Maybe more studious."

Nancy tries her own sandwich. The flavors are working. She's loving it. She takes another bite.

"Trust me, Lars is a rascal in his own way. A rascal of the *mind*." Leif taps the side of his head. "So stubborn. Always likes to get his way… Oops, I'm talking too much, aren't I? I haven't even had my martini yet."

Nancy laughs. "What was it like growing up with him?"

"Well, our parents were so strict that Lars had to run off to Africa," Leif says. "Imagine leaving a peaceful life to go live in uncertainty for years simply because you hate your parents."

"Maybe he was bored here?"

"*Njä*, not Lars. Lars loves to control and possess. He felt our parents controlled him, but he wanted to be able to control everything around him. That's why he left."

"How long was he gone for?"

"Years," Leif shares. "That's when we grew apart. We'd been inseparable as boys, but when he came back, I don't think we recognized each other anymore."

"What do you mean?"

Leif pauses to chug some water, then changes the topic. "What's your sign?"

"What do you mean?"

"Your astrological sign. Pisces? Cancer?"

"Well, I'm a Christian—I don't believe in astrology."

"You don't have to believe in it to know what your sign is." He chuckles. "I'm a flamboyant Leo, baby. What's your sign?"

Nancy hesitates. "Virgo."

"I see."

"See what?"

A smile flashes across his face. "That's why he's obsessed with you."

"Obsessed?"

"Yes, my dear. My brother can't stop talking about you. How he's gotten his creativity back. His spark. How he's been painting up a storm."

"What has that got to do with me being a Virgo?"

"He's a Scorpio." Leif observes her over his glass. "Passionately intense, jealous, vengeful. For a control freak like him, a Virgo is the ultimate challenge."

"He's my professor. This is highly inappropriate."

Leif raises his hands. "I know my brother. I know how he moves and how he thinks." He links his fingers. "Plus, I'm beginning to grow fond of you, Nancy. You're bringing out my mother hen instincts."

Nancy laughs out loud.

Leif smiles. "So, tell me all about that dashing man of yours, Malik."

FIFTEEN

TINA, 2006

Tina grips Seb's hand tightly when the pilot announces ten minutes to landing at Stockholm Arlanda Airport.

She isn't ready. She has already declined all press requests for interviews and in-studio appearances, adding fuel to the burning fire of her defeat. Meanwhile, industry experts and far-removed acquaintances have been gracing TV studios, adding their two kronor to the debate. Everyone is interested in the aftermath. A celebrity psychologist on a radio show wanted to know the reason behind Tina's performance, if it was deliberate sabotage. An intentional protest and show of activism.

When the automatic doors of the Arrivals Hall open, Tina drops Seb's hand and flies into her brother's arms. Tobias embraces her without a word, before planting a quick kiss on top of her head. She starts to hiccup into his chest. He tightens his hug.

"It's okay," he whispers into her hair. "It's okay. You did your best."

"I don't want to talk about it." Tina pulls out of their embrace and puts her sunglasses back on, shielding her from eyes all around them. The low whispers might as well be blasts from a megaphone; they reach her anyway. Whispers of disdain and disappointment from strangers.

Seb and Tobias give each other reluctant hugs. "So." Seb is pensive. "How's the heat?" He rakes his fingers through his hair. The exasperated look in Tobias's brown eyes is all they get in response.

Normally a chauffeur from the record company would be waiting to receive her. Now they have to flag down a taxi to shuttle them to Nancy's apartment in Norsborg.

They stroll in to wafts of fried catfish and Nancy wearing a flowing batik-patterned boubou. Tina rushes into her mother's arms and sobs, her wails filling the living room. After letting Tina release her emotions, Nancy holds her at arm's length and peers into her daughter's eyes, her own brimming with tears.

"Food is ready. I made *chakri* for you too. Your letters are on the table" is all she says.

Nancy is back to her nonchalant self, Tina notes. *At least she tried*, Tina thinks, as her mother returns to her task of hosting them. At least she made *chakri*—a sweet couscous-with-raisins dish from Gambia—specially for her.

Over the clanking of cutlery and Seb surgically picking out catfish bones with his knife, Tina unloads. About how she felt on that stage, her trash producer Pelle, and her passive-aggressive assistant Lotta. She leaves out the bit about Darryl and ONYX.

"I mean," Tina takes a bite of the fried fish she's holding, "I took a risk and failed."

Tobias studies Tina, trying to read her. "So, what are we going to do about the press?" he asks. "You can't avoid them forever." She flashes him an irritated look and shrugs her shoulders in response. "They're demanding an explanation, saying they deserve one since you spent taxpayers' money."

"An explanation of why I sucked?" she fires back before popping more fish into her mouth.

"An explanation of why you made a statement, Tina," Tobias fumes. "Of why you used that stage. What was your point? What were you trying to say?"

Her honey eyes hold his walnut-brown ones. "You of all people should know." Her voice is terse.

"What do you mean?" Tobias frowns at her. She continues eating. "Tina?" His voice pitches.

"Don't you see?" Tina says.

"See what?"

"They only care about you when you're performing for them."

The room falls silent. Only Nancy continues eating, undisturbed. Tobias's nostrils flare as he takes his sister in. It's probably been a while since he's seen her like this. Makeup-free, with frizzy curls packed in a low bun at the nape of her neck.

"It's about Lars, isn't it?" Tobias says, the name barely leaving his lips.

"He only wanted me, us, when I was *something*. When the world loved me," she says, her voice raspy. "He never wanted to see us until now. Never acknowledged us until fame came knocking." Tina's voice breaks.

"Tina..."

"You know it's true," she snaps at him. She suddenly turns toward Seb, who freezes mid-bite, his bright eyes widening like a deer in headlights. "It's the same with Zlatan!" she says. "They care because he's performing."

"*Älskling*." Seb reaches for her hand. She yanks it away.

"You know it's true," she wails. "Every single time Lars shows up, bad things happen."

Nancy chuckles and they all turn to her, bemused. "You're giving him too much power over you, my dear," she says before tucking back into her rice once again.

"I wanted him to see how much he hurt me, you, by abandoning us." She turns to her brother.

"Tina, look, I hear you, but this is insane," Tobias pleads. "To give up an opportunity like that for Lars of all people? You need to fucking grow up."

"You wouldn't understand, would you?" she spits back at him. "You've always hated your skin."

"That's enough!" Tobias snaps, frowning. "What do you know? You're twenty. Still a child."

"Oh, and you're all grown up?"

"You should go to therapy to deal with your issues, not spill them out in front of millions of people. You should know better."

"You're not my dad!"

"You think I want to be your *dad*? I wish I could live my twenties as selfishly as you, but some of us actually have to grow up."

Seb clears his throat and reaches for his glass of apple cider. Tobias drags him into the conversation.

"Why didn't you talk some sense into her?" Tobias fumes.

Seb coughs. "Me? Talk some what?" He coughs again. "I don't understand. I could never understand," he says.

Tina holds Seb's gaze before muttering, "Exactly."

★

Later that night, Tina stares blankly at the ceiling as she lies in bed, one arm thrown over her head, her chest heaving. Sooner or later, she will have to face the press and own up to what she's done. She'll have to admit that Lars is her father—not that they need the confirmation.

She hates her mother's distance. Nancy had simply confirmed with a nod and a "Yes, he is." Not that they were shocked by her response—just another example of her closed-off indifference that keeps her from connecting with her. Nancy often laughs off heavy topics to avoid confronting her true feelings.

Tina lies there as tears trickle sideways down both cheeks and soak into the sheets. She sniffs loudly enough to stop Seb, who's at work between her legs. He climbs up until he hovers over her, his arms planted on either side of Tina on his bed.

"What's wrong?" he whispers, his breathing labored, beads of sweat running down his face. "Don't you like it?" She shuts her eyelids. He presses his lips to hers. She tastes herself on them. "Hmm, tell me, *älskling*."

"I've been thinking a lot about Darryl Walker," Tina begins.

Seb freezes and pins her with a laser glare. "Really? While I've been down there?" He frowns, color rising to his cheeks.

Tina giggles through the tears. "It's not what you think."

"I don't know," Seb says. "He's a sexy fine-ass brotha." He draws out the word in his Swedish accent, a bite to his tone.

"Don't be jealous. I was thinking about his offer. ONYX."

Seb cuts her off with a hungry kiss. "Can we talk about this later? Please?"

She hums against his mouth. "But…"

His movements grow more insistent against her. She reaches for his cheek. He pins her down instead. She laughs into his kiss and his eyes bolt open.

"What's so funny? Hmm?" He's serious.

"What?" Tina asks, confused.

"What's so funny while we're fucking?" His eyes are pinned to her, and every emotion is playing transparently across them: anger, disdain, glee, lust. *Snygg Sebbe*'s eyes are an aquarium of feelings.

"Why are you angry?"

"Why were you laughing?"

"I wasn't laughing." Tina frowns, still trapped beneath him. "Is this because I mentioned Darryl?" His eyes do the talking. "Are you jealous?"

She reaches a palm up to his cheek. He shifts his head away from her touch. She runs her fingers through his hair instead and rises to trail her lips along his neck. "You know I'll always be yours, right?"

Seb turns back to her. She sees his eyes fill with tears.

"What's wrong?" Tina asks. He presses his lips tightly together, holding back his tears. "*Älskling*, tell me what's wrong," she prods.

"Why—"the word catches on his breath. "Why did you do it?"

"What do you mean?" she asks, even though she knows exactly what he means.

"Now everybody hates you," he whispers weakly.

"Why should you care? I don't."

"I care because I love you. Now everyone hates you."

"And you can't handle it. You can't handle being with an outcast."

He shakes his head in frustration. "Lagerbäck called me yesterday," he says, sniffing back his running nose. "He told me not to bring you."

Tina stiffens at his words. "What do you mean?"

"You can't come to Germany," Seb says bluntly. "He says you'll be a distraction."

"But *älskling*, I want to come support you," Tina protests. "It's the biggest tournament of your career, of your entire life. I want to be there for you."

"Exactly." He holds her gaze. "The biggest tournament of my life."

The room, with its high ceiling and wide windows, dips into dense silence, as he pins her down with a steady gaze. She reads his unspoken words in it.

"I see." Tina absorbs his words.

"Do you, really?" Seb regains his voice. "Do you really see me?"

"Seb, this isn't about Lagerbäck. And it's not about those vile, evil twins. It's not about what anyone else is saying. It's about you and me."

"You can't come to the World Cup, Tina," Seb sniffs, but his resolve is stronger now.

"Why are you so scared of your coach? He isn't God. Imagine if he told Zlatan's girl not to…"

"I don't want you there," Seb says before his tears consume him once more. He plants his face in a palm, sobbing.

Tina recoils. Even her own Seb is ashamed of her. The media frenzy around her loss has claimed him too. She's become his bad omen.

She backs away from him.

"Tina." He reaches for her shoulder. She swats his hand away. "Tina, you know I love you." She leaves his words hanging. "*Älskling*, please." She pushes to her feet and grabs her lavender satin bathrobe. The one permanently parked at his place. "Tina?"

Seb scrambles to his feet. "Where are you going?" He reaches for his boxer briefs and shimmies into them as he hops on one foot after her. "Tina."

When he grabs her right bicep, she yanks out of his grasp.

"You were never ready, Seb," she cries. "You were never ready for this. For me."

"Tina, please," he pleads.

"I knew it. I knew you would break someday," she cries. "I knew it. When you didn't come protect me from those picketers," she hiccups. "I just didn't know it was going to be over this."

"I can't blow my own dream," Seb cries, shaking his head. "I've worked so hard for this. I can't blow it now."

"It's not contagious." She eyes him coldly. "And anyway, I didn't blow my dream."

"You were too risky," he says, both hands pushing back his disheveled hair, his face pink.

"How many times do I have to say this? I took a stance," Tina says. "I stood for something in the moment, Seb. And you're clearly incapable of seeing that." She reaches for her bag, still wearing her bathrobe. "Only one person saw me that night," she says to him.

"Let me guess. Darryl," he says, an ironic smile settling on his lips.

"You're not ready for me," she says. "You never were. Go build your dream without me." She leaves his apartment, slamming the door. She calls a cab and when it arrives, she clambers in, exhausted.

The cab driver catches her reflection through his rearview mirror.

"*Nämen, är det sant?!*" he says in accented Swedish, his dark eyes meeting hers in recognition through the mirror. *Gosh, is it true?* A celebrity in his car. She pops her sunglasses back on, instantly cutting off any chance of conversation.

As the driver takes her south of town toward Norsborg, Tina drags her bag closer and pulls out the two letters she'd picked up from Nancy's. She had chucked them into her bag at dinner, not paying attention, and now she freezes when she sees the same handwriting on both. *Lars.*

She peels the flap off one of them. The one with the most recent date. She scans his words, written in stunning cursive. The mark of an artist.

My dear Tina

I saw you that night. I heard you loud and clear.

I understood what you wanted to say to me.

I know you hate me. Your anger is justified.

I too understand the pitfalls of sudden fame, media backlash.

I experienced it too, as a lowly professor turned acclaimed artist.

I too understand what it means to be loved one day and hated the next.

I have always wanted you and Tobias. Always.

With all my heart, I have loved you both. I love you both.

But I was a coward. I couldn't show the world I loved you.

I wasn't ready for you.

SIXTEEN

NANCY, 1979

Now approaching her second winter in Sweden, Nancy feels reset once more.

Malik, who loves exploring the city, now has a partner-in-crime. From disco nights and jazz sessions at Alexandra's Night Club to sampling salmon prepared a dozen different ways, he shows her a whole new side of Sweden. It seems riding around with azure-blue license plates opens up the city to African diplomats and academics in a different way. She seems truly content.

Someone else has noticed this seismic shift within Nancy.

"So... what are your plans for *höstlov*?" Lars asks them both their autumn holiday plans as he shuts his notebook one Friday in late October.

"Well," Malik starts to say, stretching his arms. "I need to go back home for some chieftaincy ceremony for my father." He glances at Nancy. "I wish I could stay with my girl, but I'm the firstborn and only son, so I've got to be there."

Lars sharply sucks in air. His eagle eyes find Nancy's. "And you?" He continues packing. "Any plans?"

"Not right now," she manages. "I wish I could go with Malik, but I guess I'm stuck here."

"You're not spending it with your aunt and uncle?"

"We're not on speaking terms right now," Nancy says. "So, I'll be hanging with our friends from the…"

"Come to Vaxholm with me," Lars bursts out, then quickly adds, "and Leif. He's going to be there. He mentioned you two meet for lunch sometimes. He's fond of you, you know."

Nancy feels her skin heat up. She's immediately transported back to the basement of his cottage. She wonders what would have happened if Malik hadn't come down when he did.

"Thanks for the invitation, but I'm not sure…" Nancy protests.

"Come, Nancy. I will show you the paintings I've started working on. Remember the photos I took?" His voice is energetic, flowing with excitement. "I think I got my inspiration back."

"Are you trying to move in on my girl, Lars?" Malik is suddenly stern.

"Professor," Lars corrects him.

"Okay, *Professsssor*. You know you can't be inviting your female students over like that."

Color rapidly rushes to Lars's cheeks. Nancy sees his jaw clench, feels the air shift.

"Sorry I asked," Lars says. "I just didn't think spending *höstlov* alone would be fun."

"Thank you for your invite," Nancy replies, trying to defuse the situation. "It really is kind. If Leif will be there, maybe I'll come."

"He'll be there, and you don't have to worry about a thing."

"Are you sure about this?" Malik whispers to Nancy, reaching for her hand.

"He's our professor," she hisses back. "He's harmless; he'll lose his job if he oversteps. Trust me."

Lars clears his throat. "I can still hear you." He chuckles awkwardly, his smile brightening up his otherwise austere look.

"You should laugh more often," Nancy says. "It suits you."

He slowly relaxes his mouth, eyes on her.

"Nancy," Malik breaks in. "Let's go."

They gather their things. Lars calls out after them. "Strömkajen. 12 p.m. tomorrow. For the ferry—if you decide to come."

She tilts her head at his words and offers him a smile.

Nancy spends *höstlov* at the embassy.

Thinking about it some more, she didn't want to be with Lars in closed quarters without Malik. She remembered being with him in his basement. The energy had been intense then. Now, she probably couldn't bear it.

Her father has been released from the hospital and is home recovering, but there's no one to celebrate the news with. She's still not speaking with her aunt and uncle.

When Malik comes back from his short trip to Gambia, it is without his father.

"*Baabaa* had to stay behind to handle some business," Malik says. His expression is more serious than usual. "This means I must represent him at a special dinner this

December. He wants me to go in his place," he adds with a sigh. "He's grooming me to be his natural successor."

"No one does nepotism like us Africans," Nancy giggles. She's lying in the crook of his arm—her favorite spot—as they watch snow flurries from his open balcony door.

"Sounds like you haven't met any white people yet," Malik laughs. "Talk about nepotism and generational hoarding on another level."

"So, what's this fancy dinner about? Will I need to buy sequins with my pocket money?" she asks.

He kisses her nose. "Leave that to me." He kisses it again, smiles.

"Mmmm, so mysterious." She relaxes into his caress. He adjusts his weight to look at her.

"So, *Strömkajen? 12 p.m.?*" he says, mocking their professor.

"Wow, your Swedish pronunciations are getting really good," she jokes. He playfully nips her shoulder with his teeth.

"Seriously, did you go?" She reads insecurity in his eyes. The thought of losing her to someone two decades older must be playing on his mind, holding his thoughts in a chokehold.

"I would never," Nancy whispers before pulling his head down for a deep kiss.

When they both return to class the next week, Lars seems cold and aloof. His features are tense, his limbs awkward.

He accepts their greeting with a stiff "*hej*" in response. He doesn't ask how their autumn break went. He walks up to the board to start scribbling an outline and carries on the lecture robotically, a one-way funnel of information. No engagement, no questions. When he finishes forty-five minutes later, he claps his hands once to dismiss them, then immediately leaves the classroom.

Nancy flashes Malik a quick glance upon Lars's departure. She'd stood him up.

Now we're both in trouble.

A few weeks later, in early December, Nancy grabs on tightly to Malik's arm. He's wearing a tuxedo and dignitary medals pinned to his chest. The embassy has organized a margarine-yellow Guinea brocade ball gown for her, decking her Afro out with matching yellow daisies.

They glide into the large Blue Hall of Stadshuset, the City Hall, where the Nobel Prize banquet is being held. Two matching stupendous staircases, one at each end, lead up to a large receiving terrace. Lined up along stairways is a choir wearing red tops and black trousers. Sitting at the table of honor and dressed in shiny medallions is HM King Carl Gustaf of Sweden. He is chatting to a bespectacled woman next to him as press photographers surround them, clicking away.

HM Queen Silvia is wearing a pastel-blue sequined gown, a crown on her head. Nancy has only seen crowns on queens in books. Now she's staring straight at a queen in real life, and she is breathtaking. A gold cross rests in the V-cut of her gown. Nancy grabs on tighter to Malik's arm and he chuckles, sensing her nervousness. Nancy marvels at the fact that she's ended up in this circle simply because she returned Malik's dashing smile in class.

An usher leads them to their table, where a middle-aged white man with a sharp nose and chestnut-brown hair combed off his face sits. He rises to his feet in gentlemanly fashion once the ward pulls out Nancy's chair. They all take their seats, and the man stretches his hand out to shake Nancy's and Malik's, introducing himself.

"Olof. *Trevligt att träffas*," he greets them in Swedish, his sleepy blue eyes examining them.

"Mr. Prime Minister," Malik says, his voice pitching high in excitement. "Such an honor."

The older man laughs dryly. "Please don't call me that, otherwise we might both get into trouble. We lost the last election."

"Don't worry," Nancy jumps in. "You will win again."

"You seem confident about that, *Ms....*?" He waits for her name.

"Nancy Ndow," she says shyly.

"Well, thank you, Ms. Nancy Ndow, for your vote of confidence."

"I serve a God of miracles." She smiles at him. "I know you will win."

Waiters wearing white jackets and with cloth napkins strewn across their arms begin to serve dinner—cold turbot with fish roe and hollandaise sauce, followed by roast veal with fried potatoes and morel sauce.

Over the clanking of expensive cutlery, and under the spell of the ethereal choir, Olof makes easy conversation with them. He tells them about his travels around the U.S., which had been the best education of his about race, discrimination and integration, he explains. Traveling all around the Deep South, spending time in African American communities, listening to gospel choirs, understanding that he could never fully walk in their shoes, but he could at least walk side by side with them.

He wants to know all about Malik's diplomacy and global stations, Nancy's background in Banjul, her political aspirations, how she moved to Sweden, how she's finding it here.

"It's the pronunciation for me," she says, laughing as she spears tender veal with her fork. "How do you hear the difference between *sjö* and *tjö*?"

He laughs. "You try it."

"I try every day, I can't do it," she protests.

"C'mon, you can!" he urges her.

Nancy takes a deep breath, purses her lips awkwardly, attempts the words. Malik bursts out laughing while Olof chuckles.

"I will not patronize you and say your Swedish is perfect," he says. "I know you are learning, and I appreciate you for trying."

Nancy holds his gaze and nods, hers welling up with grateful tears. "Thank you. I also will not patronize you and declare you will win without understanding current sentiments in society."

"Tell you what, if I win the next election, I will wink into the camera for both of you. Deal?"

"*When* you win," Nancy corrects him.

Olof seems amused. His eyes tell her so. "See? You're already patronizing me."

"That would be fantastic," Malik says, cutting in. "We hope you do."

"So, Madame," he says, "what will be your sign to me when you become Gambia's first female president?"

She laughs. "Thank you for your vote of confidence, sir."

"Remember, you serve a God of miracles, Nancy," he says. "Don't lose your faith now. I, for one, believe you can do it, and you will if that's what you want." He lifts a glass of Cordon Rouge champagne to his lips.

What she wants. Is that what she wants? To become Gambia's first female president? The thought always sends heat down her spine, as if the dream is so large and scary she isn't even sure she should think it.

At university, she occasionally drops in on seminars and talks organized by the Stockholm Association of International Affairs (the UF), a politically and religiously independent association—an attempt to act on her curiosity. Her biggest takeaway, though? There's excellent *fika* at their social activities—those students know how to bake magic with cinnamon, cardamom and saffron.

About an hour into the dinner, petit fours and ice cream are brought around for dessert. A few guests swing by their table to squat next to the former prime minister and engage him in either mini debates or mini adulations, giving Nancy and Malik a chance to scan the room for other famous guests.

A flash of light interrupts them.

"This way, this way," they hear a voice calling out. All three turn to see two press photographers. Malik, Olof and Nancy lean in close.

Flashing lights rain down on the trio.

SEVENTEEN

NANCY, 1980

A sepia copy of their photo with Olof circulated around various African communities and the Gambian-Swedish Association. An A3 version had been acquired, framed and hung at the embassy.

After the holidays, that photo was also displayed on the news in Gambia. It warranted a phone call from her parents, who cooed their pride that their only daughter was rubbing shoulders with kings and queens. Nancy finally spoke to Lamin after two years of moving to Sweden, telling him how she couldn't wait for him to come visit her. The only word he had for her was *Inshallah*—if Allah wills it.

"Be patient with your brother," Fatou pleads.

"Who knows, maybe it will be too late for him to apologize once I become Madame President," Nancy says with a pained laugh.

Yaya and Benke also reach out. They offer season's greetings and a reminder that their home will always be her home. Yaya has even found her a job at *hemtjänst*, she says. Nancy politely refuses her offer.

The photo reaches Lars too.

He brings a clipped-out newspaper version of it to class

that December. He first congratulates her for her ability to rub shoulders with such a crowd, and then congratulates Malik for providing her access to them. She sees pain in his eyes as he says this, a concession that he will never be able to provide her with this kind of life. She's slowly worked her way back into his good books since she refused his offer to come to his cottage. When Lars gives her an early peek at her results, she has passed with flying colors as expected.

By January, Malik and Nancy have moved into a tiny apartment leased by the embassy. It's a rustic getup with pinewood-paneled doors and cabinets in its kitchen and bathroom, perched on a side street off a popular drag, Sveavägen.

The days pass and they begin to unpack. Nancy cradles Malik's framed copy of their famous photo in her hands as she unwraps it, remembering Olof's words: *What sign will you give me, Madame President?* She smiles before placing it on their new shelf. She loves this space, their very own to start making proper memories in.

They begin to meet their new neighbors. Most are warm and inviting. Next door is an interracial couple with four kids under the age of ten: a tall, lean academic from Senegal whose smooth, well-moisturized skin glimmers under light, and his wife, a short white Swedish woman with a mass of red curls, and green eyes behind frames too large for her face. The entire family of six appeared at their door one Sunday evening, the wife bearing a plate of home-baked sugar-and-jam cookies to welcome the couple.

When they left, Malik had leaned into Nancy to whisper, "What is it with gingers and Black people? They can't seem to stay away from each other. As if they want to experiment and see what comes out." He'd punctuated this with his deep, hearty laugh, the one she loved. She loves hearing him laugh, wants to hear his voice for the rest of her days. She must tell him that soon.

The other neighbors across the hall are also kind, two men from Chile who live together after fleeing Pinochet's regime. They *oohed* and *aaahed* in dramatic fashion over the photo of Nancy and Malik with Olof. Next door to them lives a demure blond duo from Norrbotten region in the north. The man easily clears six feet four, but his partner is a woman so petite Nancy worries for her vagina. Her concerns were quickly dispelled the first time she and Malik heard them screaming and banging their entire floor down. They had simply raised eyebrows at each other when they heard a third voice—deep and male—in the mix too.

The only cranky one is Mr. Torbjörn. He's somewhere between his sixties and seventies, supported by a walking cane, with piercing blue-gray eyes bordering on translucent and thinning gray hair. He waits with his door cracked open a sliver, so he knows when it's safe to come out of his apartment, and leaves passive-aggressive notes on their door, telling them to keep the noise down.

Mr. Torbjörn has a sphynx cat, Leo, with matching eyes he always cradles like a baby. They have never had the chance to learn more about him—he never stops around for long enough. They ignore his incoherent mumbling whenever he snarls at them, and avoid his glares in the elevator. They see people—nurses, *hemtjänst*—come by twice a day to make sure he's fed and medicated.

"That man is such a sad specimen," Malik says one evening over pizza. They'd acquired an oak dining table, and Nancy an extra few pounds around her hips and thighs. "I haven't seen any family visiting him."

Nancy thinks of Yaya. She can see why helping people like Mr. Torbjörn day in, day out must take its toll on her, though she will still never understand her unspeakable request.

So, she decides she will try. She will buy cinnamon buns for Mr. Torbjörn, knock on his door, and make sure he makes her tea. She will endure his snarls; she knows he is just lonely and has no one to talk to. She decides she will spend her Easter break getting to know the old man while Malik visits his sisters in Switzerland.

Malik and Nancy are sitting cross-legged on their camel-colored wall-to-wall carpet one day when they receive a letter from the embassy. MAX cheeseburgers wrappers are abandoned beside them, and the stereo belts out a dance remix of ABBA's "Voulez-Vous." Outside their window, late January flurries lend the scene a cozy atmosphere.

It's Malik's results. And once he tears them open, the disdain Lars has shown him officially becomes mutual.

Malik rips up the papers, casts their pieces aside, and reaches for his soda to take a swig. Nancy silently observes him as he sips, his anger palpable.

That was Malik's last class with Lars. Now Nancy must endure his lessons without Malik. And Malik's absence seems to be fueling Lars's audacity around her, always pressing her to come see his paintings.

Packing up to leave class one day before her lunch break, she senses Lars close by. She knows his scent by now. Not musky and spicy like Malik's, but a mix of the turpentine from his oil paintings and citrusy aftershave.

"Aren't you curious?" he asks her in Mandinka. The words *kumpa baloo* pull her from her task.

She freezes and turns toward him. He looks serious, portmanteau in one hand, the other tucked in the pocket of his corduroy pants.

"Curious?" she parrots.

"My paintings of you," he says in a whisper. "It's been over a year."

"I thought you were just being kind," Nancy says. "I didn't seriously think you had made me your muse."

"Eleven oil paintings so far," he says breathily. "From those photographs. I just kept painting and painting. I'm still working on more. I would love to show them to you." He collects himself. "If you want, of course."

"You're always trying to find reasons to lure me to your cabin, Professor." She attempts a jovial tone.

Color floods his face. "If you feel that way, then I need to work on my skills," he laughs. "I would at least hope you consider me a friend after all our *fikas* and cultural field trips."

She enjoys this side of him, hearing him flow comfortably in Mandinka.

"I'm proud of this set. Enough to exhibit them," he says. "And I want you to be the first to see them."

She holds his gaze for two seconds before muttering, "Okay."

"Okay, we're friends, or okay, you want to see them?"

"Yes, okay, both. Before I change my mind."

"*Kana wo foo*," he says softly, a glint in his eye. *Don't say that.*

She promises to meet him at Strömkajen for the ferry to Vaxholm sometime during their Easter break. He tells her exactly which day he wants her there and where to meet. There's a brunch cruise he would like to enjoy on this particular ride with her. She's nervous yet excited, because to reinspire an artist as his muse feels invigorating.

After class, she stops by a grocery store to buy cinnamon and cardamom buns for her neighbor. She knows she must find a job soon—she lives off a monthly allowance from the government as part of her scholarship, but that doesn't stretch very far. Malik covers everything else.

As she expects, Mr. Torbjörn doesn't answer the door, though she hears him behind it.

"I'm not leaving," she yells through the door. "I have *fika* for you. Freshly baked."

"*Lämna mig i fred!*" he growls back from behind the door. *Leave me in peace!* She hears a meow as well; Leo acting like a wingman, meowing her away.

"I have something for Leo too," she adds. The tinkering stops. The door creaks open a sliver. He's carrying Leo, who is sporting a feline turtleneck to keep his naked skin warm.

"*Kanell eller kardemumma?*" he asks, eyeing her paper bag suspiciously. *Cinnamon or cardamom?*

"Both," she answers, smiling at him. He glares at her for a second before opening the door.

Stepping into Mr. Torbjörn's house is like stepping into

a museum. Beyond the slight whiff of cat piss, the house smells fresher than she imagined it would. It's decorated with furniture frozen in time. Touches of a woman who once lived there are peppered around the place: lace trimmings, delicate teacup sets in a glass sundry cabinet. She spots large black-and-white photos on the walls, most featuring a beautiful woman with long, dark, maybe black, hair. A younger version of Mr. Torbjörn, who would have turned heads in his day, is beside her. The house is a shrine—as if his wife went out to go buy them groceries and never came back.

"Coffee or tea?" Mr. Torbjörn asks, grabbing the paper bag from her as he limps with his cane toward the dining table. He's much younger than he first appears at this close range. Mid-sixties, perhaps.

"Tea, please." She pads behind him. "You have a beautiful apartment, Mr. Torbjörn," she adds, looking around. Her eyes land on another monochrome photo of him in uniform and goggles. "A fighter pilot?"

He turns to her, light in his eyes, and for a moment she sees the dashing man in that photo. The vision evaporates as quickly as it surfaced. Soon the whistle of a small copper kettle fills the apartment.

She rushes to help him. He snaps back at her. He doesn't want her assistance. It must be traumatic, she thinks. Once gripping the difference between life and death in a gear shift, and now grabbing the handle of a kettle with shaky fingers.

"I was in Congo," he says in English. Those words stun Nancy. He's never spoken anything besides Swedish to her. "Many years. Air Force."

She warms her cup between her palms, silently pleading for him to say more. He splays a few fingers toward her. They're covered in light-blue veins and brown liver spots. "Three years," he clarifies. "*Sen* Egypt," he adds in Swenglish. "My wife, Asenath. Egyptian."

"Two years." Nancy lifts two fingers. "Stockholm," she says, giggling.

"Pilot," he says. "Congo. 1961 to 1964." He switches to Swedish. "United Nations." He takes a deep breath, then points to one of the shelves. She gets up to retrieve the photo he's pointing at. Two men. Torbjörn is in uniform standing stoically next to a man in a suit. Beneath it is scribbled the words: *FN:s generalsekreterare Dag Hammarskjöld.*

"Rhodesia," Torbjörn adds from the dining table. "Plane."

Nancy turns back to the veteran as tears cloud her eyes. As someone with her own eyes set on a career in international relations and the United Nations, she knows that name all too well. Swedish Dag Hammarskjöld died in an air crash in Northern Rhodesia while flying there to negotiate a ceasefire between United Nations and Katanga forces in 1961 as UN Secretary General.

Torbjörn lifts his bun toward her in a toasting gesture. "*Jerejef.*" He thanks her in Wolof.

She doesn't correct him. "*Njo koo boo ka,*" she replies. *You're welcome.*

When she leaves Torbjörn, she thinks about his loneliness. So when Malik gets home later that night, she clings onto him, refusing to let him leave her side.

EIGHTEEN

TINA, 2006

Thirty-two years after hosting the FIFA World Cup, Germany is once again the site of the games this summer. The crowd goes wild as Sweden and Paraguay's football teams stroll onto the field at Olympiastadion in Berlin.

"Look at that sea of yellow," the sports commentator's animated voice begins. "It's looking like the Swedish fans will be voted the best during this World Cup," he yells over the collective chanting of *Heja Sverige! Heja Sverige!* "Sweden needs this win. After last month's fiasco, the Swedes will take any victory they can get."

Tobias flashes Tina a quick look. They are at Nancy's apartment because Tobias wasn't going to miss Sweden playing and as he's scolded her, it's the least she could do. Root for a win.

The national anthem starts playing and the camera pans from player to player as they stand heroically. Seb comes on. He's grown stubble. She hates it on him.

"See our fine boy," Nancy says nonchalantly before tossing popcorn into her mouth and chewing loudly.

Tina turns at Nancy's sign of resignation. *Our fine boy?*

Since Tina slammed Seb's door weeks ago, though, she has ignored his calls and voice messages. His desperate pleas for her to talk to him. She can't handle hearing his voice right now because she knows that beneath his layer of remorse lay the shame he feels on her behalf.

She did finally find the strength to crawl out of her hole and go on one of the most popular evening talk shows, *Efter Nio med Malin.*

"What happened?" the host asked. "Why did you take that risk?"

"Because I'm an artist. If I didn't want to take risks, I'd be an accountant."

The interview continued in that terse fashion for another fifteen minutes, which felt more like an hour to Tina. The interviewer even dared to ask about the Wikström twins, their claims, if they were ever going to meet in person. Tina had simply glared at the host in response.

By the next morning, the press had labeled her "arrogant" and "immature." A few more media interviews and radio slots, and Tina quickly realized why other celebrities hired PR agencies to coach them and clean up after them. Realizing she wasn't going to change anyone's opinion, she has taken to spending her days holed up in her childhood room, mulling over Darryl's offer. An initial sign-on fee of $100,000 from ONYX to help sweeten her decision. Then forty percent royalties. More generous than the standard deal. She kept his number, but sometimes she wondered if his offer had since been rescinded, if he'd finally woken up to her mediocrity.

Then, that morning, she received a text message from
Darryl. She calls him back when she's had some time to
think.

"What time is it in New York?" she says into the receiver.
"Way past midnight?"

"I'm in LA, baby!" He seems jovial, music with a heavy
bass beat in the background. "Have you considered my
offer? I can't hold on to it for too long."

"I thought I was worth the wait?"

She hears him chuckle. "Fair enough. I like you, Tina.
You've got a bite to you. Your African side."

"I've been thinking about it," she says. "I'm not sure
there's a career for me here. No one wants to book me right
now. I'm waiting till their hurt blows over, but maybe that
day will never come."

"Come to LA and I'll make them crawl on their
knees to have you back," he says. "I'll make you the Swedish
Siren. America will fall in love with you, Tina. I promise."

Heat spreads within her. Excitement? Fear of the
unknown? She isn't sure, but she's feeling more than she
ever did on the Eurovision stage.

He speaks again. "It would mean moving to LA. City of
Ange—"

"I don't know anyone there," she cuts in.

"You've got me. I got you, Tina. We'll make your move to
the States as smooth as possible. We'll take you on a press tour
introducing you to the big players in the U.S. Letting them
fall for you too. Tell you what... How about I fly you to
LA next week? Give you a taste of life here? Bring you into

ONYX Records, have you meet some of the producers behind your favorite pop stars? Show you around?"

His words jumble in her ears. Los Angeles? Flown out?

"For a week," Darryl says. "All expenses paid. You're my next star. The next Erykah Badu."

"Let me think," Tina protests weakly.

"I've given you enough time to think. Say yes!"

This time, Tina giggles, then takes a deep breath. "Yes," she says, and is met with a whoop of glee on the other end from Darryl.

"And will your bodyguard be joining us?" Darryl smirks. She hears it over the phone.

"Why do you care about him so much?"

He merely laughs before saying he'll send her details. He'll fly her to LA, give her a glimpse into her new life as the next hot star, and present a contract afterward to her lawyer. She makes a mental list of everything she needs to prepare. First on the list: *Get a lawyer.*

She's pulled back into the room with her mother's screams. "Our boy scored a goal!" Nancy is doing a shimmy-dance on the couch.

Tina turns to her mother, confused. Nancy is clapping animatedly. Tobias is on his feet punching the air. On screen, Seb's arms are spread out like wings and he's running, dipping left, then right. Flying into his dream.

Sweden beats Paraguay, one–nil. Seb had carried the team to victory. Tina heaves as tears fill her eyes. She wipes them away with the back of a finger. She hasn't told them yet. Not about Darryl and his offer. Not about her rift with their *boy*. And not about the man she has agreed to meet for dinner tomorrow.

EIGHT THIRTY P.M., THE FOLLOWING EVENING

Tina walks into a classic restaurant tucked away in Östermalm's back streets. Heavy mahogany furniture, white linen sheets, a menu of mostly potatoes and pork served in various pretentious ways. She avoids the glances being thrown her way. They'll survive, she thinks as a waiter leads her toward the back where Lars sits.

He stands, clearing six feet. Mid-sixties. A cyclist's physique. Fit. Clean-shaven like the last time. Pleasant to look at, but not head-turning. He still has a full head of hair and there are freckles splashed all over his face.

"Tina," Lars says, his matching eyes hooking hers. "I'm so happy you came." He steps forward to give her an awkward hug. She returns it with a loose one of her own and gives him a half smile. "Thank you," he adds.

She settles herself across from him and fully takes him in. Up close, she sees their resemblance goes beyond their coloring; their bone structure is identical.

"How are you?" Lars asks, linking his fingers, leaning forward.

"Let's cut the bullshit," Tina responds.

"I understand you're upset. And you have every right to hate me."

Tina pulls out the last letter he wrote to her. She unfolds it, then gently passes it over. Lars slides it closer, glances at her with a crooked smile, and reaches into his pocket for reading glasses. He unfolds and settles them on the bridge of his nose. He makes a humming sound of recognition in the back of his throat.

"What did you mean by this?" Tina asks him. "*I heard*

you loud and clear. I understood what you wanted to say to me."

Lars sighs. "Exactly what it says."

"I don't have time for this," Tina fires back.

"I mean, I heard you. I saw you. I saw all the pain in your eyes. Heard it in your voice. You didn't want my *honey*. My eyes. My features."

She holds his gaze. He continues, "You were telling the world your story. The story of what it feels like to be not one or the other. Of what it feels like to be both." He clears his throat. "I'm so sorry I failed you, Tina. You and your brother."

"Tobias," she adds. "His name is Tobias. And he fucking hates your guts. He never wants to meet you. *Ever*." She draws out the last word. "You abandoned us."

Lars presses his lips together, accepting her reprimand. "I've seen pictures of him. Very handsome. He's got Nancy's features… Isn't he a swimmer?"

"What do you want from me, Lars?" Tina cuts in.

"I—I—er, I want to start afresh. I want to do right by you and your bro—. Tobias," he says. "By Nancy, too."

"It's too late."

"I hope it's not," he says. "Because you're here."

"I can leave."

"But you won't," he challenges her. "Because you're tired of not having answers. Of not knowing all of who you are. Ask me what you want to know, Tina. I'm tired of lying."

Tina holds his gaze for a couple of uncomfortable seconds before speaking. "Why did you hurt her?" she asks. "Why did you leave my mother alone to fend for herself in this country? Away from her family?"

She sees his Adam's apple jump as he processes her words.

"I don't know what to say." Lars's voice is low. "I never wanted to hurt her."

"My mother loved my *dead pappa*." Tina's eyes are covered in a wet film. "She loved him so much all that's left is indifference. He drained her of her love."

"I know," his voice begins to crack. "I know. I couldn't choose her."

Tina twists her lips in anger. "Why not? Is it because of… Frida?" She surprises herself by remembering the woman's name.

His eyes fill. "I was married," he admits. "I still am."

"Why would my mother have done this—had us—if she knew you were married all along?" Tina can't hold back her anger now and finds she doesn't want to.

"She didn't know," he says quickly. "Leif called me a coward and said he never wanted to speak to me again." He pauses. "He could forgive the mistake with Tobias. He couldn't forgive me a second time for having you. I deserved to be called a coward and cut off," Lars continues. "I lied to Nancy for years."

Tina absorbs his words, his disposition. *Uncle Leif.* Her heart hurts when he mentions her dear father figure. He must want something from her, because sitting across from her is the most selfish man she's ever met, and selfish people always want something in return. *Always.*

"Why did you do this to her?"

"I loved her. I wanted to be with her," he says. "I've always loved Nancy. I'm Gambian here." He clutches his chest. "Here." He pats right above his heart.

"Then why didn't you leave your wife?"

"I couldn't. The boys."

"You mean your Nazi spawn?"

"Please don't call them that." Lars's voice is stern. He takes a breath. "We're estranged."

Tina laughs sarcastically. Heads turn in their direction. "Estranged from them too? You seem to be the common problem."

"Look, I don't expect you to forgive me. I don't deserve it right now, but seeing you hurting right there, on that stage... I wanted to let you know that I understood you. And that you are loved."

"I don't need your love, Lars."

"I was a coward."

"You still are." Her tone is firm. "You could have made a statement when your evil sons were trying to bring me down. But instead, you hid away from it once again. Like you always do."

"I get it. And I'm sorry," Lars starts. "Look, I understand how hard it is to get famous so quickly. I was just an anthropology professor who sold one painting for an insane amount of money at auction, and my life changed in an instant. I had no one to guide me, to help me through all these sudden rushes of feelings, emotions with no solid footing."

"And so, you want to be my sage?!" Tina cackles in disbelief. "Do you hear yourself?"

Lars has no more words.

She pulls the menu toward her, not breaking eye contact.

"Buy me dinner," she finally says, flipping it open, "and stop writing me letters."

Lars claps. Once. "Right," he says, his eyes washing over her once more. "Let's eat."

NINETEEN

NANCY, 1980

Nancy pokes at the fancy pickled herring on her plate. Beneath them, the steam engine hums as the boat cuts through the gentle waters of the Baltic Sea. Curiosity keeps her picking at the *smörgåsbord* of cold cuts, cured salmon, lukewarm meatballs and yellow almond potatoes on her plate.

Lars has painted eleven portraits of her so far, and she can't wait to see them. A piece of her—vanity, perhaps—wants to see what he sees.

She was worried about telling Malik, but she had received his blessing after some convincing. "You have absolutely nothing to worry about," she had said, chuckling into their kiss. "Nothing." Malik's grip on her upper arms had tightened, as he'd rested his forehead on hers. "He's just being kind."

There's nothing to talk about on that ferry ride. They are a long-time divorcee and his student. From the outside looking in, he probably seems like a man caught in the throes of a middle-aged crisis desperate for the gaze of youth on him once more. Maybe a man with a lot of money who has finally bagged a woman out of his league. Or, maybe it looks like an unlikely friendship budding as they each start seeing each other with new eyes.

Resting by Lars's feet is a grocery bag with cider, grapes and a six-piece strawberry cake for *fika* at his cottage. They'll stay there for a few hours, then catch a different ferry back to the mainland.

Lars's cottage is a fifteen-minute walk from the port, along the water's edge and through woods that are slowly regaining their brush of spring leaves. He lets them in to the cabin and makes a fire to heat up the small living quarters. No electricity, he says. Nancy hadn't noticed last year. They'd been basking on the deck in the sun with his brother Leif.

"How is Leif doing? I haven't seen him in a little while." Nancy breaks the awkward noiseless void. "He's so much fun."

"He asks about you too," Lars says as he stokes the fire. "I wonder what you two talk about." He frowns. "I hope not me."

"I hope he's all right," Nancy says, avoiding his question. She shifts in her armchair. She could never stay in this place at night by herself. It's so isolated, and she can't help wondering if Lars gets lonely out here.

Lars makes her tea and coffee for himself. He dishes out the cake and grapes, and then rushes down to the basement. One by one, he carefully carries out large canvases until they form a makeshift gallery around her. Nancy balances on the edge of her chair as he brings up thick, richly layered oils: it's her, in that white-and-black polka-dotted romper. And the light. The low orange glow framing her portrait, spilling in from that basement window. She jumps to her feet and covers her mouth with a palm.

Lars poses with the last painting, a hand on his hip, collecting his breath, his eyes shining as he looks to her for validation.

"You like them?" he asks giddily, a boyish grin on his face. She turns to look at him. Every part of her wants to rush up and press a chaste kiss of gratitude onto his lips. "Which one is your favorite?" he asks.

She clasps her hands tightly in front of her, spins around to assess all his work, then points to the one where she's backlit facing Lars, her arms held above her head. The shot Malik had interrupted.

"That one," she says. "It's beautiful. They're all so beautiful. I can't believe it's me."

"Well, you better believe, Nancy." He smiles. "You are beautiful."

She beams back at him, reaches up to plant a quick peck of gratitude on his cheek. His hand leaves his hip and tightens around her waist, pulling her to his side. He turns his cheek away from her peck and plants his lips on hers instead, featherlight.

"Nancy," he whispers against her lips, pressing her tighter to him, kissing her. She startles, pulls away. He releases her as swiftly as he'd grabbed onto her. His face changes color. Bright pink.

"Oh God, I'm so sorry," he begins to apologize, his voice low, panicked. "I'm so sorry. I was caught in the moment."

"It's okay, it's okay," she says. But she knows she needs to flee. "When does the ferry leave again?"

They return to Stockholm in awkward silence.

★

When Malik returns from Switzerland, she can't tell him
about Lars and that stolen kiss. It sits heavy on her mind.
Fortunately, Malik is distracted by the energy shift in their
apartment building.

"What happened to Mr. Torbjörn?" he asks her, genuine
surprise in his eyes before he places his suitcase on their
shag carpeting. "He smiled at me in the elevator just now."
He points behind him. "What's going on?"

Nancy giggles. "I may have warmed him up with some
cardamom buns a couple days ago. He's actually quite
harmless. Former Air Force pilot who served in Congo. His
wife was an Egyptian goddess."

His eyes pop wide open at her intel. "A what?"

She laughs at his reaction, happy to have him home again,
but she can tell his mind is elsewhere. He starts tugging at
his tie to loosen it, to get more air. His voice turns serious.

"Something is brewing back home, and *Baabaa* wants us
to avoid the embassy," he says. He casts the tie onto the sofa
and pulls her closer by her hips.

"Okay?" She tries to read his eyes, her hands moving to
cup his face. "What's going on?"

He shrugs. "I don't know." He seems forlorn. "*Baabaa*
just says the sentiment back home is getting heated and he
doesn't want his family caught in the political crossfire."

"Are you scared?" she asks him softly.

He winces. "I don't know what to be scared of," he says.
"And that's what scares me." His grip tightens. Nancy
studies him before pulling him by his collar down for a kiss.
She instantly breaks it off when she feels Lars's lips on hers
instead.

"What's wrong?" Malik whispers back, pulling her closer

to continue their caress. Nancy's thoughts spin. Malik is kissing her. In her mind she hears Lars whisper her name against her mouth instead. Though her panic afterward had prompted her to run, the truth is that she loved his taste in that moment. His feel. The smell of turpentine mixed with citrus. His warm skin and its galaxy of freckles. His wide palm spreading against her back.

Emotions course through Nancy as she realizes the gravity of what seems to be happening. Warmth and kindness from unusual sources are distorting forces that play with the mind and prey on the heart. She doesn't doubt her love for Malik, his loyalty, but her footing in Sweden remains loose since her rift with her aunt Yaya, and he is a transient diplomat, after all. With his friendship and presence, Professor Wikström has simply seeped into her cracks of loneliness.

TWENTY

TINA, 2006

Tina is at Nancy's for dinner, tucking into her potatoes quietly. Tobias made them oven-baked salmon with lemon and dill, the only dish he has perfected. Soon he'll head off to his job as a bouncer at a swanky nightclub in Stureplan. At twenty-three, her brother is a looker. Tall, broad torso, low-cropped hair, a few freckles compared to her generous dusting of spots, a slight open gap between his top front teeth matching Nancy's, along with their mother's full lips. His boisterous laugh makes his eyes squint from joy. He recently got out of a six-year relationship with a blond named Klara. They'd been squatting in her family's basement until her father threatened to kick them both out. She stayed, and Tobias came home. Now Tobias is a walking bag of raw nerves. Klara had been his first love.

Tina knows this isn't the time to tell them that she met up with Lars. After their dinner, she met him once more for coffee. His elation that she'd been willing to meet him again thawed a bit of her heart. Only a tiny sliver. He spent their *fika* date profusely apologizing for the past once again. Which is the lesser evil? she wondered. An asshole of a father who acknowledges your feelings, or a lukewarm mother who loves you but never truly sees you?

As for the World Cup, Seb and the boys come home earlier than anticipated. Two goals from Podolski and their German hosts snuffed out his dream. They didn't make it to the quarterfinals. Back-to-back global defeats. Everyone is planning to recuperate with a low-key Swedish summer.

They eat in silence, disappointed by the team's loss.

"How's Sebbe?" Tobias breaks it. "He's not picking up my calls."

Tina shrugs.

Nancy and Tobias still don't know about her fight with Seb. Tina isn't sure if they've officially broken up, but time apart to reflect might hasten that decision or, like every single time they fight, bring them closer once more.

Tina switches topic instead. "I'm going to LA next week," she drops over clinking cutlery.

Tobias's fork pauses mid-scratch on his plate. He turns sharply toward her. "LA?" He scrunches his face. "Los Angeles?"

Nancy continues eating before casually asking, "Who do you know there?"

"I'm being flown out," Tina says.

"Flown out? By who?" Tobias is tense. When she doesn't answer him, he growls at her, "Tina!"

"A record label, okay? They want to sign me."

"A record label? What's going on?"

"In Athens, I was approached by ONYX Records," she says, taking a bite of potato. She thinks of Darryl. Lush skin, smooth swagger, dazzling smile. She catches herself. "They want me. They offered me a 100K sign-on bonus and royalties that sound good." She shrugs.

Nancy stops eating at the sound of the money. "Dollars or kronor?"

Tina swallows. "Dollars." This time, Nancy's fork hits her own plate, and she mutters something in her native language. A cross between praise and a chant.

Tobias glares at Tina wordlessly. *Keep talking*, his eyes say.

"There's nothing for me here, Tobbe," Tina says. "Our evil twin brothers—"

"They're not my brothers," Tobias snaps.

"Whatever." She rolls her eyes. "Even though they've backed off over the last few weeks, the second I try to put myself out there again, you know they'll be trying to tear me down."

"Look, Tina, people were shocked, disappointed, *yes*. But you fucked up, now clean up." He turns back to his meal. "So, what do they want from you?"

"No congratulations first? You can't even say that you're proud of me?"

"You know I'm proud of you," he assures her. His tone is fatherly now. Deep down they both know he's like her surrogate dad.

"Then say it! Say you're proud of me." Her voice pitches higher.

"I am proud of you, and I love you, okay?" He makes eye contact. "Now tell me, what do they want?"

"They want to fly me out and woo me." A smile creeps onto her lips.

"This is huge, Tina! And you waited this long to tell us?"

"I didn't want to get our hopes up."

"This could change your life," Tobias says, happiness slowly creeping in.

"You know they represent Alana and DJ Kamid, right?"

She begins to giggle, filled with relief at his reaction. If Tobbe is this excited, she's making the right decision. "Oh my God! Me and Alana on the same label. America's biggest pop star. They even have a name for me. The Swedish Siren."

"Siren?" Nancy jumps back into their conversation. "You know sirens are evil spirits."

"Mamma, please." Tina rolls her eyes at her. "You know what they mean. At least show that you're happy for me."

"This is wonderful news, my dear, but are you sure you're ready? Will you have to move to America?" Nancy's voice sounds shaky.

"Yes. To go record my album with them, right? Oh my God!" she squeals. "My own album. It sounds insane." Tina sees the worry play across her mother's eyes. She leans over to give her a hug. "This might be the break we all need. The break you need." Nancy's dark eyes hold hers, shining with tears. She doesn't say a word. She simply receives her daughter's hug, then turns back to her salty salmon. "Mamma?"

"Tina, let's pray about it. The world gives you your heart's desires, then violently rips it away from your hands when you're most vulnerable. Please stay vigilant."

She feels Tobias's palm on her back. He pulls her in for a hug and kiss on the head.

"I'm really holding back from screaming right now because nothing is signed yet, but…" He flashes that handsome grin and pumps a quick fist in the air.

"*Fan!*" Hell!, he curses.

★

159

The crowd roars as Anders, the legendary host of *Allsång*, the revered, gleeful sing-along show, leads them in a buoyant chorus of "*Stockholm i mitt hjärta*," Stockholm *in My Heart*.

Tina can feel their energy as she waits backstage, getting final touches to her makeup. She opted for a short summer frock with plumes of red feathers all around it, slowly slipping back into pop star mode. Covering a song of Swedish pop icon Carola will be her peace offering. "Honey" is too bitter to sing right now.

She isn't even sure if the crowd will cheer or boo. Since Eurovision, she hasn't sung in public. She did hop from show to show, interview to interview, doing damage control.

"And now, our Melodifestivalen star, Tina Wikström!" Anders announces in his strident manner. The crowd cheers, albeit weakly. They clap too. But a pop star knows her claps. That was forced applause. Once the band starts, she strut-hops onto the stage, her hair in loose curls flapping around her in the slight evening breeze. Her short dress bunches around her, making her look like a red robin. She claps her hands over her head, gearing the audience up, fueling them to continue. Soon enough, they're clapping along, singing and watching Tina wear someone else's skin on stage.

She finishes to wolf whistles, cheers, and a standing ovation from the crowd.

"Tina is back," Anders says, joining her as she takes a bow to more applause.

After a few more platitudes and jovial banter with the host, Tina rushes backstage to her room to find Seb there.

She freezes at the door. He's sitting on a barstool and rises to his feet, brushing sweaty palms on his thighs.

"*Hej.*" His stubble is now a mini beard, his hair swept off his face. "You weren't taking any of my calls."

"You had a dream to prepare for," she says. "I didn't want to distract you with my presence," she adds coldly.

"I'm sorry, I needed you there. By my side. We've been through so much together… I should have been braver and I'm sorry." She takes him in, her eyes warming. "God, I missed you," he says, inching closer.

"Missed me or missed sex?" she murmurs, her voice lower.

He bursts out laughing, color rushing up his cheeks. He turns back to her with his aquarium-blue eyes.

"Seb, I can't always be there to indulge you," she says. It's been clear to her that Seb has had a staunch dependence on her ever since she first found him beaten and bloodied back in high school. He's like a skittish kitten. His smile drops. "You're more than enough. You scored an amazing goal. You saved the team."

He peers at her. "I'm sorry for being a coward."

"I know it's not easy to go against the group"—she holds his gaze—"in many ways."

He closes the gap between them and grabs her forearms tightly in desperation. Then he softens his grip on her.

"Tina." He leans in. His lips barely graze hers.

"I'm going to LA later this week," she says abruptly.

He pulls back, staring straight through her for a moment, processing. "ONYX?"

She nods. "They want to show me around. Woo me." She

smiles, her eyebrows dancing at the word *woo*. Planes of worry and fear race across every inch of Seb's face.

"It sounds like the opportunity of a lifetime," he finally says, the words delivered in broken snatches. "A dream." She glides a palm across his cheek, her fingers crawling into his hair. He turns his face slightly to kiss her wrist.

"Should I go?" Tina whispers. Seb's eyes turn back to her. "Should I?"

"What would it mean?" he mumbles. "Besides Mr. Hotshot Producer," he adds. "What would it mean for you? Us?"

"I would have to move to the U.S. To Los Angeles." She steps closer to him, her voice low. "You'll come visit me, right?" But besides his rigorous training schedule, she knows he can't afford to fly over every other week, even with his place on the national team.

His face crumples. He pulls her hand from his cheek and plants a kiss in its palm. And another kiss. And another.

"You'll be fine without me," she says. Seb shakes his head. "Should I go, Seb?"

He studies her with eyes glassy behind tears. "This place is too small for your brilliance, *älskling*," he says. "You're too big for Sweden." His voice breaks. "Go live your dream. You deserve the world."

She gives him a tearful smile. Seb presses on. "Promise you'll call me every day?" He attempts a happy grin, but his eyes give him away.

"Promise." She crosses her heart. "Every day."

"You're my best friend. I'll always be your biggest fan." At his words, Tina kisses him. He wraps his arms around

her waist, pulling her into his chest where she can feel his
rapidly beating heart.

"Go," Seb whispers against her lips.

TWENTY-ONE

NANCY, 1981

A few minutes past midnight in the early hours of July 31
Loud banging on their door jolts Malik out of her
arms. Nancy sits up in bed, pulls the sheets around
her shoulders as Malik slips on a T-shirt to go investigate.

"Be careful," she whispers after him.

Malik opens the door. She hears several male voices. Malik
doesn't sound concerned. He must know the late-night
visitors. She launches out of bed and grabs a robe.

When she makes it to the living room, all eyes turn to her.
She recognizes an attaché and two security guards from the
embassy. Malik's brows are knitted in worry as he peers at
her.

"What's going on?" she asks.

"I've been summoned back to the embassy," he says.
"Until further notice."

"What?! Right now?" Nancy rushes into his arms.

Malik cups her cheek while she clasps his hand on her
face with both of hers. "Nancy," he murmurs. "It's only for a
short time. Please don't worry. You're safer here. I'm safer
there."

He gives her a slow, sensuous kiss while the three men

make their way into their apartment, looking for suitcases to start packing Malik's belongings.

Nancy starts to sob. "Right now?"

"I'll write to you from the embassy every week," Malik promises as he grazes her nose with his. "It's too risky for you to come visit me there, but it will be as if I'm just away visiting my sisters."

"Tell me what's going on."

"I'll explain later, my dear. I promise."

Those are Malik's last words to her before the embassy men lead him away.

Coup d'état attempt.

It had happened on July 30, when Malik's father was in London for the wedding festivities of Prince Charles and Lady Diana Spencer alongside Gambian President Jawara. Members of the Revolutionary Party and Field Force had carried out an insurrection back home, catching everyone off guard, her father Omar explained weakly over the phone a few days later. She sensed the fear beneath his stoic delivery.

When the news of the attempted coup broke, Malik was instantly considered a potential target.

Malik's unease had always been an undercurrent to their relationship: through their first Christmas together in their tiny apartment off Sveavägen; through the following spring when he took many trips back home with his father to handle business; through their first Midsummer together, joining hundreds of people hopping like tailless frogs around the maypole at open-air museum Skansen. And Malik had been so tense since she'd returned from that trip to see Lars, she never told him about the incident.

Lars had never invited her back to his cabin. Though they still saw each other for lectures, the atmosphere was awkward now. He stopped talking about his paintings of her.

Nancy now cradles the large receiver tightly as she cries over the phone to Omar. He is the only one composed enough to talk to her. Fatou is already on the floor, wailing. Lamin has been taken from them to go serve in the Gambian Army alongside the Senegalese armed forces who had swept in to save the country, and her mother is devastated.

"Allah is in control, my dear. Don't be scared," Omar comforts her. He breaks to cough and clear his throat. "Senegal sent troops to help us. Nancy? Nancy? It's okay," he calls out, as his daughter's sobs punctuate his message. "Lamin will be fine."

"How can you be so sure?" Nancy demands as she cries back in the phone booth. "Why did they have to draft him?"

Omar goes silent over the phone. She senses the fear in his voice too once he comes back on. "Lamin will return to us, *inshallah*. Don't worry," he says. "He will come back to us. Keep your faith, my dear. Keep your faith."

Lamin getting drafted stokes a new worry within her. They may never get the chance to fully repair their relationship if he doesn't make it back to them whole.

Being cut off from Malik, even for a few never-ending days, makes Nancy realize how cocooned her life in Sweden has become. She has no social network beyond their bubble, his friends from the Gambia-Swedish Association, and the UF international affairs club she occasionally attends on campus. She suddenly understands how dependent she and Malik have become on one another. How they carved a hole from reality and buried themselves beneath the soil of utopia. He's been gone a few weeks—ripped out of her arms—and she misses him desperately. Misses his easy laughter, his warm brown eyes, his touch. Who is Nancy Ndow without Malik Barrow?

The Swedish prime minister goes on national TV to give a speech. He implores his fellow Swedes to open their hearts as they prepare for an influx of Gambians. A new wave adding to the existing set of academics and scholars, of the businessmen and women bankers.

He also shares some news. Malik's father is being held as a political prisoner. He'd decided to return home to help stabilize the government while the president stayed behind in London—a foolish move, it turned out. Probably why they had yanked Malik away from her. The Swedish government promises to come to Gambia's aid alongside Senegalese troops as peacekeepers.

Malik did keep his promise to write letters—one has arrived every week since his departure. Nancy holds onto Malik's letters like a lifeline to their love. A reminder of how real it was—is—and that it hasn't been a figment of her imagination. The day she spent at the elegant Nobel banquet, laughing with a former prime minister, eating roast veal, seems impossibly distant.

Then his letters suddenly stop.

The first missed week, she writes it off as him being

concerned with more pressing matters. After all, his father is still being held prisoner by insurrectionists. The second missed week and Nancy starts to worry they reached him too. Maybe stormed the embassy and dragged him out. But that could never happen here. Not in Sweden. Not in the Nordics. Right?

A month after his first missed letter, Nancy is a fragile, broken mess. When Mr. Torbjörn asks her while in the elevator where her *dark chocolate* man is, she bursts into tears. The man presses himself against the wall, bothered by her discomfort, unsure of what to do or say. His Sphynx Leo seems uncomfortable too as it glares at Nancy and meows softly.

She tries dialing the embassy from various phone booths sprinkled around town, begging for someone to pick up and tell her where her love is. Someone to promise her he is okay. The line is always engaged. It seems she isn't the only one inquiring about loved ones around the clock. She takes the bus over to the embassy in Danderyd and is left standing at the wrought-iron gates.

When Nancy returns to her department the following week to turn in a thesis report, she sees a band of professors huddled by the photocopier, holding steaming mugs of coffee. Lars is one of them. He adjusts his glasses upon seeing her. He is no longer her professor for any modules.

She walks up to the trio and excuses herself before barging into their conversation.

"Thank you, Nancy," one of the professors, a tall, lean white woman with a bowl cut, sharp bangs and coral beads around her neck, says as she reaches for the report. Her research laboratory had been in Lamu, Kenya. "Well done for turning it in on time." She pauses after grabbing the sociology report. "Especially with all that's going on back home," she adds. "Is your family okay? Safe?"

Nancy nods. She wipes a rogue tear that slips down her cheek. "Yes, thank you. They're safe."

"I'm sorry about Malik," Lars says.

Nancy turns sharply toward him, trying to process his words. Malik? Sorry? What could have happened to Malik—and how would Lars know before she did?

"Sorry?" Nancy asks. "What are you talking about?"

"I'm sorry, I thought you knew," Lars continues, adjusting his glasses. "He had to pull out of school."

"What do you mean *pull out of school*?" Nancy feels her heart beating faster. "What happened?"

"Oh, Nancy." Lars pauses. "Malik was deported. They found drugs on him."

PART TWO

TWENTY-TWO

TINA, 2007

Scanning the Arrivals crowd at Los Angeles International Airport, Tina spots Darryl. He's wearing sunglasses and is dressed in a white short-sleeved linen shirt and army-green cargo pants.

"Damn, Tina" are his first words once he takes off his shades. "You really do turn men into fools," he says before leaning in to give her a peck on each cheek. His ride is equally suave—a dark, sleek Range Rover matching the man himself. En route from the airport, they speed past palm trees and shiny convertibles, all gleaming in the misty haze, reminding her she is now in the California of movies. Tina presses her nose to the window, absorbing it all. The sun, the lightness, the possibility of a new life wrapped up in Hollywood fairy dust. Unrestrained, untethered and free.

She turns back to Darryl. "How far is the hotel? I need to freshen up."

"Our first stop is ONYX, actually," he says, eyes on the road. "You can clean up there. There are a few people I'd like you to meet before I drop you off at the hotel."

After showering and preening in an en suite on location, she pulls on a peach-colored silk pantsuit and pulls her straightened hair into a high ponytail. Black eyeliner intensifies her amber-colored eagle eyes. She loops her hand in the crook of Darryl's arm. He walks her around, introducing her to producers, sound musicians, voice coaches and mixing artists dotted around the building.

They reach one of the studios where DJ Kamid is rapping animatedly behind a soundproof box, the producer with headphones on, bobbing his head along, and pushing dials up and down a 32-channel digital mixer. Darryl catches the attention of the artist, who waves a hand to stop his mixing producer. He steps out of the booth and gives Darryl a handshake-hug combo.

"Here she is," Darryl says.

"Ms. Tina." Kamid rubs both palms together, gives her a quick, dramatic bow. "So honored to meet you. Darryl won't stop talking about you." The famed Egyptian American rapper's dark eyes shine. He has a full beard and lush black hair in two large cornrows that reach past his shoulders. She fights the urge to pull at one of his plaits, realizing how the brain pushes people to touch strangers' hair, oblivious to the violation in the moment.

Tina can't fangirl in front of this icon-turned-colleague. "The feeling is mutual." She smiles, her cat gaze hooking him, not breaking contact even though her insides are burning up.

"Bro, I need to get back in, but Ms. Tina"—Kamid turns back to her—"hope to see you around? Maybe collaborate on a track and video?"

"That's the plan," Darryl answers before she says a word. "Get back in there."

The rest of the week Darryl takes her around the hills and talk shows to introduce her. Tina wonders how he's going to bob and weave around her Eurovision fiasco. But watching him in action, drawn to his lips moving as he talks about her, she feels her chest pounding. He can turn anyone into a mushy fool, including her.

"I mean, Jimmy," Darryl says, as they both sit on one late-night talk show. "When she sang that song on stage, everyone wanted the pomp and pageantry of Eurovision. She showed her raw talent. That incredible sultry alto. Our siren." The show often ran a special segment, highlighting rising stars recommended by top industry producers. With his deep connections, Darryl had bagged her the slot.

The talk show host smiles and points to the stage. Tina, wearing glittering silver sequins, steps up there and is met by applause. She sings her own song, "Honey"—not as an emo ballad this time, but a soulful R&B rendition with vocal runs and riffs that sweep the audience into a frenzy.

She finishes to standing ovation and wolf whistles from the crowd. Her face flushes red as she clasps her hands in front of her chest, soaking it all in. She hasn't even signed anything yet, but she's already getting swept away, giving Darryl so much of herself.

The next morning, Darryl's phone rings nonstop, his assistant Kasha batting off press. Everyone wants to know who his new pop star is and how he brought her to the States.

On her last night, Darryl takes her to West Hollywood for a goodbye dinner before she returns home to Stockholm. "Do you trust me, Tina?" he asks as they eat sashimi at an overpriced seafood restaurant on Melrose Avenue. Tina smiles, her crimson lips widening. He swallows before continuing. "Are you convinced now?"

"Thank you," she says. "I can't wait to move here. I'll have my lawyer look over the contract." She thinks about Seb. This would mean leaving him behind, probably for good. He told her to go follow her dreams. She would want the same for him, wouldn't she?

"Good." He smiles, his eyes locked on hers. With that look, Tina knows her life is about to change once more.

SIX MONTHS LATER

Tina is settled in a sectioned-off apartment attached to the Bel Air mansion of a music industry acquaintance of Darryl's. She hugs a mug of lukewarm coffee as she stands on her tiny patio overlooking verdant rolling hills, savoring the feeling of her new freedom.

Lars is still writing her letters, even though she told him not to. How did he even get her new address? she wonders, though a part of her wants him to continue writing. She loves reading his cursive handwriting, talking about how he met Nancy, how he hopes to see her again, and about his life as an artist. He asks her about her new life in LA, if she's taking time to bask under the California sun. She never writes back, but she keeps hold of his letters.

As for Tobias, she calls him every day and Nancy, once a week. She promises to fly them both to LA for Christmas.

And then there's Seb.

"You should see my view right now, Seb," she says into the flip phone at her ear as she sips coffee. "The sun is out."

"Describe it to me." Seb's voice is husky over the phone. She feels his smile.

Before she moved to LA, Tina had pitched her case to him. She needed to experience all California was offering her, she said. She needed to jump in with both feet and commit to self-discovery. A long-distance relationship would be too much of an emotional distraction from her dreams, her art. And that meant he couldn't be her boyfriend anymore.

Sebastian had protested before finally nodding, his clear eyes clouded by tears, then pleading to at least stay friends.

"Well," Tina starts. "The hills look like the curves of your muscles down your back."

"Hmm, tell me more," he purrs.

"The sunlight brushing them... like those tiny hairs on your shoulders."

"I've got hair on my back?" Seb cuts in. "I thought you said I reminded you of a mole rat?"

"Well, yeah, but a sexy mole rat?" she giggles.

"I've never heard of a sexy mole rat before," Seb laughs.

"Well, you are a—"

"There you are." Darryl's deep bass comes from behind her. "We gotta be in the studio. We still need to get those last three songs cut," he says.

"Shit, gotta go. *Love ya*." Tina abruptly disconnects Seb before slipping the phone into the pocket of her robe. She pivots briskly and pushes loose strands behind her ears, makeup-free, still in her pajamas.

"You're not ready," Darryl says, his eyes roaming over her.

"I need only five minutes." She sets her mug down and

walks toward him barefoot. She notices he's holding a stack of magazines. He pulls out *Rolling Stone*.

"They're comparing you to Badu. The look, the voice, the whole package." His attempt at small talk is totally failing—his gaze is locked on hers to avoid her barely-there outfit, sheer over taut nipples. "Go get ready." He cocks his head in the direction of her apartment. "We've got a full day. Kasha will brief you once we get to the studio."

Kasha, his assistant. Always in fresh braids. It was Kasha who had settled her in, showing her the ropes of her new life stateside. Kasha's number was the second one she'd saved as a local contact, and she often texts her late in the night looking for answers to mundane questions. Kasha still holds herself apart from Tina, simply doing her bidding or whatever Darryl needs her to do, but Tina hopes she'll let her in. Because she needs friends. In Stockholm, she and Seb had created their bubble, blocking out all other friendships. They had both been so focused on their careers that they'd only had time for each other.

A quick shower and forty-five minutes of traffic later, Darryl and Tina meet Kasha at the ONYX studios.

"*Hej*, girl," Tina says, leaning into Kasha for a hug. The "older" woman—she's only twenty-nine—receives her hug and pats her on the back.

"How you holding up?" she asks Tina.

"I've watched too many shows at home alone," Tina admits. She must seem tragic.

"We need to get you a driver's license fast," Kasha giggles. "You need activities."

"Well, I can't drive," Tina says. "I didn't need to back home. It was all trains and buses."

"Girl, you're in America now," Kasha says. "I'll sign you up at a driving school. Okay, this way. The producer is waiting."

Once they settle Tina in with headphones behind a booth, the producer comes over the speaker.

"Kamid wants you on his current rap track," he says.

"Okay?" Tina is unsure. "Like, right now?"

"Yes," the producer says flatly, "we need just a few sounds from you." He's a stoic, bespectacled white man with wisps of shaggy, dusty-blond hair and an equally unkempt beard that belies his age.

"What sounds?" she asks, shifting. The plan had been to keep working on her album.

"Just some moaning sounds, like, *oooo baby, you da man, you it, you the eight-figure nigga that make me go, ooo baby*," the producer says, his face serious as he mimics for her benefit.

Tina bursts out laughing. "Are you joking?"

Darryl comes on over the speaker. "We're paying G by the hour. Please do what he says."

She turns to look at the producer, who looks like a furry Muppet wearing glasses, his face unsmiling.

The grin slides off Tina's face. "You can't be serious."

Darryl comes back on. "He's the hottest rapper in the U.S. right now, Tina. Imagine DJ Kamid and the Swedish Siren. Together. This track will be off the chains."

"*Oooo baby?*" she asks. "Is that even a legit lyric or just fake orgasm?"

Kasha comes on over the speaker. "Just get your coins, *gurl*," she adds. Tina looks at her. *Getting her coins* could win Kasha's respect and get her one step closer to what she wants—some form of friendship.

"Okay, let's take it from the top," the producer, "G," says into the speaker.

They spend over an hour correcting her moans until she gets it right. She sees Darryl squirming uncomfortably in his seat until he excuses himself for the toilet. After a water break and a revitalizing session with the on-site vocal coach, Tina is back in the booth, now belting out the lyrics an ONYX-designated songwriter has penned for her. They've already released her first single, the R&B rendition she performed live on Kimmel months ago. It quickly climbed the charts, as Darryl had predicted, a good sign for the upcoming release of her album, *Honey*.

Six songs down and she's now riffing on the lyrics to "BUTTER."

"At this rate, your album will be used as a recipe for baking cakes," Kasha had cackled in the studio when they presented the full list of songs:

HONEY
SUGAR
SPICE
SWEET
BUTTER
CINNAMON
BLACKBERRY
HEAT
RISE
CREAM

Tina shrugs. Darryl clearly knows what he's doing. If she wants this life, she needs to let him lead. Six hours in the studio leaves her drained and famished.

"Get some rest," Darryl instructs her. "I'll see you at Kamid's bash tonight. Everyone you need to know will be there. Kasha will help you with clothes," he says curtly before leaving.

Kasha swivels toward Tina, her waist-length braids still whipping in the air long after she pivots.

"Well, let's go shopping then." She smiles at Tina, her plum-colored lips widening. "Rodeo Drive's calling!"

They crisscross Rodeo Drive looking for something befitting of the Siren.

Wearing this life still feels off-balance for Tina. Yes, she was a public figure back home in Sweden, but she lived in a three-bedroom, no-frills apartment with her mother and brother. Here, she has her own swanky Bel Air place with access to the main mansion it's attached to.

Everything feels too easy, too effortless, but the memory of the disaster at home sits uncomfortably in the back of her mind. The Wikström twins resurfaced after her talk show performance, balking at the fact that she was now being touted as the Swedish Siren.

Their joint statement had been swift:

The question isn't about identity because clearly, she can't prove hers.
This is simply an issue of fraud.
She has deceived this great nation of ours and we

refute any claims of familial links or her representation.
We will continue our investigation into whether Ms.
Wikström violated any codes of conduct and cost us the
opportunity to shine at Eurovision…

She expects their hunt is being driven by a deep-rooted need to protect their mother's integrity. Their statements had to be a projection of their loathing for their father for hurting their mother. And it's not like Lars swooped in to help, even after she mentioned it to him.

Still, she's not surprised to find he's let her down again.

Later that night, Tina sits cross-legged in the back of a limousine shuttling her and Kasha to Beverly Hills well past eleven p.m. According to Kasha, Darryl is already there because he has business with Kamid. The stretch limo pulls in through Tuscan-style luxury wrought-iron gates to a long line of cars waiting to be parked. Behind the stream of Ferraris, Bentleys, Bugattis and Lamborghinis sits Kamid's four-story mansion. It's so stupendous in size it looks like a hospital. Music with earthquake-simulating bass blasts across the whole compound through outdoor speakers.

Herregud, Tina quietly mutters under her breath. *Oh my God.*

A valet rushes to the door and extends his hand. She gingerly takes it and steps out in a platinum-colored leather catsuit, her hair slicked back in front and blown out into a large Afro in the back. A few heads turn her way as she strolls in behind Kasha into a rococo-styled hall. Some guests are holding drinks, a few are wearing sunshades, others are weighed down under hefty jewelry. She recognizes a rapper here and pop star there.

"*Hej*, gorgeous," someone intercepts her. Tina recognizes him. A drummer, all tatted up save for his face. She gives him a meager smile. "The Siren," he cackles before lifting a sludge-like drink to his mouth. It leaves behind a green mustache, and he licks the residue off. "My mom's Swedish," he shares, stepping in closer. "How are you liking it here?"

"Let's go." It's Kasha, linking arms with Tina and dragging her along. "Stay away from that cesspool of disease. Always trying to hit on anything in a skirt," she whispers curtly as they continue, passing waiters carrying trays of champagne and hors d'oeuvres, guests flaunting every designer brand under the sun, and the drunk ones gyrating to a DJ playing out on the patio. Beyond the DJ, there's a bottom-lit pool full of people in various stages of undress.

They follow the thick smell of cigar smoke to a billiards room, where Kamid is leaning over a snooker table, about to shoot, a cigar perched in the side of his mouth. He sees them and straightens back up. "There she is!" He takes the cigar out and spreads his arms dramatically before swaggering up to her. He leans in for a peck on each cheek. She catches the glitter clipped on his right ear. "You were incredible on the track."

"I didn't really sing."

"Oh, you definitely did," Kamid cackles, his eyes roaming her figure-hugging suit. "You sure did." They settle back on her eyes. "*Damn*, you fine."

"Where's Darryl?" Tina asks, glancing around the dim room, distracting him. She feels Kamid's hand on her arm.

"I was thinking..." He lifts the cigar back to his lips, drags in smoke, his dark eyes studying her. She assesses him too. Easy on the eyes, but he's no Darryl. "Can you dance?"

"Dance?" Tina laughs. Her eyes continue to search for her manager. A waiter sneaks past. She grabs a flute of champagne from his tray.

Kamid chuckles. "You know what I mean." He blows smoke. "I'm working on the video for '8-figa'. You know, with Jonas Jonsson." That name gets her attention. "He's the hottest guy in town. I told him about you... Well, he already knew, actually. All about you." He takes another drag of the cigar. "Maybe a little too much." He winks at her.

Everyone knows Jonas Jonsson's work—music video director, famed within the industry for his frantic style and sharp transitions. A fellow Afro Swede—father from Dalarna, mother from Uganda.

"Jonas!" Kamid booms across the den. Deep in conversation in a corner, Jonas spins at the sound of his name. He has shoulder-length dreadlocks, two gold loops in his ears. His eyes are drooping—he's clearly high. "Jonas!" He takes the spliff out of his mouth and moves slowly toward them. "Look, your country-girl!"

Jonas towers over them. "*Tjena*," he mumbles in Swedish. *Hello*.

Her lips part to say something, but no words come. Only a soft sound escapes her as she stares back up at him.

"*Äntligen*," he says. "*Skitkul att träffas. Alltså, du är...*" He stops mid-speech, laughing before dragging in smoke once more. *Finally*, he'd said. *So fucking cool to meet*.

I mean, you're so... Then he'd stopped. He couldn't find the right adjective for her.

"*Detsamma.*" She smiles back. *You too.* Her eyes survey him. From his turquoise eyes against his bronze skin. Down the loose-fitting wheat-colored Cuban shirt open at the nape. Over khaki capris ending at his calves. Down to his... bare feet?

When her eyes meet his once more, he responds with a smile, a single dimple surfacing.

TWENTY-THREE

NANCY, 1981–1982

Lamin never returned to them.

The despair in her mother's breathless wailing over the phone is something Nancy never wants to experience again. She cradles the receiver in shock as Fatou screams and screams. Fatou's only son. Her only sibling. Claimed by the attempted coup. Despite 3,000 Senegalese troops marching to their aide, Gambian forces sustained devastating losses. Lamin was one of over a thousand who would never get to see another day, would never get to grow old.

Nancy had frozen at the news. Numbed. Shocked. In disbelief. She told them she would be on the next flight out there.

"Don't come home," Fatou wails. "Don't come home."

Omar grabs the phone from his wife. "Nancy, things are finally beginning to settle. You will come home, but not right now."

"*Baabaa*," Nancy says, finding her voice once more. "*Baabaa*, I need to be there. I need to bury my brother too."

Omar sighs, before saying words that will haunt her soul forever.

"There is nothing left to bury, my dear child." Omar's voice breaks. "That Marxist Sanyang and his cronies ran to Guinea-Bissau. Allah will catch them! Allah will…" He coughs to conceal his tears from Nancy. "Allah will catch them!"

"You will come back home someday, but for now, please stay in Sweden," Omar says firmly. "It is better for you there. Safer, my dear. Please learn all you can from them. Enhance your diplomatic skills. Grab the world in the palm of your hands, my Nancy." His words catch on a sob. "You will enter politics in due time, Madame President."

Her father has never called her that before.

"*Baabaa*, I'm graduating this June," Nancy protests in tears. "There's nothing left to stay here for. I can move back."

"Stay and continue your studies," Omar implores her. "Get your master's degree. Maybe a PhD too. Give the world a reason not to deny your brilliance."

Nancy starts to shake, her shoulders dancing as she sobs. She holds on tightly to the receiver as her body convulses in fits and waves at her father's words.

"May his soul…" Her father breaks down. "May my son's soul rest in peace."

They both sob over the phone until Omar composes himself. He forbids her once more from entertaining any thoughts of coming home and promises to keep her abreast of any news.

Her grief is twofold. Once she disconnects from her parents, her thoughts turn to Malik.

Malik never returned to her either.

When Lars told her the previous year that he had been deported because of drugs, the world began to make less sense. Her Malik, who had never once dragged a cigarette. Drugs? What drugs? She was desperate to find out more, but she didn't have any contacts at the embassy, and Lars didn't have any more information for her when she'd asked.

"Do you have a few minutes?" Lars had asked her as she'd stood frozen. The other two professors he had been drinking coffee with had promptly excused themselves.

"Nancy, I'm so sorry you had to find out like this." He reached out a hand to stroke her forearm in comfort. She tensed under his touch. Not that it wasn't pleasant; it was warm and inviting. But she'd rather have Malik's large, soothing palms on her.

"If you need anything, I'm here for you," he continued, gently caressing her arm. "Friends?"

Nancy had nodded in agreement. Yes, they were friends.

"Come next week for *fika*," he said. "I'm worried about you. I need to know you're all right."

Nancy simply nodded once more.

After finding out, she rushed back to her apartment and wailed so loudly someone came knocking on her door. Mr. Torbjörn and his cat Leo on a leash, wondering if she was okay. At that, she wrapped her arms around his torso, startling the old man whose arms remained frozen by his sides. After a few moments, he gave her two light pats before resting his palm on her back as she sobbed.

"Thank you," she says after composing herself.

Mr. Torbjörn nods before peering down at this cat. "*Kom nu, Leo. Nu går vi.*" *Come on, Leo. Let's go.*

Once Nancy settled down, she decided it was time to let Yaya back in. She was driven by selfishness; she didn't want to be alone anymore. She needed the company of someone familiar; to be tethered once more to the solid ground of her culture. Malik had been her anchor, foundation, rock and cement. Nancy now realized she'd swapped her agency for his love.

"My dear Nancy." Yaya's words the second she hears Nancy. "My heart is filled with joy to hear your voice. I hope you're well?"

Yaya sniffs quickly to cover her tears.

"I know it's been a while. I wanted to let you know that I'm no longer upset with you."

"You're not?" She hears her aunt's voice weaken.

"No, I forgive you."

Nancy remains silent while Yaya cries on her end. Once Yaya composes herself, she comes back on stronger. "Come on Sunday. Benke has finally learned how to make *domoda!*" Peanut lamb stew.

Nancy accepts her dinner invite but declines her subsequent offer to move back in with them.

She's still living in the embassy's leased apartment; they signed a multiyear lease for the place. But Nancy knows her days there are numbered. Staying there feels like basking in his aura every day. Moving out feels like severing their memories. Once a new administration is voted in and new diplomats welcomed to Stockholm, she will have to leave. Right now, Malik's name, his father's status as a high-profile political prisoner and Sweden's involvement as peacekeepers negotiating his release are what keep her living in that tiny apartment off Sveavägen.

Nancy calls the embassy often, and they never pick up.

She once showed up at the gates asking for him, and the guards advised her it would be wise not to come back.

At least she gets to stay in the apartment for now.

Months later, it's her graduation day. It feels so strange without Malik standing by her side. Lars, newly appointed head of the international relations department, is announcing the graduates.

"Nancy Ndow," Lars calls her name out loud in that auditorium. Applause follows. She hears Yaya in the crowd, louder than everyone else. Lars's eyes slowly reel her in as she moves across the stage toward him. He cut his hair for the occasion, slicked it back away from his face.

"Congratulations." He mouths the word tenderly to her, the corners of his eyes creasing, as he hands her a rolled-up diploma. *Bachelors in international relations with a minor in political science.* His fingers brush hers during the handoff and she looks down, noticing a glimmer around his finger. She's seen his hands many times over the years—scribbling on the board, thumbing through schoolwork, or lifting canvases upon canvases out of his basement for her—but she's never noticed this ring before. It must be new. Maybe this is the reason he has stopped pestering her for her company. The lifelong bachelor seems to have settled down. She's not sure how to feel about it. She simply extracts her hand from his and returns to her seat.

"I'm so proud of you." Yaya pulls her into a bosom-crushing hug after the ceremony. She's wearing a navy-blue traditional wrap beneath a white lace blouse cinched at the waist with more blue traditional fabric. Benke is wearing a white dress shirt with a blue tie matching Yaya's textile.

Since making amends with them, Nancy has been dropping by their place every week, mostly to eat food from home and take leftovers with her. Benke is no longer awkward around her. His shoulders seem to have relaxed now, his eyes no longer holding the fear which Yaya had incited with her uncomfortable request. Their first few meetings, she had divulged more about her relationship with Malik and her heartbreak about him being deported for drugs. The words sounded foreign when they left her. *Her Malik would have never done such a thing.*

"You never truly know the heart of a man," Yaya said when she'd told her. "Power corrupts. He comes from a long line of politicians. When you have tasted power, everything else tastes bland."

Nancy also listens to Yaya talk incessantly about her patients. At those dinners, she often fills them in about her professor, the artist, who has been working on a portrait series inspired by their niece.

Nancy is brought back to the present with Benke coming in for a hug. "We're so proud of you. You did it, Nancy."

She beams at her aunt and uncle, her proxy parents. All she has left to root her in some sense to home.

"Yes, you did," a third voice joins theirs. The three of them spin round to see Lars standing close by.

"*Trevligt att träffas,*" Benke greets Lars in Swedish, stretching his hand out to the younger man. Lars slips his left hand into Benke's. Nancy scans for the ring she'd spotted on stage. Where is it?

"*Hon brukar prata om dig,*" Benke adds. *She always talks about you.*

"*Är det sant?*" Lars's eyes widen at the perceived compliment. He turns to her. *Is it true?*

Nancy feels her skin prickle. She isn't sure if it's from anger at Benke or the look the clean-shaven, freshly clipped Lars is giving her.

"*Bara att du kan Wolof och Mandinka flytande,*" she quickly adds in rough Swedish. *Only because you can speak both Wolof and Mandinka fluently.*

"But you said he was a marvelous artist, am I not right?" Yaya says. "That he's painting you?"

"Marvelous artist?" Lars raises a brow, his eyes finding Nancy's.

"You must join us for dinner," Yaya says to Lars, breaking their moment. They are taking her out for a celebratory meal.

Nancy mutters into her aunt's ears. "Must he?"

Yaya turns to Nancy, scanning her expression. A smile begins to slowly carve itself across Yaya's face. Like a parent who has just discovered their daughter has a cute crush on their neighbor. Her pleading goes unheeded. They dine at pint-sized Formosa in Gamla stan, one of the oldest Chinese restaurants in town.

Benke and Lars get right into politics. Apparently, Olof Palme gave a speech about why he is a democratic socialist. Lars deconstructs the speech line by line for Benke over sticky rice and hotpot.

Nancy pushes around her broccoli in oyster sauce under Yaya's probing glare. She knows what her aunt is thinking. No, she doesn't like him that way. She must convince herself that Lars is nothing more than a caring professor-turned-friend. She must read nothing more into his kindness. She can't let him slip into those deep cracks left by Malik's disappearance.

"I like him," Yaya whispers to Nancy. "I think he might be good for you. To you." Nancy rolls her eyes. Of course Yaya would think Lars is perfect for her—her own husband is fifteen years older.

Forty-five minutes later, after Lars pays for their entire meal, ignoring Benke's and Yaya's pleas, the group gather their belongings.

"Nancy, can you walk? You're not too far from here," Yaya says. "So, you can save some money."

"I can walk Nancy home," Lars instantly offers. "For safety."

"I can walk myself home," Nancy counters. "Don't you have somewhere better to go? Your wife or something?"

Lars tenses, his eyes hard. "I'm not married. I told you and Malik..." She winces at the sound of Malik's name. Lars catches himself, but Nancy knows it was intentional. "I told you I've been divorced for years."

"Let him walk you, Nancy," Yaya says. "Benke and I are too old and tired. We need to go sleep."

Nancy lets out a sigh of defeat, her own eyes hard on Lars. She's angry that he dropped in Malik's name and peeled open her healing scar.

Once Yaya and Benke huddle off to go catch the *tunnelbana* to Odenplan station, Nancy stands staring after them.

"You look really lovely this evening." Lars's voice floats over from behind her. Her Afro has grown out and is now pushed back with a comb-toothed hairband decked out with miniature plastic gerbera daisies. She's wearing a minidress made of black satin with slight shoulder pads.

She turns to see Lars taking her in, golden summer sunrays bouncing off his eyes in the fading evening light. She silently accepts his compliment. He reaches out a hand to her. She hesitates.

When she slips her hand into his warm palm, he grasps it tightly.

They stroll across Gamla stan in silence, down Drottninggatan, past several blocks until they reach her tiny apartment. When the elevator door opens, they're greeted by the sight of Mr. Torbjörn and his cat, Leo, wearing a jacket. His eyes immediately go to Lars's and Nancy's clasped hands. She quickly slips out of his grip.

"*Grattis*, Nancy," he says, his voice chirpier than normal. "I still owe you cardamom buns. I will make Asenath's Egyptian tea for you," he says in Swedish as he shuffles out of the narrow elevator. "Come tomorrow," he orders before letting Leo jump out of his arms to the floor.

Nancy bends low to help him hook Leo's leash on. When she straightens back up, she meets his interrogating glare. "We will toast in *Dark Chocolate*'s honor," he adds before leaving, totally ignoring Lars.

Nancy swallows, turns back to Lars. "Thank you for walking me home."

He doesn't answer. His pupils do. They grow larger, his eyes darkening as he peers down at her. She feels herself blushing. She turns and steps into the elevator. He follows her.

"Lars," she whispers.

"*The heart wants what it wants, or else it does not care,*" he mutters beneath his breath as the doors creak close behind him. Nancy remains silent. "Emily Dickinson," he continues, his voice low and heady, pupils widening, golden irises shrinking. "American poet."

"Professor," she says, putting distance between them

His hand moves to her cheek. *Stop calling me that*, his hand says.

"I didn't want to fall for you," Lars says softly. "Looking into your eyes for months as I painted you from those photographs." He pauses, sucks in air. "I didn't want to fall. But I did, and now I don't know what to do." He moves his thumb across her mouth, across her full bottom lip.

Nancy gazes into his eyes, slowly opening her mouth. He gently slides his thumb between her lips. He lets out a low groan when she closes them around his finger. She feels his thumb run along her warm tongue in a tender gliding motion. She doesn't recoil from his touch, instead enjoying the shock of pleasure.

Lars steps in closer. She feels his breath on her face.

"*Naa jaŋ*," he whispers against her lips in her language. *Come here.*

She can sense from his kisses that he is a man who knows what he is doing. But what is she doing? Is grief driving her senselessly into his arms? Her desire to be loved, to be reminded that she is not alone?

She moans into his kiss, and he responds with vigor, pressing her against the wall. The elevator door pings open. They break apart for the very blond couple and an equally blond female friend to take their place. They all exchange silent nods of acknowledgment. Nancy fumbles for her keys once they reach her apartment. Lars's hand comes in to hook her waist, to pull her in for another knee-weakening kiss against her closed door, his mouth soft, his tongue exploring.

She turns back to her door. Words tumble out of him. *A batu. Wait. Kana taa. Don't go. N be jaŋ. I am here.* He explores her curves against her door, both hands roaming while he pins her with a kiss. When his hands reach her waist, he grabs on tightly, locks her against him.

"See what you've done to me," he whispers against her ample lips before pressing his mouth to them once more. She feels him hard against her stomach. "See what you do to me, *Nna kanuntee.*" *My darling.*

She cups his face in her palms, stopping his roving mouth. "*I ñiiñaata,*" she hushes back. *You're handsome.* He grins, the years falling away as he smiles. Then his eyes fill, and she realizes he has been disarmed by her comment. Has no one else thought him handsome enough to stick around?

"*I diyaata,*" he mutters. *You're sweet.*

Lars lets her open her door. The apartment is relatively dark, save for late-summer sunlight streaming in through the windows. The sun won't be setting until 10 p.m.

"Coffee?" she offers. The look in his eyes tells her coffee is the last thing he wants.

He takes her hand and leads her to the soft, mustard yellow velvet couch. He sits and pulls her onto his lap. His hand starts to explore her leg, up her thigh, while his lips plant featherlight kisses down her neck. She arches her back when his hand dives underneath her satin dress, grazing her inner thigh, inching upward until it finds its target.

"*Ḍa i kanu le, Nancy,*" he says breathlessly against her shoulder as his fingers explore her. *I love you, Nancy.* "Let me love you. Let me show you." His voice is more sharp breaths than words at this point.

She shifts in his lap to straddle him. His hands grab her backside tightly, not wanting to let go. Not wanting to lose her again. Malik's love had kept her out of reach for so long.

Nancy runs her fingers through his soft strawberry curls. His Pippi Longstocking red tresses. She watches his eyes darken into Bamse honey gold. She leans in to press her permission against his lips. *Yes.* She will let him love her.

Lars kisses her again, roughly, desperately this time, as if to consume as much of her as possible before she changes her mind. He makes quick work of her black lace panties. He guides her against him, shows her how to move in his lap. He lays her on her back and tastes her hungrily until she writhes, her back arching off the couch, her fingers gripping his short locks tightly, her nails scratching and leaving marks across his tender, sensitive skin. He takes and takes until he exhausts her.

Hours later, she lies in the nook of his arm on the sofa, her chest expanding, seeking more air for her lungs. He peers down at her as she lies there naked, collecting his breath. When her eyelids flutter open, she finds him studying her intensely.

"*Du är så jävla vacker,*" he whispers in Swedish. His own mother tongue. His palm roams her exposed torso, touching her, cupping her as his eyes fully take her in. *You're so fucking beautiful.*

TWENTY-FOUR

TINA, 2007

"The heart wants what it wants, or else it does not care."
Emily Dickinson, an American poet, Lars writes.
I remember speaking those words to Nancy many times.
The first few times, it disarmed her.
The last time, she laughed in my face and walked away.
Every month, Tina gets a new letter from him.

She never writes back, though temptation gnaws at her. But what would she say? He hasn't earned access into her life yet, so she can't brief him on her escapades in California.

Standing up to his sons would have required bravery. Writing was the coward's way. He often commiserates with her in his letters, describing his own rise to fame within tight art circles. His paintings fetched hundreds of thousands of kronor, especially his most well-known series, painted in the 1980s: *Aja: The Pilgrim*. Tina knows nothing about the art world, so this is news to her.

"Inspired by his love for Gambia," the series description reads, "*Aja* is short for *Ajaratu* in Mandinka, denoting a female pilgrim. His pilgrim never made it to her promised land, her face concealed." Tina doesn't know if it's pain, disappointment, anger or sadness she sees in the painting. The woman's features are so blurred and unrecognizable that she remains an object.

The painting is done in heavy oils of varying shades of brown, the *slightly exaggerated* busty outline of the woman unmistakable beneath sheer wisps of white cloth. Low-cropped hair, lush curves filling each canvas. A series of twelve limited-edition paintings in this collection that all sold at auction. She'd found all of this out when she continued googling him, piecing his life together, running a thread back to when he was a professor at Stockholm University. He'd received harsh backlash for the series, with people criticizing a white man profiting off the body of a Black woman.

That Black woman. Nancy. Tina's mamma. The pilgrim who never made it to the promised land of her dreams.

Is this why Nancy told her children their father was dead? Because the man was selling naked paintings of her mother? Knowing Nancy, she probably didn't want her children to know. Is this why Nancy wanted Seb out of her life, too? So, he didn't derail her from her own dreams? What would Nancy think if she knew Tina was in touch with Lars now?

His letters always end with him saying how immensely proud he is of her. *Now I am someone worth cherishing, because others cherished me first*, Tina thinks, despite herself. The man who had robbed her of her mother's warmth.

Nancy rarely initiates phone calls, instead expecting Tina's weekly check-in. She wished the letters from Lars were from her mother instead. Telling her just how much she loves Tina, despite the fact she looks just like the man who hurt her. Whenever Tina feels homesick, she isn't sure what she's missing, since her mother is often cold with her. At least that was a constant she could faithfully rely on.

And now she's at Jonas's home studio, in utter disbelief of what she's seeing on his wall. It takes Darryl tapping her on the shoulder to snap her out of it. Because there, hanging on the wall in Jonas's home studio, is *Aja #8*. This time, the sheer white cloth has slipped off the subject's derriere.

"Tina? You okay?" he says, before following her eyes to the painting, the faceless woman looking over her shoulder at them.

"Yes, sorry. It's just…" she begins, then composes herself. "That painting is, it's so, it's stunning."

Jonas pads over and stands beside her, a smile etched across his face.

"Yeah, same way I felt when I saw it at Sotheby's." He beams. "I had to have her."

Tina's skin bristles at his words. Her mother. A thing to be *had*. A thing to be hung up on walls and gawked at. Before she saw this, a small part of her was considering writing Lars a letter of truce, but that faceless look over Nancy's shoulder has snuffed out any desire to further their connection.

Maybe, she thinks, this was why she had sabotaged her own song on stage. Because she was tired of being *a thing to be hung and gawked at*. A walking painting to be picked apart physically, stared at while all proceeds go to the creator—the label, producers, *Lars*?

She turns to Jonas. He drinks her in, those eyes roaming across her freckles, down to her lips, and slowly climbing back up. "Can't wait to work with you, Tina," he says softly before lifting his mug of tea to his lips, his eyes giving her a glimpse of what he's thinking—*a thing to be had*—over its rim. She sees herself in him; wants to have him too. Tina turns away shyly from his gaze, only to meet Kasha's. She's waiting, a wry smirk on her face. Was their chemistry that obvious?

"Let's get to it." Darryl claps hard to break their standoff, his voice gruff.

They're here to shoot a video with Jonas, but ever since Darryl walked in on her first meeting with Jonas at DJ Kamid's, she's sensed a new distance between them. He is still civil and collegial, but his eyes betray him. She assumes he's fighting whatever he's been feeling since they met in Athens.

Kasha organizes lunch while DJ Kamid, Jonas, Darryl and Tina sit around a glass table in Jonas's lush garden. He already tramped barefoot through the dirt—*I need to ground myself before we get started*, he had said, plucking a few leaves off his plants, rolling and lighting them up. A choreographer whips and gyrates in front of the group. She pauses to explain her vision for the music video, before continuing her writhing.

Tina feels eyes on her back and turns to look. Jonas is leaning halfway back, blowing tendrils of smoke into the air, legs spread apart, inviting her in. She lets her gaze linger on him for a few seconds, her skin heating up. His attention is electric.

"The fuck are you doing, Jonas..." Darryl isn't really

asking. Jonas shrugs, revealing bright teeth as he adjusts his position in the lounge chair and sits up straighter.

"Got distracted, that's all." Jonas glances her way once more, a tiny look of glee. She wonders what he would have done if Darryl hadn't interrupted their moment; she craves a taste of whatever he's offering.

The men plan out the music video while Tina sits pretty, twiddling her thumbs, looking around. The sun begins to dip, coating everything in gold. She excuses herself and strolls through Jonas's garden. It's a sprawling property with hundreds of hectares—the man is clearly in tune with the earth. He'd requested a vegan option when Kasha had taken orders. Verdant flowers are scattered around. Roses, gerberas, magnolias, lilies, marijuana patches.

She slips out of her silver goddess sandals and burrows her toes into the soil. So much history in this land. The raw earth warms her soles. It feels comfortable. All she knows about Jonas is that he left home to go discover himself in the Americas and Caribbean. His name isn't one that regularly graces entertainment reports back home. Maybe a passing mention here or there whenever he wins a Grammy or MTV award. And when he does, the news always leads with "*Den svensk producent främst känd för sina musikvideor…*" The Swedish producer mainly known for his music video…

Son of our land, Tina reflects. It makes her wonder; would he still be worthy of Sweden's love without his accolades? She feels the same about herself. If they weren't performing and striving, were they still enough? She can feel a thread between her and Jonas begin to form, seemingly out of thin air.

Tina feels him behind her. She wants to lean back into his chest—this statuesque, broad, handsome stranger. As they float between two worlds, not sure which one will claim them, he feels like home. She pivots to face him. Golden sun rays play across his face, turning turquoise into peridot green. She basks under his gaze.

"I want to take you out to dinner," he says, his voice heavy, low. She knows what he means, sees it in those gorgeous eyes. *Let's fuck our pain away. If we belong to no one, at least we'll belong to each other.*

"I can't have dinner with you, Jonas," she whispers back, pushing loose strands of hair behind her ear. She watches his handsome features soften.

"Why not?" he protests.

"You know why," Tina says softly. Those goosebumps surface once more.

"Is it Darryl?" he asks, reading her face. "Are you two together?" She breaks away from his gaze. She knows Darryl would never approve of this pairing—too much of a distraction.

"I think Kasha's back." She moves around him and starts to walk away, back toward his patio, but she can feel his eyes burrowing into her from behind.

Two more hours of planning after dinner. Darryl gives both Tina and Kasha a ride afterwards, with Tina riding shotgun.

"So, I've got exciting news for you," he says. His eyes scan the traffic, now pinheads of spotlights in the night.

"More news?" Tina beams back at him, hoping he catches her elation in the dark car.

"ONYX's big thirtieth anniversary bash is planned for next year," he says. "Guess who they want as the opening act?"

"No way," Tina squeals once the news settles in. "DJ Kamid and I are performing the track?"

"No," Darryl says. "Just you." The car falls dead silent once more. 'Honey.'

"I don't know what to say." Her voice begins to crack. "I don't know what to say."

"It means ONYX is ready to do everything for you beyond this album," he continues. "We're ready for you to own the world," he adds. "But you have to want it. You must truly, deeply want all of this."

"Oh, I do, I do," she cries. "This is my dream."

"Really? Sometimes I'm not so sure, Tina," he says sternly.

"What do you mean? This is all I've ever wanted."

"You let yourself get distracted easily."

"Distracted? By what? Who?" Tina's flustered. She already dumped her gorgeous Seb for this opportunity. She needs Darryl to believe her commitment. She hears him take a pronounced breath, sees his brow furrow as he contemplates his next words to her.

"Please don't fuck Jonas," Darryl says. "He's a troubled man. And a druggie."

Tina visibly bristles at his sharp words. Kasha in the backseat chimes in. "They're perfect together. Don't you see it?"

"No, I don't fucking see it, because Tina is gold and Jonas will bury her, okay?" Darryl sounds exasperated. "Yes, he's a creative genius, but he's also been in and out of rehab on the down-low far too many times. I don't want him near her outside of this video shoot."

"Now you're overreacting," Kasha chides. "They're both grown-ass adults. Let them do whatever they want." She touches Tina's left shoulder. "He probably feels like home to you, don't he? A gorgeous home at that." She chuckles to herself. Darryl doesn't share her amusement. Kasha continues, "I see the way you two look at each other. Your chemistry is insane…"

"Are you done?" Darryl snaps, his grip tightening on the steering wheel. Kasha ignores him and promises to get Tina Jonas's number.

When Darryl and Kasha drop her off, Tina beelines for her bathroom to wash off Jonas's smoke. Once bundled in a plush bathrobe, she preps an espresso, thinking over Darryl's words. So jealous. Why won't he make a move himself? He clearly wants her, she assumes.

The phone rings until Nancy picks it up after the fifth chime. Her mother sounds absent when she answers.

"Are you okay, Mamma?" she asks, concerned. "Is this a good time?"

"I'm fine, my dear, how are you?"

Tina hesitates. "I saw them," she says quickly. Mumbles of confusion from the other end.

"Saw what? What are you talking about?"

"I saw his paintings of you. Is that why you cut him off? Was Lars a pervert?"

"Which paintings?" Nancy asks, her tone unsure.

"Did Lars ever paint you?" Tina's question is clearer now. Silence from Nancy.

"Hmm, Mamma? Did you let him paint you?"

"No," Nancy says in a low, heavy voice. "I mean yes, I let him paint me. But no, I didn't give him permission to sell me to the world. How did you find out?"

Tina's nostrils flare as a gasp of despair escapes her. "Mamma, your naked body is hanging on a stranger's wall in California."

TWENTY-FIVE

NANCY, 1982

Lars invites her back to Vaxholm. "Come spend a weekend with me," he'd pleaded against Nancy's damp skin after loving her raw on her couch. "Last weekend in August," he added, before nipping her swollen lips again.

He was working on more paintings and wanted her *once again* to be the first to see them. He kissed her fervently before leaving.

Nancy meets Mr. Torbjörn for coffee in his apartment a few days later. The old man can smell the deception on her skin. He'd grown to like Malik and always asked if Nancy had heard anything yet about his condition or his potential return.

He pours her chamomile tea in silence. He'd already chastised her in his own grumpy way for still not drinking coffee after all these years in his country. He's back to speaking only Swedish to her, and she understands much better now. Yaya was right that she would take to it quickly—now they converse with ease in his language.

"Who was that new man?" Torbjörn asks her once he settles in with his mug of black coffee. She lifts her tea to her lips under Leo the sphynx's judgmental glare. The cat is decked out in a Selbu Rose knitted sweater, perched on the dining table, staring daggers at her.

"He's not a stranger," she says defensively.

"I could see that," he says before taking another sip of coffee. He points to the buns which he had portioned out into quarters—easier for him to take bites. She grabs a meager piece.

"He's an old friend of ours," Nancy says. "He's an artist. An oil painter."

Torbjörn grunts after another sip. "Has he been lurking in the shadows all along? Waiting for you?"

Nancy winces. "I wouldn't put it like that."

"You don't have to," Torbjörn chuckles. "You forget I am a military man. Trained to read and identify threats." He gives her a meaningful look.

"So, what are you planning this summer?" She switches topics.

He shrugs. "Baaa, I need to find something to do. Maybe take Leo on a trip back to my family's village. Maybe finally go back to Asenath's family in Egypt." His eyes glimmer. "Spend my last days there with them in Aswan."

"You're not even seventy yet, Mr. Torbjörn," Nancy giggles.

"Ha, my body feels ninety, though," he says. He seems to droop with the admission. She reads it in his eyes; years spent in the best shape of one's life as an Air Force pilot, now reduced to skin and bones because of undue stress and grief. Those eyes must have witnessed unfathomable horrors around the world.

"You still have plenty of mischief to get up to. You'll be

around a long time, growling at all of us on this floor." She laughs before taking a bite of her bun.

"You all deserve it," he says, pointing a finger at her. "That Norrbotten couple," he says, meaning the blonds. "They have heard my cane banging many times." He shares a wall with them. "I remember those times *very well*," he chuckles into his mug. "And the Chileans, Jose and Jose."

"Jose and Joseph," she corrects him.

"Baaa," he grunts again before launching into another inappropriate tirade. The Senegalese-ginger couple aren't spared either.

Above all, Nancy knows he is trying in his own twisted way to make her feel less alone since *Dark Chocolate*'s disappearance. She misses Malik desperately, wants more than anything for him to write her a letter explaining that it was all one big misunderstanding.

Their *fika* is interrupted by the sharp buzz of Mr. Torbjörn's doorbell. "Baaa," he grunts. Nancy gets to her feet to answer. She opens the door to a nurse, a middle-aged white woman in uniform.

"*Visste inte att hemtjänst var redan här*," she says, pushing past Nancy, padding into the apartment. *Sorry, I didn't know home service was already here.*

"*Hon är inte jävla hemtjänst!*" Mr. Torbjörn curses from his dining table. His fury fills up the room. "*Ut med dig!*" he screams at the woman who freezes, her eyes wide in shock. *She is not fucking home service! Get out of here!*

Nancy hears the woman exchange words with him; his response is heated. The woman mumbles something about coming back with his medicine. She turns to leave, gives

Nancy a quick once over, grumbles some sort of apology for the confusion, and leaves.

When Nancy turns back to Torbjörn, she finds him with a hand over his face, his shoulders jumping slightly, weeping, and she wonders if he's missing his wife in that moment.

Late August. A Friday afternoon. Low rain clouds hang overhead.

Nancy takes the ferry alone over to Vaxholm. The dark aquamarine waters of the Baltic Sea are choppy beneath the rudder.

Lars waits for her at the pier. He's wearing a white short-sleeved shirt left unbuttoned over khaki shorts and leather sandals. On his head is a straw fedora; white-rimmed sunglasses hide his eyes. He's looking unusually stylish. Quite dapper.

He greets her with a chaste hug once she disembarks with the rest of the crowd. Once inside the shaded woods on the way to his cottage, away from the busy pier, he gropes her against a tree trunk and ravages her mouth.

"I've missed you," he groans. She writhes uncomfortably beneath him as tree bark scratches her bare back, exposed by her halter top.

He pulls back, his eyes glittering. "Sorry, I was too excited." He peels himself off her. "Come on, let's go." He grabs her hand and continues the last few yards to his cabin.

"I should get some electricity in here," Lars says once they're inside and he's stoking the fire. "I had planned for dinner out on the deck. Maybe tomorrow, once Leif joins us."

It's been a while since she met up with his brother

for lunch—Malik's absence has kept her holed up and antisocial, besides attending the occasional event thrown by the Gambia-Swedish Association here and there. But Leif did reach out, wrote her a letter of support which Lars delivered to her over one of their *fika* dates. She had read it in silence under his intense gaze.

Nancy listens, a weak smile on her lips. Lars packed only what they need to eat for the next few days. There's a portable generator for his fridge. He's planning on catching trout for dinner tomorrow. Right now, though, he's on his knees in front of her, satisfied with the size of the fire he's set. He dips low to kiss her thigh, trailing his tongue.

"I've painted some more." He whispers against her skin. "Two more. I think I'm ready." He licks her softness. "There's a gallery here in Vaxholm that wants to exhibit me this autumn. My first ever. A solo exhibition." She feels his smile, his excitement, against her.

"You must be so proud," she mutters, her fingers raking his soft hair while he explores her thigh.

"Thanks to you." He pulls away from his task to look up at her. "Thanks for being my muse." He rises to kiss her.

A loud bang startles her. She grabs onto his neck tightly. A sharp flash of lightning has hit too close to his cabin. Lars pulls away to shut the windows before the rain starts. And when it does, the downpour is so thick and dark, they can barely make out his dock in the distance.

"Looks like I might have offended the weather gods," Lars chuckles. "I must apologize," he says to her, his eyes shining in the low light. Lars starts to strip until he's standing stark naked in front of her. She averts her eyes shyly. This energy feels different; released from an invisible shackle, free.

Lars unlatches the deck door and heads out into the storm. He spreads his arms wide like an eagle, his face pitching upward toward the heavens, his chest bouncing with laughter. Nancy leans against the doorjamb, in the safety of the indoors, watching him do his rain dance.

He spins, jumps, wiggles as large drops pelt him from all angles. He pushes wet hair off his face. He turns sharply toward her. Her breath catches. He yells words in the rain toward her. She doesn't hear him. He yells some more. When she still doesn't understand, he slowly pads up to her, water sliding down his long, toned torso, until he's standing inches from her face.

"*Naa jaŋ,*" he whispers softly. *Come here.*

She shakes her head. He grabs her. She yelps, giggling as he drags her into the pouring rain with him. She tries to wriggle free, but he holds tight. When she gives up, he presses her against his bare chest, drops falling off strands of hair plastering his face, his eyes luminescent in the dark air. He makes love to her roughly on the patio table as rain pelts his back and rumblings of thunder drown out her cries.

The storm intensifies. They move indoors, onto blankets he pulls off armchairs to make a nest in front of the fireplace. This time he's more tender, trailing and outlining her features with his fingers under the crackling fire. "Tell me what you want, Nancy," he whispers against her cheek as his fingers roam lower.

"Tell me, *njusoo.*" *Sweetheart.*

She shows him. Gripping his head, pushing it southward as the storm churns the sea outside.

Afterwards, Lars desperately tries to console her, to no

avail. Nancy weeps and shudders in his arms, her tears overwhelming her. After a few moments of holding her while she sobs, he asks in a defeated whisper, "Do you miss Malik?" He sounds so small now. "You still do, don't you?"

Hearing Malik's name on Lars's lips feels so wrong. She covers her face with her palms. He lies quietly by her side, his fingers trailing her arms, letting her know he's there for her, even though Malik is gone.

"Why won't he write me?" she cries. "Why?"

He takes a moment before responding. "I don't know, *njusoo*. I wish I had more information for you, but I don't." He pauses, ponders his next words. "Don't forget what he did."

"Malik would never do such a thing," she says, sniffing back tears. "Never."

"Sometimes we don't truly know the people we love," he says. "I know you want to think the best of him and the lovely times you had together, but *sweetheart*, he was caught trafficking drugs. It's best you start to move on from him. Politics has a funny way of digging up your skeletons, especially if you want to become *Madame President*." His voice turns light.

Nancy drops her palms to peer sideways at him. He reaches to trace a finger down her jaw. "I miss my brother too." Nancy forces the words out.

She tells Lars all about Lamin. Her older brother who let jealousy consume him so deeply that they lost contact, and then the war claimed him before they could stoke the fire of that relationship once more.

She feels Lars swallow.

*

In the early hours of the next morning, a series of flashing lights stir her. She wakes up to Lars swiftly putting his camera aside.

"What are you doing?" She looks down at her body. The blanket has slipped off sometime during the night. She quickly drags it back up to cover her nakedness as goosebumps surface

His face turns bright red. "Oh, those are just for me," he explains. "I promise not to show them to anyone," he adds before leaning in for a kiss, which turns into another early-morning lovemaking session. They fall back asleep in each other's arms.

When they wake, the sun is high, as if yesterday's storm never happened. The only evidence is the few raindrops that are crawling across leaves.

"*Kori i siinoota baake?*" Lars asks her when she stirs. *I hope you slept well?*

"*Haa n siinoota baake,*" she answers softly, a smile spreading across her lips. *Yes, I slept very well.*

Leif arrives later that morning like a tornado bearing bags of groceries: some pre-cooked couscous, carrots, broccoli, sinful amounts of butter and bread, ingredients for a summer salad and backup filets of trout because he knows his brother will catch nothing. He's wearing super-short hotpants cut close to his butt cheeks, an exercise band across his carrot-orange hair, which is now shoulder length, and a loose-fitting blue singlet.

"Mother Hen is here," Leif whispers to Nancy before

pulling her into a bear hug. He barely acknowledges his brother as Lars watches the pair embrace.

She can't stop thinking about her brother. She regrets not telling Lamin that she loved him. Hopefully while he took his last breath, he realized she'd always loved him. That she wished he too had found the opportunity to study abroad and expand his horizons in life, and never wanted her own success to come between them.

Lars abandons his bid to fish for their dinner after thirty minutes in his canoe. He pulls out the filets Leif brought and starts to grill them. The brothers have barely spoken to each other all day, each talking mostly to Nancy. There's a tension in the air she can't quite put her finger on.

"*Kan du andas i de där?*" Lars drops once Leif starts setting the table. *Can you breathe in those?*

"*Vad?*" Leif shrugs, straightening back up. *What?*

"*De där,*" Lars smirks as he flips trout on the grill. He nods toward Leif's hotpants. *Those.*

"*Vad?! Gillar du dem, eller?*" Leif smirks back. *What? You like them?*

Lars snorts audibly. "A man your age should know better," he continues in Swedish.

"Know what better?"

"You want me to spell it out to you?!" Lars yells in a sudden flash of anger.

Nancy startles at his outburst, shrinking into her patio chair. She sees pink spread across Leif's face as he stares his younger brother down.

"The nerve," Leif says, his tone deep, low. "The nerve of you to say anything to me. One word from me—or rather, three words—and your fairytale would be over."

Lars cuts her a quick glare. "Please excuse us," he says in English.

"Lars, is everything—"

"Go in now," he commands, his tone firm.

Nancy scrambles to her feet and makes her way back into the cottage. Once the door shuts, she hears the brothers arguing. She begins thumbing through a few novels she finds on a nearby shelf to feign nonchalance.

Leif is yelling at his younger brother, screaming words and names. Lars bangs his fist on the patio table so hard she hears glass breaking. Maybe plates flying off. She stays planted inside while they verbally attack each other. She moves closer to the window to spy on them. Lars is aggressive. Leif has his face buried in a palm while Lars is only inches from him, spittle flying, a finger pointing sharply at his brother. She can't quite make out what he's saying but his fury is clear.

Leif turns to go, his hands flailing about him as he makes his way back into the cottage. She catches his teary eyes, and they take each other in for a few seconds before he scurries off to shut himself in the bathroom.

She'd seen fear and sadness in Leif's face. What secrets is he protecting?

That evening, she and Leif wave at Lars as the ferry pulls them away from Vaxholm.

Away from him.

TWENTY-SIX

TINA, 2007

They're back in the studio recording "CREAM," her last song for the album.

"I'm not sure." Darryl shakes his head. "Again," he says over the speaker.

"Again?" Tina is exasperated. Four hours in, her voice is teetering on turning hoarse. She's beginning to hate these four walls. "What's wrong with this take?"

"Too breathy. A little nasally on the bridge. I don't like it. Again." He whips his right index finger in the air in a circular motion. Tina rips off her headphones and bursts out of the booth, planting herself squarely in front of him.

She glares at Darryl. "And if I don't?"

The studio goes silent. The producer, G, freezes his fingers on the dials. Kasha excuses herself and leaves the room.

"The label is betting millions on you and paying G a month's salary by the hour, so don't play with me, girl." Darryl's voice stays calm, measured.

"Girl?" Tina crosses her arms over her chest. "I'm twenty-one. I'm not a child." She can't seem to shake the label of petulance which has clung to her like Velcro since Eurovision.

"Get to work, Tina," Darryl says sternly. "I ain't got time for this bullshit."

"Well, I do," Tina practically shouts. "First, you make me *ooooh* and *aaaah* on Kamid's stupid rap, and now you want me to twerk in his video with Jonas? Who do you think I am? You think I'll just do anything for fame?" She catches her breath. "I fucked up a whole country on stage at Eurovision. Kamid is nothing!"

"You need a minute?" G asks.

"Please," Darryl says, not turning to look at him. The door shuts, leaving them in a standoff.

"What are you doing?" Darryl's eyes are hard, his voice low.

"I know you want me," Tina says, cocking her chin to the side, a coy smile on her lips. She sees him catch his breath before a chuckle starts building up within his chest. It turns into a laugh, and soon he's cackling in a way that sends color rushing up her cheeks. Her smile drops, her eyes widening at his mockery.

"Seriously?" Darryl glares at her. She wraps her arms tighter around herself. "Is that what you think? That everyone in the industry just wants to fuck you because you're this young hot thing?"

She fumes silently. He presses on. "I brought you to LA because you need to fully stand in your own body, in your power. You're still waiting for validation from *them*, from me." He jabs a finger into his chest as he moves closer to her.

"Then why would you degrade me on Kamid's rap album? Why would you have me dance like that in his video?" Tina finds her voice. "And you know I can't say no because you're my manager. You set the rules. I simply follow."

"Because you don't even know what you want, Tina," he counters. "You have no clue."

"Oh, so now this is all my fault? Damned if I do, damned if I don't?" she spits out angrily. "I'm an artist, Darryl. I came here to create art. To create something with depth, with meaning."

"This is how the music business works," he says. "Collaborations between the biggest acts. I scratch your back, you scratch mine. DJ Kamid is the number-one DJ and rapper in the world right now." He throws his hands in the air. "Imagine, the Swedish Siren appearing in one of his videos?"

"So now Kamid is validating my stardom."

"No, Kamid is teaching you business. I am teaching you business," Darryl yells. "There are thousands of starving artists out there who would do anything to be in your position, including... whatever you're insinuating." He studies her face. Her lips are pursed. A tear escapes. It races down her cheek, dignity be damned. "Light-skinned girls come here by the dozen every hour. You ain't extra-special."

"Now you're just being cruel on purpose," she says, her voice dipping to a whisper.

"I'm being real with you, Tina. What do you want? You have no fucking clue. Do you want to be a star, or do you want to sing live in empty pubs on Fridays? That's where you'll end up if you let Jonas distract you."

She holds his gaze defiantly. Darryl laughs once more

before placing a palm on her cheek. "You've got a silly crush," he says, his voice low. "It will pass."

"Why do you keep invalidating my feelings?" Tina cries. "I know what I want and who I am."

"I'm twelve years older than you," Darryl says, "and trust me, I get my fair share of chicks. If you're looking for a daddy, I ain't him. If you don't want better for yourself, I do." He takes his soothing palm off her cheek. "Do you know how many women come in here, into this record label, saying they want to fuck their agents, managers, producers for their big break?"

"So, they don't have agency, but you men do?" she spits.

"I'm saying…" His voice breaks. He composes himself. "I'm saying you don't have to go low to go high. That's all I'm saying to you, Tina. You don't. Even if you dance in Kamid's video, you still have full control. Your own agency. You don't have to do anything you don't want to do, okay?"

She doesn't answer. A mixture of embarrassment and fury courses through her bones. All this time, she thought he had a secret crush on her. Now she realizes her appearance means nothing to him. She can't play that card with Darryl. Gorgeous women of all shades stroll through the doors of ONYX every single day. She needs more.

"If you want to be successful, you need to start sucking it up and doing the work. It's not always going to be fun and games." Darryl glances down at his shiny wristwatch. "So, do you want to work or not?" he presses.

"I'm not sure, Darryl. Right now, I don't. How's that for agency?" She spins around and storms out.

Tina cries all the way to her Bel Air apartment.

"Miss? You okay?" the taxi driver asks, peering through his rearview mirror as they pass lush, rolling hills.

"I'm okay, thanks for asking," Tina sniffs. She pulls out a tissue to wipe away her tears. The paper takes some blush with it.

The driver wants more. "Where you from? I detect an accent. Me, I'm originally from Baja California. Mexico, baby!" he says with pride.

"Sweden," she answers half-heartedly, wiping away tears.

"Sweden?" he asks. "Really? They got Black people there?"

Tina bristles at how easily he dismisses her other half. "My mother is from Gambia and my father was"—she pauses, thinking of Lars's letters—"is white Swedish."

"I have learned something new today," the driver guffaws as he switches lanes. "Black folk in Sweden. They got Mexicans too?"

Tina rolls her eyes. "I'm sure there are one or two."

He chuckles, unbothered by her tone. "How is Sweden? Cold? What do you eat there?"

She ignores his questions and stays silent the rest of the ride to her apartment. Mulling over what Darryl had said to her: *If you're looking for a daddy, I ain't him.* In that moment, she'd wanted the ground to swallow her whole. His rejection made her want to rip off her own skin.

Is that why she keeps Lars's letters close? Because she's been looking for unconditional love wherever she can find it?

When the taxi drops her off, a navy-blue McLaren she doesn't recognize is parked in front of her apartment. Tendrils of smoke escape through an open window. She steps cautiously toward her front door. Once the taxi driver speeds off, clearly vexed by her unresponsiveness to his inquisition, the doors of the McLaren flip open. Jonas Jonsson unfolds his long limbs from the tight sports car. He's wearing aviator glasses, a loose white linen shirt, khaki shorts, and flip-flops. His dreadlocks are pulled into a bun. He flicks the joint he's holding onto the gravel path and takes off his shades.

"*Tjena*," he greets, his teeth blindingly white.

"*Hur fick du min adress?*" she asks him, wondering how he landed at her place.

"Kasha," he says. He glances with brief regret at the joint he disposed of.

"*Vad vill du?*" *What do you want?*

"A proper chat. Kamid's party was batshit crazy. I didn't hear a word of what you said." His blue eyes roam her curves as he continues in Swedish. "At my place, it was all business, and we didn't get time together." He pauses, runs a finger across his lips. "You remind me of home. I want to reminisce."

She eyes him before unlocking her mahogany door and letting him in. "*Kaffe?*" she offers. Jonas hums in response, while slipping out of his flip-flops. He pads around her small space, then spots the patio.

"*Vilken utsikt!*" he exclaims at the view. "*Bor du ensam, eller?*" he asks. *You live alone?*

In response, she asks him if he wants sugar and milk. Jonas pulls open the sliding door and strolls out. Standing with both hands on his hips, he takes a pronounced deep breath. "I love it here."

"When did you leave?" Tina comes out with two mugs

of black coffee. He grabs his, takes a sip, drinking her in over its rim.

"Not soon enough," he says before his eyes fix on nothing in the distance. She observes him. "Sorry about Eurovision." He suddenly turns toward her, catching her off guard.

"Old news." She waves it off awkwardly. "I'm trying to build something here. Make it here. Like you," she says.

He smiles, revealing a dimple. "And how do you feel here?"

"Feel?" she asks. He steps closer, mug in hand. She studies his peculiar features borne from when North and South fall for each other.

Tina shifts on her feet. She hasn't paused long enough to reflect on this new feeling, this new land. What is this feeling spreading within her? Freedom? Possibility? Tilled soil to nurture the seeds of her success?

The soil back home was patted down, undisturbed. Did it have enough air for Tina to grow? It seems her mother's seed never sprouted there.

"This place," she starts to say. "California... it feels so different in ways I can't express yet." She pauses and cradles her cup in both palms. Jonas nods back indoors toward her kitchen island. They relocate. "I guess I feel freer."

"Just say it," Jonas challenges her in Swedish, his eyes clouding with emotion. "Say it."

"Say what?" She feigns ignorance.

"Say you feel like a queen here," he says. "You know you do. You were in the music business back home, right?" She nods. "Did you ever hear of Jonsson Productions?"

She thinks for a bit, then shakes her head, a lie. She'd always known who he was. After all, he was an Afro

Swede making it in America, even if he wasn't getting the recognition he deserved. But it would be too embarrassing to admit that.

"Exactly." He leans back and sets his mug down. "And here, I drive a motherfucking McLaren. My videos have swept the MTV Awards every single year since I broke into this market. I've won four Grammys." He splays out four fingers. "They'll finally recognize me when I'm dead," he concludes bitterly.

Tina absorbs every single word, every emotion etched across his face.

"They pick and choose, *älskling*," he adds. "You're only good enough when everyone else wants you."

Älskling.

That word reminds her of Seb. How he often called her darling. She thinks about him. They haven't spoken in days now. How quickly he had left her mind when Jonas came into focus.

She thinks about her quest for unconditional love again. Had she projected her insecurities onto Seb? Her feelings of distrust, questioning his loyalty and commitment? Or, had he truly been ashamed of her when she lost at Eurovision? Abandoning her when she'd needed him the most?

"Do you really believe that?" she whispers back to him. She sees his chest heave, his eyebrows relax, sadness play across his eyes. Did he feel neglected too?

"Do you believe that's true?" she asks again. All she really wants to do, though, is kiss the pain away. She needs the ego boost after Darryl's rejection. But she pities Jonas now. She knows what it's like to feel unwanted.

Jonas must have read her thoughts because in one fluid motion, he steps in, his arm encircling her waist, pulling her gently toward him as he backs up against the kitchen island. She presses both palms against his chest, her head barely grazing his shoulder.

"*Vad gör du?*" she asks breathlessly. *What are you doing?*

He pulls her closer. "What I've wanted to do since I saw you at Kamid's," he whispers against her lips. "I saw it in your eyes. You miss this." He runs his tongue across her bottom lip. "You miss home."

Tina responds hungrily, her palms cupping his face, cradling him, her mouth seeking his. Jonas lets her lead, opening to her when her tongue wants in. He runs his fingers through her straightened hair, falling like silk through his fingers. He lifts it in both hands, tightens his grip, and pulls back to look at her.

"Do you want this? Over the curls?" he whispers. He tugs her straight hair softly. "Do you?" She knows what he means. That physical proximity to the white part of herself. The part that was missing for decades because it didn't want her. Or maybe Nancy didn't want *it*? Because it had thrown her mother off course, stolen her dreams and immortalized that fact in brown ochre and burnt sienna?

"You don't know me," Tina says, her voice low. "You don't know what I want." She remembers Darryl's words. He'd warned her about this distraction.

Jonas lets go of her hair. He runs both palms over her backside, pulls her close, locks her to him. "I feel like a king here, Tina," he whispers back against her lips before pulling her into a sensuous kiss. "I feel free here." He lifts her, spins around, plants her on the island. He hikes up her skirt, his fingers grazing her outer thighs, his eyes pinning her in place.

"And what do you want?" She kisses into his mouth.

Jonas doesn't answer. He simply returns her question in his touch, his caress, his rhythm. He feels different. He's not Seb. She knows his answer. Jonas wants to find his way back home.

Afterwards, she catches her breath, her arms still wrapped around his neck. Jonas's shirt is on her tiled kitchen floor. His dreadlocks are out of their bun. Those half-lids are back as he peers at her, trapped between his arms on her kitchen table, basking in her afterglow. He plants soft kisses down her neck, across her shoulder.

"Do you have a lighter?" he mutters before another press of his lips on her skin. This time around her collarbone.

"A what?" She pulls back to read his face. Eyes still on her, he reaches into his back pocket, fumbles for something, pulls out a small bag of white powder.

"A lighter." He presses a kiss to her lips. "And a spoon."

Later that evening, an hour after Jonas leaves, Tina finally peels herself off the kitchen island, reeling after what transpired between them. Her first one-night stand. Her first hit. She still doesn't know why she did it but, looking into Jonas's familiar gaze, she'd felt safe, seen, less alone.

She picks up her phone and dials. "Mamma?" Tina wipes her nose as her eyes begin to fill, her appearance disheveled.

"My dear." Nancy's voice is upbeat. Dare she say it, excited? "I've missed your voice. How are you?" Tina clutches her chest to stop from hyperventilating. She remains silent. "Tina?" Nancy seems distressed. "Are you okay?"

Tina hears the fear in her mother's voice. Too far away to pull her child into a hug.

"Why did you let him do it?" Tina's tone is cold, desperate as she rakes fingers wildly through her hair.

"Let who do what?" Nancy's confusion sails through the phone.

"*Aja*," Tina manages. The phone goes dead silent. "Why did you let him distract you from your dreams?"

"I promise you, my dear." Nancy's voice is low. "I didn't know he painted them."

"Don't bullshit me, Mamma! I'm tired of all the lies. Just tell me!"

Nancy collects herself before answering. "He took pictures when I was sleeping. He made those paintings later. I only knew about them when they talked about the auction on the news." She pauses.

"He's such a pervert!" Tina screams angrily. "Such a disgusting pig!"

"This is exactly why I want you to stay away from that Sebastian boy." Nancy grows agitated over the receiver.

Tina is taken back, confused. "Why do you hate Seb so much?" she demands. "Why? What has he ever done besides love your daughter—something you've never done!"

Silence. Nancy processing her words. "What are you saying, Tina? Why are you talking like this?"

"Do you even love me, Mamma?"

"Of course I do. What a question! You and Tobias are my everything."

"Every time I came crying to you, wanting you to hug

me," Tina sobs, "you always pushed me away. Told me I should act like a big girl."

"Tina, I want you to grow thick skin. The world is not a kind place," Nancy says. "You can't be weak all the time."

"So, you think I'm weak?"

"I think that boy is making you weak," Nancy says. "Men like that only come to steal what you hold close to your chest."

Oh, Seb, Tina thinks sadly. Not because of her mother's words, but because she'd given herself over to Jonas so easily. The one who may well be the thief.

"Is that what Lars did to you, Mamma? *Hmm?* Did he steal the thing you loved the most? Your dreams?"

Nancy hangs up.

TWENTY-SEVEN

NANCY, 1982

The wink.

He does it. He winks for them during his speech.

"Oh my God!" Nancy screams, sitting taller in her chair. "Oh my God!" She hopes Malik also saw that wink, wherever he is. It was meant for him too.

Nancy claps and cheers as Olof is announced prime minister of Sweden once again. She's watching the breaking news over at Mr. Torbjörn's apartment. She convinced him to invite the Chileans too. The men cheer in support, one of them holding onto Nancy's framed photo of her, Malik and Olof.

After spending that torrid weekend in August with—and under—Lars, she decided to switch out of his department for her postgraduate degree. Sleeping with the head of said department was probably against the rules. So, Nancy switched to political science, which was more in line with her path toward *Madame President*. She gets goosebumps whenever she thinks it. A new degree outside his jurisdiction also means guilt-free quickies in his office. Against his wall. On his desk. In his chair. His hand clenched tightly over her mouth to keep her quiet, Malik slowly fading into the deeper recesses of her mind and heart.

But Lars never takes her home.

"I need my space," he said when she built up the courage to ask. "I can't be seen letting a student into my apartment."

"But your office is okay?" she retorted.

"Yes," he responded after a long pause. "In my office, I'm your mentor. No one would think anything of it."

Skål. Cheers.

Joseph's gleeful voice pulls her back into the room. "Nancy is a proper celebrity now," he says before downing a cheap red that tastes more like rancid juice. He'd said so himself. All he could afford since he was still hunting for a job.

"*Baaa,*" Torbjörn adds in his signature style. "I am the real celebrity." He pokes a finger into his chest. "You all won't leave me alone."

They laugh. She and her neighbors have formed an unlikely bond. The embassy currently pays for the apartment, her largest expense, but Nancy knows her days within these walls are numbered. She must find a proper job soon.

"So, what are you kids doing for *höstlov?*" Torbjörn asks them before a sip of coffee.

"We're going up north," Jose beams. "We hear it's already minus thirty degrees." He turns to Nancy. "Come with us!"

"Never," Nancy replies in mock horror. "You want to kill me? That wine is making you mad."

The Chileans manage to drag her to Kiruna, into calf-deep snow already in early November, to go husky sledding and chasing the aurora borealis. Both firsts for her. She wears every single layer of warm clothing she has.

She screams her lungs out when the huskies race across frozen lakes and Arctic tundra at full speed. She cries at the sight of the aurora, huddled close to the two men as ribbons of green and red shimmy across the indigo-dark northern sky.

She calls her parents from the hotel lobby the next morning, excitement still ravaging her body. Omar laughs softly as his daughter launches on her joy-filled tirade. About those celestial curtains swaying in the sky. A reminder they serve a God of miracles. "Live your life, my dear," Omar tells her.

Since Lamin, whenever she calls home to check on how they're doing, it is Omar who picks up. Fatou finally got off the floor but remains a fraction of herself. Deep grief is making her mother indifferent to her daughter.

Nancy arrives home to her eviction letter.

She knew it was coming sooner or later, but it's still a blow. At first, she felt excitement at the embassy seal on the envelope, praying and waiting for word from or about Malik.

When she tears it open, she finds a rather kind letter telling her time is up. She needs to move out by December 31 for the new staff moving in. Since Malik had essentially bought all their furniture and they weren't legally joined, they "strongly encourage" her to leave the place intact and fully furnished.

She makes herself lemon tea, sits with the news for a few minutes, then bolts over to Mr. Torbjörn's place.

"I know you're in there," Nancy says as she pounds. "I'm not leaving you alone."

She hears the cat, Leo, come closer to the door. He starts to meow, louder and louder. She squats down and pushes the letter flap back to peek in. She locks eyes with the sphynx. A strong waft of piss and something else hits her. She sees a mini pile of about twelve letters. She straightens back up and keeps pounding.

"Mr. Torbjörn? Mr. Torbjörn?" She hammers away, loud enough to draw the blond couple out of their own apartment. The man is topless, and his wife is adjusting the shoulders of her robe.

"*Hemtjänst* couldn't get in either for two weeks," the man says in a drawl. "I think he told them he was traveling for *höstlov*. They came and knocked a few times, but then stopped coming. They must have thought he'd gone away for the holidays."

"He would never leave Leo behind." Nancy's voice rises in fear. "They should already know this."

"Leo?" the man asks, puzzled. "Does he have a son?"

"His cat," Nancy snaps. She turns back to banging and calling his name.

Another door across the hall opens. The Chileans. "*Amiga*, what's going on?"

"I think something has happened." Her eyes are wide in panic. They all hear Leo meowing. They also hear scratching on the door. Leo trying to get out. "Please help me open the door."

Five minutes later, two men are shoving their shoulders into Torbjörn's door, trying to break it down. The blond wife has dialed 112 and is now on the phone with paramedics on their way.

"Argh!" the men grunt in unison as they hit and hit until the door gives way, taking some wall with it. "*Gud! Vad det luktar!*" The blond man pinches his nose. Joseph and Jose unsuccessfully try to stop their gag reflexes.

Leo springs back into the apartment toward the living room. Nancy rushes after the cat. She freezes when she finds Torbjörn on the ground, a soiled towel around his waist. The apartment is filled with a distinct smell—a mix of decomposing fish, rotten eggs, and feces.

Her neighbors, hot on her tail, freeze behind her. Joseph lets out a gut-wrenching scream as Jose bolts back out.

Nancy clenches her mouth tightly. She feels vomit rising, filling her throat, as she steps closer to Mr. Torbjörn's body. Leo hops on his back and starts to meow again. A deep, sad sound emits from the feline. He knows it too. His best friend is gone.

Nancy tiptoes closer, hand over her mouth, to assess him. His piercing eyes are open to slits and glazed over by some film. His head is turned toward the large photo of Asenath hanging on his wall. His mouth slightly ajar. She spots movement around his mouth. White blobs like grains of rice. One drops into his mouth, and her own instantly fills with puke.

She thinks again about Yaya's mental health. Coming from a place rooted in community to find people dying in isolation, from *it takes a village* to this, is so cruel.

She turns and rushes back toward the door, the vile liquid squeezing through her fingers. First, her Malik. Now her dear friend Mr. Torbjörn. Is Lars next?

She feels her heart tighten as she starts to hyperventilate.

Is the universe forcing her to grow thick skin? To stop being weak around men—both lovers and friends? To be a big girl?

She meets paramedics at the door who immediately clear them all out of the apartment. The Chileans help her clean up in their own apartment while paramedics get to work over Torbjörn's body.

"He has no family." Nancy grows hysterical. "He has no family." She collapses into their arms and sobs. Once she settles down, the trio head back across the hall to watch the paramedics at work. Two police officers have now joined them, their hands splayed to keep curious neighbors from inching closer to the scene.

She hears Leo meowing once more from somewhere deep inside the apartment. "Leo!" she screams. "Leo! *Kom hit!*" she calls. *Come here.* Leo meows some more, then rushes over to Nancy, clawing at her trousers. She bends low to sweep the cat into her arms. His loose wrinkly skin is cold and clammy to the touch. She peers into his large bright-blue eyes, a feline replica of Torbjörn's, and hugs him to her chest to warm him up.

Nancy moves out of that apartment one week after discovering Torbjörn. There is no need to stay until December 31. Instead, she knocks on the door of that historic apartment in Odenplan.

Yaya opens it up to find Nancy with a turtleneck-wearing sphynx in her arms.

TWENTY-EIGHT

TINA, 2008

Nancy has never hung up on her before.

When it happened, Tina held her flip phone in shock. She climbed into bed, curled up in a ball facing the wall, and finally fell asleep at 2:54 a.m.

Barely four hours later, she bolts awake. She dials Jonas.

"Hmm?" he answers drowsily. "Tina?"

"Come," she whispers.

"What? What are you saying?"

"Come to me."

"Now?" He pauses, comes back on. "It's seven in the morning."

"Don't make me beg you, Jonas," she says, her voice low. She hears him murmur and stretch in the background.

"I'm on my way," he says. "I'll bring a little something too."

Thirty minutes later, his McLaren arrives at her door. She knows he must have raced through the hills over 100 miles per hour to get there that quickly. He's in sweatpants, a T-shirt, and hemp flip-flops. His locs are loose and fall past his shoulder. He's holding a canvas pouch.

They stare at each other wordlessly. His eyes roam Tina's silk teddy as she leans against her door. She opens it for him. He strides quietly past her to her living room and flops onto her large sofa. She trails him. He proceeds to spread out his supply, pulling out white powder, carving perfect lines across her glass-top coffee table.

He follows a line up a nostril, sniffs, and lets out an audible gasp. Then he turns toward Tina standing by the sofa and pats the spot next to him.

She shakes her head.

"What's wrong, baby?" he asks. "Why did you want me here at the crack of dawn?"

"I didn't want to be alone," she says, wrapping her arms around her chest.

He scans her face. "Don't you want to feel better?" He points at the coffee table.

"I want you to make me feel better," she says. She looks at his cocaine. "I'm stronger than that."

Jonas chuckles. "So, I'm weak? Is that what you think?" She sits next to him, cups his cheek, plants a kiss on his lips. He laughs against her mouth. "But not weak enough not to fuck?"

When she doesn't answer, he pulls out of her caress and turns back to her table, bending low to finish his task.

Weeks later, her album is cut after she's apologized to Darryl for walking out. When it hits the airwaves, a star is born. She makes the rounds on late-night shows again. She shimmies in skimpies on morning talk shows while America eats breakfast.

This was not what Tina had envisioned as a pop star. But her name is splashed in neon.

Several feelings course through her. Gratitude for the attention. Happiness that "CREAM" showcases her artistry. Sadness that Nancy still hasn't called to apologize for cutting her off. Anger that Jonas read her for filth and showed her—rather strongly on her knees on the polished marble floor—that he wasn't "weak" once his lines were gone. She's angry that she let him, but she can feel him seeping into her, pushing parts reserved for Seb to make space for his own brand of love.

Through it all, seedlings of pride begin to sprout. She's resisted his feelgood remedy after that first stupid lapse—which she'd coughed through, slowly reclaiming her agency.

"*Eurovision Star Turned Swedish Siren,*" headlines read once DJ Kamid drops his raunchy rap video, "8-figa," featuring her. She moans his anchor notes smeared in baby oil, gyrating alongside other dancers in a mass of human flesh, indistinguishable from the rest. Her first video under Jonas's guidance—and gaze—as music video director.

She finally sees him in action. His turf. Trying to prove his genius to non-listening ears, while those in front of him adore him. Here, he is beloved. And at her place, whenever he makes hard love to her, he gives her a glimpse into his void. She feels her heart swelling for him, despite his terrible habits. She needs him to know he matters to her too. Deeply. Passionately.

After that risqué video, she's not going to fly Tobias and Nancy in for Christmas as promised. She can't look them in the eye after her performance.

"Next year, I swear" is all she says, promising Tobias she is sorry for embarrassing him with soft-core, swearing never to appear in another vixen video.

"You better not," he says. "Miss you."

"Miss you too. How is Mamma?"

"Stubborn as always," he laughs. "She says she's fighting with you but won't tell me what about."

"Did she tell you she hung up on me the last time I called?"

"She's waiting for you to call her and apologize."

"Well, she's gonna wait a long time. Love you, Tobbe."

"Love you, too."

Click.

Seb reaches out too. "*Hej.*" His voice is heavy. It's been a while.

"*Hej,*" she answers. "Let me guess, you've seen the video too."

"I have," he says before a long spell of silence.

"And?" Tina's petulance surfaces.

"I just want to say I'm happy for you. You know, I guess you're now living your dream." Seb pauses. "If that's your dream."

"What's that supposed to mean?"

"I don't know," Seb sighs. "If that's what Jonas wants from you."

"You don't know him," she says defensively.

"I think I know all I need to know about him, *älskling.*"

"Stop calling me that," Tina snaps. More silence from his end.

"Okay?" He seems perplexed.

"We're not together anymore, you know that." Tina's voice is brittle. "We're just friends."

"You know I love you." His voice deepens. She can tell he's trying to hold back tears. "I just want you to be happy. And if dancing naked for that *jäveln* makes you happy, then…"

Tina disconnects the call abruptly, her decision made the second Seb called Jonas a bastard. She grabs a plush pillow and screams into it. She feels warmth on her bare back. Jonas runs a soothing palm over it. She peers at him over her shoulder. He's leaning against the headboard in a mist of marijuana smoke that's enveloping him like a halo.

Come here, he mouths to her, reaching to rake his fingers through her hair, pulling her to him.

She obliges Jonas and starts the painful process of excavating Seb from her life. *Her Seb*. She's barely thought about him for the last few weeks, but now he swims in her consciousness.

She can't shake him.

TWENTY-NINE

TINA, 2009

Several months have passed, with Tina sinking deeper into Jonas and his life. She enjoys his aura, his touch, his intensity. But in love? She isn't sure yet.

Jonas has been traveling a lot, scouting out locations for new videos he's conceptualizing and going on silent retreats when he feels guilty about the drugs. He'd flown her out a couple times to meet him; from Bali to Bermuda. They haven't officially stepped out in public together yet. They never roam around holding hands. She knows her budding career would never survive another headline-worthy scandal.

The only people who know of her situationship with Jonas are Darryl and Kasha. Any news about them as a couple would be too volatile to manage PR-wise, considering Jonas's drug history. So, since Tina isn't a *child*, had *chosen* him, and *can't* let him go, Kasha begged her to at least keep him on the down-low.

Four hard knocks rattle her door after the doorbell gets no response. "Hmmm," Tina stirs. Jonas is spread-eagled across her bed, barely making a sound. She shoves him to make sure he's still breathing. He mumbles in discomfort and shifts his weight. She reaches for her phone.

Eleven-something at night. The numbers blur into each other. She turns to look at Jonas once more. He snores lightly. He's been urging her to move in with him. She keeps refusing, knowing she isn't ready to be completely consumed by him.

Earlier that day, he'd gotten the news. Yet another Grammy nomination. Not for Kamid's video, but for a futuristic, edgy video he'd dreamed up for another artist on another label. Tina wasn't sure how he made it safely to her place. His car was a mist of smoke and he swagger-slumped his way to her door. When she opened it, he grabbed her, kissed her hard, and took her roughly from behind against the wall by her front door. They moved on to the kitchen, the patio, her sofa, then ended in her room before he finally told her about his nomination for the classy music video. Now she wonders if she writhed in baby oil for nothing.

The hard banging continues. Tina slides out of bed naked. She reaches for a T-shirt lying on a pile of clothes, others littering the floor. She treads over them, palms on the wall, guiding her toward the front door.

She opens it to Kasha, mid-knock. Kasha is wearing a floor-length black ball gown, her braids piled into an elegant updo. Beneath the do, smoky makeup and nude lips. The other woman's eyes glance up and down Tina. Her hair is tangled and there are tracks of makeup across her face. Kasha sniffs. She probably smells the smoke.

"Is he here?" Kasha's words are firm.

"Who?" Tina scratches her scalp. It feels itchy. The itch moves to her forearm. She remembers she hasn't showered in days.

"Don't play with me, Tina," she says. "I had to stop Darryl from coming himself." Tina glares at her, trying to understand what's going on. "Otherwise, he would have killed Jonas."

"Why are you here?" Tina is confused.

"You've got to be kidding me," Kasha says before pushing past her and letting herself in. She clips her nostrils shut with two fingers. "*Jesus*, Tina. Did you fire your cleaners? What's going on here? Where is he?" Kasha starts marching toward her room. "Where is that bastard?!"

Probably hearing the commotion, Jonas meets her at the door, eyes drooping, a newly lit joint hanging from his lips. He blows out smoke.

"You crackhead!" Kasha screams into his face. "I never should have given you her address, never!" He chuckles at her, scratches his torso, and slowly pads toward the bathroom. Kasha goes after him. "Jonas? What are you doing? She missed the event because of you!" Kasha's voice booms around the small space.

Tina sees a side of Kasha she's been craving access to for over a year. Protective, vibrant—a friend. Tina trails them, trying to decipher what Kasha is yelling about.

The event. Which event? What had she...?

"Oh my God." The fog lifts. "ONYX's thirtieth anniversary!" Tina exclaims.

"Your team was here hours ago." Kasha turns to her. "Your stylist and makeup artists couldn't get in. They tried calling you. They said they banged on the door, walked around the property, and peeked in through the windows." Kasha stands in front of her now, her dark eyes scanning Tina's face. "They were going to call the cops." Kasha lets out a sigh. "I couldn't let that happen, knowing what I was going to probably find here. With you and that motherfucker." Her face twists in fury once more. "I didn't want the press tearing you apart."

"I—I—I didn't hear anyone." Tina wraps her arms around herself. "My phone must have died or something. God, I'm so sorry. I must have, I must have—"

"Passed out? From those?" She points to white powder coating her kitchen island. The countertop is littered with the stuff.

"They're not mine. They're his. I don't use," Tina says. "Kasha, I'm so sorry."

"But you smoke, right? Right? Are you high now, Tina?" Kasha stands inches from her face, peering dramatically into her eyes. "Are you? You're a mess. Why aren't your friends checking in on you from Sweden?"

Tina begins to shake as sobs overwhelm her. Kasha's eyebrows scrunch as she takes her in.

"You were the opening act." Kasha's voice changes from its reprimanding tone to something softer, laden with pity. "You are ONYX's golden girl. And you didn't even show up."

Tina cries, her hands clasped in front of her face. She teeters on the edge of losing it all. Since her spat with Darryl in the studio, he drew away from her, becoming more distant with each passing week. She wants him in her orbit once more. She craves friends, and Darryl's dark gaze and Kasha's boisterous warmth are the closest thing she's got.

"Where are your friends?" Kasha asks, her voice filled with concern. "I can't be your only one."

Seb flashes across her mind. After she'd disconnected his

call, Seb kept trying to reach her, probably wondering what he'd done to make her grow so cold and distant. Days had turned into weeks. Then he'd stopped trying at all.

Tina knew why she'd let him go. She couldn't bear the weight of his judgment, knowing she probably deserved better than what she'd sunk herself into. The sinking sand that is Jonas Jonsson. But Jonas is soul food. And she is famished.

"I'm fine, Kasha, I swear to you. It won't happen again." Tina wipes snot from her wet nose. "I swear to you."

Kasha pursues her lips as she glares at Tina. "It better not happen again. You hear me? Now we need to put out a press release."

"I promise you, it won't," Tina sniffs. "Let me buy you brunch some time to apologize."

"Girl, please, you can't afford me," Kasha says, lightness returning.

"Please, you pick," Tina insists. *I want you to be my friend.* That's what Tina wants to scream out loud.

"Fine," Kasha concedes. "Fine. But don't ever pull this stunt again."

"I swear to you," Tina whispers.

"You owe Darryl an apology," Kasha finally relents. "I'll set up dinner for you two."

Tina nods vigorously.

Kasha's eyes soften. "I also owe you an apology." Her voice breaks. "I never envisioned Jonas pulling you into all of this when," she pauses, "when I connected you both. I thought you being Swedish would create a bond. Maybe you would help him climb out of his darkness. I'm so sorry, Tina. This is all my fault."

"I chose him too." Tina's voice is terse.

"Please drop him," Kasha whispers. "Please."

Tina stares down the older woman. "I can't," Tina says. "I—I love him." The words shock her the moment they leave her lips. She's witnessed the pain behind his facade, and she doesn't want him to struggle alone. Yes, she does love Jonas. He's hers now.

They hear the toilet flush. A couple of seconds later, Jonas pads back out naked and scratching himself in full view of the women. Even Kasha can't ignore how impressive he is.

"*Älskling,*" he starts. "What did I miss?"

The next day, a press release goes out.

The Swedish Siren suddenly fell ill and was unable to perform at the anniversary bash, it says. Pop sensation Alana had graciously stepped in last minute to belt out two impromptu songs. She'd been plucked directly from the audience, unprepared, instantly shutting down lip-synching rumors. In the weeks following Alana's performance, her name was back in the spotlight while Tina's began to dim.

Christmas is a low-key affair stateside. Darryl and Kasha both retreat to their families, so Jonas and Tina spend the holiday eating pizza, drinking coffee, and exploring each other in bed. Watching Jonas's back bent over her coffee table, she thinks about *jul* in Sweden. Christmas with her family. Their *julbord*, which Uncle Leif took charge of preparing every year—meatballs, pickled herring, cured salmon—with his assistant Tobias, who was responsible for all the trimmings. If they'd left it to Nancy, it would have been fried chicken and rice for their Swedish Christmas.

Uncle Leif.

She misses his laugh. His warm, dark maple eyes watching them tear into their Christmas gifts. The way he flailed his arms dramatically when he was excited about something. The succulent Christmas ham he prepared with glee. It's been close to five years now.

She sighs audibly, the memories haunting her. Jonas turns toward her, his eyes wild, and crushes her with a kiss.

"*God Jul*," he mumbles against her mouth. *Merry Christmas.*

On New Year's Eve, they toast the new year with expensive champagne, a deep kiss and long stretches of silence sitting out on his back patio, gazing up at constellations in the clear California night. Fireworks pop in the distance, echoing all around, magnifying the sound of their loneliness.

THIRTY

NANCY, 1983

Nancy moved in with Yaya and Benke before Christmas, Leo in tow. Yaya avoids the cat like he's a demon. Nancy had grabbed onto her aunty, crying, telling her she now understood the emotional toll of bonding with patients; the elderly, the disabled, how upsetting it was that they left just when you were beginning to fully understand and love each other.

Weeks later, it is Yaya who notices the change in her first.

"Your breasts look big," Yaya mentions over dinner one evening in early March. Yaya had opted to cook them *yassa ganarr*, seasoned fried chicken with white rice, instead of Benke's tasteless cod. The seasonings have Benke reaching for his glass of water after every bite.

At Yaya's words, he chokes and launches into a coughing fit that has nothing to do with the spiciness of the meal. Nancy glances down at her chest. Yes, they've been more tender than normal, but fuller?

"Is it that professor?" Yaya continues, spooning rice into her mouth, not looking up at Nancy.

"What are you talking about, Aunty?! Of course not! He's my—*was* my professor," Nancy flares. She notices color rising up Benke's cheeks as his eyes dart down to her bosom and away again, fighting distraction.

"Then whose is it?" Yaya asks.

Nancy doesn't respond, so Yaya reaches over to grab a boob. Nancy smacks her hand and backs away from her. Yaya chuckles and turns back to her rice and chicken. This is the part that still grates on her, that quintessential lack of personal boundaries. If there is one stereotype she believes is justified, it's that. The African Aunty. A cause of many generational traumas.

"Yes, you're definitely pregnant," Yaya says. "Have you missed your period yet?"

"No," Nancy responds curtly.

"Don't worry, you will," she says smugly. "I need to figure out how to inform your parents. They're not going to be happy."

By the time Nancy misses her second period and fights bouts of morning sickness, her body has violently announced that Lars's child has taken root within her.

She heads to his department after spring break. She finds him making paper copies, his glasses resting on the tip of his nose. Studious, serious, intense. "We need to talk," she says, her disposition skittish.

"I'm busy right now." He continues his task, not looking at her. "Come back during office hours."

"It can't wait," she says, her voice low.

"*A batu*," he switches to Mandinka. "*Nka naa le.*" *Wait. I'm coming.*

"*Nej*," she says firmly in Swedish. *No.*

"Damn it, Nancy." Lars punches the machine with a fist. He seems to be getting more irritated by her presence with each passing month, as if the luster that once enveloped her is dulling. Meanwhile, her heart only beats faster for him. "I have an exam to run this afternoon. I don't have time for—"

"I'm pregnant." She drops the word like a rock into a still pond. Lars turns sharply toward her, his brow furrowed.

"What?!" The words leave him in a whisper. He steps in closer to her. "Stop talking like that."

"It's true." She peers up at him, her chest heaving. She hadn't been anticipating this reaction. Their standoff continues for a few more seconds before he grabs her by the forearm and leads her to his office.

Once Lars shuts the door behind them, he pushes his fingers through his soft curls, then rests them on his hips, staring straight up at the ceiling. She watches the muscles in his lean back tense. She isn't sure what reaction she expected, but this isn't it.

Lars turns to her. "Are you sure? I mean, have you been seeing anyone else?"

Those words stab her right through the chest. A new feeling begins to bubble up within her. *Contempt.*

Nancy starts to laugh. A deep cackle welling up from within her. It turns manic when it reaches her lips.

"Keep it down," Lars whispers through clenched teeth. "What are you doing?"

"You bastard," she says through her laughter. "You sad bastard."

She watches his nostrils flare. "Nancy, I'm sorry this has happened to you."

"Happened to me? Happened to me!" Nancy cries. "Why are you acting this way?"

"I'm so sorry." He is breathless. "So sorry. You caught me by surprise, that's all." He pulls her into a hug. At first, she struggles, then relaxes into his embrace. He kisses the top of her Afro. They stay in that position for several minutes until their racing hearts calm down.

He pulls out of their hug, holds her at arm's length, peers into her eyes.

"We will get through this, Nancy. I promise you," he starts. "I'll take care of you. Of our baby. Things are just a little difficult right now." He stops to adjust his glasses.

"Have you met someone else? Is that it?" She wipes a tear away before it lands on her cheek. "I've never even been to your place," she says abruptly. She hears him sigh loudly.

"I know, I know. I just… It's complicated," he chokes. "It's complicated with my ex-wife and our joint apartment," he says, his voice low. "I can't explain it right now, but I promise you, I will. And I will figure out a solution."

"A solution?" She eyes him skeptically. He leans in to give her a peck. She pulls away from his kiss. It lands in the air. "What solution?"

"Please trust me, Nancy," he begs. "I will take care of you. Always. I promise you."

Later that evening, his solution arrives at Yaya's house.

She hears Yaya in low conversation with a man at the door while she and Benke sit in the living room, watching *Dallas* on their square box of a TV set—one of a few American imports that unite the nation in the evenings.

Benke cranes his neck curiously. Nancy sits up. Yaya leads the man into their living room. Nancy is stunned into silence when she is met with Leif's walnut-brown eyes. His reddish mane is clipped low, his face is clean-shaven and he's wearing a suit.

"Benke, meet Leif," her aunt introduces him. "He is the father of Nancy's baby." She turns to her niece. "Thank you for inviting him to come meet us." Yaya's gaze lands on Leif once more. Leif. An apparition in their apartment. "This is a very serious matter for us Africans, you know. Having a child out of wedlock."

Nancy glares at her aunt—the same one who had been suggesting she use her body as a surrogate for her. Had she planned on keeping that secret from their family back home?

Nancy pushes to her feet, rubs her hands on the thighs of her plush pink flared trousers. She sees Leif swallow as she strolls up to him.

"Leif," she says. "What are you doing here?"

"Mother Hen." He smiles weakly. "I had to come." His tone is heavy, laden with sadness. "I had to come for you."

"Why?" Tears begin to fill her eyes. She knows why. A tiny sliver of suspicion had crept into her the day she walked across that grand stage to grab her diploma from Lars, one that's only grown since catching sight of the glimmer on his finger. "Why are you doing this?" she whispers, her voice shaking. "Why?"

Tears fill his eyes too as he peers down at her. "Because he can't," he says in a hush.

Nancy twists her lips as she studies Leif. She throws her arms around his neck and weeps against his chest. He runs a large palm over her back, soothing her.

Once she pulls out of his hug, she turns to her aunt and uncle. "This is Leif. We're in love."

"Yes," Leif says. "Yes," he repeats as if to convince himself too. "I love your niece and I will marry her as soon as possible. We will get it done at City Hall, so our child is delivered under our union." He pauses to collect his breath. "This will not happen out of wedlock. She deserves the world."

Yaya clasps her hands. "You're a good man, Leif," she says, her voice brittle. "You are a good man for making an honest woman out of our Nancy."

Then she spreads her arms dramatically toward him. "Welcome to our family."

"Her name is Frida," Leif confesses the next day, lifting a mug of coffee to his lips.

Nancy had made the forty-five-minute train journey from central Stockholm to his modest apartment in Norsborg south of town.

Leif continues, "They've been married since our parents forced him to return from living in Gambia. They have twin boys, Lukas and Ludvig."

"All this time?" Nancy winces, cradling her own mug of green tea. He nods at her, his eyes sad. "But why would he lie?"

"My brother is a spoiled and entitled control freak," Leif says before reaching for an almond cookie. "Vaxholm is his hideaway. Where he can live the life he feels he deserves."

"But why would he lie to us? To Malik and me?" Nancy
wants to understand, needs to understand why Lars would
tear her apart this way. Has she been this stupid all along?
Not wanting to see it, even though it was quite transparent?
The double life he's leading? Nancy feels weak. Utterly
spineless, powerless, helpless.

"I know it sounds twisted but"—Leif stares at her
intensely—"but he fell for you, Nancy. He loves you so
much and doesn't want to lose you."

"Why are you doing this for me, Leif?" she asks. "It can't
simply be from the goodness of your heart."

The air around them shifts, laden with untruth. He
raps his finger on his mug, tapping out an inaudible tune,
pondering his next words.

"I have my secrets too." He takes a sip. "And Lars holds
them over my head because the world is cruel."

"It is your brother who is cruel," Nancy spits.

"The world too, my dear," he says. "He is but one of
millions who hate the likes of me. Regardless of whether
we're family or not."

"Tell me your secret, Leif." Nancy holds his gaze. "I will
take it to my grave."

Tears well up in his own. "Oh, Nancy. I don't know what
to say."

She reaches for his hand, clasps it tightly. "Is it tied
to your hotpants?" She sees a smile carve across his face
before he nods in response. "So, he is blackmailing you?
Is that it?"

"He can make life very difficult for me if he chooses,"
Leif confesses, "and for us Scandinavians, exclusion from

our tight-knit circles is our biggest fear. No one ever wants to feel isolated."

"So, what do we do now?"

"Move in with me. Lars has promised to pay for your expenses."

"To live a lie together?" she challenges him, her voice sour.

"To survive together," he responds. "The world is a very unkind place for the likes of us."

Unkind indeed, but when her baby boy screams his lungs into the world later that year, she names him "Tobias"— *God is good.*

Leif puts his name on Tobias's birth certificate, making her son legally Swedish and legally his.

The nurse places the boy on her bare chest. He is dotted in freckles, dark-copper hair plastered against his soft scalp. When he opens his tiny eyes, Nancy lets out a cry of relief. Warm, dark brown like hers. She couldn't bear raising a child with Lars's eyes, that unique feature of his. Staring into them every single day would break her over and over again.

Leif squeezes her hand tightly as she weeps. He finally breaks down and turns toward the wall, sobbing as well.

The night Leif showed up at her aunt's door was the last time Nancy ever uttered Lars's name. His memories are poison, his entire being dead to her. His sweet honey eyes, now bitter. Nancy watches Leif cry, her chest tightening, knowing he will have to continue living his real life in the shadows while this false fatherhood gives them both the respectability they need to survive.

Her heart expands with empathy and, in that moment, Nancy realizes what she must do to grant Leif freedom. To live his life and his truth. He will be *Uncle Leif.*

Her son will never call him *Pappa.*

THIRTY-ONE

TINA, 2010

A few weeks before the Grammy Awards, Tina is up early on a Saturday morning, poring through her box of letters from Lars. She hasn't spoken to Nancy in over a year, since her mother slammed her phone after their discussion about the paintings. She wonders what her mother must be thinking. Probably reliving that violation again because Tina had dredged it up out of curiosity. Tobias keeps her updated about their mother. Nothing new—her days are mundane, working her shifts as *hemtjänst*.

Tears occasionally surface when she thinks about Nancy. The one person whose approval she craves the most doesn't even want to hear her voice. Does her mother's hatred for Lars run that deep? The audacity of Lars to think he could ever develop a relationship with her when he'd stripped her mother bare for purchase. But still, Lars's letters are filling the void Nancy's emotional absence has left behind.

Tina googles more of his work. He's represented by three galleries in Sweden and internationally. She pulls up more articles about him and his various art projects, mostly inspired by Black and Brown people. In several interviews, he says it's his tribute to the "incredibly warm people of the Gambia." He'd kept the fact that he could speak both

Mandinka and Wolof at an advanced level private from the public. It had eventually been dug up by a journalist, who claimed his entire stance as an artist was cultural appropriation—that he was hiding this information, only wearing it at opportune times.

Of course he kept it private. The coward, she thinks. The same way he couldn't publicly claim Tobias and her. At least his sons have calmed down their campaign against her—for now. Out of sight, out of mind—they'll be onto their next hate-filled campaign.

Tina notes the time and quickly closes out her Google search, then rushes into her closet. She pulls out slip-on wedges and a white summer frock patterned with orange flowers. She still hasn't gotten her driver's license, so she calls a taxi, which ferries her off to the breakfast joint Kasha picked for their makeup brunch.

Tina's hair is pulled back into a ponytail and she's sporting see-through, red-tinted aviator glasses. She spots Kasha in a corner booth fashioned from red pleather seats. She scuttles over, her smile reaching the other woman first.

"*Hej*," Tina greets her in Swedish.

"Howdy," Kasha responds, cocking her head to the side. "You look fresh."

Tina laughs and settles in. She pulls the laminated menu toward her. It's been a while since she's eaten somewhere this unpretentious. It makes her feel more like the Tina who once flipped burgers in Sweden as a teenager. Her eyes scan the menu, which promises grease, fat and heightened cholesterol.

"Their creamy eggs Benedict with butter king crab is to

die for," Kasha suggests. "Figuratively speaking," she adds. Tina giggles, her mind made up, calories be damned.

The waiter rolls over on skates to take their order. Tina turns back to Kasha with her eyebrows scrunched. "I really am so sorry," she says.

"I know you are." Kasha sighs. "I'm sorry too for setting everything up between you and Jonas. Darryl can't stand me right now either."

"It's not your fault. Besides, we're grown adults. We both wanted this."

"But Darryl is trying to protect you." Kasha is serious.

"He hates me." Tina's voice dips low.

"On the contrary." Kasha holds her gaze. "Darryl is doing everything he can to shield you because he thinks you're talented. Trust me, I've known him for two decades and worked with him the last ten years. Darryl is married to the job."

Tina's eyes soften as she takes Kasha's words in. "I wish he would just let me know he doesn't hate me." The waiter interrupts them with two tall glasses of mimosas and skates away backward from their booth. "He's hot though." Tina takes a suggestive pull from her straw, eyebrows arched. "I won't have minded if he'd actually been interested."

Kasha laughs. "I thought you were happy fucking Jonas? I mean with that *thang* he's swinging?"

Tina bursts out laughing, spraying mimosa onto Kasha, who squeals and reaches for a napkin.

"I'm so sorry." Tina stretches out her hand, touching Kasha's arm, cackling. Jonas pops into her head... *At least we'll belong to each other...* Her laughter simmers down. "Jonas and I are doing good. One year on the down-low because we can't go public yet. I've grown to love him in my own way. But he's no Darryl."

"Look," Kasha starts. "Forget about Darryl. Yes, he cares about you, but you're never going to have him."

"What do you mean? Is he gay?" She drops her voice to a whisper.

"He's got discipline, Tina. He's got integrity and he understands his power. He'll never misuse it or put you in harm's way if you can't handle things yourself," Kasha says. "Trust me, many girls have tried it with Darryl. He's a fine-ass brotha who is also picky as hell. He knows what he wants."

"What about you?" Tina asks. They spot the waiter rolling over with their plates. Tina resists the urge to childishly stretch out her leg and trip him just to test his reflexes. "There you go," he trills as he places a plate of eggs Benedict in front of Tina. He does a half spin on one foot and slides banana pancakes in front of Kasha. "For you, my lady." With that, he sidesteps and rolls away.

"So, what about you?" Tina repeats. Kasha starts cutting into her pancakes and shrugs.

"At first, yes, I thought he was the finest thing since Morris Chestnut. But now"—she takes a large bite—"he's like my big brother." The words come out muffled as she chews. "Don't chase him. Let him come to you if he wants to," she continues between bites. "Then you'll know he's serious."

"What about Jonas?" Tina asks.

"Stay away from that life with him. Don't let him suck you in. I've been in this industry long enough to see it happen to the best," she says. "He does some crazy shit."

"I don't do drugs, Kasha, please trust me, I don't. He wants me to but I'm stronger than that."

Kasha shakes her head. "You're fighting the same thing he's fighting. He doesn't know who he is, and now he's dragging you into the abyss with him." Kasha pauses. "I think he's become your own drug." Tina considers Kasha's words. "Who are you, Tina?"

Tina is silent for some time. "I don't know," she eventually admits. "I hated my face for so long. All these freckles. They called me *fire crotch* in high school. I never knew my dad, and my mom lied to us, told us that he died when we were young," She waves a hand in front of her face. "I look exactly like him, and I hate him for it," she exhales. "She hates me for it too."

She sees Kasha's look of pity but keeps going. It feels good to finally get all of this out. "For years, I longed for him. He abandoned us. Didn't want to acknowledge us. He robbed my mom of her love," she sniffs. "She loved him in her own way, and he abandoned her. He took a part of her with him, leaving us with a detached shell." She pauses, audibly sucks in air. "He keeps writing me letters. I just throw them in a box."

"He writes you letters?" Kasha asks, perking up. "He clearly wants to make amends."

"Yeah, every month. I've gotten over two dozen so far." Tina exhales audibly. "For years I barely thought about him. Now he's shown up in my life and I'm at a crossroads. I'm tired of not knowing, but I also think he's a bastard."

Kasha rests her chin on her clasped hands, elbows on the table, silently encouraging Tina to go on.

"I've never felt fully Swedish, you know," she says softly.

"I feel like I always have to explain my existence, even to taxi drivers, and it's exhausting." Tina pauses. "When I performed at Eurovision, I was telling the world my story, but no one wanted to listen. They just wanted me to keep performing. That was when I decided I was done."

"Darryl heard you. He heard your story," Kasha says. "But he's afraid you're already done performing, even though you want to be a pop star." Tina takes this in. Kasha is probing a truth she isn't ready to confront.

"I've been questioning the *pop* part lately," Tina says, air-quoting the word. "I need inspiration. I need to know who I am as a storyteller."

Tina is surprised at the ease of offloading on Kasha. It feels cathartic, and long overdue. She takes a deep breath, and it feels like the first one she's taken in months.

"I have so much to say, Kasha. So much bottled up inside me," she goes on, her voice breaking. "So much anger at my father. So much—*I don't know*—sadness that he robbed me of my mom. Sometimes I wonder if she ever loved me, or if she always hated me because I look so much like him. I see it in her eyes when she looks at me, then turns away," Tina sniffs. "I want to get all these feelings out. I need to be free of them. I just don't know how."

Kasha reaches her palm over and places it across Tina's hand. "I think I know how," Kasha says, squeezing gently.

A few days later, Tina sits quietly, almost holding her breath. The basement room is dimly lit. At one end, a standing microphone. Behind it, a heavyset Black woman with waist-length locs and a gold ring looped through a nostril. She's snapping both her fingers, the sound echoing and ricocheting off those dark walls.

I rise, rise to fall, to fall and rise.

To see a light, light so bright, so I kneel, kneel to see…

She continues with her spoken-word; the room is filled with other artists and poets. Open mic night. Kasha dragged her here on their quest to discover what truly stirs Tina.

To remain as inconspicuous as possible—after all, she'd been gyrating half-naked in DJ Kamid's video and done the rounds on TV—Tina goes makeup-free, wears tinted glasses and leaves her hair in its natural coils for their outing. She gets a few stares of recognition, but she's grateful people leave her in peace.

"Thank you, Lorraine," the host says after the artist finishes to scattered applause. "Next up, we have Trisha." Heads whip around looking for Trisha. Kasha elbows her. "Oh, that's me." Tina jumps out of her seat. She gingerly makes her way up front. She's wearing an ankle-length bohemian goddess-cut dress with spaghetti straps. She clears her throat, closes her eyes, and pulls in a deep breath before reciting the words to a new poem she hastily cobbled together. A poem titled "Aja."

Each word grows stronger, lands hard as it leaves her lips, the genre suiting her lyrics. Beads of sweat start to collect over her brow, her cheeks flushing with warmth. Her fingers roll into fists, eyelids still shut, as she performs.

When Tina finishes, her ears feel like they need popping. Her eyes flutter open to limbs moving in slow motion, coming together. They seem to be clapping. Once the fog lifts and the muffled sounds become precise, booming applause envelopes her. Her eyes search for Kasha in the crowd. Kasha is clapping and jabbing two fingers toward her in slow motion.

This energy is different. Compared to the rather lukewarm reception at Eurovision, this buoyancy welling up within her feels grounding. It feels *oh* so real. So right. She wants more of this poetry coursing through her veins. Is this who she is? A poet trying to emerge? Singing "Honey" as a pop chorus hadn't felt right in her soul. Was that why she had switched it to a ballad on that stage? Had the poem simply forced itself out at the oddest of times?

Tina rushes back to her seat next to Kasha, giddy, her body tense with excitement.

"Girl, you killed it," Kasha exclaims. "Same time next week? Seems like this just might be your side thing." Tina beams, her eyes darting around the small room. She smiles at each person she makes eye contact with. She could get used to this air.

She wants her celebratory fix. She needs Jonas.

She leaves the show well past midnight. His house is closer by taxi. She has a key, which he'd given her in anticipation of her moving in with him one day. She lets herself into the dark hallway.

"Well, hello there." His voice emerging from the void startles her. He's wearing plaid pajama bottoms, nothing else.

"*Jesus*, Jonas! You scared me." She clutches her chest before shutting the door behind her.

He flips on the lobby light. "I've been calling you all night. I even swung by your place on my way back from ONYX…" His eyes roam her body. "New look?"

"Maybe." Tina smiles. She walks up to him, throws her

arms around his neck. "I had an incredible night." She gives him a feather-soft kiss. "Come with me next time."

"Where did you go?" he asks, humor in his tone, wrapping his arms around her waist to pull her closer.

"Open mic night. Spoken-word," she says, burrowing him into. "I loved it."

"You did?" he chuckles. "You didn't find it pretentious?"

She shakes her head. "I'm still trying to find my way of telling stories." She kisses him. "I don't think pop is all of it." She slightly opens her mouth. "So, I'll keep exploring." Her tongue seeks his.

He returns her caress, then pulls back. "Want some?" he asks. Not sex, she knows. She peers into his eyes. Darryl's words surface in that instance. *Distraction.*

"No." She shakes her head. "You don't need it either."

He holds her gaze seriously, his lips cocking into a sly smile. He snorts before pulling out of their embrace and padding away. Tina trails him. He heads over to his bar area.

"Jonas," she calls out.

"Go to bed, Tina," he says over his shoulder. He starts pulling out his apparatus. Tools. Lighters. A syringe.

"Jon..."

"Go the fuck to bed!" he yells, suddenly spinning around. She jumps at his aggression, words caught in her throat. His eyes, piercing with fury, pin her in place.

Tina backs up at his anger. Barely seconds before, they'd been cuddling. Now he's in a fierce rage. She can't stay here with him. Not right now, not in this state. She beelines for the front door, her steps hurried. She hears him behind her. He reaches for her bicep. She struggles to free it as she reaches the door.

"Tina, please," he calls out. "I'm sorry. I'm sorry, okay?"

"I need to go home." Once outside, she fumbles for her phone in her bag, standing in the cool California night.

"It's almost one in the morning," he pleads. "Come back in here." He pulls her back by her arm. She wrenches herself free and starts down the gravel driveway toward his iron gates. Hears the chirping of crickets. The cawing of some bird in the distance. The distinct night sounds of the early witching hour. He follows her down the path. He could easily catch up with a few calculated long strides, but he lets her scurry ahead like a nocturnal creature.

She reaches the gate. He traps her there between his arms.

"*Snälla, sluta. Kom in*," he whispers in Swedish, urging her to stop and come back in. "What are you scared of? You know I'll never hurt you."

"You're different when you take them," she finally says. "You're not you."

"Heeyyy," he says softly in her ear. "I'm me. I'm always here. Hmm?"

She turns around to face him. "I can't carry on with this if you keep using." She remembers the few times she'd let his smoke fill her lungs. He wanted her to try something stronger. To numb their pain together. Her answer was always the same. *No, Jonas. I want you instead.* She realizes now he doesn't believe her. That she could ever love him unconditionally, drugs and all.

"Promise me you'll stop?" she pleads.

He has her locked between his arms and the gate. She

knows he can't promise her that because he isn't searching for his own answers, isn't doing the work yet. His pad, rides, lavish lifestyle are all ways to leapfrog over the painful work he needs to do.

"Let's go back in," he says instead. "It's late." He grabs her hand, starts to lead her away.

"No." She yanks out of his grasp once more. "No." Her voice breaks. "Promise me, *älskling*."

The air between them grows thick, denser in the night when she utters that word. *Darling*. She wonders when he'd last heard that word said to him, about him. Had anyone else said it to him here in California? Because right now Jonas looks deprived, loveless.

He cups her cheek, rests his forehead against hers. She feels his breath feather across her face.

"I promise you," he mutters. "I promise." He keeps repeating those words as he carries her back to the bungalow. As he pulls that boho dress over her head. Braless and perky underneath, almost always. He runs his palms over them. Kisses down their groove, his lips traveling down her stomach. He promises once more while looping his fingers through her lavender panties.

As her fingers tighten in his maple-brown locs, holding on for dear life lest her knees fail her, he promises yet again.

And for the first time in their passport-sharing, trauma-bonding, colleagues-with-benefits situationship, Jonas moves tenderly against her. Painfully slow. This time, she fully enjoys his size and shudders uncontrollably beneath him.

He makes love to her again and again until she falls asleep with him inside her.

★

Four forty-seven a.m.

Tina wakes up sore and ready for a pee break. Stretching in bed, she reaches over to his side. She pats around. Warm but empty.

"Jonas?" she calls out softly, sitting up in bed. A whimpering sound in the low-lit room reaches her. She sharpens her ears, looking for its source. It's louder the second time. The low grumbling sound of chattering teeth. "Jonas?!" She peels off her covers, rushing to his side of the bed.

She finds him naked on the floor, shivering.

PART THREE

THIRTY-TWO

NANCY, 1985

Leif has gotten himself a mobile phone. It's the Roaring 1980s—*Glada 1980-talet*—and they call those phones *yuppienalle*. *The yuppie's teddy bear*. He doesn't need to work—Lars has made sure they're financially secure—but Leif remains a man, and his ego won't let him be a kept one, so he goes to work each day as a financial analyst.

"*Farbror, farbror.*" The chubby toddler wobbles on his feet the second he hears the door latch. *Uncle. Uncle.*

If there was one thing Nancy vowed to do in their sham of a marriage, it was to never tell her son that Leif is his father. No, Leif deserves his freedom, so he'll always stay that way. As for Tobias's father, once he's old enough to ask about him, Nancy will tell Tobias his father is dead. She'll kill him off in a car accident in Gambia.

Leo meows and trots after Tobias as he makes his way on pattering feet toward the door. Leif gently pushes it open, swoops down and swings Tobias into the air. He spreads his chubby arms wide, a sweet giggle escaping him.

"*Min pojke!*" Leif mutters as he tosses him up a few times. *My boy!*

Nancy watches from the doorjamb of their compact kitchen. "Hope you're hungry?" she calls out. Leif's eyes light up. "Always. *Benachin?*" he asks. Leif now sports a mustache, his normally cherubic face looking leaner with each passing month.

She nods. "With *dahar* and *rangha*," she adds, mentioning her spicy tamarind sauce and greens. "And make sure you eat properly. You're getting too skinny to be living in an African woman's house."

As he had promised her family, Leif made an "honest woman" out of Nancy during her second trimester. Omar and Fatou were thrilled that their daughter had ended up with a respectable man. But Nancy had to drop out of school while pregnant with Tobias, her dream of becoming *Madame President* feeling ever more distant.

"Dreams can wait, my dear," Omar said to her over the phone when she'd called them after their swift court ceremony. "Dreams can always wait. Live what Allah has dealt you right now. He has a higher purpose for your life. Trust him. As your mother always says, you know we serve—"

"Yes," she interrupts him. "A God of miracles."

It's okay, it's only for a short while, Nancy said to herself for the first few months. *It's only a season. Right now, God wants me to have this child. There must be a lesson in all of this*, she reflects. A lesson she could impart on her kids— both Tobias and any future ones; especially if she ever had a girl. She'd teach them that men can stymie you so swiftly. That while you're left picking up the pieces, they're on to the next, shining brightly.

She remembers the first time the toddler called Leif *farbror* in front of Yaya and Benke. He had just turned one. They had invited her aunt and uncle to a Sunday roast of lamb and rosemary potatoes in Norsborg. Tobias had been clinging onto Leif while he cooked in the kitchen, crying for *uncle* to lift him up. Carry him.

"Farbror?" Yaya had wrinkled her nose at Nancy. "Is the boy confused?"

Nancy held her aunt's gaze before saying: "Aunty, I need to tell you something."

So, with Leif sitting next to her, clasping her left hand, Tobias now comfortably on his knees, Nancy confessed that Leif was a dear friend who wanted to help her because Tobias's father couldn't.

"It's that professor, isn't it?" Yaya had muttered after a long spell of silence. "I remember the way he looked at you at your graduation."

"That's the past now," Nancy said. "Leif is my husband."

"But why doesn't he call him *Pappa*? Why won't you let your son grow up with a father?"

Nancy and Leif had exchanged a quick glance.

"It's better this way," Nancy said.

"Better this way? What do you mean, *better this way*? So that boy will grow up never knowing his father?"

"Aunty, please let's eat."

"Eat? Are you listening to yourself, Nancy?"

"Please drop it."

"So, I can't talk to you again? I can't tell you anything anymore because you're a mother now?"

"He's my child. I get to decide what I do with my own son and how I raise him, not you."

"Nancy..."

"No, Aunty! Go get your own child and stop trying to control my life."

The room grew quiet, the air so dense Nancy knew

something had permanently shifted between them. She saw Yaya bend her head low, hiding tears. Benke reached a hand over to stroke her back, soothe away his wife's hurt.

When Yaya looked back at Nancy, she saw it clearly. The damage irreparably done.

"I'm not feeling well," Yaya said. "I think I need to go home and lie down. Benke, please drive me home."

Two years since their court marriage and Malik now a distant memory, Nancy and Leif have settled into a mutual domesticity that gives Leif freedom to find the love he desires. Nancy, on the other hand, becomes a young stay-at-home mother, living with a man nearing fifty years old. Their neighbors automatically assume he is her husband of convenience because she is African. Technically, yes, but their assumption still grates on her.

Their shelves are lined with photos of their own loved ones. Of her and Malik. Of her family: aunt and uncle. Of Nancy, Malik and Olof at the Nobel banquet. She sets some ground rules. Leif can't bring men into their house. A jarring disease, which scientists are still figuring out, is claiming young and middle-aged men faster than they can research it. She doesn't want him bringing it home, whatever it is.

Beyond that, Leif works a lot, and he often works late. Lars's monthly allowance keeps all three of them plus Leo fed, clothed and satisfied for now. He quit his job as head of department when one of his paintings broke a record at auction in Sweden.

Nancy doesn't keep up with his news, but Leif gives her any necessary updates. Apparently, Lars painted a series "so provocative, so sexy, so iconic," according to the Culture section of newspaper *Expressen,* that the art world couldn't get enough of it. The series was first exhibited in a small gallery on Vaxholm. It later traveled to Stockholm proper where two wealthy patrons, fueled by other attendees, got into a huge bidding war. Lars instantly became "that Swedish artist" and the value of his paintings soared.

Leif read a newspaper clipping out to her as they dined on kebab pizza one night. The resentment and disdain in his voice was clear. Why did Lars get to live in the limelight while his own deceptions forced them to live in the shadows?

Aja #1 in the series sold for over one million kronor. Nancy had cringed when she heard the name of the series— *Aja.* Her language. Short for *Ajaratu.* Female pilgrim. Why would he name his work that?

She avoids looking at images of the paintings. She's seen enough in newspapers and on the news to recognize that the abstract form is hers. Smooth, shimmering cocoa curves, layered thickly. Dark pecan brown blended into various ombré patterns and ochre colors. Breasts fuller in his fantasy than reality. The suggestive poses. That late August morning in his cabin when she caught him snapping photos of her. She had felt unsafe in that moment, but then she'd rationalized it away. He could never hurt her, could he? He simply wanted to continue his artwork with her as his muse. He'd showed her tenderly afterward that she had nothing to worry about, that he loved her and would always be there for her.

She hasn't seen him since that day in his office when he swore to find a solution to her pregnancy news. He's hardly ever written or called. It seems Leif is his liaison. Lars gets all the news and information he needs from his brother. The occasional Polaroid photo of Tobias, a cute teddy bear of a boy.

When he was born, Lars sent flowers and a note promising he would grow to love Tobias someday. When all this dust settles, he says, he will pry himself from Frida's right-winged claw. He sent a toy fire truck to Tobias for his first birthday. Leif had helped Nancy set fire to the letter over their sink. The toy still sits in its original box one year later, unopened.

The brothers talk on Leif's mobile phone occasionally. They no longer scream at each other in anger. A new emotion is filling up the cracks between them—less tension, more indifference. Civility. A chasm widening and deepening with each call. They are dead to each other as siblings and instead interact like business partners.

Nancy plates out generous portions of *benachin* while Leif sets the boy down, loosens his tie and glides toward their dining table. "How was work?" she asks as she hefts a spoon of rice, lamb and vegetables onto her own plate. "You've been working later and later each day." She catches the glint in his eyes.

"I think I've met someone worth working late for," he says, clearing his throat, reaching for a glass of water.

"Hmmm," Nancy mutters. "At your office?"

Leif chugs water. "Yeah, we're working on a very intense project together." There's a skittishness about him that feels uncharacteristic.

"Is everything okay?" Nancy grows suspicious.

He quickly spoons up a mouthful of rice. "Hmmm?" he asks as he chews.

"Is everything okay?" she repeats. He shrugs his shoulders.

"Let's just eat, Nancy," he says after swallowing. "I can take Tobias for a stroll for some fresh air afterward."

"At nine at night? Is everything okay?"

"It's June," he counters. "The sun barely sets. Do you trust me, Nancy?" He locks eyes with hers. Brown on brown. She nods. "He needs some air too."

After dinner, Nancy bundles Tobias up while Leif whisper-talks on his mobile phone in another room. She eyes Leif suspiciously as he loads Tobias into his mini stroller. The toddler yawns. She knows he'll pass out the minute cool summer air hits his lungs.

Leif gives her a peck. "We won't be long," he stresses before putting on a thin beanie.

When he shuts the door, the apartment is thrown into silence. She pats her head, her hair in thin cornrows, and pulls off her apron. She decides to go wash off the smoky smell of cooking. Warm water pelting her is what she needs right now, to distract her from thinking too much about the life she could be living if she had followed a different path. Maybe once Tobias starts first grade, she'll pick up her master's program and rekindle her delayed dream.

Nancy hears noise coming from the living room once she turns off the shower. *They're back already? Barely ten minutes have passed.* Leif must have left Tobias's water bottle. He always does. She grabs a towel and wraps it around her.

"His water bottle is on…"

She freezes when she sees him. He's cradling one of the photos from her shelf. She pulls her towel tighter, crosses her arms in protection. Leif had betrayed her. He had given Lars a key.

Lars spins toward her when he hears her footsteps. His hair is longer now, brushing his neck in large, wispy curls. He isn't wearing his glasses. His eyes look darker from this distance. Tired. Red-rimmed. They glance over her bare shoulders, down the short towel she has wrapped around her, trying to hold her in.

"Get out of my house." Her voice is dark and deep. "Now."

He places the frame back and falls onto his knees in front of her. "Nancy."

"Get out," she screams. "Now!" It doesn't deter him. "What are you doing?"

"I'm leaving her," Lars says abruptly, still on his knees, his arms now spread out, palms up. She tenses. "I'm leaving Frida for you," he cries.

Nancy freezes at those words. She finds her voice once more. "Get out!"

"Please, Nancy." He clasps his hands together as he kneels, begging.

"You pathetic man," she spits out. "Get up and get out of my house."

He launches off his knees and advances. She shuffles backward as he reaches her with large strides.

"*Ḍa i kanu le, Nancy*," he says as he inches closer now, backing her up against her wall. "*Ḍa i kanu le*."

I love you, Nancy. I love you.

"Stop speaking my language," she screams into his face. "Don't you *ever* speak it to me *ever* again!"

Tears pool in his eyes. "Nancy."

She slaps him. He accepts it. She slaps him again. And again. He grabs her hand and pins her to the wall.

"Let go of me, right now," she growls at him. "Don't you ever touch me. Ever again."

"Please listen to me," he cries, his hand still locking hers firmly to the wall. "Please," he says again into the crook of her neck. "I'm leaving her. I want you. I want my son. A life with you."

"You can't even lie to yourself," she says, her racing heart calming down. "You'll never leave them for me."

"If I didn't want you, I wouldn't take care of you and our son." *Our son.*

"Money is not love." She chokes on the word. Money could never replace missing him. His touch. His eyes like golden suns when they land on her, enveloping her fully in their warmth.

"Let me go," she demands, her voice cracking as she feels tears come on. He clamps down harder on her hand, presses it tighter against the wall. His other hand starts to roam, down the nape of her neck. She slaps him once again with her free hand. He grabs it and now pins her by both to the wall. She feels her towel loosening, slipping. She wiggles in his arms so she can cover her nakedness once more. *What's the point?* she thinks, *when he has already put my body on display for all the world to see?* He follows the towel with his eyes as it slides down her body.

When his gaze crawls back up to meet hers once more, she holds her breath. He frees one of her wrists. He needs his own hand back. It travels down her soft stomach toward the valley between her thighs.

"What are you doing?" she whispers. His mouth inches

closer to hers. She feels his breath on her face. A slight whiff of alcohol. The liquid courage he needed to come into her apartment. She gasps against his lips when she feels his cold fingers. His eyes pin her in place. "What are you doing?"

He answers her with a rough kiss. One which reeks of desperation. She can't keep up with it as he moves brashly against her freshly showered skin. It has been two years since she's felt a man's touch. His touch. She fights it. Pushes him away from her body.

"What do you want, Nancy?" he asks her breathlessly. "Tell me what you want. Should I stop? Should I stop?"

"I don't know," she whispers, her feelings at odds with her body. She remembers lying on his patio table in the pouring rain. He'd unlocked something divine within her then.

Lars presses closer to her once more. This time, his kisses work their way down her body, and she throws her head back, presses it against the wall, her fingers intertwining in his curls.

"I promise you, Nancy," he mutters against her. "I swear to you. I am coming for you. For our family." His movements grow hurried against her. "I swear to you." They join together, desperate. On her fallen towel. In the living room. Under Leo the Sphynx's judgmental eyes as he watches from his perch on a cabinet.

Lars pulls her toward her room, worships her curves, whispers words in Swedish she doesn't understand. He drowns out each scream. Swallows them with his mouth on hers. They fall asleep, limbs tangled. He was supposed to have left before Leif and Tobias got home.

It's the first night Nancy doesn't tuck her own son into bed.

★

The next morning, Lars and Nancy stumble out of her room to the smell of coffee and cinnamon. He's wearing his clothes from the night before, his hair a disheveled mess. She's in a batik-print bathrobe.

Leif doesn't say a word to his brother, quietly flipping pancakes instead. Tobias is on the floor playing with technicolor wooden blocks, trying to stack them as high as he can.

Lars moves past Leif as if he doesn't exist. He gets down on his knees in front of his son, holds the boy, and assesses him for the first time.

"He's so beautiful," he says, the words punctuated by tears. "So beautiful."

Nancy shoots Leif a sharp look. She glides over to him. "Why did you do this to me?" she asks him in a low voice.

He casts her a sideways glance. "He told me he's finally grown the balls to leave Frida. They've separated." He moves a cinnamon pancake off the pan to join the rest. "You're the love of his life," he whispers. She purses her lips at those words. She dare not start believing them—she's already been hampered by Lars's love once before.

She turns toward Lars, who is now on the floor with a nonchalant Tobias. When he reaches out to the boy, Tobias yelps, turning from his father's touch. Leif leaves the spatula and picks Tobias up. The boy instantly calms down in Leif's arms.

Lars buries his face in his palm, overwhelmed. A few seconds later, he gets off his knees and presses a hard, close-lipped kiss onto Nancy which jerks her head backward. He bolts from their apartment without saying a word to his brother.

Nancy and Leif exchange a look.

Their quiet standoff says everything she needs to know. The boy has rejected the stranger. Her plan is working. Uncle Leif and a *dead father*. Lars will have to work hard for their son's love.

If he sticks around this time. And if he does, he will have to work to regain hers too.

THIRTY-THREE

NANCY, 1985

"*Blatte-älskare*," Lars says. "I will never forget their words." He stares into the distance before lifting coffee back to his lips. *Dark-skin lover.*

She bristles at the slur. He's sitting at her dining table one Thursday afternoon while Tobias is at *dagis* and Leif at work. For proximity to Tobias, his daycare, his needs, Nancy has found a part-time job at their neighborhood grocer as a cashier. Perfect for her kitchen because she can pick up okra, scotch bonnet peppers and catfish there too.

She studies Lars's profile as he drinks. He must work for her heart once more. Her love. The one he stole from Malik. On occasion, her first love flashes across her mind, and she wonders where he is, what he is doing, if life is treating him any better.

Nancy says nothing when Lars drops that derogatory phrase. Since their torrid reunion, Lars has let himself into their apartment a couple more times. Conveniently when Leif isn't around. He tells her he is about to start moving his things out after the separation as they lie together after making love. Staring at the ceiling, collecting their breath.

Soon, they'll move in together and become the family he has always craved, he swears to her.

She sees age lines slowly crawling across his features as he stares off. Those creases at the corners of his eyes deepening. A few darker copper spots on his hands, his chest.

He turns back to her. "They were ashamed of me. Of us," he says of his parents. "I remember the day they summoned me back home from Gambia to meet Frida. Her parents were prominent socialites."

Nancy says nothing. She often wonders why she let him back into her bed. Was it desperation to feel like the chosen one? Had she internalized being his muse? Did he remind her of her old self, when she was on her way toward a career? Did she crave intimacy?

Or, was she only giving him another chance to do right by his son and their friends-turned-lovers tale?

"I swear to you, Nancy. I never loved her. I was so afraid to be cast out of their world simply because I followed my heart. I was a coward."

"You're still a coward."

He presses his lips together. "I know, and I will spend the rest of my days, our days now, making it up to you. I swear, *njusoo*."

He's now back to whispering sweet nothings to her in Mandinka, trying to make her feel safe and seen once more. Besides meeting up occasionally with an acquaintance here and there from the Gambian-Swedish Association, she's back to cocooning herself once more in a single relationship. Since she'd said those hurtful things to Yaya that Sunday afternoon, her aunt has distanced herself.

Nancy now realizes she'd rather take anger over indifference.

She reaches for a sugar cookie with a free hand, her teacup in the other. Lars intercepts her hand, links his fingers with hers, pulls them to his mouth. He brushes his lips lightly over them, slowly trails to her wrist, kissing her hand.

"I've missed you," he whispers against her wrist. "So much. Every single day. Touching you, kissing you, feeling you." She doesn't respond, simply observes his display, his Vaxholm cottage surfacing. His mouth reaches hers. She tightens her lips, not giving him access.

"I know, I know. It's going to take time to win you back, my love," he mutters against her clenched lips. "Please let me kiss you."

"I need to go pick Tobias up." Nancy sets her teacup down. Lars pulls back, nods, a sly smirk on his lips, color rushing to his cheeks, as he looks at her.

"Can I follow you?"

"Why?"

"I want to see my son. I want to hold him."

"He only knows Leif," she says, eyes hard. "I'd like to keep it that way."

"I swear I will never hurt or abandon him ever again. Please believe me."

She shuffles to her feet, adjusts her bubblegum-pink dress with its puffy shoulders. He gets up as well, pulls her close.

"Please let me come with you." His hands grip her waist. "I promise not to upset him again."

She nods. He dips down for a kiss. She obliges him.

Lars waits, shifting from foot to foot outside the building. His hands leave his pockets when Nancy emerges with the boy on her hip. Tobias is squinting against the sun, his fist in his mouth, a lush crop of dark-copper curls on his head.

"*Hej, gumman.*" Lars bends low, runs his fingers through his son's hair. *Hello, sweetie.*

Tobias observes the stranger for a few moments before saying *hej*.

Lars looks at Nancy. "Can I?"

She holds his gaze before nodding. Lars reaches for Tobias, pulls him close to his chest, sniffs his hair. The toddler pulls back to assess Lars's face before reaching a chubby hand to feel his stubble.

"*Heeejjj.*" Lars bounces him lightly in his arms. "Do you want to play?" The boy smiles and bobs his head. Lars grins, his face brightening up in his own handsome way. "Let's go to the park!"

Over the next few weeks, Lars meets Nancy and Tobias in the neighborhood park after she picks him up from *dagis*. He pushes Tobias on the swings, rides down the slides with him, tosses him in the air, plays *kurragömma*—hide and seek—with him as Nancy watches from a bench, her heart swelling.

Mammas kompis. Mommy's friend. That is all Tobias needs to know right now.

Lars and Leif continue to keep their distance, their relationship perpetually on ice, while Nancy's heart begins to thaw. Even though Leif hates his brother, he's happy to see the light slowly return to Nancy's eyes. He tells her this over a late dinner one evening, after he's tucked Tobias in for the night.

"He makes you happy, doesn't he?" Leif says before taking a bit of *falu korv* sausage.

"Your brother is an intense man," Nancy responds.

"It's that mad Scorpio energy," Leif chuckles. "Well, I never thought I'd ever say this, but I'm happy you found your way back to each other. Finding true love is rare. Even if it's with my asshole brother."

"You only want me to move out of your apartment, that's why," she laughs. "So, you can bring your lovers here." Her eyebrows dance up and down in jest.

"Yes, I am ready to evict you."

"You can't get rid of me." She grins before another bite. "I am your *wife*, Mother Hen."

Leif laughs out loud before a coughing fit seizes him. Nancy pushes a glass of water forward.

"Thanks, just food down the wrong pipe," he croaks before grabbing the tumbler and chugging water.

They resume dinner in silence.

The doors chime. A customer struts in. Nancy looks over from her cashier till. *Lars.* He's advancing toward her with wild eyes. His hair looks different. A crop cut that reminds her of pictures of Roman emperor Julius Caesar. His face is clean-shaven.

"Are you okay?" She laughs as he reaches her.

"Come with me," he demands.

"Are you crazy? I'm working. My shift ends in two hours."

"Where is your manager?"

"What are you doing? Are you trying to get me fired?"

He storms behind the counter, grabs and pulls her into a tight embrace. The only other customer, a man in his seventies or eighties who had been muttering something to himself, freezes upon seeing the couple caress in the store. Lars kisses her against the till, his hand grabbing and groping at her backside.

"Fine, fine," she whispers against his mouth. "I'll close up now. Stop it." She pushes him back.

She checks the old man's items out—a newspaper, an orange and a lottery ticket—then flips the sign to "Closed."

Once outside, Lars drags her toward a shiny white Ford Mustang. Nancy pauses on approach and stares at the car. "Wow."

Lars beams. "What do you think?" His chest rising and falling in excitement.

"It's beautiful. Congratulations."

He crushes a kiss on her in response. "Come, let's go for a ride."

Zero to 130 kilometers. Nancy screams as Lars careens across the highway, away from Norsborg, heading east. They enter Tyresta National Park barely thirty minutes later at that speed, Nancy's chest heaving, collecting her breath after their joyride, Lars cackling after each of her screams. He pulls a wicker basket and a rolled-up plush blanket from the trunk, flashing her a grin. They hike in silence until a still lake emerges through pine forest. No other soul for kilometers. Lars clears away brush and builds them a spot close to its shores. She spreads the blanket out and anchors it with the picnic basket. She spins round to find Lars unbuttoning his gray checkered shirt, his eyes on her. Then he unbuckles his dark belt and starts to shimmy out of his stonewash jeans.

"What are you doing?"

"Appeasing the weather gods," he says breathlessly, a twinkle in his eyes. He strips naked and dashes toward the lake, hopping with every step as cool water hits him. He dives in, then surfaces a few moments later, pushing wet hair plastered like mud off his forehead.

"Come in," he screams. His voice echoes through the park. A few birds respond to his call.

"I can't swim," Nancy yells back, her hands cupping her mouth.

He waves once more. "It's not deep. Come in."

Nancy laughs before peeling off her logoed employee T-shirt and nylon skirt. She tiptoes toward Lars in her bra and undies. "Everything," he yells. "Now."

She giggles before unhooking her bra, stepping out of her lime-colored cotton panties and padding trepidatiously toward him. He swims for her, grabs and crushes her to his chest before treading further out until her feet can no longer feel the lake's murky soft bottom. She wraps her arms around his neck for support.

"Do you trust me, *njusoo*?" he whispers against her lips, drops of water racing down his face. She opens her mouth and his tongue dives in, his kiss slow, sensuous, possessive. She threads her fingers through his hair. He runs his fingers through the tracks of her cornrows, one by one, exploring every inch.

"Never hurt me like that again." She kisses the words against his lips, his arms the only thing preventing her from drowning.

He nods against her, his eyes sparkling gold. "Never."

They bob quietly in the lake, her arms around his neck, her head resting against his shoulder.

THIRTY-FOUR

NANCY, 1985

Six weeks later

Nancy misses her period. When she sees two pink lines, she clasps onto Leif's *yuppienalle* tightly in excitement, waiting for Lars's voice on the other end of the line. Leif is equally excited, sitting by her side.

Frida picks up instead. "*Det är Frida?*" she says into the receiver. It's the first time Nancy has heard the other woman's voice. It is silky, authoritative.

Nancy swallows, then asks for Lars.

"*Vem är du?*" Frida inquires. *Who are you?*

Nancy freezes on those words, the phone in a death grip. Leif's eyebrows furrow at her. He pries the phone out of her hands, lifts it to his ear, and answers.

He shares a few words of Swedish with Frida. She puts Lars on the phone. Leif mouths *Lars* to her and hands it back.

"Jesus," Lars mutters quietly when she tells him the news. "How fucking fertile are you guys?!" His tone is angry. Brash. Alien. *You guys?!* His words hit her like a slap. The exact way he responded when she'd shared the news about Tobias—irritated. She's no longer his muse but his burden.

She realizes that he has lied to her once again.

After swimming in the lake at Tyresta, they'd moved to

his plush blanket, out of view of the walking trail. He lied and lied and lied… until they both shuddered their release together.

She hears a female voice distant in the background. "*Jag kommer, älskling,*" he yells before coming back on the line. *I'm coming, darling.*

"Look, Nancy, I have to—"

She disconnects the call abruptly, severing his voice, cutting him out of her life forever. She turns to Leif, who is waiting for news with wide eyes. "He didn't leave her."

"What?" Leif seems confused. "What are you talking about?"

"He didn't leave her." Her voice is flat, indifferent. Her shell hardening.

"He looked me in the eyes," Leif says in disbelief. "He promised me. He looked me dead in the eyes and told me they'd separated. That they're over." He races fingers through his hair in exasperation. "That's why I gave him a key. So you could find your way back to each other."

"I know," she says softly to him. She can't blame Leif. Like a true Swedish diplomat, he had tried to broker a negotiation, a peace deal between his brother and her. One that would give him his own life back as well.

"Tobias needs me," Nancy says. She stands and gives Leif a light pat on his cheek, before brushing past him.

THIRTY-FIVE

NANCY, 1986

How many times can a heart shatter into a million shards?
Nancy wonders. *You spend days, months, years picking up those fragments, piecing them back together like a puzzle. Lots are missing. Holes left in your patchwork. You can never fully love the same way again.*

She reminisces about all the men she's loved in different ways—friends, family and lovers.

Her first true love. Malik. He had simply disappeared into oblivion. As if he'd never existed in her arms. Never laughed that full-bodied sound in her ear. Her first true friend, Mr. Torbjörn. He didn't bother to be a people pleaser. A man so hardened by time and what he'd witnessed in the Congo it aged him beyond his years. She found maggots crawling over him, after he died looking into the eyes of his Egyptian love.

Lamin. Her brother. A light extinguished too soon. One they could never fully reignite. Their relationship had simmered on low heat until the coup violently snuffed his life out.

Now Lars. He had seeped into those cracks, patching up her heart with his own kind of glue. A different kind of love that wanted to be what it wasn't. Wearing her culture, she realizes now, was never going to make him of her culture. The ease with which he had slipped back into his world of privilege at the sound of his wife's voice told her everything he really was—a master fraudster of the heart. Leaving enough hearty slices of bread to make you believe he baked it himself when, really, he'd simply stolen the loaf.

Yet his monthly allowance arrives right on time. Paying off his lifelong penance for pushing them into the shadows. The margins.

And Leif. Her best friend. The only one rooting her in this place, where she's slowly sinking from the prestigious worlds of academia to the periphery of mere survival. Her cashier job gives her purpose. And right now, she has another child on the way.

Leif also severed all ties with his younger brother. True love is never conditional, Leif tells her one evening, before launching into a coughing fit. He gets up and rushes over to the kitchen sink. There is a sliver of blood in his spit. She catches it before he turns on the faucet to wash the evidence away. She runs a palm down his back, where she can feel his ribs. She soothes him, letting him know he needs to rest and take it easy. That he has been working too much. Leif turns toward her, lays his head on her shoulder and sobs while she cradles him.

Christmas comes and goes. The city is a vision, covered in glittering lights all December long. By January, it plunges into its customary dreariness. Darkness prevails. People smile less.

Leif grows weaker.

One evening while Tobias is resting in his lap as they sit on the couch, digging into a bowl of popcorn, Nancy turns toward him, stroking her seven-month bulge.

"How are you feeling, Mother Hen?" she asks. He closes his eyes, takes a deep breath, hugs Tobias tighter. The boy is drowsy, on the verge of falling asleep but still fighting it.

"Exhausted," Leif chuckles. "No energy. I just want to sleep all day." He is suddenly serious. "I think I will go to the doctor next week."

"Is it that bad?" Her concern grows. "Are you still coughing blood? Maybe a lung infection?"

Leif turns back to the movie they're watching and sighs.

A few moments later, they hear commotion by their front door. Two voices, one male, the other female, arguing heatedly in Swedish. They hear someone fumbling at their lock with keys. Only one other person has a key to their apartment. *Lars.*

Leif hands Tobias over and gets to his feet. Frida lets herself into the apartment, Lars hot on her heels, before Leif can reach the door. Her blond hair is blown out in a large updo. She is wearing a shoulder-padded watermelon-pink dress cinched at the waist with a belt. And her face is a picture of horror. Her hard blue eyes settle on a heavily pregnant Nancy on the couch as she hugs a now sleeping Tobias on her chest.

She freezes a few steps from Nancy, takes one look at Tobias, his rust-colored hair and reddish-brown freckles. There could only be one man responsible for that coloring. Frida must know it isn't Leif.

"Get out of here." Leif is firm. He grabs her arm. She yanks it away from him, spinning to stand inches from his face.

"*Du omoralisk lögnare!*" she spits at him in Swedish. "*Lögnare!*" *You immoral liar! Liar!*

Leif presses his fingers into his chest in defense. "*Fråga din jävla make!*" *Ask your fucking husband!*

Frida turns back to Nancy, now a frozen statue on her sofa. She meets Frida's eyes. The tiny hairs on her skin rise at the look Frida is giving her.

"Do you speak Swedish? English?" Frida's tone is condescending.

Nancy peers wordlessly back at her. The same Nancy who had dined with dignitaries. Who had loved an ambassador's son.

"Do you speak English?" Frida continues. "Do you know that in this country, we don't do polygamy? Is that what they do in your country, Africa?" *Her country? Africa?* "We don't condone polygamy in civilized societies. This is Sweden," Frida continues. "This is the north. We are not savages!"

Nancy remembers her neighbors, the blond couple, who were always entertaining multiple partners. Was that the only acceptable form of "savagery" in the north? But she remains quiet, gives the disappointed wife space to rail and pour out her anger. After all, Lars deceived them both. Her desperation had made her believe he wasn't capable of it. That he truly loved her.

"You are the slut behind all those vile paintings, right? Right?" Frida screams in her face. Nancy's sleeping child and pregnant belly are invisible to Frida in that moment.

Tobias wakes up and starts to whimper from all the commotion.

Leif intervenes. Grabs Frida and pulls her away from her spot, where she is looming over Nancy.

"Get out of our house!" Leif yells, pushing her toward the open door where Lars parked himself all throughout the exchange.

"You slut!" she screams over her shoulder. "Those paintings need to be burned. Destroyed. Every single one."

Leif pushes Frida into Lars's arms. He grabs onto his wife. The brothers exchange a long, loaded look.

"*Din jävla fegis,*" Leif says calmly to his brother. He need not scream at Lars. His tranquil delivery conveys the gravity of his words. *You fucking coward.*

When Leif pushes them out of the apartment, he simply picks up Tobias, who has now fallen back asleep, and carries him to his room to tuck him in.

Nancy doesn't cry. She is tired of tears—her well has run dry. She digs back into the bucket of popcorn perched on the couch and continues watching the movie. The cat hops right onto the sofa and curls himself in the warmth Leif left behind.

The next week, in the early hours of 1 March Leif violently jolts her from sleep.

"What is going on?" she asks, trying to process the world, coming back to life.

Leif is crying uncontrollably as he tugs on her arm. "Come now, Nancy. Come!"

She shuffles out of bed in her boubou of a nightgown and slowly pads after him into the living room.

The TV is on. Reporters solemn, reporting on the breaking news from the night before.

February 28. The prime minister of Sweden was shot at eleven twenty-one that night while on his way from the cinema with his wife. The next morning, he was dead.

Olof Palme är död
Olof Palme is dead
Palme mördad
Palme murdered

The headlines. The breaking news tickers. His face plastered across their screen. On newspaper cover pages shown on the TV as well. Those sleepy blue eyes. That sharp nose. His chestnut-brown hair always combed off his face. That smile immortalized next to hers and Malik's in the photo that sits on her shelf.

Olof. Assassinated.

Nancy's world darkens. She lets out an animalistic growl of sorrow so deep that she clenches her stomach in pain afterwards, and her waters break six weeks before her due date. When the paramedics arrive, Nancy is breathing shallowly. They rush her to the hospital. Two hours later, her daughter Martina—*Tina, warlike*—is cut out of her stomach and hooked up to a life-saving ventilator. And when Nancy sees her daughter's honey amber eyes, she screams.

Her eternal haunting, Lars's eyes in her child's.

PART FOUR

THIRTY-SIX

NANCY, 1989

Nancy stares at the fragile woman.

Early nineties, maybe. Wizened in appearance. Forgotten by her children and grandchildren. She is sobbing quietly, her gray eyes obscured by tears. Nancy knows it's from shame that she has shit herself again, for the second time that day.

"*Ursäkta, en sekund.*" Nancy excuses herself for a second and rushes out to the woman's wooden patio. She clamps a palm over her mouth as she stifles her cries.

Hemtjänst.

This couldn't be her future. Her life as a cashier is long gone, and her master's degree remains on hold while she muddles through life with two kids. Tina has just turned three and is now in *dagis*. Six-year-old Tobias is in pre-elementary school. Nancy needed work with flexible hours.

Leif had promised to find her something else to do in line with her first degree. "International relations is so hard right now," Leif had said over *fika*. "Unless you find something academic or within the government, and right now, USSR is all they have on their mind."

It was Benke who had reached out to her. He tried to help her understand just how much she'd hurt Yaya at their last dinner. As a peace offering, Yaya pulled strings at her work, and now Nancy composes herself before going back in to wipe the woman up.

Last she heard, Lars sold some paintings for an exorbitant price at auction.

When she picks Tobias up from school, the boy seems downtrodden. He's sporting a buzz cut and wearing khaki shorts. He's kicking a small, jagged rock along as they stroll home, he in front while Nancy holds Tina's hand as she waddles along beside her.

It had taken Nancy a couple weeks to fully warm up to her daughter. The freckles, the hair, the bone structure, those eyes—bitter honey. Her girl must sense this. The thick wall between them. Words of affirmation don't come easily. She can't think of games to play with the girl. So, she's grateful Tina often seems more relaxed in Leif's arms than hers. But her Tobias…

"*Gumman?*" Nancy calls out to him. "*Vad är fel? Är allt okej?*" *Sweetie? What's wrong? Is everything okay?* He shrugs his shoulders in response. "You know you can tell me anything, right?"

He stops kicking the stone, spins around, stares straight up at her. "I don't want to be brown anymore."

Nancy freezes as she peers back at him, his mouth in a taut line, his eyes hard, trying not to cry—at only six years old.

"What are you saying, Tobias? Why? You're so beautiful." She squats low to meet him at eye level.

"Olle said I look like a *bäjskorv*," he says, his voice breaking. *Poop sausage.* "Do I?"

"Of course not." She pulls him into an embrace. "He's just jealous of you. Do you see how beautiful and unique you are?" She feels his hug tighten, absorbing her words. "My dear Tobbe. Do you know that eggs come in different colors—brown, white, spotted blue—yet all have the same delicious yellow yolk inside. Right?"

He looks up at her with a smile. Nancy feels a light tug, Tina trying to get her attention. "*Inte nu*," she snaps. *Not now.* "Can't you see Tobbe is upset?"

"Mamma," Tina begins to cry.

"Tina." Nancy gets agitated. Only three years old and already so needy and possessive, like her father. As if no one else mattered. As if she's the only child and... Nancy notices the blood on her right hand. "Tina!"

She pulls the toddler closer, inspecting the cut. Tina's cries intensify as pain wracks her body. Nancy finds the culprit. A quartz stone with a sharp jagged edge she plucked from the concrete sidewalk. She fishes in her purse for a Band-Aid and wet wipes.

"What were you doing with that rock?" she scolds as she cleans Tina's sore. "Hmm? Why did you pick it up?"

Tina keeps hiccuping through her tears. Once Nancy is done, her daughter rushes into her arms, grabbing on tight.

"See, just like Tobbe," Tina cries. "Just like Tobbe."

By the time Nancy gets home with two exhausted kids, her nerves are raw and exposed. She unlocks the door. A lean young white man squeezes past her the minute she flings it open. Leif is on his feet, running fingers through his hair.

"*Hej*," he greets them, flustered, adjusting his shirt. She gives him a deathly glare. The one thing he promised not to do.

"Who was that? Hmm?" she demands from the door. Tobias and Tina are already running toward their uncle, arms spread out, with Tina clamoring to show him her *boo-boo*. Leo the Sphynx comes to join the trio as well.

"No one important. *Heeejjj!*" he greets the kids, scooping both up at once.

"No one important?"

"No one important. Nancy, not right now," he says firmly. "I'll start making dinner. Salmon?"

"So, you're bringing friends here now?"

"Not in front of the kids. What happened today? Rough one?"

She drops her bags, pushes past him and the kids, and races over to her room to go call the parents of the kid who hurt her son.

Later that night, Tobias refuses to eat and insists on taking his bath early. Leif runs him a warm bubble bath filled with vanilla-scented foam. He leaves the bathroom door open so they can hear Tobias, and he rejoins Nancy at the table where Tina sits in her high chair, counting peas.

"I'm sorry about today," Leif apologizes as he tucks back into his pesto salmon.

"I'm sorry too," Nancy says. "I know it's difficult to live this lie with me. I should be more understanding."

"I broke my promise, Nancy. That is why. You've been left with so many broken promises, imagining I also contributed to that would be too heavy for me to bear. I'm sorry."

She nods, reaches for his hand, gives it a gentle squeeze before returning to her own rice and fish. "So, who is he?"

Leif's face flushes. "A co-worker. Executive assistant to our boss. Young. Eager." He pauses. "I'm in my fifties and he makes me feel so desired, so wanted."

Nancy listens. It's all she can do. Leif barely shares his private life and relationships with her. For years, she thought he still didn't feel completely safe with her. Maybe he thinks she'll judge him, being African with stricter values.

"Do you love him?" she asks.

"I like him. That's a very good start."

Nancy exhales audibly. "You're right. I've had a rough day."

She recounts it under his gaze as he eats. He glances at Tina warmly and plants a kiss on her little Band-Aid. She giggles and squirms in her chair for him.

"A boy at school called Tobias a *bäjskorv*."

The room grows silent. Leif seems to have frozen on the word. She sees his eyebrows dip. Concern and anger. That is also when Nancy hears it through the quiet. The absence of Tobias's splashing. His voice singing tunes from the bath gone.

She launches onto her feet, her napkin hitting the floor and beelines to the bathroom in panic. Leif is getting up as well.

"Tobbe? Tobbe? Tobbe!"

She spots his outline below the bubbled surface, back up, face down, floating. She dives in still wearing her *hemtjänst* uniform and drags him into her chest, shaking life back into him.

"Tobbe!"

He starts to cough and then laughs. "*Mamma, vad gör du?!*" Tobias says. *Mom, what are you doing?!*

"Praise God, praise God." Her lips begin to quiver as she hugs him. "You scared Mamma."

"I was only holding my breath." He wipes water off his face. "I wanted to see how long I could hold my breath."

She senses a presence and turns to see Leif hovering over them. He reaches to stroke Tobias's hair, then turns to Nancy.

"I'll enroll him in swimming school next week," Leif says.

THIRTY-SEVEN

NANCY, 1993

I can't swim.

Sunshine glimmers across the lake, streaks of light bouncing off his eyes as he breaches the surface, peering at her like an alligator.

Do you trust me, njusoo?

Three years later and Tobias has taken to swimming like a pro. Barely ten years old and he's already competing in his little league. She often drags Tina to watch his swim meets in support. Whenever he adjusts his swim goggles and shuffles over to his spot to get set, she beams. Her pride and joy.

"Your son is so handsome." A white woman leans over to share, her bleached blond hair bone straight. "I find mixed kids so beautiful." She turns her attention to Tina sporting a single French braid. "All that red hair and freckles. She looks like a doll," the woman continues before reaching to tug at Tina's braid.

Nancy gives her a weak smile, wraps an arm around Tina and pulls her away from the woman before saying, "She's not a toy."

The stranger returns an awkward grin and turns away, feigning interest in the competition.

Tobias wins. Again. And all the girls on his team line up to make sure they don't miss a high-five from him.

The air still feels particularly electric, even among parents at the swim meet. Barely four years prior, in 1989, the Berlin Wall had fallen, and Europe is still jubilant, years after. That energy of hope also reached otherwise neutral Sweden too. When it happened, the prime minister gave a speech. Leif had rushed home, ecstatic because his executive assistant friend could now finally go visit his family in East Berlin.

Heading into the holiday season, as Stockholm plunges into darkness, bright lights spring up all over town. Candles adorn sidewalks. Christmas trees blink with tinsels and bulbs. The sounds of chimes and classical orchestras playing instrumental versions of Christmas songs float around town.

The energy is so palpably invigorating, Nancy decides to take the kids to the *julmarknad*, a Christmas market forty-five minutes away, in the heart of the old town. Right in Gamla stan's Stortorget square, the market has opened for the season. The strong cinnamon waft of candied almonds fills the narrow cobblestoned streets. The sweet spicy smell of *glögg*—mulled wine—too. The kids are handed free *pepparkakor*—gingerbread cookies—by a generous vendor. They nibble in excitement while Nancy keeps them from disappearing into the crowd.

Flashes of copper-red hair catch her eye. Two boys. Teenagers. Same height and build. They are both eating from one bag of almonds. Most definitely twins. They're not alone. A tall, lean man wearing a fur hat is holding the gloved hand of a blond woman next to the boys. He's drinking *glögg* from a paper cup, steam rising into the cool air.

As if sensing being watched, Lars swivels in her direction, the cup still at his lips. They make eye contact over its rim. He freezes, eyes widening as he takes her in from that distance. His wife is preoccupied with the boys, digging for almonds too.

In that split second, she sees terror in his eyes. They wash over the little girl by her side. Tina. His replica. Nancy realizes that this is the first time he has ever seen his daughter. His features soften as he stares at the girl.

Nancy notices Frida starting to turn in his direction. As quickly as his warmth surfaced, it's gone. He reaches an arm to grasp Frida's shoulders and keep her from following his distraction. As if living in a parallel world, another dimension where their love never existed. He is simply a family man Christmas shopping on a lazy Sunday afternoon.

The Wikströms disappear into the crowd, leaving Nancy staring after them. She feels a light tug on her gloved hand. She looks down at its source.

"Mamma?" Tina asks. "Who was that?"

"We've decided to fly to Germany to go celebrate with his family and go to the concert," Leif says as Nancy watches him pack a small suitcase. All Leif would tell her was that it was a band of six male performers who dressed up as women. Drag queens.

This will be the very first Christmas Leif spends away from them since they built their family. That young man has his heart. Leif still won't share his name with Nancy—he seems to be protecting his identity—but Leif's elation is contagious. It forces a smile out of her. "So, what are you going to do in Germany?"

"Well," he starts. "Our own mini rail trip. First, Hamburg and the Reeperbahn." He folds a pair of cyan-colored trousers. "Then on to Cologne, Frankfurt, Munich, hopefully Berlin and Checkpoint Charlie, if they'll let us."

"I'll miss you." Nancy rushes into his arms. He hugs her, kisses the top of her head as if she's a child too.

"*Hej*, Mother Hen is always near." He gives her a peck. "You know you can always reach me. It's just for the holidays. I'll be back by mid-January." He pads over to his closet and pulls out a large navy-blue plastic bag filled with wrapped boxes. "Here, these are their Christmas presents. Please set them under the tree for me."

When Leif leaves, the house feels stark and empty. His energy filled it with so much love and warmth that his absence is now reminding her of all what she's lost. From Malik and Torbjörn to Yaya, Benke—even Lars.

Julafton—Christmas Eve—is equally quiet. She makes the kids a modest spread of meatballs, cured salmon and potatoes. She adds fried chicken to the mix. They watch *Kalle Anka* together—a cultural tradition played every Christmas Eve at 3 p.m. Tobias grabs a stack of Batman comic books and retires to the room he still shares with his sister.

Tina sits cross-legged in front of the TV watching a show. Leo the cat, wearing a Christmas sweater and mini moose antlers, is lying next to Tina. That's all he has energy to do these days. Simply curl up and lie for hours. Nancy clears up and occasionally glances over to chaperone what she's watching.

"Mamma?" Tina calls out.

"Yes?" Nancy snaps back, irritation building as she scrapes leftovers from their dishes.

"Did you have snow in Gambia?"

"No, my dear. We have so much sunshine you just want to sit out all day and do nothing. Everyone who goes to Gambia loves it there."

"Is that why Pappa doesn't want to come back?" Tina asks. Nancy takes a deep breath. *Right.* The lie she has told her kids. That their father is living somewhere in Gambia, unable to check up on them. "Hmm, Mamma? Is that why, Mamma?" Nancy remembers that look in the Christmas market, Lars peering over the rim of his *glögg*. "Mamma?"

"Your father is dead!" Nancy blurts out.

Tina turns toward her mother with drowning eyes before getting to her feet and racing toward her room. Nancy shuts her eyelids, breathes out audibly. When she opens them, it's to Leo's judgmental feline ones. He squints at her before moving over to his corner. He laps up some water, and then curls himself to sleep on his cushion. She tosses the kitchen cloth aside, sets herself down on the sofa and cries. Leif would know what to do, know what to say, and she misses her friend desperately. She falls asleep on the sofa.

The next morning, in the early hours of Christmas day, a piercing scream jolts her up. It's Tina crying, carrying a lifeless Leo.

"Mamma, Mamma, Leo doesn't want to wake up," Tina cries. "Leo doesn't want to wake up!"

THIRTY-EIGHT

NANCY, 1999

"Get your feet off my table." Nancy pushes Tobias's long limbs off her dining table. "So dirty."

He has headphones on, listening to music from his Walkman which Leif bought him when he turned sixteen earlier that year. Leif looks up at the sound of their commotion from the newspaper he's reading, *Expressen*, his glasses resting on the tip of his nose.

When Leif squints at him in judgment, Tobias raises his eyebrows. "*Farbror?!* You just channeled Leo with that look," he says. "You're freaking me out."

Despite his death six years ago, Leo's presence is still felt. The kids had loved picking seasonal outfits for him. They'd perch little hats on his head. Leo would sit still until they finished entertaining themselves. Then he'd shake their little hats off to regain some semblance of dignity.

The vet said it had happened suddenly. Sphynx cats often have a heart condition, he'd said. Nancy had gotten him cremated and sprinkled his ashes next to Mr. Torbjörn's gravestone with Leif by her side. The kids had been too distraught to tag along.

Leif shakes his head at Tobias. "Don't you have a swim meet tonight?" he asks. The teenager shrugs, gets up and stretches to his full height, towering over his mother. He pads off to his room without a word. Leif scoffs. "Those girls won't leave him alone. That's why he doesn't want to go."

The children becoming teenagers meant rearranging their three-bedroom apartment once more. Leif has now moved into Nancy's room, sharing her bed, giving up his for the growing boy and leaving one room for their pubescent Tina. When the move happened, Leif and Nancy had laughed about it, with him promising she had nothing to worry about in bed.

"Sleep naked for all I care," he'd chuckled. Nancy's laughter had weakened. She noticed him observing her. Since Lars, she hasn't touched another man—out of exhaustion and lack of energy, but mostly out of fear of being hurt again. "That doesn't mean you're not a sexy mama," Leif had said, reaching for her hand in comfort. "If you need me to help you out, I can sacrifice my pleasure and martyr myself on occasion." He winked.

She had smacked his shoulder in playful jest. She hasn't taken him up on his offer.

As for Leif and his executive assistant lover, they split up immediately after that Christmas in Berlin. Nancy dared not ask what had gone wrong in Germany, if their collective jubilation had gone too far. Leif was back to working his long days and his promise of not bringing anyone home. But she notices his exhaustion too. He's growing leaner each passing year. His once cherubic self is now giving way to a tauter frame, his likeness to his brother more evident.

"I'm getting tired of Tobbe's attitude," Nancy says once she plops into a chair next to Leif, wiping sweat from her brow.

She has just returned from her *hemtjänst* shift, exhausted. One of her wards keeps pretending to swallow their pills, and it took her physically prying the woman's mouth open to find the pills hidden under her tongue. Unfortunately, her fingers left bruises on the woman's delicate skin, and she received a warning from her supervisor.

"Tobbe is fine," Leif says. "Tina is who you need to worry about. You never spend time with her."

"She's too needy," Nancy says, reaching for Leif's glass of cider. She chugs the rest.

"She's a child who wants her mother to spend time with her."

"Tina needs to toughen up and learn that the world is more difficult for girls, for women."

"She's only thirteen."

"I was already at boarding school away from my family at ten years old." Nancy is exasperated.

Leif's look turns serious. "What are you doing, Nancy?"

"What do you mean?"

"You're already pushing her away. The same way Yaya pushed you away. Your mom has barely spoken to you since Lamin's death."

The room grows quiet as she mulls over his words. Was she really doing that? Subconsciously alienating her girl?

"I'm trying, Leif. I'm trying." Nancy's voice cracks. "But…"

"He's all you see when you look into her eyes, right?"

She pivots toward Leif, holds his gaze sternly. "Your brother has no control over me."

"He clearly does."

Nancy, outraged, pushes off her chair. "Don't ever talk to me like that again."

Leif lifts both hands up in a gesture of surrender, repositions his reading glasses, and turns back to his newspaper. How dare he pick at her scab? Nancy fumes as she observes his profile. How dare he? She doesn't want to admit to the semblance of truth she isn't ready to face.

A few moments later, they hear the lock turn. It's Tina with a backpack wearing a yellow crop top, black baggy jeans, large loop earrings and her curls in a bun.

"*Gumman*," Leif calls over his paper. She beelines for him, gives him a tight hug, and sits on his lap. She sighs and he pulls her closer. "*Gumman*, what's wrong?" Leif shares a look with Nancy over her shoulder. "Is it those girls again?" Leif asks Tina.

"Girls? What girls?" Nancy feels excluded. It makes sense that Tina has been confiding in Leif instead of her, but it still grates her, makes her skin heat up that her daughter naturally chose him over her. *Mother Hen.*

Tina ignores her mother, keeps addressing Leif. "They called me *fire crotch* today."

Leif exhales. "*Gumman*, you know they're jealous, mean girls, right?"

"In the locker room," she adds, exasperated. "They saw me changing."

Nancy observes as Leif consoles her daughter, cups her face, whispers that all will be all right.

Then Tina turns to Nancy. "Will you come tonight?"

"Come to what?"

"My choir recital. It's tonight at 6 p.m. *Farbror* Leif is taking me and I'm practicing the solo."

"I'm sorry, dear. I didn't know. I'm very tired. Maybe…"

"You never come to any of my solo performances."

"I try, Tina."

"No, Mamma, you never try. You never try for me! You never miss any of Tobias's swim meets," Tina screams back at her.

"Go to your room and calm down," Nancy orders. "You're just upset about those girls." Tina purses her lips at her mother, clearly trying to prevent more tears. "Go to your room."

Tina launches off Leif's lap and storms off.

Leif turns sharply toward Nancy. "You should know better," he says, his voice low, deep.

That night, Nancy carries a tray of spaghetti and meatballs to Tina's room. The girl has holed herself in there and missed her recital. The door is unlocked, and Nancy gently pushes it in with her shoulder as she balances the tray.

Tina is lying in bed, curled up, facing the wall. Nancy sets the plate down, coasts over and sits next to her. She runs fingers through her daughter's loose curls, silky like her father's.

"I'm so sorry, my dear," Nancy whispers. "I'm so sorry."

"They said no one will want me," Tina says softly. "*Who would want that furry, spicy-looking thing?*" she paraphrases.

"You're too young to be thinking and talking about these things," Nancy says. "You're such a gift, Tina. Of course, you are loved and wanted."

"Before he died," Tina starts. "When Pappa moved to Gambia, did he not want us?"

Nancy swallows. "Yes, he wanted you both very much.

But he chose to go to Gambia. *Sometimes the heart wants what it wants, or it doesn't care."* Nancy repeats those words.

"So, he wanted Gambia more than us?"

Nancy mulls over her daughter's innocent words. He wanted the idea of Gambia, the idea of her, the idea of their relationship more than the reality of it all. He wanted the fantasy so much more.

"My dear Tina, to be honest, I don't know what your father wanted most of all," she says. "But know that you are deeply wanted and loved by Leif and me."

She feels Tina smile before burrowing herself deeper into her bed for the night, her spaghetti forgotten on her desk.

After showering, Nancy climbs into her own bed, turns on her side and sniffs back her tears. Several minutes later, she feels Leif settle in beside her. Then his arm rests over her, pulling her into a spooning hug from behind, trying to comfort her.

In that moment, she feels just how scrawny Leif has become, and Nancy finally lets her tears fall.

THIRTY-NINE

NANCY, 2002

Nancy stops in her tracks when she rounds the corner toward her kitchen.

The teenage boy, seventeen maybe, is startled by her presence. They wordlessly take each other in. Nancy's eyes roam his face, both eyes swollen, slivers of piercing blue peeking through, his lip bloodied. His hair is very light, the color of whipped butter or margarine.

He gets to his feet, unsure, unsteady. "*Hej*," he greets.

"*Vem är du?*" Nancy asks. *Who are you?*

"Sebastian." Nancy waits for more. "*Tinas kompis.*" *Tina's friend.*

They hear footsteps. Tina comes out of the bathroom with a damp face towel.

"*Hej, Mamma.*" She goes to give Nancy a peck in a seemingly good mood. "You've met Seb. We also met today. I found him at school like this."

"Today? He said he's your friend?" Nancy questions.

Tina glares at the boy, then smiles at him. "I guess you can say that now."

Nancy turns back to Sebastian. "Are you okay? Have you eaten?" He shakes his head. "Okay, give me that." She grabs the towel from Tina and shows Tina how to clean up his face. Then she pops a few frozen ham-and-cheese mini pies into the oven.

She watches as Tina gently tends to the boy's bruises, gingerly sweeps blond strands off his face, her fingers lingering on the "friend" she met for the first time that day.

"Tina, come." Nancy nods toward her bedroom.

"Right now?"

"Come with me," she repeats before leading the way.

Once in her bedroom with the door shut, she turns toward her daughter. "What are you doing?"

"What do you mean?"

"Bringing strange boys home?"

"Mamma, I found him beaten up!"

"And you didn't think to call an ambulance? Take him to the school nurse? Instead, you skip the rest of your classes and bring him home?"

"Why are you so angry, Mamma?"

"Don't you see? You have just met him and already he is derailing you."

"Derailing me?"

"Yes! You're not in school right now, when you should be." Nancy pauses to collect herself. "Boys who look like that do lifelong damage to girls."

"Look like what? Blond? Cute?"

"Tina." Nancy draws out her name. "That boy has already latched on to you. Calling you his friend. He's traumatized, and now he has forced you off your path as well."

"Mamma! It's only one day of school. I'm not going to be a dropout because I missed classes today."

"That was what I thought before your father derailed me."

The room is cloaked with silence as Tina peers at her. "Seb is not like that. You don't know him."

"But you do? Hmm? After only a few hours you think you know him because he's staring at you like a puppy?" Nancy is breathless. "I know the likes of him and what they grow up to be. You find them in the depths of their trauma, and they pull you into the abyss with them."

"Is that what Pappa did to you? To make you so cold and cruel?" Nancy pursues her lips in anger. "I wish *Farbror* Leif was here instead. He would understand."

"What do you mean?"

"You're such a hypocrite. You never complain about Tobias or the stupid girls he brings around. I bring one guy who isn't even my boyfriend home, and this is how you treat me."

"I don't want that boy in my house," Nancy says. "Take him back to where you found him."

"You don't know him," Tina screams. "You're just a miserable woman who can't find a man!"

Nancy's fingers curl into her palms, containing herself, restraining herself from hitting Tina across the face at those words. *Miserable woman.*

Was it that obvious? Her light had been extinguished over the years, but was she communicating to her daughter that she had no agency of her own outside of men? Leif was right. Lars still had such a stronghold that she refused to release herself by letting go of his memories. Was she truly making herself miserable by not forgiving herself?

By the time they leave the bedroom, Sebastian is gone, and the fire alarm is ringing at the forgotten pies.

★

Those stinging words keep them apart for months. They flit around each other, barely speaking, with Leif acting as mediator. She knows Tina sneaks off with that Seb boy. Despite her initial disdain, she backs off, leaving her daughter alone. If Tina doesn't want to learn, then life will teach her.

For her school's performance, Tina is crowned *Sankta Lucia*, honoring the long-revered Swedish tradition. She's wearing a flowing white gown with a crown of faux candles on her head. Her voice, that ethereal alto, fills the auditorium as she leads the choir of teenagers, her maidens and star boys in matching white gowns, some dressed like gingerbread men and *jultomte*—Santa Claus.

"Our Tina is a star." Leif's brown eyes warm as he leans over to mutter in her ear. Nancy beams back at him before leaning onto his shoulder. She feels his body begin to spasm. Leif tenses his muscles, trying to control himself for several seconds.

"Nancy, I don't feel well," Leif whispers before launching into a coughing fit.

PART FIVE

2010

FORTY

TINA

Tina learns a cardinal rule of being famous the night she finds Jonas shivering on the floor:

Don't call an ambulance before your agent.

One of the hospital staff leaks the news before they finish pumping Jonas's stomach clean. Darryl and Kasha find Tina rocking in a blue plastic chair at the ER, wringing her fingers, her face wet from tears. Kasha is instantly on her knees, throwing her arms around Tina.

"He promised me," Tina wails into Kasha's shoulder. "He promised me." She doesn't dare look at Darryl, his disappointment already searing her from a distance. He plants himself in a chair next to her, takes an audible deep breath, and places a palm on her back without a word.

"I'm so sorry," she cries, her tears shaking her whole body.

"It's not your fault," Kasha says kindly. "It's not your fault. This isn't his first time."

"Why isn't anyone helping him get better?" Tina's voice rises. "After all these years?"

"There's only so much support you can give someone who isn't ready to help themselves." This time, it's Darryl's deep voice. "We've all tried."

A bespectacled young doctor strolls over. They all perk up upon his approach, Kasha getting back to her feet.

"Ms. Tina," he says, clasping his clipboard with both hands in front of his torso, "you can see him now."

Tina nods her thanks. They follow the doctor down two halls until they reach Jonas, connected to an IV drip. She reads shame in his piercing eyes, now cloudy from pain medication.

"*Hej*," he calls out softly to her. Tina stands rooted to the spot. Kasha walks in and places a hand on his shoulder.

"How are you feeling?" Kasha asks. He closes his eyes instead of answering, shakes his head. "You gave us all a scare," she continues.

He rubs both palms over his face, parks them there, then begins to shudder with sobs. Darryl moves in and places his hand on Jonas's other shoulder. Tina doesn't leave her spot by the door.

"Hey, bud, you're safe now," Darryl consoles him. "Don't be pulling this shit at night when we can't come get you," he adds, a bit of levity in his tone.

"That bad, *uhn?*" Jonas asks between his sobs. Darryl locks eyes with him and nods.

Yeah, it is that bad. They're only four days away from the Grammy Awards and he needs to get clean in time. It's already quarter past nine on the East Coast and all the early-morning talk shows break the news:

Multiple Grammy Award-winning music video director Jonas Jonsson was rushed to the ER early this morning in Los Angeles.

Sources tell us it was from a drug overdose. We have no new information about his current state.

Jonsson has been nominated for yet another Grammy, and the ceremony will be held this weekend.

Our thoughts and prayers are with him for a speedy recovery. We hope he turns up at the ceremony. That would be a triumph, wouldn't it? one of the hosts, an airy blond, says, her voice morning-show shrill.

Jonas is discharged two days later. He turns up at Tina's house sober, face forlorn. She leans against her doorjamb, staring straight at him, saying everything she wants to through her gaze.

"*Hej*," he greets her softly. She presses her lips together tightly, arms folded across her chest as she peers up at him. "*Förlåt mig*," he whispers, begging for forgiveness.

Tina's eyes remain hard. He moves in closer still, close enough for a hug. She doesn't oblige him. She turns on her heel, door still open, and walks back into the apartment, to her kitchen island. He follows her.

"Tina." He reaches for her arm. This time, she doesn't yank away from his touch. She lets him pull her into an embrace. She hears him shuddering, crying, and she hugs him back. They stay intertwined for a few minutes.

She pulls back to look up at him. "*Du lovade*," she whispers. *You promised.*

"I know." He nods. "I know. But some things are easier said than done."

"Then why did you promise me?" Tina demands. "Why?"

"Because I wanted to believe I could do it." He sobs unabashedly. "I wanted to believe I could be strong enough." He wipes his tears away with the back of a palm. "God, I really wanted to try for you."

"Not for me, Jonas, for yourself," she says, her tone bitter with disappointment. "All you had to do was try."

Jonas sighs. "*Älskling*, it doesn't work that way."

She absorbs his words. "How long?" she asks. He pads past her. "How long?" she repeats.

He drags a palm over his handsome face. "Too long," he replies before dropping his duffle bag and helping himself to a bottle of apple cider from her fridge.

Two days later, Jonas is wearing a gold-sequined tuxedo jacket, a low-cut V-neck black shirt underneath offering a teasing peek of his defined pecs, his brown dreads pulled into a neat bun at his crown.

"Are you sure?" he asks her as they hide in the cool dark of a stretch limousine. He squeezes her hand tightly, a look of joy on his face. Tina knows he has to show up. To show the world that he's in control, whether he really is or not. She presses a featherlight kiss onto his lips in reply, then wipes away her slight lipstick stain. She's wearing a matching gold-sequined catsuit, her natural curls piled high on her head. Since her night at the spoken-word jam, she stopped straightening her hair. This is going to be the first time the world will see her—the pop star—in her natural tresses.

The limo pulls up to the red carpet. An usher opens the door on Jonas's side. He steps out to flashing lights from paparazzi, adjusts the nape of his tuxedo jacket while Tina observes from inside. He waits a few seconds before coming round her side to help his date out. Once Tina's gold-strapped feet hit the red carpet, the crowd goes wild.

"*Look this way! Smile for us! Yes! Hand on hip! Tina!*

Tina! Smile with your eyes! You look great, Jonas! We're happy to see you back on form, Jonas!"

Jonas hooks an arm proudly around her waist as he leads her down the red carpet, occasionally stopping to rearrange limbs in various poses for the cameras. They hear several entertainment reporters buzzing with excitement as Tina officially steps out with Jonas at the Grammys.

"Tina Wikström! The Swedish Siren and Jonas Jonsson!"

The journalists rush over, angling to be the first to break this celebrity gossip. The questions come flooding, making Tina rethink her show of support. She wanted him to know he'll always have her so he can start to beat this beast. She didn't anticipate this level of attention.

"Jonas! Was Tina by your side that night?" That question floats to the surface. The other reporters pipe down, waiting for his answer. *"Was Tina with you when it happened? Did Tina take some too?"*

Jonas's grip around her waist tightens. He glances toward her, his mouth cocking into a smile. Then he presses a hard kiss against her lips under the strobing flash of a dozen cameras, confirming their suspicions and throwing Tina off guard, leaving her exposed and unprotected. As they continue down the carpet, she feels her phone vibrate endlessly in her clutch purse. She reaches in and shuts it off for the rest of the festivities.

Jonas wins his fourth Grammy that night.

On their limo ride to DJ Kamid's place for an after-party in his honor, he can't get enough of her in the backseat of the limo. He wants to celebrate. Her tight bodysuit isn't cooperating. He abandons his mission with a groan, and she laughs as she pulls out her phone.

Sixteen missed messages and calls in total. Several from Kasha.

One voice message from her that simply says, *"Jesus, Tina! What were you thinking?!"*

A single text message from Darryl reads, *"What in the actual fuck?!"*

It makes news back home in Sweden as well. Several texts from Tobias, which amount to *"Call me!"*

Two missed calls from Nancy. Two voice messages. One singing a praise-and-worship song. The other saying Tina should call her back when she gets a chance.

Seb sends a congratulatory message. *"You looked beautiful,"* he writes. *"So beautiful. Jonas is a lucky man."* His voice breaks on the word "Jonas." She knows Seb doesn't mean it. His words amount to *I miss you desperately and Jonas is a jackass.*

She also gets an elated text from Lars. He wants to hear her voice. He wants to know if she's okay. If she's been reading his letters. How cathartic it has been for him to spill his heart into the void of her silence.

"What the fuck?!" Tina is surprised. "How did Lars get my number?" She has never once written him back. She turns to Jonas and sees the mischief in his eyes. *How dare he get into her private business?*

"*Farsan, eller hur?*" Jonas asks. *Your dad, right?* "*Bara ring honom.*" *Just call him.*

Jonas urges her to call, before planting another kiss on her neck, then downing his flute of champagne. He'd been leaning over her shoulder, reading her text messages, hands roaming.

"Why did you give him my number?"

Jonas lifts both palms up. "Not me. Probably Kasha. She's always in your business," he snorts. "Ring him."

"*Nej*," she protests softly. "*Inte nu*," she says. *Not now.*

"You have a box full of letters from him," Jonas whispers. "You never write back but you keep him close, so just call him." He rubs a soothing palm down her thigh. "Make his day like you made mine."

Jonas's giddy energy drives her to do it. Tina cradles the phone nervously to her ear, listening to that slight buzzing ringtone, praying he doesn't pick up.

"Tina?" Lars asks gently into the receiver. He recognizes her number.

Tina waits a second or two before responding. "*Hej, Lars*." She can't call him Lasse yet. It feels too personal— and calling him Pappa is off the table.

"I've dreamed of this day since you moved away," he says, his voice unsteady. "I'm so grateful to Ms. Kasha for giving me your number," he adds. "Thank you for calling me. Have you been getting my letters?"

"Every single one," she says, and she swears she feels him beam over the phone.

"Good, good," he says. "I hope you didn't throw them away," he laughs awkwardly.

"I should have when I learned just how much of a creep you are," she spits back.

He goes silent for a few seconds. "What do you mean, Tina?" His voice is stern, fatherly.

"*Aja*," she says. "Your shameless artwork. My mother." She hears him sigh on his end. "Why did you do it?"

Lars meets her with reflective silence before finding words for her. "I knew she was going to leave me someday because I wasn't good enough for her," Lars says. "So, I wanted to keep a piece of her with me."

"Bullshit." Tina's anger cuts through his excuses. "You were the married one. You're still married."

"I love your mother."

"Bullshit!" she exclaims. "If you did, you wouldn't sell her to the world. Limited editions. Thousands of dollars. Even hanging here in Los Angeles. At Jonas's house."

She feels Jonas tense up by her side. "*Aja? Aja #8?*" Jonas asks, confused. Knowing Jonas, he'll connect this news to divine intervention from a goddess and say it's the reason they're together. Tina ignores him, turning her focus back on Lars. "Why would you do that to her if you loved her? You made her the pilgrim. You failed her by having us and leaving. You killed her dreams."

Lars takes his time formulating a response, probably wondering what more he can say to keep Tina in his orbit.

"I was a man trapped in love like a wild animal in a cage," he begins. "When you open that cage door, you never know how the animal will act once free. I hurt Nancy deeply and I dream of seeing her again one day. If she would let me."

"That will never happen." Tina is screaming into the phone now. "Never. She barely even looks at me because I look like you." Jonas's arm wraps around her in comfort. Tina is tired of crying over the last few months. No tears come this time. She is simply done feeling weak and helpless.

"I'm so sorry, Tina," Lars says. "I don't expect forgiveness from you. I know I—"

"I forgive you," Tina cuts him off. "I forgive you."

His shock is palpable over the phone. "What—What do you mean?"

"I forgive you. You no longer have power over me." Her tone is brittle. "She was miserable because you wielded power over her. Not me, Lars. Oh no, not me. So, stop writing me and never, ever contact me on this number."

"But..."

She disconnects the call and buries her face in Jonas's chest.

They arrive at Kamid's hospital-sized mansion for his post-Grammy bash with its bevy of stupendously expensive cars, rap blaring out of speakers, scantily clad celebrities, the world's hottest performing acts, a few hired models milling around, and heavy liquor flowing like waterfalls.

Tina loses Jonas in the crowd as several groups form in different corners around Kamid's house. Those with their noses to glass tables. Some dragging from thick cigars, others inhaling from bongs. She grabs a stem of fizzy champagne from a waiter. He winks at her before gliding through the crowd with his tray. She lifts the drink to her lips, takes a sip and walks over to the outdoor pool, which has now become an opaque mass of bodies rubbing against each other.

FORTY-ONE

TINA

Five thirteen a.m.

Tina stirs. She feels coolness across her skin and lifts her eyelids. She's outdoors, lying on the patio. Disoriented. Her eyes adjust to her surroundings and she sees the pool, a shimmering translucent aquamarine, lit from the bottom. A man wearing only his boxers, with dark curls across his chest, is sprawled out, passed out maybe, across an inflatable unicorn bobbing gently on the water. Other bodies are strewn across the concrete deck and lush lawn. Most are sleeping, a few still moving against each other.

She glances back at the house. Lights are off, save for a few strobes here and there, remnants of the rave. A sharp, pounding headache seizes her. She plants a palm across her forehead and winces. The throbbing continues. She tries pulling herself up onto her feet but notices her golden straps are off. She winces once more, trying to understand. She feels a draft against her chest and looks down. The low V-cut of her catsuit now reaches her belly button. How had she ripped it?

Tina feels a palm on her back as she grabs her clutch purse and attempts to get to her feet by kneeling. She spins to take in the source. Recognition washes over her. The tattooed drummer she'd met in passing at one of Kamid's previous parties. "Heyyy gorgeous." His voice is slurred, clearly high. His hand roams her back. She pulls away from him.

"What happened?" she asks, trying to drag the two halves of her suit as close together as possible. "Where is everyone? What's going on?"

The drummer giggles, half in this world, half gone. His eyes roam around him, his fingers looking, reaching for something invisible. An object glitters on the ground. A pair of scissors. Was that what had ripped her catsuit?

The man chuckles once more. "See? You win," he says. "You cut more than I did." He lifts his fingers up and clumps of hair fall out. Clumps of reddish-brown auburn curls. Panicking, she plunges her fingers into her hair and more ringlets fall off. He'd cut off her hair—or rather, they'd done it together. She peers down at her handful of curls. She's morphed into a cliché before her own eyes—the pop star spiraling out of control.

Tina backs away from him, launches to her feet and staggers into the main house. She rushes into thick smoke and the rank, spicy stench of marijuana. She begins to feel herself hyperventilate. She needs a mirror. She feels hair falling off her shoulder as she rushes through the mansion's endless corridors, her movements crazed.

There's low music playing in the background, but no people milling around. They've all found corners, spots on the floor or on the sofa. People become a single mass. Her eyes can't separate individuals. As her ears adjust, the moans reach her. Intense, deep grunts, adding bass to the lo-fi beats over the speakers.

Her skin begins to heat up. She needs to leave. She goes in search of Jonas in that maze of a mansion. She folds into herself when a hand or two randomly reach out of the dimness to touch her, to pull her toward them. She bunches her shoulders in fear.

Tina rushes past a behemoth of a mirror and backtracks to assess herself. Her fingers begin to tremble when she touches the remnants of her hair. All gone. She's a ragdoll whose tresses have been violently pulled out. Her face is puffy. Tracks of black mascara have reached her chin. She lets out a gasp of despair, then clasps a palm tightly over her mouth.

She needs to find Jonas. They need to leave. Her mind whirls, trying to make sense of where he could be. She feels her way back to Kamid's den. The first place she'd met Jonas. When his eyes had sought hers, looking for home.

She makes her way down narrower hallways and passageways, deeper into the bowels of Kamid's place, squeezing past people pressed against walls. Guttural sounds and high-pitched screams reach her first as she stands in front of the door to the den. She stops in her tracks, scared to push the door in.

It creaks open to her nightmare.

Women outnumbering men. Surgically enhanced curves. Too many limbs for one leather sofa. Sounds she never wants to hear ever again. That scent as old as time, perfuming the dark den.

Jonas.

Turquoise locks with honey from across the room. He is unrecognizable. A stranger. He doesn't process her, can't decipher who she is. So, he turns away, back to his task. *Tasks*.

Tina rushes barefoot out of the mansion, racing past all the sports cars toward those Tuscan-style wrought-iron gates. She reaches them, grabs a few bars and screams into the night. She reaches into her clutch purse, pulls out her phone.

He picks up on the second ring. "Tina?"

She starts to hyperventilate. "Come get me," she screams into the receiver, her voice sounding frantic and disembodied even to herself. "Come get me!"

"Right now?" He seems confused. "What's going on? *Älskling?*"

"Seb... Please... Come for me."

The night grows darker, sounds around her flutter into whispers. Her legs can no longer carry her, and Tina's world turns pitch black.

FORTY-TWO

NANCY

Four days later

A mother should never see her daughter like this. It was Tobias who had told her. A girl called Kasha had reached him to let them know Tina had been hospitalized. She'd been found unconscious on the premises of an acquaintance and had been transported to a hospital. Apparently, she hadn't eaten properly for days and was severely dehydrated. She had been subsisting on alcohol, tea and apples leading up to the party.

According to the examining doctor, she had also been drugged at the party, though there were no signs of sexual assault beyond her ripped golden suit. Normally she wouldn't have bothered them with minor incidents, Kasha had told Tobias, but she felt, this time, Tina's family needed to be by her side.

Tobias and Nancy arrive at Tina's hospital room, Kasha trailing them. They find Tina sleeping, snoring lightly. Seb arrived before them and is sleeping on a chair next to her, his head resting on folded arms on her bed. Nancy's eyes wash over her daughter, her head shaved down to a low crop.

"What happened?" Tobias turns toward Kasha. He stands tall, broad and angry. Nancy watches the other woman become flustered by her son. Women tend to do that around her boy, she has noticed.

"She cut off her hair. She must have been disoriented when she did it." Kasha pauses, her eyes roaming Tobias's face. "From the drugs," she adds.

"Dear God," Nancy mutters, holding back tears. She needs to stay strong for when Tina wakes up and sees her. The hospital has shaved her head nearly bald to even out her handiwork, and Nancy notices her bone structure, her freckles, her nose and eyebrows. All Lars.

Seb stirs. When he registers his surroundings, he gets to his feet. Tobias pulls him into a hug and Seb breaks down. "Tobbe," Seb cries into their hug. "I thought I was going to lose her."

"*Heeej.*" Tobias draws out the word. "Thanks for being here for her," Tobias whispers back to him. "Thank you."

"You should have seen her," Seb says, his eyes near invisible, swollen from crying. "She was broken when I got here, Tobbe, broke—" Seb loses himself once more and sobs into Tobias's shoulder. Tobias cradles his head, holds him tight against his body until the younger man composes himself.

"Did she tell you anything?" Tobias asks, his voice heavy.

"Not at first." Seb wipes his eyes, then pushes his hair back. His blond hair now grazes his shoulders. His beard is gone. "She didn't want to." Seb pauses to clear his throat. "I asked her if it was Jonas, and she won't say anything. I swear if he hurt her... If he..." Seb's voice breaks.

"Where the fuck is he?" Tobias fumes. "Where is he?"

"Darryl told him it would be wise not to show his face," Kasha chimes in. "Ever again. And that's putting it lightly."

Tobias grits his teeth. "And where is Darryl?" he asks.

"Giving her space to be with you all," Kasha says. Tobias holds her gaze. She avoids his by turning to Nancy. "He's been dropping by to see her every day."

"Thank you," Nancy says softly. "And what is your name again?"

"Kasha," she says, her eyes back on Tobias. "If you need anything while you're all in town…" The sharp buzz of her phone interrupts her offer. "Excuse me." Kasha picks it up, backing out of the room before speaking.

Nancy moves toward a sleeping Tina, giving Seb a quick, comforting pat on his arm. Her eyes roam her daughter's face. She reaches her palm over, cups Tina's right cheek until she stirs. Tina turns toward the heat, her eyes fluttering open. Once her eyes lock on Nancy's in recognition, she grabs Nancy's wrist and leans closer into it.

"Mamma," she says softly. "Mamma."

"I'm here, my dear." Nancy plants a kiss on her forehead. Tobias rushes over and strokes Tina's buzz-cut head.

"*Heeej*," he says, soothing her. "*Hur känns det?*" *How does it feel?*

"Have you eaten anything?" Nancy jumps in. "I need to get you proper food. Do you want *chakri*?"

Tina chuckles, a pained sound. Her face contorts as the laugh turns into an ugly cry.

"It's okay." Nancy moves in, hugging her to her bosom. "All will be well, my dear," she says. She will cry later. Right now, her baby needs her.

"Thank you for coming."

"*Självklart*." Tobias's deep voice sinks lower. *Of course.* "We would have come sooner if we could. You're safe now.

We're all here." He throws Seb a quick glance. The other man is leaning against the wall, arms folded across his chest, his face a map of fear and sadness.

"Your boss has been kind to us," Nancy says. "Putting us in a fancy Hollywood hotel," she beams, hoping to lighten Tina's spirits. "Is this how you've been living out here without us? All that Hollywood money?"

"Stop." Tina laughs. She reaches to push her hair behind her ear and feels nothing there. Phantom tresses. She's pieced together some details. She'd haphazardly clipped it all off over a game of truth-or-dare with an asshole. "I can't believe I did this," she says, caressing her head with a flat palm. "I can't believe…" She breaks down again.

"It will grow back, don't worry," Nancy says. "Right now, I need to make sure you eat something."

"I'll go grab a sandwich," Tobias offers. He turns to go, dragging Seb out of the room with him.

Barely five minutes after Tobias leaves the room, they hear a low knock on her door.

"Visiting hours are probably over," Nancy mutters in frustration, adjusting her floral gown and getting to her feet.

The door slowly swings open. Behind it stands a tall, lean man in his sixties with terracotta-blood-colored hair peppered with gray and golden eagle eyes Nancy hasn't seen in over fifteen years.

Nancy freezes, the tiny hairs on her arms standing up. They drink each other in. Kasha comes around from behind him.

"I had to call him too," Kasha says. "I'm so sorry, Tina."

FORTY-THREE

NANCY

If Nancy could travel back to the night of her graduation in her tiny apartment off Sveavägen, to that stormy afternoon in his Vaxholm cabin when she and Lars lay in each other's arms for sixteen hours straight, to the time they bobbed in the lake at Tyresta and made love on its shores. To all the times he pulled her close, ran his palms over her, explored her with his touch. To the times he'd softly whispered *Naa jaŋ—Come here*—in Mandinka to her, pulling her closer.

She would have resisted him. Even if it meant Tobias and Tina vanishing into thin air, never existing.

Sensing the atmosphere in the room, Kasha excuses herself, giving Tina a quick hug on her way out of the room.

"Nancy," Lars calls her name softly. "*Yamfa n ma*, Nancy." His first words to her after all these years. *Forgive me, Nancy.*

Nancy presses her lips tightly together for a moment, not trusting herself to speak.

"Your audacity must be studied." The words taste bitter once they leave her. "The nerve to show up here." He moves closer. She puts out a hand to stop his advance.

"I know, I know," he whispers. "I had to stay away."

"No!" Nancy yells suddenly. "No. You chose to stay away. Leif took care of us."

"Yes, he did it for me," Lars said. "I sent him funds to take care of you. Of them."

"You blackmailed him," Nancy yells. "Told him you would let everyone know he enjoys the company of men. You are no saint."

"I swear, I wish I could go back and do it all over again," Lars says.

"Yes, because I would have cursed you the day I saw you." Nancy's eyes are wide, her chest heaving. She wishes she could blink and make him disappear.

"I wanted to come see my daughter," Lars says. "I had to rush over to be…"

"She is not your daughter!" Nancy's voice is cutting. "She will never be yours. You lost access to both of them that day when you let *her* into my home."

Lars stands stoically, and Nancy wonders if he's realizing how much pain he has caused his children. Now his ghost of a life stands before her, seeking forgiveness in its delusion.

Lars turns to Tina. "*Hej gumman.*" Hej sweetie.

"Don't talk to her," Nancy seethes, forming a physical barrier between father and child.

"Mamma," Tina says from her bed. "I need to rest. Can you both leave me alone please?" She turns to her father. "Now? Before Tobias gets back and sees you? You don't want him to see you," she adds. "Trust me."

Lars nods in defeat and backs up toward the door. Tina turns to Nancy. "You too, Mamma. Go!"

"Me? Why me?"

"Because he has been sending me letters for two years talking about you, and I need you two to go talk to each other and leave me out of it!" Tina is exasperated.

"Letters...?" Nancy processes Tina's words.

"Yes, letters. Apologizing for his *Aja* art series. Apologizing for someone called Malik. Apologizing for..."

"Malik?" Nancy gets chills at the mention of that name.

"Please go find a room somewhere and talk." Tina grabs the pale green covers, pulls them over her shoulders and turns toward the wall, a child cowering away from fighting parents.

Nancy pivots to Lars. He holds the door open for her. She tucks her purse under an armpit and hurries past him into the hallway and into a private waiting room.

"Can I get you some coffee?" Lars asks, running his fingers through his hair, still thick and lush. She remembered loving the feel of those silk red threads as he smiled at her, eyes glittering like amber, freckles adding to his boyish charm.

"Don't waste my time," Nancy says hotly, planting herself in an armchair. "Say what you have to say. About the letters. About Malik. About everything."

Lars sighs before walking over and crouching down next to her. Her arms are crossed, her eyes not meeting his.

"Nancy," he starts, his voice soft, unsure. "I hurt you so much, and I know I don't deserve your forgiveness. But you have to understand, *Aja* was my way of loving you from afar. Because I knew I would never get the chance to love you this close again." His fingers reach out to graze her arm. She pulls away.

He continues, "If I could rewind time, I never would have taken that first photo. In the cabin. You, standing there." His eyes roam her face.

"Why were you writing my child letters?" Nancy ends his trip down memory lane. "Why have you been upsetting her? What did you write?" Nancy presses her lips tightly. "About Malik?"

"Umm," he starts, stumbling over his words. "I—I umm…"

Nancy sits up taller. "What did you do to Malik?"

His eyes meet hers once more. "It was all my fault. I was a very small jealous man and…" His voice breaks. "I was jealous of him. So jealous."

Nancy feels her chest tighten at his words.

"I got him deported."

The room is silent. Nancy feels a void so heavy she is sure she will pass out.

"The drugs…" she starts, processing his words.

"I planted them," Lars confesses, voice shaking. "I wanted him—needed him gone because I wanted you. I wanted you so much." He reaches for her hand. "I still do."

She slaps him. He accepts the blow, then turns back to look into her eyes, which are raging with fury.

"I'm so sorry, Nancy," he whispers. "I'm so sorry I couldn't give you the life you deserved."

"What else have you confessed to my daughter? Uhm? What else?" she demands, her voice sharp.

He lets out a deep breath, wipes a few tears with the back of his hand, composing himself.

"I knew it was too late to fix all this with you," he says. "But with Tina—our Tina—I know I still have some time."

"And what about Tobias? He needed you more. He longed for you all these years. But you abandoned him too. He kept asking about *Mammas kompis*. He remembered you as my *friend*."

"I know, I know," he says. "I have such lovely memories of us picking him up from *dagis* and playing in the park." He audibly holds his breath for a beat, then continues. "Anyway, I knew they would never let me back in. If I can't be there physically, I will take care of them financially." He pauses to look at her. "I have put you in my will."

"What are you talking about?" Nancy furrows her brows at him. "What is this nonsense?"

"You're in my will. All three of you," he says. "You will soon be hearing from my lawyer. Frida has no idea, nor do the boys. I had to make sure they weren't involved. I swear. I am going to do right by you and my children this time."

Nancy sits with this news, not sure how to absorb his words. "Is that why you've been writing to Tina all this time?" she asks.

Lars shakes his head, bends it low, then lifts it to look at her. "I'm dying, Nancy." His voice breaks. "My doctor says I've got less than a year."

Nancy holds her breath, her mouth dropping slightly open.

"Tina doesn't know," he adds after a long spell of silence. "I wrote to keep her close to my failing heart."

Nancy presses her lips tightly together as tears rise. She

refuses to let them fall, keeping her eyes focused on Lars. She struggles to her feet from the deep armchair. Lars rises as well.

"Is that all?" Nancy says. "*I be heera to, Lars?*" she adds in her mother tongue. *Are you at peace now, Lars?*

With that, she grabs her purse and tramps out of the room.

FORTY-FOUR

NANCY

After her chat with Lars, Nancy presses herself to the wall outside, trying to process what transpired between them. He admitted to violently removing Malik, her true love, from her. It's too much to process after all this time and her head spins.

My brother is a spoiled and entitled control freak.

Leif's words. She places her palm on her chest, eyes closed. Love isn't jealous like he was of Malik. Love isn't vengeful the way he feels about his wife Frida. Love isn't transactional as portrayed by the way he treated his brother. And love certainly doesn't feel entitled to her and her body just because he knows her language. Lars had tried to control them all. Tried to conjure up his own reality of what love was—*what art is*—with him right smack at the center of his own feelings and emotions. *Like an artist.* Because only an artist truly knows why he creates what he creates.

She senses a large, broad shadow hovering over her. "*Mamma, vad gör du?*" Tobias asks, a turkey sandwich and takeaway coffee in his hands, Seb close behind him. *Mom, what are you doing?*

348

Lars had better not leave the room at this moment, Nancy thinks. Tobias cannot see him.

"Nothing, my dear." She collects herself, linking her arm in his to pull him away from the door. "Nothing, let's go."

They find Tina sleeping, huddled like a baby, in her hospital room. Nancy pads closer, strokes her head, then bends low to kiss her child.

She remembers the day Tina came home crying from school. Jealous girls, she'd cried. Mean girls, she'd sobbed. Teasing her because they'd caught a glimpse of her while changing in the locker room. Her fire crotch. They'd laughed. *Who would want that furry, spicy-looking thing?*

Tina had cried herself to sleep that night. Nancy had run her fingers through her child's loose curls as she'd slept her sorrow away. The same way she strokes her daughter's head now.

Nancy glances at Seb and gives him a small smile. His face looks puffy and tired. She sees his eyebrows begin to crumble at her gesture, and she beckons him to come in for a hug. Seb pads over to her, his mouth contorted, trying to hold back his emotions. She pulls him into an embrace.

She remembers the day Tina brought Seb home after school. Nancy had peered at the boy, who looked like he'd never seen hard work in his life. Looking like butter. Staring at her with intense eyes like he was reading her soul. She didn't want him around. Not in her house. Not around her daughter. If Lars could snuff her dreams, imagine the lifelong damage boys who looked like Seb could do to her daughter?

Tina had shut her out for months. Barely spoken to

her. Called her a hypocrite for opening her door up to the bubblegum-chewing, hair-twirling white girls who came looking for Tobias.

How could Nancy fully explain to her daughter that she didn't want her flatlining like she did? Over a boy who latched onto her like his dying breath, bonding with her simply because she found him in the depths of his own trauma?

She remembers the day Leo the Sphynx grew too old to judge her with Mr. Torbjörn's eyes and the kids couldn't get him to wake up.

"*Hypertrophic cardiomyopathy*," the vet had said.

Nancy had scrunched up her nose in confusion. *What?*

"Heart disease caused by the thickening of his heart muscle," the vet had explained. "The disease often shows no outward signs, so it causes sudden death sometimes." The vet had watched Nancy collapse into herself. "I'm so sorry."

She remembers that phone call from Yaya. Omar's heart had finally failed him too.

"Go home." Leif had kissed her on the cheek. "They'll be fine with me," he assured her. A few days later, he drove her to Arlanda Airport. The first leg of her journey back home to bury her father in Gambia. She'd had to stay strong for Fatou, who was moorless without Omar. Without her head of household and anchor. Together, they also visited the plaque which had been put up in Lamin's memory. Nancy finally planted her lips on the cool, metallic stone, kissing her brother goodbye.

She remembers the day she realized she'd failed Leif too.

All these years. Without being fully aware of it. Failing him every single day he spent with his nephew and niece.

His children. The day she realized she should have let them call him Pappa all along. *Father*. Because Leif was the only father figure they'd ever had. He was so active in their lives and raised them as his own. He deserved the pleasure of being called Pappa.

It was on December 13, 2002. Tina had been crowned *Sankta Lucia*. She was singing a solo, her voice so rich and velvety, it enthralled the audience sitting in the dark.

Our Tina is a star.

A coughing fit had seized him. He tried stifling it, not wanting to embarrass his niece on stage. He clamped a palm over his mouth. Nancy helped him up and out of the crowd. They rushed to the lobby together.

"Leif! Leif!" Nancy shook him. She saw trails of blood seeping through the fingers of the hand he had over his mouth. Within a split second, his eyes rolled back, and he hit the floor.

Nancy knew what it was. That disease now had a name. She watched it slowly claiming him over the years. Whittling him down to a shell of his former ruddy self. Now it had come to collect her best friend.

Leif stayed in the hospital throughout Christmas. Tobias and Tina brought his gifts to him. They shared *julafton* dinner together in his room. Tina belted out his favorite tunes; Gloria Gaynor's "I Will Survive" always got him bobbing his head and biting on his lower lip in unison.

"Please forgive me," Nancy cried into his hospital sheets as he lay back. "I failed you, Leif. I failed you." Leif glanced at the kids as they stared at him, their faces forlorn. He nodded toward the door. He wanted to speak to Nancy alone.

Once they left, he turned toward Nancy, reached out and stroked her braids. "Nancy, please," he said, his voice low, soft. "It was my life's pleasure to be their uncle. You gave me my freedom."

"You deserved to be their father," she wept. "You are their father."

Tears had welled up in his eyes as he looked at her.

"I know all you see is Lars when you look into her eyes," Leif rasped, his words coming out as broken sobs. "Please take care of her for me. She is not him." He began to shiver. "She is not Lars. Please take care of my Tina."

When Leif took his last breath on New Year's Eve that winter, it was with Nancy holding on tightly to his hand, his face turned toward his window where snow flurries fell from the sky. He never got to see the fireworks.

Now, as Nancy watches Tina sleeping in her hospital bed, her chest rising and falling, Nancy silently promises to honor Leif's final plea, to embrace the child who simply wants her mamma to see beyond her father's likeness.

Lars had already torn Malik away from her. She isn't going to let him take her daughter too.

FORTY-FIVE

TINA

Tina runs a brush over her shaved head. She sees her features prominently now. Isn't sure what to make of her face. She adds moisturizing lotion to her scalp, then the rest of her skin, staring at her reflection in the sliver of the mirror in her hospital room. She remembers the deadness in Jonas's eyes when she found him at the party. They were missing that spark of life. As if he had nothing left to live for.

As Tina peers into her own in the mirror, she wonders if she's becoming like him.

She catches Seb's sad eyes in the reflection, observing her from a chair. She's known him long enough to read the look on his face. He's not sure he knows who she is. Who she's becoming.

Darryl will arrive any minute to pick her up. Seb has offered to stay with her until he does. Tina thinks Seb may also be feeling territorial.

When Lars appeared yesterday, the spite and anger she expected to feel didn't surface. Instead, she merely felt she was seeing a pen pal—albeit a one-sided pen pal—in person. He looked a little thinner than the last time they met up for *fika* in Stockholm a couple of years back. She wondered what her parents had discussed, because when the conversation was over, Nancy had rushed back to her room, her face back to normal—as if Lars hadn't returned to upend their world.

Nancy can't come to be with her as she's being discharged, she says. She's under the weather, jetlagged, has a headache—all the usual excuses. Tobias stays back at the hotel with their mother.

She recognizes his scent before she sees him. Darryl. She spins to take him in, in a crisp white dress shirt that's fast becoming his signature. It contrasts deliciously against his smooth skin.

"Hey, Tina." A broad smile stretches across his face. He's holding a bouquet of yellow lilies for her. He takes a few steps in before noticing Seb in the chair. "Ha, it's our bodyguard," he jokes. Seb gives him a crooked smile before launching to his feet for a handshake.

"Good to see you again, David," Seb says.

"You know my name," Darryl says with a wry smile. His handshake is firm enough to rock Seb's entire torso.

"Thank you so much for coming," Tina says, rounding her bed and giving him a hug. "Thank you for everything." She feels him tighten their embrace and run a soothing palm over her back.

"Don't mention it," he says, giving her a peck on her cheek. "I've taken care of Jonas as well." She doesn't dare ask what that means. "You ready?" he asks. Tina responds with a grin.

Darryl shuttles them to the hills in his shiny Range Rover, Tina riding shotgun. Seb sulks in the backseat, gazing out the window as they speed down the highway.

"Kasha has been chucking his flowers out," Darryl laughs. He's wearing dark aviator glasses, an elbow resting on his rolled-down window. Apparently, Jonas sent a bouquet every day she was in hospital.

"I want to ask what happened at Kamid's party, but I know better," he says as he switches lanes. "Kamid is livid. You're his opening act on the global tour this fall. He's understandably concerned you might have been hurt."

"Really?" Tina's tone bites with sarcasm. "After that hedonistic binge he hosted at his own mansion?" She rolls her eyes.

"Kamid wasn't there when they found you," Darryl says. "He and I had left earlier to talk business. His posse went wild after we left."

"What kind of business do you talk about at eleven p.m.?" Tina is skeptical.

"Welcome to Hollywood, baby," Darryl chuckles. "So," he is suddenly serious, "are you really ready for all this, Tina?"

She remembers Kasha's words, about Darryl fearing she was done before she even started. She considers his question for a few seconds before responding.

"I am," Tina says. "I really want this. If ONYX will give me another chance. I got swept up in him." Jonas's striking face flashes across her mind. His eyes, always hooded from being high. His body. Her desperation for familiarity whenever he orbited her.

"It's been one round of damage control after the other since you hit the scene," Darryl says. "We can't afford much more drama. So, I'll ask you again: Are you really ready?"

"I am." Her answer comes swiftly. "I can be on top form practicing with the dancers this summer, ready for tour this fall."

Darryl flashes her a quick smile and places a hand on her knee.

"Tell you what. How about you take two weeks off? Go get some sun. ONYX has yachts docked around Europe. Maybe head over to Croatia for a few weeks, center yourself?"

"And my new look?" she asks, running a palm over her scalp. He glances at her. His eyes are hidden behind shades, so she can't read them.

"Own it," he says before breaking into another dazzling smile. "Or wear a wig. You choose."

Tina sits tall in her seat, her shoulders squared. Yet another second chance, but first, a yacht in Croatia? Is this really her life?

Darryl's eyes drift to Seb through his rearview mirror. "So, *Bodyguard*, how are—"

"I have a fucking name," Seb snaps back uncharacteristically. It catches both Darryl and Tina off guard. She swivels to look at him.

Why am I here, Tina? he seems to be asking.

Why did you call me when you have him?

I knew you before all this, Tina.

Before this version of you.

She turns away from his searing gaze, not wanting to confront those feelings, and focuses back on the road. In that moment, she sees their teenage selves, the ones desperately clinging to each other against the world.

"My bad," Darryl apologizes. "I was just messing with

you. I've clearly outstayed my welcome." He gives a weak laugh, then clears his throat. "Sorry, man."

Seb turns back to the view of the rolling hills outside his window.

They leave Seb at the hotel first. Tina gives Tobias and Nancy quick hugs and kisses at the drop-off. They are all heading back to Sweden in two days. Nancy had insisted on staying an extra week to be by Tina's side—out of character, Tina had thought. She reminded her mother that Kasha and Darryl would be there for her so Nancy didn't need to worry.

Darryl drops her off at her apartment. A bouquet of red roses and bluebonnets awaits her at her front door. The accompanying note is scribbled hastily in Swedish.

Tina, Jag älskar dig. Jag är så ledsen. Förlåt mig älskling /Jonas

Tina, I love you. I'm so sorry. Forgive me darling /Jonas

She smirks after reading the note, then turns to Darryl with the generously sized bouquet. "Can you give this to Kasha to add to the pile, please?"

"You're so shameless," Tina whispers to Kasha as they sit at their reserved table covered in expensive white linen. "Plus, he's my brother, so, *eeewww*. That's nasty."

Kasha pumps her shoulders and taunts in a low voice, "God, he's so *fooine*."

They're at the leaving dinner Darryl had arranged for Tina's family, and Darryl has ordered an expensive Bordeaux for the table. Nancy sits quietly, something clearly weighing on her mind. Tina yearns for the version

of her mother that had materialized in her hospital room—
the protective mother hen ready to pluck eyes out for her
chicks. Now Nancy's back to being the nonchalant version
of herself Tina's always known. Tina is sure Nancy is hiding
something about her conversation with Lars—she wishes
Nancy would discuss it with her. It doesn't matter though,
she reasons—sooner or later, Lars will write her another
letter spilling his soul.

Since his outburst in Darryl's car, Seb has been detached,
only speaking when spoken to. She wants his friendship
back. The version of him that beams like a blond sun, ready
to warm everyone and everything around him. Unlike most
of his teammates, who are playing for top leagues around
Europe and the Middle East, Seb stayed home, playing for
one of Sweden's premier football clubs, AIK. She knows the
Allsvenskan football league season is going on and he needs
to head back to camp as soon as possible. He'd taken a few
days off to be by her side.

She reaches over to touch his arm. "*Hej,*" she says softly
to him. "Thank you for coming."

He cups his hand over hers. "*Självklart,*" he whispers
back. *Of course.* "Whenever you call me, I'll answer. I'll be
there." His eyes, sad.

"You can always say no too," she whispers back. "We
will be friends forever, but we can't always be each other's
pillow."

Seb bobs his head with a pained smile on his lips. He
leans into her again. "You once said '*I'm yours, always*' to
me," he says. "I'll never forget those words, Tina. I'm yours
as well. Always will be. So, when you call me, I will always
come. Where you lead me, I will go because"—he lifts her

palm to his face, presses a kiss into its groove—"my heart is here." He kisses it again. "Right here in the palm of your hand." He leans back to look at her. "Please don't squeeze too tightly, otherwise you'll stop it from beating."

Tina stares at him, mouth agape, eyes wide, processing his words.

"So, what's this spoken-word venue?" Tobias says, breaking up all other conversations. Kasha has finally moved in for her kill. "Sounds intriguing," he adds. "Let's go there after dinner."

FORTY-SIX

TINA

Smooth, dark pebbles massage her feet. The light seafoam-green waters of the Adriatic wash over them. They're swimming in waters pristine down to twenty feet. Sea salt tickles her throat. Croatia is offering her soul glorious rejuvenation. Late mornings. Lavish breakfast spreads with the other guests on the yacht anchored in Hvar, Croatia.

She's spent the past week sailing the Dalmatian Coast on a sleek black yacht owned by the record label. She isn't the only guest, though. This seems to be one of ONYX's floating recovery centers, where they send their artists and producers who are on the verge of spiraling out of control. They're surrounded by luxury—spa treatments and wellness activities, daily massages and yoga. Reiki healing sessions to redirect and manipulate their energy flow. Tina has been soaking it all up, letting her face finally breathe, makeup-free, during her stay.

Now, past eight in the evening, Tina is back in Hvar, this time sporting evening makeup and a black shoulder-length wig with sharp bangs. She dines alone, a few steps from the yacht docked by the party island. From her view on the terrace of Gariful, the island's priciest seafood joint, she sees the Pakleni islands in the distance like sleeping giants. She tucks into her lobster carpaccio and takes a sip of locally produced white wine. She wishes Darryl was here. Even though she knows he'll never see her as more than a friend and his artist, she loves being around him. Soaking up his confidence, admiring his discipline, basking in his dazzling grin.

He'd sent her here as her last chance to reflect and figure out who she is, if she's made for this life in the limelight. He'd warned her about letting Jonas distract her and she hadn't listened. But she's listening now. Joining Kasha at those open poetry and spoken-word nights—after the first time, they'd been back every couple of weeks—has felt like a revival of her creativity, somewhere she can read her words clearly without the distraction of music. At her last reading, sharing those words while her family had beamed back felt invigorating, validating. Tobias had crushed her into a hug afterwards, Nancy had patted her on the back, and Seb had simply kissed her hand.

After this week in Croatia, she's sure she'll be ready for an intense summer of rehearsals.

"Madame." A tall, smartly dressed waiter interrupts her thoughts. "This from the gentleman over there." He sets a purple lavender-infused cocktail down in front of her. She turns toward her benefactor, a smile across her lips.

Shit.

She can't cause a scene at this fancy restaurant, so she lets the "gentleman" saunter toward her table. He takes a seat next to her.

"I had to track you down, *älskling*," Jonas says, leaning in close. "You weren't responding to any of my calls, texts, flowers..."

"Can I get you anything, sir?" the waiter offers. He orders a glass of the wine she's having. He turns back to Tina once the waiter leaves.

"Darryl threatened to kill me if I contacted you," he continues. "Tina, what happened at Kamid's?" He seems genuinely concerned. "All I know is that an ambulance was called, and you were rushed off the property." He leans in closer, trying to catch her eyes. "Did someone hurt you, baby?" he asks in a whisper.

Tina looks away. She tries to scrub out the image now forever lodged in the deepest recesses of her mind whenever she thinks of Jonas. Not his turquoise gaze warming whenever he sees her, or his easy-going countenance, but that vision of him at the party, his hips moving and pounding against other bodies. She can't look at him.

"Tina." Jonas is insistent. "Please tell me. What did I do?"

She lets out a strained laugh. "*Skojar du?!*" *Are you joking?*

His hard look tells her he's not. She needs to leave, and she looks around for a waiter.

"*Snälla*," he pleads. "Was it the drugs?" he mutters quietly. "Was I with another girl?"

"Correction—girls," she clarifies. "Jonas, I want you gone. Right now."

He reaches for her fingers, and she recoils sharply. He tightens his grip and moves closer to her, their knees brushing.

"I'm a mess, Tina." His voice breaks. "Since you left. I've got no one. No one understands me the way you do." She thinks of Seb. Is this what trauma bonding looks like?

He's still talking. "I can't lose you like this. Over

something dumb I did when I was high. I can't. I've beaten myself up every day since it happened." He reaches to squeeze her knee under the table linen. She curses herself for responding with heat. The way her body always responds to his, regardless of what her brain and heart want.

"I can't fix you," she says to him. "I can't, Jonas." His hand moves from her knee to the hem of her peach-colored summer dress. "Stop it," she murmurs breathlessly to him. He moves his chair closer to hers.

"Please don't leave me alone back there," he pleads. "In that world. Please don't." He leans in to kiss her ear. When she swivels to face him, he tugs her with a soft kiss.

She pulls back from him. "*Stooop*," she mutters, drawing out the word, ashamed she's accepting his distraction once more. "I can't do this anymore."

"Please come back to me. I swear I can beat this," he whispers, his hand working her thigh underneath the table. "I can beat this with you by my side."

They're causing a scene. Other dining patrons are throwing curious glances their way. Some squinting their eyes in recognition. In these parts, Eurovision reigns supreme— some probably recognize her as Sweden's failed star.

Tina turns back to him and looks directly into his eyes. Sees the emptiness behind them, because he hadn't been ready for any of this. He hadn't found his footing and identity before being thrust into the rushing waves of the industry. Now, like a tsunami, it has overcome him, and he can't escape.

At that moment, she realizes she doesn't want this stardom enough because she isn't ready for it. Her grounding feels like fine grain sand easily washed away by each receding tide. She wasn't ready in Athens, and she still isn't ready now.

She needs to find solid ground. Discover who she is beyond looking to others for clues and validation, the way both Seb and Jonas keep searching for themselves in her eyes. She yearns for more beyond gyrating in videos and being relegated to a vixen behind DJ Kamid. She needs to find a different way of telling her own story.

Her eyes wash over Jonas with pity and she decides to give him one last night, the hedonistic party vibe of Hvar momentarily softening her for him. Though unlike Jonas, she still has a chance to turn back around and reach for higher ground.

They dine in silence. Fingers intertwined. Palms roaming under the table. Eyes locked over the rims of their glasses. He trails her silently to the sleeping yacht. He watches as she peels off her dress. In the dimness below deck, he matches his rhythm to the gentle bobbing of the vessel. He drowns her every cry with his mouth covering hers. The sounds of the rippling Adriatic fill her quiet cabin, coupled with the beating of their hearts.

Jonas lights up afterward. He drags deeply, his cheeks concaving with the motion, before blowing tendrils of smoke from a blunt into the air. He turns to her, his eyes twinkling like diamonds, his skin absorbed by the darkness. He passes it on to her. She hesitates, her head resting on her folded arms, her stomach pressed to the sheets, peering at him, wondering if this is love, lust or the end of her old life.

That image resurfaces as she stares at him waiting for her to smoke. Those dead eyes in Kamid's mansion. She had seen it in his eyes—a sad man with no control. A man who has become a slave to his weakness. This isn't the life she dreamed of when she won Melodifestivalen. Falling back into Jonas's arms means fully losing herself. One must go. And if there is one life lesson Nancy has inadvertently taught her, it's that giving yourself over to a weak man will derail you forever.

Unless you take back control.

Tina reaches out a slender hand and grabs the smoke from him. She doesn't lift it to her mouth. Instead, she crushes it into an ashtray on the bedside table, taking one giant metaphoric leap forward, before turning back toward him.

"You're pathetic," she says. "So fucking pathetic." He stares at her. "You can't even try. Not even for one night."

"Tina…"

"I never want to see you again. Ever."

"*Älskling?*"

"You will not make me a miserable woman."

"Miserable? What are you talking about?"

Images flash through her mind. A bloodied Seb at her dining table. Her teenage fight with her mother, who she had called a miserable woman because she let a weak man wield power over her.

She shoves Jonas.

"Tina? What are you doing?"

She keeps shoving him until he falls out of her bed. She goes for his beige Cuban shirt, his khaki capris, flings them at him.

"Get out, Jonas!" she screams. "I never want to see you again."

"Fine, fine. I promise," he says, gathering his clothes.

They part ways, and he promises to pretend they never existed.

Tina leaves Croatia five days earlier than planned. Darryl and Kasha are surprised to see her strut back into ONYX so soon. She's wearing her shoulder-length wig with the bangs. Beneath them, her makeup messy and face puffy from tears.

"Croatia didn't do it, *eh*?" Darryl asks, his voice taking on a jovial tone. Kasha smiles too. Their faces turn serious when they read Tina's look. "What's going on?" he asks.

She pulls the wig off her head and rolls it into a fur ball in her hands. Beneath, her short reddish-brown fuzz is growing in.

"I'm sorry," Tina cries. "I can't do this." She gasps for air, shaking. "I'm done."

PART SIX

2011

FORTY-SEVEN

TINA

She moved back into her room at Nancy's. Her first few months home, she hid from public view like a vampire, refusing all requests to perform. She's been taking her time, moving at her own speed, rewriting her own story.

She remembers Darryl's words that summer sharp and clear. His dark eyes, warming as he took her in. A mess; mascara tracks racing down her cheeks. Her wig in her hand. Standing in his office, throwing his dream for her back at him, Kasha standing by his side. While she cried, Darryl slowly rose to his feet, fingers pressed tightly into his desk.

"I'm so sorry," she'd wept, her face pink from shame. Kasha had stood frozen. Stunned into silence. "Please forgive me, Darryl," she cried. "I have so much work to do. So much." She wiped her wet nose.

"Then go do what you gotta do, baby." Those were his only words for her before he came around his desk to pull her into a tight brotherly hug.

When the news reached home, the media tore her apart once more. The petulant girl who still wasn't content with her hotshot producer-agent Darryl Walker and Grammy-winning music director boyfriend, Jonas Jonsson—or, *son of a bitch*, as Tobias likes to call him. The Wikström twins surfaced yet again as well, calling her a stain on their land's pristine image.

Her former apartment, with its enviable view of those Californian rolling hills, feels like a dream. Like she'd conjured up the parallel life in which she donned sequins, partied with DJs and got swept up into Jonas's darkness.

Last she heard—from Kasha, no less—Darryl had finally found love with a redheaded Norwegian songstress he met while on a scouting trip in Europe. Tina had laughed into the phone when Kasha mentioned that he'd been touting her as *the Norse Rose*.

Lars never came back after the scene in the hospital. He'd simply vanished into thin air once more, as if whatever he and Nancy had discussed erased him from existence entirely. There'd been no more letters either and, truth be told, Tina missed his gorgeous calligraphy.

The pieces of her heart where she'd slowly let Lars slip in were now sealing over. She tried searching for news about him, but there was nothing new. His artwork still sold. The occasional journalist penned an opinion piece about his cultural appropriation. Otherwise, nothing noteworthy. Lars was gone from the public eye. She still has his phone number—she could text him. But who would it benefit? He needed her forgiveness and grace more than she needed his love and money.

Seb hasn't been in touch either. Since that dinner in Los Angeles where he'd promised his eternal allegiance into her palm, she has only seen him running after a ball on TV. Some gossip spread had caught his hand roaming low on a "blond bombshell" he was seen partying with in Stureplan. Tina had scanned the article hungrily, cigarette in hand, trying to work out what Seb's body language and disposition meant in those paparazzi photos; scanning his features to see if he was truly happy.

She thought she read it in his eyes: *I miss you, Tina.* Then she pressed the burning butt of her cigarette onto the blond's face, watching it singe off the paper.

Tina wondered why she had called Seb first when she'd been alone, scared and confused in Los Angeles. Perhaps it was because he knew the vulnerable Tina, the real version of her, who had been figuring herself out from the start. She misses him fiercely. Hates when his photo is flashed across her TV screen or printed next to some chick at a red-carpet event.

She hates it, but pride will never let her admit the truth. That they belong to each other.

Tina twiddles her thumbs. She's waiting in a back corner of an Asian fusion joint in the heart of Stureplan. She isn't sure why she set this up, but now back in Stockholm without hearing his voice or seeing his face feels odd, unsettling, not right.

He took a full week to respond to her text message asking for a meeting. His response had been curt. *Sure. Where and when?*

She hears male voices and looks up from her fingers. She sees him pause on approach, shaking hands with two other patrons, clearly football fans. She squints, studying him as he moves closer. A man bun? On her Seb? Well, just *Seb* now. He's also sporting a matching mustache and beard.

He pauses at her table, expressionless. "*Hej*," he greets her. Tina bristles at his chill.

"*Hej*. Glad you could make it."

He gives her a half smile and settles in the chair across from her. A waiter promptly delivers a menu to him. He shakes his head. *No*. He isn't planning on staying long. Tina feels uneasy as she stares at this different version of the man who used to be her lover, her best friend. Is this how growth manifests—in the form of a man bun and beard?

"So," she starts. "How have you been?"

Seb shrugs. "Good. The team is good. I'm good. Life is good." He holds her gaze.

"Well, that's good," she says, sounding unsure. "You're probably wondering why I called you."

"After a whole year? Not really." His tone is flat.

"Look, Seb. It's been rough, you know this. It took me a while to fully land back home."

He toys with a fork on the table, a coy smile on his lips. "I see. Tina first. Always."

"It's not like that."

"Then what is it like? Hmm? To be honest, I don't understand why you invited me here."

"I—I—just…"

"You never cared about me, Tina," he says, his eyes leaving the fork. "You never did."

"You know that's not true." She leans in closer. "I care about you. I love you…"

"Stop it."

"Seb?"

"Tina, please stop. I'm done with this bullshit. I dropped

everything to be by your side in LA. You didn't even ask how I was feeling, what I've been through, how life has been."

"But you just told me 'Life is good,'" she says sarcastically, with air quotes. He holds her gaze with hard eyes. She instantly regrets it.

"Who do you think you are?" he starts.

"I'm sorry."

"Life is all about you, isn't it? So immature, so miserable."

"Miserable?" Tina flinches at that word.

"Yes, Tina. You're a miserable person. I fear you'll end up alone and on drugs like that son of a bitch."

"Seb?"

"Why didn't you call someone else that night in Los Angeles? Hmm? Jonas? Or Darryl? Even Tobias?" He glares at her. "Am I that usable?"

Tears well up as she peers at him, her lips pursed. She sees emotions play across his own eyes. Seeing her cry seems to be thawing him. She reaches for his hand across the tablecloth. He pulls it away, looks over his shoulder, adjusts in his seat.

He continues, "You can't manipulate me anymore. You can't." His voice is brittle.

"I'm sorry," she mutters in a low voice as a few drops race down her cheek. "So sorry."

He clears his throat, trying to compose himself. "I can't do this with you anymore."

"You're my best friend, Seb. I miss you."

"I tried." His voice is hoarse. "But you squeezed too hard." He pauses, then whispers. "You crushed it."

Tina shuts her eyes at his words and nods. The one act he

begged her not to commit. When she opens them, it's to his glassy wet gaze, eyes rimmed red.

"I'm yours, Seb. Always."

Those words trigger him. He pushes back from her table, jumps to his feet, then looks down at her in a wordless standoff. Tina knows she has broken his facade. She has cut right through him. It's the start she needs. With the look he's currently giving her, she knows his loyalty is unwavering.

Sebastian wipes his eyes with the back of his right palm before storming off and leaving Tina staring after him.

FORTY-EIGHT

TINA

"Jesus, what witchcraft is this?!" Tobias exclaims as he opens the door to the intense woody waft of incense that has filled up Nancy's apartment.

"Don't talk like that in my house. This apartment is covered in the blood of Jesus," Nancy yells from the kitchen where she's prepping the meal. Nancy has summoned both Tina and Tobias for this "special" dinner, perhaps wanting to unload the weight on her mind.

Tina strides out of her room, a cigarette perched in the side of her mouth. The only habit she kept from her days with Jonas. Her hair has grown in, sprouting fast. It's currently twisted into mini locs of copper. She wears a golden loop ring in her right nostril, her face makeup-free. Fresh. Lots of water daily. Her lean, taut frame is hidden beneath one of Nancy's overflowing boubous. She has taken up Pilates.

"Seriously, Tee." Tobias starts to peel off his brown aviator jacket. "Sage? Incense? Are we missing myrrh? You dabbling in black magic?"

"Shut the fuck up," she hisses at him. "I need a smoke."

"Please!" Nancy screams back from the kitchen. "No cursing in your mother's house. Why all this disrespect? Tina, you should treasure your older brother before it's too late."

"Yes, Mamma, I know, I know." Tina rolls her eyes as she pulls her lighter off a shelf. She pauses by one of her favorite photos of Uncle Leif and her. She couldn't be more than ten years old or so. They're both wearing sunglasses, dressed up as Ghostbusters for a party. She lifts the corner of her lip in a crooked smile at him.

Uncle Leif always knew what to say to make her feel better. Always.

"Yes, you should know." Nancy pads out of the kitchen, her face hard, her eyes puffy red. Both Tobias and Tina pause, her sadness palpable. "I miss my brother Lamin. I wish I told him I loved him every day. You two are all you have left when God calls me home."

"Mamma, please stop being dramatic," Tobias chuckles. Tina knows he's trying to lighten the mood. Tina reads something else in her mother's expression. *What is going on?*

"Are you okay?" Tina asks, her voice soft.

"I'm fine." Nancy composes herself. "I'm fine. We'll talk over dinner. Come help me with the fish."

"Can I go smoke?" Tina protests, exasperated.

Nancy cuts her a glare that instantly changes Tina's mind and propels her toward the kitchen.

While the women finish up, Tina hears sounds of a soccer match coming from the living room. She hears the commentators mention AIK, Seb's team. Some words about him having a tough season, distractions of the "Östermalm" variety, one of the sportscasters says, chuckling. The snooty part of town with its overpriced restaurants, girls with lip fillers and chic nightclubs. The ones where Tobias worked on and off again as a bouncer on the weekends.

She hears Tobias switch to a news update as she drizzles olive oil on Nancy's tomato-and-onion salad. Something about the Arab Spring. More updates from Egypt now. A surprise uprising that had caught the Middle East by storm in January. News was still trickling into Sweden, everyone trying to decipher what was going on. What this was going to mean for the rest of the world.

It had started in Tunisia. A street vendor had set himself ablaze. This sparked protests across the entire region. Now there were protests every week in town as well in support of Arab civilians who dared to stand up. Shaken by the news, she'd gone to a few of them at Sergels torg, waving flags alongside Syrian and Libyan strangers who, in those few hours of protest, became friends and family.

She hears Tobias curse as he listens to the news.

"What's going on?" she shouts from the kitchen.

"You should see the images from Tahrir Square in Cairo," he calls back. "*Damn*."

"Food is ready." Nancy cuts off their conversation. She carries stewed fish and white rice to their dining table. Tina trails her with fried plantains and the tomato-onion salad.

"*Tack, Mamma*." Tobias stretches to his height before leaning over to give Nancy a peck. "Smells great." Then he tugs at one of Tina's locs. She slaps his hand. Once they settle in and plate up, they dine in silence for a few minutes before Nancy breaks it.

"Your father is dying," she says abruptly.

Tina pauses mid-bite. She turns to Nancy with a puzzled look. Tobias continues eating. "What do you mean?" Tina asks.

"His heart is weak." Nancy shoves rice into her mouth

with a spoon. "That's what happens when your heart is wicked like his." She continues chewing.

"Wait, wait, what?" Tina feels herself flushing.

"Why do you care?" Tobias says dryly as he spears a piece of fried plantain.

Tina turns back to Nancy. "How do you know? What is going on?"

"He told me at the hospital." Nancy scoops up more rice with her spoon.

"At the hospital? You've known for over a year?" Tina's voice is shrill.

Was that why Lars stopped writing her letters? Had he been waiting for Nancy to tell her? Tina isn't sure what to think, but the emotion bubbling up is one she hadn't anticipated. Sadness. A fleeting feeling of empathy for a man who had to live under the weight of his actions for two decades. Was that why his heart was failing him? In all the letters he'd written her, dozens upon dozens of letters—enough for a memoir— it was clear Lars Wikström had loved her mother so deeply he had selfishly destroyed the lives of those closest to him in service of his wants, his desire. Now his heart is probably losing its light because it couldn't get the love it desperately desired. It couldn't control love. She thinks about her own meeting with Seb. You can't manipulate love, she reflects.

Nancy breaks through the silence to add, "Since that day at the hospital, he won't stop writing me letters."

FORTY-NINE

NANCY

Her son finishes his meal in silence, then leaves his dirty plate in the sink and walks over to get his jacket. "Thanks for dinner, Mamma," he says, slipping his arms through the sleeves and adjusting its wool collar.

"Where are you going? I'm not done yet," Nancy says, her voice shaky.

Tobias doesn't stay for the rest of her news.

When Nancy swivels to Tina, she instead sees the tears welling up in Lars's eyes peering back through her baby's face. Nancy wants to avert her gaze, return to her meal, pick up her spoon and brush it all off. Leif's words surface in that instant.

She is not him. She is not Lars. Please take care of my Tina.

Nancy shuts her eyes, breathes out loudly, then turns to her daughter.

"Has he been writing you letters?" Tina asks. "What has he been saying? Begging for forgiveness?"

Nancy purses her lips, then shakes her head. "No."

"No?" Tina seems perplexed.

"My dear, your father no longer has power over me," Nancy says, her voice uncharacteristically weak. "I forgave him the day your uncle died."

Tears obscure Tina's glare. "I miss *Farbror* Leif so much," she says in broken snatches. "I miss him."

"I know, my dear." Nancy reaches to grab her hand. She gives it a gentle squeeze. "He was my best friend. I miss him too. Some days I wish I had lied and called him your father."

"Have you been writing him back too?" Tina asks, wiping away tears.

Nancy shakes her head. She fiddles with her fingers before turning to her child once more. "His lawyer has reached out to me." She drops the bombshell and notices Tina's face scrunch up in confusion.

"Lawyer? Why?" Tina asks, her voice dipping into a whisper.

Nancy blows out air before responding. "He has finally decided to stop being a coward."

The following week, Tina squeezes Nancy's hand in support.

They're standing on a side street in Norrmalm in front of heavy mahogany doors bearing the plaque *Melander Advokatbyrå*—the law firm where Nancy has been summoned. Lars's lawyer wants to meet her to go over documents he has drafted at his client's request. Nancy couldn't face the lawyer or whatever Lars was planning to bequeath her alone.

"How are you feeling, Mamma?" Tina leans in to ask. Nancy gives her a smile.

Nancy had opted for a floral blouse over black trousers, her hair cropped low. Tina is wearing a body-hugging dark-green crochet dress beneath a white blazer. Her locs are rolled up and packed into a small bun. Today, she wears makeup. Black cat eyeliner. Nude lips. She turned heads as they strolled the streets.

Once they are received and signed in by reception, they wait five minutes before a tall, heavyset man wearing glasses, with jet-black hair, clearly dyed for his age, strolls toward them. His eyes dance over Tina in recognition before turning to Nancy.

"Ms. Ndow?" He stretches his hand for a shake. "Thank you for meeting me today."

"Did I have a choice in the matter?" Nancy says before taking his hand.

The man chuckles. "You always have a choice. Kristoffer Melander, partner at the firm," he introduces himself. He turns to Tina and bobs his head in greeting. "Ms. Wikström." She nods back at him. "Would you like some coffee? Tea?"

"Can we please get started? I have to go to work," Nancy says.

"Yes," Mr. Melander says. "My client mentioned you worked as *hemtjänst*. Hopefully not for much longer. Right this way."

He leads them to a meeting room at the end of the hall. They hear noise coming out of the room, muffled voices, upon approach. Mr. Melander pushes the door open for Nancy and Tina to step in. The hushed voices instantly fall silent. Nancy chills.

Frida.

The last time both women confronted each other was over twenty-five years ago when Frida had stood over her, screaming, while she held Tobias in her arms and Tina in her belly. Time has not been good to her. Though she is dressed in expensive textiles with white pearls around her neck like a true Östermalm socialite, there are bags under her eyes and her hair has thinned out.

Nancy's glance moves from Frida to her sons. The twins, Lukas and Ludvig. Hard-faced, same hair, eyes, freckles as their father, but with a severity in their gaze, which now tracks down her skin. Is this how suffocating it feels to be around people who hate you because of the color of your skin? Something you have no control over?

The looks the woman and her sons are giving her are a mixture of shock and disgust. Lars has deceived them yet again. He sits next to Frida, looking gaunter than when she saw him at the hospital in Los Angeles. His hair is slicked off his face. He gives her a sly grin from his chair. He still looks good. Living longer than his doctor had estimated. *It is always the ones awash with wickedness who look their best, leaving their victims haggard and trying to pick up the pieces of their lives*, Nancy thinks.

"What on Earth is going on?" Frida starts to get to her feet. Lars places a hand on her arm to stop her. She yanks it away. "Why is this whore here?"

"That's enough," Lars yells at Frida. "You will respect her in this room. Please."

"Respect?" Frida is exasperated. "Respect? Are you out of your mind? Did you bring her and her bastard here to torment me?"

Nancy turns to Tina, who stands frozen by the door. She and the twins are in a silent standoff of shock. Nancy tried to do all she could to protect her daughter from this vitriol, but yet again, Lars has tricked them all. He knew she would

never set foot in that room if she knew his entire family was
going to be there.

Mr. Melander jumps in. "Please, Mrs. Wikström, let's
refrain from insults and keep it civil here." He directs Nancy
and Tina to one end of the long table. He sits between both
families.

"We're gathered today because my client Dr. Wikström
would like to discuss the details of his will while he is still
alive," the lawyer starts.

Dr. Wikström. Doctor of Anthropology. Professor. Nancy
shuts her eyes at his name as an image flashes across her mind.
Raindrops racing down ringlets of red hair as he dances naked
and gleefully in pouring rain before turning toward her, telling
her to *come here. Naa jay.* The moment she fell for him.

The lawyer continues, "Knowing the nature of your
relationship, my client is concerned about the affairs
of his estate once he passes. Particularly about a new set of
artwork."

The silence in the room is dense. She hates Lars for doing
this to her. Forcing her into this room again. Forcing her to
deal with his own selfish mistakes.

"What is it you want from us, Nancy?" Frida jumps in
unexpectedly. "What do you think we owe you?"

"Nancy knows nothing about this," Lars interjects. "She
didn't know we were going to be here."

"She is not your wife," Frida snaps at him. "How long
will you keep disrespecting me like this? How long do I
have to live with this pain?"

This time, one of the twins jumps in to defend his mother.
"*Du är en skam.*" The vitriol in his voice is acidic, his eyes
harsh as he stares his father down. "*Du är en skam för ditt*

folk. En jävla nationell skam." You are a disgrace. You are a disgrace to your people. A *fucking national disgrace.*

Lars swallows his son's words. Doesn't respond. He simply purses his lips, links his fingers. "Please proceed," he urges his lawyer. The lawyer rings for his assistant. A younger man joins them in the room, then heads over to a packing crate in the corner.

"My client would like to bequeath the following collection to Ms. Ndow," Mr. Melander continues as his assistant slips on gloves and gently slides one of the oil paintings out. Nancy recognizes it at once. Her lush skin wearing a white terry romper outfit with large black polka dots. She bites her lower lip to prevent tears.

"Eight oil paintings from the estate of artist Lars Wikström collectively worth ten million kronor," the lawyer reads off his documents, his glasses resting on the tip of his nose. "A complete collection called *ju-sö.*" The lawyer struggles with the pronunciation.

"*Njusoo,*" Lars corrects him. Then he trains his eyes on Nancy, probably looking for validation.

There's sudden whispering in the room. It's the boys, presumably distraught about potentially losing out on ten million kronor from an existing estate already valued at over sixty million.

Nancy lets out a sigh of despair. How dare he do this? At this moment, she realizes Lars may very well be a narcissist. He must be one to orchestrate such a gathering, while sprinkling salt into her open wound and somehow still looking for adulation.

Njusoo. Sweetheart. A sick inside joke only she could ever share in because she and Lars are the only ones in that room who understand Mandinka, and what those images mean. The moment he stalled her, and she had let him.

Nancy turns to Frida sharply, her face hardened. She's transported to her living room when the betrayed wife's pain had rained down on her, Leif holding her back.

"You were right, Frida," Nancy says, quieting them all. "They are vile. They need to be destroyed."

FIFTY

TINA

The twins—or Satan's spawn, as Tobias likes to call them—look less menacing in person.

When she walked into that conference room, they had zeroed in on her like Siamese cats. It must be blowing their mind, she reckons. Staring at a darker, *way prettier* version of themselves reflected in her.

But their menace can't match Nancy's in that conference room. Tina watches her mother as if she's a stranger. Nancy launches onto her feet and dashes toward the young assistant wearing gloves, holding one of the oil paintings.

Once the twins realize what's going on, they're on their feet. Lars springs up as well and spreads his arms wide, stopping his boys from rushing toward Nancy and hurting her.

"No," Lars screams at the top of his lungs. "No." He pulls one of his sons back. The other breaks loose and Tina rushes for him. She grabs him by the jacket, stalling him with both hands, digging her heels in. He stops, spins toward Tina and shoves her into the wall. Their matching eyes lock, as if in slow motion, once he realizes what he's done. Tina hits the wall hard.

The other twin struggles for freedom from his father, pushing Lars down. The older man stumbles and hits the ground, letting out a sharp cry of pain.

It's already too late. Nancy is stabbing each canvas with a pen she has grabbed from the table. Tearing into the first one with all her might, then forcefully pulling more out of their gently wrapped crate. The assistant tries to stop her.

"Leave her alone," Lars cries, his hand gripping his chest as Mr. Melander helps him up. "Leave her alone." At his command, the assistant turns to the twins, yelling that they could be charged for assault if they touch Nancy. Defeated, they sit down once again, forced to watch Nancy's show.

"Let her be," Lars croaks, clutching his heart. He winces and whimpers while Mr. Melander props him up and leads him back to his chair. Frida watches Nancy in horror, a palm over her mouth, as the other woman destroys each painting one by one. Nancy is making a guttural sound, tears streaming down her face as she rips and rips while everyone waits with bated breath.

She reaches a particular painting. One with her arms over her head and light flooding in behind her. In it, she is gazing at the painter, *Lars*, through downcast, hooded eyes. Nancy is taking it in, breathing heavily, studying it. Analyzing every surface area spread with oils. Then she stabs both her eyes in the painting with the pen and drags it downwards, ripping her face.

Once Nancy is done destroying all eight oils, she pauses and collects her breath. She spins toward Frida, makes eye contact with the woman. Frida's hard shell seems to have broken. The woman is sobbing, her eyes glassy as she stares at Nancy. It seems rage against Lars is something the two women share.

Tina watches Nancy as she pulls the straps of her purse further up her shoulder. Once she struts past Lars, she mutters something to him in her language, one which Tobias and Tina hadn't bothered to learn. Uncle Leif had learned a handful of words for fun, and mostly to make Nancy smile on occasion. Tina has never wished more that she had learned Mandinka too. So she could be closer to her mother in this moment. So her mother feels less alone.

"Come, Tina," Nancy calls her without turning to look. "Let's go." She slams the door behind her.

"Wait," Lars calls out to Tina. "Wait. I have something for you." He reaches into the inner pocket of his jacket with his free hand, the other still firmly rooted on his heart, Tina notices. Can't anyone else see he's in pain? Or are they all too focused on their inheritance?

"Are you all right?" Tina asks him. "Should we call an ambulance?" It's only when she says this that the twins spin around to see their father doubling over while pulling out an envelope for Tina.

"Lasse? Lasse?" One of his estranged sons is back on his feet, rushing toward Lars.

"Tina, take," Lars pushes out the words. "Take." Then he falls back. Mr. Melander catches him before he hits the floor. Frida yelps and jumps to her feet as well, trying to pull him into an embrace.

"I'll call an ambulance." The lawyer's assistant is quickly on his phone while everyone else tries to stabilize Lars. Tina stands pinned in place until one of the twins turns to her.

"You're free to leave now." His tone is cold and harsh. "This is a family matter."

Tina purses her lips. She reaches for the envelope Lars dropped on the table for her, her eyes never leaving her half brother.

She finds her mother in the lobby, silently weeping. As if whatever had possessed her in the conference room has now released its grasp. Tina plants herself in the soft chair next to her mother and pulls her into an embrace. At first, Nancy hesitates out of pride. Then she softens into her daughter's hug as both women sit for a few more moments, arms wrapped around each other until the paramedics arrive.

Lars is unconscious and the paramedics get to work, stabilizing him and using a defibrillator to bring him back to them before rushing him off to the hospital.

Once home, Nancy retreats into her bedroom for the rest of the day. Tina hears her soft sobs through the door. A few hours later, she emerges, dressed for her work shift, and leaves. Inside her own room, Tina pulls out Lars's letter and rips it open. That beautiful cursive style. She'd been expecting some lengthy musing, more conversation, maybe yet another apology for disappearing from her life again.

Only a few sentences written out. Tina flips the letter in search of more. Nothing.

She turns back to Lars's note.

Kära Tina,
I knew Nancy would destroy them.
I am so grateful she did.
Love, Lars

FIFTY-ONE

TINA

She hears the update on the seven o'clock evening news when she emerges from her room later that day.

Acclaimed artist Lars "Lasse" Wikström had suffered a heart attack and mini stroke. He was admitted into Karolinska Hospital.

Tina isn't sure what to feel. She finds Tobias sprawled out on the sofa, watching the update. He quickly switches channels once Lars's face is projected onto the screen.

"Where were you today?" he asks nonchalantly before popping a potato chip in his mouth. "I tried calling both you and Mamma."

"Nowhere important," she says, settling on the couch next to him.

"*Hmmph*," Tobias grunts, turning back to the news broadcast. She observes his profile, studying his handsome outline munching on chips until he senses he's being watched and turns back to her.

"What?" he asks, brows furrowed, his face bunched up in suspicion.

"Nothing," Tina says. "I love you, that's all. I can't remember the last time I told you."

Tobias tries to read her face, his features twisted in confusion. "Like, never?"

She punches his bicep, then leans her head on his shoulder. He senses her need and wraps a large arm around her, pulling her closer to him. He kisses the top of her head.

"Are you okay?" he asks softly, lowering the volume on the TV.

"I think I'm ready," she whispers into his shoulder. His grip tightens. "I'm ready."

"To sing again?" he asks. She shakes her head against him. "Poetry?" She nods.

"Yes," Tina says. "I think I want to have my own show. Perform my entire album as a spoken-word set. Read those lyrics as poems instead."

"Are you sure?" Tobias adjusts to look in her eyes. "Can you even earn a living doing that?"

Tina sits with his words, thinking about the inheritance that Lars had promised them earlier that day. *Well*, the inheritance that Nancy destroyed.

"Lars put us in his will," she says. The TV goes mute. Tobias needs to properly hear her.

"What?" he asks sharply.

"Mamma and I were at his lawyer's office today," she confesses. "We didn't know they were going to be there."

"They?" Tobias is shifting his weight, repositioning himself. "What do you mean *they*?"

"The evil spawns. Their mother. Him," Tina says. She reaches for a potato chip from his bag. Tobias smacks it out of her hand.

"Start talking!" He gives her the look she knows so well.

"Fine." She digs into her pocket for a cigarette instead.

"Apparently Lars painted an entire series of Mamma. Unexhibited. Eight canvases of her in white-and-black polka dots. Valued at ten million kronor."

Tobias's eyebrows arch into his hairline. "Sorry, what?!" he asks.

"Yeah." Tina shrugs. "But Mamma destroyed them. Right there. She took a pen and just stab, stab, stabbed away." Tina mimics the gesture with her cigarette in hand.

Tobias starts to chuckle. A sound building deep within him before it surfaces, squinting his eyes and revealing that gap-toothed grin. It's contagious because Tina begins to giggle as well. Soon, both siblings are laughing uncontrollably, Tina repeating the stabbing motion with her cigarette, clutching her stomach from laughter.

"You should have seen her," Tina cackles. Tobias wipes tears from his eyes. "Stark raving mad. Like a crazy Black Chucky doll."

"And the evil carrots?" Tobias asks.

"First time in their lives they went diving after Black booty," Tina laughs. Tobias guffaws loudly, bouncing on the sofa, probably to keep from peeing himself.

"*Mammas kompis*," he snorts. *Mommy's friend.*

She watches his amusement morphing into something else as his shoulders start to shake. He's sobbing. Crying. Unraveling in her presence. Tina reaches out to run her palm over his back, soothing him. Consoling her older brother. The one who had stayed *oh* so strong for her all these years. Uncle Leif did what he could, but she knows why her brother has broken down.

Deep down, he must have missed their father's love the most.

*

"We're beyond thrilled to have you back on stage next year." The director at Kulturhuset shakes Tina's hand enthusiastically.

Once Tina decided how she wanted to tell her stories, she personally reached out to the director at the iconic cultural house, which also houses a library, theater and arts center. Within minutes of hearing her pitch her idea to perform her entire album, *Honey*, as on-stage poetry, the director had slotted her into the following year's spring programming.

"Thank you for staying true to yourself and your craft," the older woman, decked out in black, says to Tina, her bright eyes twinkling. "It takes bravery to make a stand."

Tina smiles as she takes the woman's hands. The creative outlet she has been yearning for—to write her own performance, tell her own stories, plan out her one-woman show—is officially hers.

"Once we announce next year's schedule, I guarantee you will sell out your show," the woman assures Tina over chanting coming from outside. Right in front of Kulturhuset, the square Sergels torg is packed once more. Protesters in support of the Arab Spring and uprising. They're shouting chants of allegiance.

"I think it's time to go now," Tina says, rising to her feet. She's wearing her favorite spaghetti-strapped goddess dress, the one she wore to her first poetry session with Kasha. The one Jonas loved stripping off her. She sighs, pushing the memory of him to the back of her mind once again.

Once she exits the building, she meets a crowd packed like

sardines in the square. People are waving flags of different countries—Tunisia, Libya, Afghanistan, Syria. White, Black, Brown standing shoulder to shoulder. Some linking arms in a show of solidarity.

Their voices aren't the only ones raised in protest. While the crowds fill the open-air basement, lined around its upper railings are counterprotesters. Mostly young white men wearing white shirts tucked into black trousers. They are screaming, throwing salutes, flicking their right hands up in signs of white power. The police presence is massive. Officers, hands tucked into their pockets, radio cables stringing down from their ears, line every corner.

A few activists recognize her as she begins to mill through the crowd.

"Tina? Tina!" they call out to her. "*Tack för ditt stöd!*" *Thank you for your support.* Simply by being present, with her relatively big profile, she has become part of the protest. Some launch themselves into her unprepared arms for hugs. Someone thrusts a megaphone into her hands.

"*Säg nåt! Säg nåt! Sjung för oss!*"
Say something! Say something! Sing for us!

Tina freezes, her fingers tightly wrapped around the megaphone. The chants continue. The opposition equally charged.

Say something!

Those words propel Tina forward. She can do it. She takes the stairs two by two, squeezing through people until she gets up high. Her eyes wash over the crowd, the flags, the sea of bodies, of colors, already saying something.

The first words that enter her mind are the lyrics from her song "RISE." She lifts the megaphone to her lips and begins humming. A low humming sound that begins to quiet the protests down. She riffs the sound, turning it from an R&B tone into a Middle Eastern vocal run. The crowd goes wild at her chanting.

They quiet down once Tina begins to speak the lyrics of "RISE," her eyes tightly shut.

> My fingers bleeding
> Soul pleading
> Sinking into steel bars
> Caged by your fear
> Dammed by your righteousness

Three minutes of silence as Tina recites her lyrics of caged souls, trying to break free.

Once Tina opens her eyes, she instantly receives her new label. *Activist*.

FIFTY-TWO

NANCY

Nancy finds Tina biting her fingernails as her daughter watches her face plastered over the news. No longer a social pariah, she is now being touted as a champion of democracy.

"What possessed you to do this, Tina?" Nancy asks, her voice filled with fear. She is looking at her daughter, a woman, no longer living in the shadow of her own life. Does hiding away rob you of your voice? Nancy isn't sure. She once had dreams too.

"Nothing possessed me, Mamma." Tina rolls her eyes. "I got swept up in the moment. Now my phone is ringing nonstop for interviews."

"Protests are dangerous places," Nancy reprimands her. "You could have gotten hurt or arrested. Remember, you're still a celebrity."

"Mamma, I thought you would be proud of me for standing up for something. For refusing to cower away and hide. Aren't you tired of hiding and living a small life?"

Nancy pins her daughter with a hard glare, her nostrils flaring, angry that Tina is picking at scabs from her own heart. "I didn't choose this life," Nancy says between clenched teeth. "I didn't choose this life," she repeats. "It chose me. All because I let a man disrupt me."

Nancy joins Tina on the sofa. She notices her daughter studying her, scanning her face, silently begging her for more.

"Everyone joked that I was going to be the next president of Gambia once I returned home." A smile creeps onto Nancy's lips. "I already had my first degree. I was working on my master's degree when I had Tobias. I had to drop everything and delay my dreams." Nancy twists her fingers as she considers her next words. "I never got back on track."

"Did you ever love him?" Tina asks, her voice soft. "Do you still?"

Nancy closes her eyes at her daughter's words.

I didn't want to fall for you. She remembers Lars murmuring those words to her. *I didn't want to. But I did and I don't know what to do.* She remembers him moving his thumb across her bottom lip. She hadn't wanted to fall for him either. But she did. In his cottage out in Vaxholm. On that stormy August night as he danced in the rain, she did.

"I don't love him," Nancy says, finally opening her eyes. "I don't. Maybe I cared for him in the past. I must have, enough to have two kids with him," she chuckles weakly. "But no, I don't," she says, trying to convince herself.

"What was your dream, Mamma?" Tina asks. "Was it to become president?"

Nancy presses her lips together and shakes her head. "My dream was much simpler than that," she says. She remembers her *baabaa*'s words: *Stay and continue your studies. Get your master's degree. Maybe a PhD too.* "I wanted to give the world a reason not to deny my brilliance. But I ended up in a cage of my own making."

Tina sits taller. "Don't say that," she protests. "Don't ever say that, Mamma. You can't keep blaming yourself for what your heart wanted in that moment. What is that Emily poem you keep quoting again about the heart wanting what it wants?"

Nancy can't repeat those words. Not right now. "I know."

"Tell me about Malik," Tina probes. Nancy tenses at the mention of his name. "Was he the man you loved? Lars didn't tell me much in his letters. Just that there was a man named Malik who he considered his competition."

Nancy crumbles when she hears those words. Lars had ripped Malik out of her arms because he could no longer take it. Not fully having her. He had confessed in detail in the letters he wrote. How and where he had planted the drugs. And how Malik had been quietly deported back to Gambia because the embassy didn't want their son tarnished this way. Malik had a diplomatic legacy to uphold.

Lars had thrown his own demands into the process. He had requested Malik cut all ties and not attempt to get in touch with Nancy. If Malik truly loved her as he said he did, he would spare Nancy the heartache of a scandal. In hindsight, she wished Malik hadn't been such a gentleman.

"What do you want to know about him, my dear?" Nancy asks.

"Who was he? What did he look like?" Tina asks. Nancy gives her a crooked smile before getting to her feet. "Wait, where are you going?"

Nancy shuffles off in the direction of her bedroom. A few minutes later, she comes back bearing a frame. A photo. Nancy hands it to Tina and settles back in her spot next to her.

Tina has never seen this photo before. She sees her mother wearing a bright-yellow gown with flowers in her hair. She's sitting next to two men. One white, the other Black. The Black man is strikingly handsome. Dark, luminous skin, bright white teeth, his chest cocked out in pride. Reminiscent of Darryl. And the white man?

"Olof Palme?" Tina stares at her mother in shock. "You and Malik had dinner with a prime minister?"

Nancy thinks about that fateful night when her water had broken at the news of his assassination and Tina had to be cut out of her belly to save both their lives.

"The Nobel banquet. Malik was the Gambian ambassador's son," Nancy explains, steering the conversation away from Olof. It's too painful to remember that night. "We met in university. Lars was our professor."

Tina stares at her, wide-eyed. "Mamma, you were dining with the king and queen too?"

"Go for your dreams, Tina," Nancy says, ignoring her inquisition. "Don't let a man obstruct you. I let a man stop me from becoming who I was meant to be." She pauses. "That was why I was so hard on Sebastian. I thought he was like the others. I was clearly wrong."

Tina mulls over her mother's semblance of an apology. Her Sebastian. She's counting the days. He's simmering, piping down, planning his return... *she hopes.* Because if he doesn't...

"But it's never too late to reclaim your life," Tina adds. "You know this, Mamma."

"When I saw you dancing like a prostitute for that rapper, when you were dating that video director, my heart broke," Nancy admits. "Like I was posing for Lars and his paintings all over again." Her voice cracks.

Tina rolls her eyes. "Video vixens aren't prostitutes, okay? And I said I was sorry."

"I cried for you, my dear. I prayed and cried. I asked myself why my daughter wasn't the star. Why she just wanted to be an opening act and a background body for this man. I blamed myself for not being closer to you to help guide you on the right path."

"Mamma, you can't have known which path I needed to go down. I was still figuring it all out myself," Tina says. "I needed to go to LA to find myself."

"It was all part of God's plan," Nancy adds. Tina nods her agreement.

"Do you want to see him again?" Tina asks. "Malik? I'm sure you've been googling him."

Nancy hasn't. She knows her heart could never take him smiling happily in a photo next to another woman. Knowing the kids they were meant to have together would have been had with someone else. Curiosity had itched within her over the years, but Nancy knows discipline. Digging up Malik and seeing him moving on with his own life would have made her hate Lars even more for what he stole from her. And hating Lars even more would have made her hate her daughter. She needed to protect her love for Tina. She needed to protect her child from her indifference.

They hear the door unlock. *Tobias.*

"I swear, Tina," he starts to say as he pads angrily into their living room. "Do you want to kill me before my time?" He sounds exasperated as he tosses two newspapers onto the sofa. *Expressen* and *Svenska Dagbladet.* "You're an activist now." He's not asking.

"Damn, you should be an actor," Tina spits back at him. "You're dramatic as fuck."

"Enough with the cursing in my house," Nancy says before turning to Tobias. "You should be proud of your sister. What she did took courage." She takes Tina in once more. "I am so proud of her. She has shown me what it means to stand in your power."

She notices Tina pressing her lips together in shock.

"Standing in her power?" Tobias challenges. "By always causing a scene on whatever stage she stands on?"

"Yes, *my dear,*" Tina says to him, mimicking Nancy. "You should try it sometime. Finally grow some balls and let the world know how you truly feel."

Tobias hisses at his sister before storming off to the kitchen in search of a snack.

Nancy chuckles. Her cell phone starts buzzing in her purse. She pulls her bag closer, fishes the phone out, flips it open. An unknown caller. Probably a telemarketer. She answers it anyway.

"*Det är Nancy,*" she says into the receiver. Silence on the other end for a few seconds until a woman's voice comes on. Low, silky, authoritarian.

"The doctor says he doesn't have much time left," the voice breathes into the phone.

"Why are you calling me?"

"Days, in fact. If you want to see him, tomorrow is your last chance," the voice says. "Then we're banning all visitors and keeping his last days for us. His family."

Nancy considers Frida's invitation as she grabs tightly onto the phone. A single tear starts to crawl down her cheek.

FIFTY-THREE

TINA

Tina sees her mother's disposition change toward whoever is calling. She quickly pads away in the direction of her bedroom, passing Tobias, who is leaving the kitchen with a bowl of baby carrots.

He crunches loudly, agitating her on purpose. "So, what possessed you? Your incense?"

"Grow up," she says to him. "Take a stand for something. Or are you just happy coasting through life being mediocre?"

Tobias stops munching. She knows she hit a nerve. "Mediocre?" he repeats.

"What turns you on, Tobbe? *Hmm?* What turns you on in life?" Tina asks.

"Besides beautiful Black women and curves for days?" He pops a carrot in his mouth, looking at her tersely. She holds his gaze at that confession. His dating history has suggested otherwise.

"Yes, Tobbe. Besides sticking your—"

"Ssssh, my ears," he says, mimicking Nancy's frequent reprimand. "*Not in my house.*"

"I'm serious, Tobbe." Her eyes turn hard on him. "It took me fumbling Eurovision and finding myself in LA to realize I want to live life on my own terms and create art in my own way. To use my voice so others feel seen too." She collects her breath. "A very expensive lesson."

His dark-brown eyes are thoughtful as he listens to her words.

"Do you stand for anything at all?" she says. "Do you even have dreams besides making coffee for people and pushing people out of clubs?"

"I am content, Tina," he finally says. "I am content. I am happy living my life without having to prove myself to anyone."

"So, you're living the privilege of mediocrity?" she says.

"I am living the privilege of a free man," he counters. "I am living free. Not bound by rules. Not having to prove my worth to anyone. Not looking for validation in anyone else's gaze." He pauses in his typical dramatic way. "You should try that sometime, Tina. It is liberating. So fucking liberating."

The room falls into dense silence. "You hated your skin for years," Tina says softly. She notices something flash across his eyes. She can't decipher it.

"I did," he confesses. "I did. Because Lars didn't want me. He never came looking for us. So, I assumed he didn't want us. Didn't want our skin," he confesses. "That was before Mamma told us he was dead. But then, Tina, I grew up. I realized I never needed him or his money, and never will. True love only comes from within. Unconditional love comes from deep down inside you. When you stare at yourself in the mirror. When those eyes are all you have peering back at you, you have no choice but to love them because no one else will, the way you want them to."

Tears quickly well up in her eyes. "Damn, Tobbe." She

wipes her cheeks. "Who knew you're such a teddy bear behind all that brawn."

He flexes a bicep, smiles at her, and pops another carrot into his mouth. He kisses his bicep and its galaxy of freckles.

"*Mwaah*," he emphasizes his kisses. "I love you." He smooches it again while chewing. "Damn, I love you so much. You're making me horny," he says to his bicep. "You might need to excuse us, Tee."

"You're disgusting." She rolls her eyes. He chuckles and keeps munching carrots.

The doorbell rings. Tobias glances down at his watch before padding over to the door.

"Finally," he mutters as he reaches it. *Finally?!* Tina wonders. Who is Tobias inviting over at close to ten p.m. at night?

He opens it and gives the visitor a half hug. And that's when she sees him. *Seb*.

He's in his AIK black training jersey with yellow stripes over matching track pants. His butter-blond hair is now long enough to be pulled back into a heavy bun. Stubble a couple days old covers his chin. He looks tired. Tina feels blood color her cheeks. She's not sure if it's from anger, because Tobias is not respecting her boundaries, or from finally seeing Seb again after their terse standoff.

"*Hej*, Tina," he says softly once he kicks off his sneakers and steps into their place in socks.

She feels her skin heating up in excitement. She feigns nonchalance instead. "Don't you have someplace to be? Some ass to grab in Stureplan?" she says before turning away from him and back to the TV. She hears him chuckle.

"Jealousy looks so sexy on you," he says, inching closer to where she sits. His tone is different, as if he hadn't stormed off at their last meeting. Tina studies this new version of Seb.

"Why are you here?" she asks, lowering her voice to keep it from shaking. She reads the reason clearly in his aquarium eyes. "I thought you hated me?"

"Want a beer?" Tobias offers. He heads off into the kitchen without waiting for Seb's response.

Seb takes a seat next to her. She inches away from him.

"I saw you on TV today," he says under his breath. "Activist." He draws out the word.

She rolls her eyes. "Did I embarrass you? Were you ashamed of me?"

His eyes lock on hers. He moves closer. She holds her breath. "I was so proud of you, *älskling*," he says. "So proud of you. I wished I was standing right next to you. Where I should have been all along. From the start. Showing the world just how proud I was and am of you." He's close enough for her to feel his words on her face. Her skin. "You've finally grown up."

He lifts a hand to her left cheek, cups it, moves in closer.

"Did you miss me?" he whispers against her lips. "Did you miss me too?" He rests his forehead on hers. She nods against him, her hand moving up to cover his own. "Did you suffer?" His tone grows shaky. "Have you suffered like I have?" His voice, breaking.

She nods once more against him.

"I'm so sorry for letting you go," Seb whispers before pulling her into a soft kiss.

"I'm so sorry for letting you suffer." She shakes her head against him. "I had to go, Seb. I needed to grow. You had to grow too."

He looks at her and bobs his head. "Yeah, I did," he agrees.

"While squeezing bombshells in between?" She smiles in jest.

"I thought I'd lost you forever," he whispers. "To them. Darryl Walker. Jonas."

"Hmmm," she murmurs, leaning in for another kiss. "Jealousy looks so sexy on you."

Seb grabs her. Kisses her fervently. Hungrily taking control. He sure has grown, Tina thinks. He's handling her with much more experience than his skittish-kitten disposition allowed for in the past. The Seb in her arms clearly knows what to do with a woman.

"Will you take a walk with me, Tina?" he asks, his voice is shaky now. Tobias, on his unusually long quest in search of beer, is entirely forgotten.

The "walk" is a taxi ride back to Seb's apartment on Kungsholmen. The driver sits in discomfort as Tina tries and fails to contain her moans, while Seb pins her with his eyes to the backseat, his fingers wreaking havoc under her skirt, his hair loose and wild from its bun.

She pulls his head down for a kiss, her palms gripping him tightly as the taxi shuttles them north along E4 from Norsborg.

"Don't quit loving me," she gasps against his lips, his

fingers between her thighs. "Don't you ever stop loving me, Seb."

He peels one of her palms off his cheek. "My heart is here." He kisses it. "Right here."

His breathing is labored against her lips. "The only way I'll ever stop loving you is if you squeeze my heart and stop it beating yourself."

FIFTY-FOUR

TINA

Five a.m.

Seb's alarm goes off. Tina stirs and reaches across his side of the bed for him. Still warm. He's probably getting ready for practice. The national team will be playing a friendly match against Belgium later that evening at Friends Arena.

Normally Seb would be a bag of nerves before an important game, but by the time they got back to his apartment past eleven p.m. last night, adrenaline had kicked in. He couldn't get enough of her. As if he wanted to catch up on four years of missed sex in a single night.

They went at it on every available surface area in his spacious open-plan apartment. First against the wall by his front door. On the dining table. Lying on his sofa. Flat on the rug in front of his TV. And finishing off in his bedroom where they grunted so loudly a neighbor banged furiously on their connecting wall. They giggled, then cuddled for the rest of the few hours left before his five a.m. wake-up call.

Tina hears buzzing coming from his bathroom. She gets out of bed and goes in search of him. She finds a trail of thick wheat-colored locks on the cold tiles. He's shaved it all off and is now sporting a crew cut. The way she likes. Her *Snygg Sebbe.*

A white towel rides low on his hip. He's freshly showered, the muscles in his toned back working. He is shaving his stubble when he locks eyes with her through the mirror. His gaze travels down her naked reflection and back to her eyes.

Seb misses practice.

He gets benched by his new coach Hamrén for missing team training that morning. Seb had no legitimate reason to give him beyond a gleeful "*fucking my girlfriend like a rabbit.*" He had said those exact words to his coach, he later tells Tina. This new Seb doesn't seem to give a damn what anyone else thinks, even when he's placed on the bench. They've both grown, she thinks.

That evening, the stadium is a sea of yellow jerseys and chanting fans screaming, "*Heja Sverige! Heja Sverige!*" Tina is sitting in the VIP section reserved for family and close friends of the players, hiding behind sunglasses.

The crowd quiets for the national anthem. The boys are projected across the screen, their hands behind their backs, as they sing along to the lyrics. His new look is on show and the crowd roars with cheers for him, clearly loving clean-shaven Seb. Once the anthem is over and applause fills the stadium again, one of the sportscasters gets on the microphone to talk about Seb and his crew cut.

He is projected onto the screen as he stretches his calves with the team. The crowd goes wild, chanting, "*Heja Snygg Sebbe! Heja Snygg Sebbe!*" He waves, his face red. Tina clasps her hands together and smiles into them, her heart swelling with pride.

Barely ten minutes into the friendly match, the worst happens. Their star player Zlatan is injured. The Belgians have been out for blood, and one of the opposing team's players is so enthusiastic on the field, he inadvertently takes the star out with a hard kick. He immediately gets red carded for the foul.

Two more Swedish players are felled by fouls from the opposition and are carried off the field. The energy in the arena shifts from friendly to pure competition. Coach Hamrén warms up his bench. Seb springs to his feet and starts lightly jogging parallel to the field to get his blood pumping. Tina feels the energy he's emitting as he twists and hops. Life has seeped back into her Seb. That need for validation, always in his eyes, is slipping away.

The substitutes are sent in and Seb rushes like a ferret on drugs onto the field, energy clearly coursing through him. The game suddenly picks up tempo. As a midfielder, he's all over the pitch, running to assist, pulling the opposition with him, tiring them out on an unstoppable adrenaline rush. A high from their reconnection. From hours of sex. From finding each other again. She knows him, can read him like the back of her hand. That Seb racing around like a maniac on the field is one who has found his stride in life.

Twenty minutes before the end of the game, still at *noll noll*, Seb scores the goal of his life. He follows the ball backward as it sails over toward him. It's a cross pass which he intercepts from Belgium with a bicycle kick. It hits its target. The back of the net. The entire stadium goes wild and begins chanting *"Heja Snygg Sebbe! Heja Snygg Sebbe!"* once more. Even the broadcasters can't hide their excitement, counting this goal as one for the history books of Swedish football. The new revved-up tempo works to

Sweden's advantage. Seb makes two more beautiful assists, finding and passing to his strikers, who finish the goals.

Once the referee blows his whistle to end the game, Seb instantly becomes a star. His face is projected onto the screens, his clear eyes near transparent, filled with happy tears. Seb jumps the fence into the VIP section. He grabs Tina, pulls her up into a crushing kiss, which is once again projected for all to see.

"I'm yours. Always," she whispers against his lips. Seb beams at her with pride.

One of the broadcasters calls it. Sebastian Ljungberg had to be the man of the match with that showing. No one else touched him that evening. "What an impressive feat," the sportscaster announces as the crowd watches Seb passionately kiss Tina on screen as if they're locked in the privacy of their bedroom, in a bubble of their own, and not in front of thousands of screaming fans.

"And to think he was benched because he missed practice this morning," the announcer adds. "For no reason at all."

FIFTY-FIVE

NANCY

Nancy watches the other woman rise to her feet upon her approach, her puffy face evidence of tears. She was sitting on a wooden chair outside Lars's hospital room, waiting for Nancy.

Nancy wonders why Frida called her—the source of her pain—to be by his bedside too. Perhaps it was the reaction Frida had witnessed in that lawyer's office, the ferocity with which Nancy had torn those paintings apart in her presence, that had made Frida call.

"Nancy," Frida greets her. Nancy nods, pulling her purse closer to her. "He doesn't know you're here. The boys don't either." Nancy bobs her head once more. "I couldn't do it. I couldn't let him go without seeing you." She pauses, collecting herself. "You can never know the pain of looking into your husband's eyes for decades, knowing they warm for someone else and chill for you."

Nancy takes a deep breath at Frida's words. *Oh,* she understands quite well. Having your heart beating for someone who isn't yours.

"Thank you for letting me come," Nancy says weakly.

Frida isn't done. She wants to offload. So, Nancy listens. That is all she can do. Listen to a pain that mirrors hers.

Both women loved a selfish man, not fully accessible to either of them, because he wanted to control love.

"The first child, I could live with." Frida's tone, hard. She fishes for a handkerchief. Dabs her nose. "A mistake. Swept up in a moment of lust. Confused," she says. "Then I found the key." She blows her nose. Her handkerchief takes some light-colored foundation with it. "I didn't want to believe it. I didn't want to believe he was capable of it. Of choosing to create a second family," she says bitterly. "It's one thing to look at your wife with dead eyes. It's another to despise her so much that you have not one, but two children with your lover." She sniffs again. "Why did he hate me so much? What did I do to deserve his wrath?"

Nancy lets out a breath. "It wasn't you he hated," she reassures Frida, her voice barely a whisper. "It was his parents he despised."

Frida locks eyes with her. "I knew about Vaxholm," she says. "I knew about his cottage. *His happy place.* Where he would go wear another skin and pretend he was someone else." She studies Nancy. "Is that where it happened?"

"What are you asking me, Frida?"

"Is that where you fell in love with him too?" Frida asks. "I saw it in that conference room. I saw it clearly. When you tore all his paintings of you, I saw your love for my husband."

"He is the father of my children too," Nancy starts. "I must have had some feelings for him at some point."

"Aren't you tired of lying to yourself?" Frida says. "I lied to myself for over twenty years. I know he hurt you too. He lied to us both. Did you ever know about me?"

Nancy looks at Frida for several seconds, trying to work

out the right answer. She shakes her head, deciding on the truth. "He told me he had been divorced for years when we first met," Nancy admits. "That he was divorced and childless."

Frida gasps, her hands over her mouth. As a mother, Nancy knows how this must feel. The divorce lie she could take, but lying about his children, denying her sons ever existed? It's probably more than Frida can bear at that moment.

"Our twins," Frida cries. "He said he didn't have our boys?"

"You must understand," Nancy says. "He probably saw who he had become in those little boys. They are carbon copies of their father. Maybe he thinks his actions pushed those boys to become who they are today... by not fully loving their mother."

Nancy doesn't know why Lars did what he did, but as one mother to another, she knows Frida needs to hear this. That he loves his children. Her children.

"You must have known he was married when you started living with his immoral brother," Frida says.

"Don't you ever say a word against Leif." Nancy's tone is brash, angry. "Don't ever mention his name. He saved your husband's reputation and your dignity. He was the only true father my own children have ever known."

She sees Frida reflecting on her words. Nancy goes on. "I had Tina because Lars lied again. He came crawling back, saying he had finally divorced you. That he wanted to build his new life with me, with us." Nancy's voice breaks as she starts to sob. "And I took him back. Like a fool, I took him back."

"Because you loved him," Frida says. Nancy presses her lips together tightly, angry at Frida for provoking her once more. "You still love him. I can see it."

"I hate him," Nancy mutters through her tears.

"No, you don't," Frida says softly, her own tears slowing. "You hate him because he cheated you out of the life you thought you would have together. I understand that now. I too feel cheated out of a life with him. Because I still love him too."

Nancy wipes her tears, pulling herself together, squaring her shoulders.

"Why did you call me here, Frida?" Nancy asks. "I don't need to see him."

"You need to talk to him," Frida says.

"I said all I wanted to say to him in that conference room. At the lawyer's office. I don't want his money or yours. I don't want anything from your family. I wish my children didn't have his name, but Leif signed on their birth certificates. He was giving them a fighting chance in this country as *Wikströms*," Nancy says. "I wish I hadn't met…"

"You have so much more to say to Lars," Frida says. "Now is your chance. Please take it"—she glances down at her glittering wristwatch—"before my sons arrive to see their father."

Then Frida ducks her head toward the door to his room. It's quiet, save for the beeping of the heart monitor; warm and filled with bouquets of flowers. Lars is peering out the window, watching a few small yellow birds, warblers maybe, playing on his windowsill.

He turns when he hears the door creak open. His eyes widen in disbelief.

Nancy quietly shuts the door behind her. His amber glare reels her in as she slowly walks over to his bed.

"Nancy?" He draws out her name as if looking at a ghost. "Nancy."

"*Hej*," she says softly once she's by his side. She pulls a chair closer and sits next to him. He banks his head to the left, peering at her as he lays his head sideways on his bed. He's unblinking. She sees a tear form in his right eye. It travels across his nose and hits the sheets as he takes her in.

"*Nna kanuntee*," he whispers to her. *My love.*

Nancy doesn't respond to that endearment. She studies the tears now slowly running across his nose, pooling on his sheets.

Lars continues, "I'm so glad you came." He reaches out a hand toward her. She hesitates before slipping her fingers into his.

Once she feels his touch, she's transported back to Gamla stan. Graduation night. She had been staring after Yaya and Benke as they made their way to the *tunnelbana* to take the train home. Yaya and Benke, who have both now retired and are living a quiet life in the countryside. She had turned to see Lars drinking her in, the late-summer sun bouncing off his eyes, making them glow. Lars had reached out a hand to her. She had hesitated before slipping her fingers into his warm palm. He had grasped her hand tightly back then, his possession.

The same way he does now, though his grip is weaker.

Lars pulls her hand toward his lips. He presses a kiss to the back of it, their fingers interlocked.

"The heart wants what it wants, or else it does not care," he whispers, then he winces in pain, his brows knitting together. He tenses beneath her touch. "Yours was the love that was never mine to steal."

Nancy lets out a groan at those words, but she contains her tears. She will not cry for him. He doesn't deserve it. The monitor beats faster. Nothing concerning, but she sees him beginning to writhe in discomfort, his hand still clasping tightly onto hers.

Nancy knows that look from her years of working in service to others. She has held on tightly to the elderly, the sick, as they took their last breaths before paramedics arrived. Visiting their homes, taking care of them, in the footsteps of Yaya. Many of them dying alone before she could get to their side. *Just like Mr. Torbjörn.*

Lars's breathing is labored, his eyes widening as he peers at her, his grip tightening.

"Kiss me, Nancy," he whispers, his voice hoarse. "Kiss me, my love. Please. *Njusoo.*"

She fights it. Fights every emotion that transports her back. Lying in front of his fireplace in Vaxholm, asking her to tell him what she wanted. He had whispered those words against her cheek. *Tell me what you want, Nancy.* She had gripped his head, pushing him down her body.

She knew what she wanted then. She knows what she wants now. She wants Lars Wikström to finally leave her in peace.

Nancy watches his honey eyes dim as his pupils grow

wider, darker. Dilated from pain. The same way they dilated whenever he made love to her. The same way they took her in for the first time in his class. A dying sun. They now lock on her, tear-filled, as she feels his fingers loosen their grasp, weaken in her palm.

The monitor starts to beep rapidly. She hears rushing from outside the room.

"*Njusoo.*" His last word delivered on his last breath, his eyes still open, pupils large, looking at Nancy, a final tear crawling across his nose, his mouth slightly open.

The monitor flatlines.

She never gave him what he wanted. That final kiss to let him know she loved him too. Nancy holds her breath, her heart racing as she peers into his eyes still looking through her. Extinguished.

Never hurt me like that again.

His eyes had glittered as they gently bobbed in the lake.

Never.

As the door bursts open with nurses and Frida hot on their heels, Nancy leans low and plants her lips tenderly against Lars's lifeless ones. She whispers two words back against his mouth before gently stroking his bottom lip with her thumb, sniffing back tears.

"*Nna kanuntee.*"

My love.

EPILOGUE

2016

TINA

When Nancy informed Tina of Lars's passing, and that she had been the last person to see him alive, Tina's tears had caught her by surprise.

She hadn't expected to be shaken by his death. Or maybe they were tears of release, of relief that she no longer had to fully understand why he did what he did. Maybe they were tears for all the letters she'll never receive from him now. Or simply tears of denial that she'd finally grown a bond and connection with her father.

Her *pappa*.

When Nancy told her the news, her tone had been hard, composed. Not indifferent, but dry. Like her feelings for Lars had finally emptied out and there was nothing else to draw out of them. Afterwards, Nancy mentioned she was going to pay her Uncle Leif a visit. To share his brother's passing with him at his own grave.

It's been four years since Lars passed. The news had been acknowledged by the Swedish art world. Experts and panelists were called in to dissect the importance of his body of work on radio and TV.

Frida had extended an invitation to Nancy, Tobias and Tina to attend the funeral. Nancy had declined on their behalf. It was a family affair which needed to be handled privately, with reverence and respect to Frida's station as his legal wife, she had said. Instead, Nancy, Tobias and Tina had taken pink roses over to Uncle Leif's grave and paid him a visit. Their true father.

It seems Lars's passing was what Nancy had needed to fully break free from the shadows. She is more vocal now. Following Tina to her events, cheering her on, always reminding her how proud she is of her baby. Since reciting her song-turned-poem at the square, Sergels torg, Tina has come back with an unshakable, untouchable confidence; despite the occasional hate mail from keyboard warriors, threatening murder, rape, and all sorts of macabre things. Sweden is taking in a record number of refugees, mostly from the Middle East. An aftermath of the Arab Spring that led to civil wars in several countries across the region. The once "kumbaya" sentiment that had them locking arms in the square is slowly beginning to thin out as the country begins to grapple with the enormity of the situation on its hands.

She founded the Afro Swedish Union, the ASU, for people who consider themselves such. Members might have one parent of African descent, be born in Sweden to African parents, become naturalized while having African roots, or be true allies who feel African in their souls despite their skin color.

Months after their public display, Tina moved in with Seb—much to the dismay of his banging neighbor. Now, she's sitting at Seb's dining table, sorting through stacks of fan mail and the few bills in there. "Of course they have,"

Tina scoffs under her breath as she reads the cease-and-desist letter that arrived at her and Seb's apartment that morning. The Wikström twins, it says, have promptly reported her barely three-month-old organization as a terrorist and hate group.

The brothers aren't having it. They claim her organization discriminates against ethnic white Swedes because the government doesn't differentiate by color and doesn't gather statistics on ethnicity.

"Tina," Seb calls from the dining room.

"What? I'm busy," she yells back at him.

"Tina, come." His voice is heavy. "You have to see this."

She pushes up from the table, exasperated, and pads over to him in the living room.

Jonas's handsome face is on SVT.

Breaking news.

Drug overdose.

Dead.

The music industry rocked by the news.

He had been found by his cleaners in the morning sprawled on his bedroom floor. She remembers the night she found him shivering on that same floor.

Oh, Jonas.

Tina covers her mouth with a palm as tears rush into her eyes. Seb is quickly on his feet, pulling her into a hug, kissing her forehead, rubbing a soothing hand over her back.

"Join us at nine p.m. tonight for a special program reflecting on the life of an incredibly talented music director and artist, gone too soon," the news anchor finishes before switching topics.

They'll finally recognize me when I'm dead.

Jonas's words ring in her ears. He had laughed before taking a sip of his coffee.

NANCY

Madame President.

Nancy chuckles into her cup of rooibos tea as she watches CNN. *More like Mr. President.* A major upset in the Gambian elections is underway.

Malik Barrow has been voted in as the next president of Gambia.

Malik.

His inauguration invitation had reached her through the Gambian Embassy. His first letter had come in 2011, the second he caught wind Lars had finally passed. Of course he had missed her, Malik said. He had loved her too much to break her heart. Of course he hadn't taken any drugs. He had always maintained his innocence. He knew he had been framed by someone. Nancy had finally told him who.

"You will love Binta," Malik had gone on to say in one of his letters. "She was the one who convinced me to reconnect with you. Our love is that strong."

Of course, he was happily married to a Senegalese woman named Binta with three beautiful children. A strong African woman, he had written.

She remembers Tobias bursting into her apartment a few months ago. She had invited her children to dinner, including Sebastian. Seb is now getting used to her spices. No longer fanning himself and reaching for water after every bite of her *dahar* sauce.

"I think I met someone," Tobias had said, his eyes shining, pulling off his aviator jacket. His disposition was one Nancy hadn't seen before. This *someone* must be special.

"Really? What's her name?" she had casually asked while serving out chunks of lamb.

"Kemi." Tobias beamed, taking his seat, breathing heavily.

"Kemi?" Nancy repeated. "African? A Black woman?"

"Nigerian. She's breathtaking," he added while reaching for rice. "When she walks into a room." He paused for dramatic effect. "*My God.*"

Nancy had started to cackle. She kept laughing and laughing until tears had streamed down her face. Her son hadn't been sure if it was from joy or plain amusement.

"You've finally found a strong African woman like your mother," Nancy had said, wiping tears off her cheek.

"Mamma," Tina had rolled her eyes, "stop it."

Now her doorbell buzzes. Nancy sets her mug of tea down and opens the door. She freezes.

"Frida?"

The other woman is makeup-free, wearing a navy-blue and margarine-yellow batik scarf around her neck.

"*Hej,*" Frida greets her, smoothing her hair nervously. "I brought us some cardamom buns." She lifts a brown paper bag, unsure.

"Why are you here?" Nancy's voice turns stern.

"There's something I've been meaning to say to you for over twenty years." Nancy leans against her door, the woman still out in the hallway. Frida continues, "That night I came over to your apartment. That night." She stops, exhales audibly. "That night I said all those harsh words to you... I have come to ask for forgiveness."

Nancy's eyebrows crumble in confusion. *What?*

"I am so sorry, Nancy. You didn't deserve any of that." Frida is in tears, a fragile hand covering her mouth. "No woman deserves such disrespect. Especially from another woman who should have understood that he was the one who deceived us both."

Nancy is stunned, then she quietly mutters "I serve a God of miracles" under her breath, before taking the bag and opening her door wider for the woman to step in.

This, she must hear.

RESOURCES

Here are some supportive resources for the serious themes discussed in this book.

You're never alone and always have someone to reach out to through these resources.

Substance abuse – samhsa.gov
Mental health – mentalhealthfirstaid.org
Affair recovery – affairrecovery.com

AUTHOR'S NOTE

"The rights of democracy are not reserved for a select group within society, they are the rights of all the people."
Olof Palme, former prime minister of Sweden

To say writing this book was simply a joy is a gross understatement.

I absolutely loved writing this book. Creating these characters who feel so real to me and navigating their personal struggles with identity, belonging and self-actualization with them was incredibly humbling. They lived in my dreams and every waking moment.

As my first foray into historical fiction, I truly enjoyed delving into major world events and crafting my narrative against these timelines. I anchored Tina's story during the revered Eurovision Song Contest in Greece and the FIFA World Cup in Germany, so I could tease all those activities and weave them organically throughout the story. I also drew on the Arab Spring where many people found and used their voices, prompting Tina to find hers too.

For Nancy, it was all about politics. From the attempted coup in Gambia to dining at the Nobel dinner with former Swedish prime minister Olof Palme. There was a

Gambian consulate, not embassy, during this time frame, but I fictionalized it into an embassy with a prominent ambassador so I could tie him back to the events of the civil war and have him attend the royal wedding in England.

Researching Mandinka phrases through various publications as well as fact-checking them with experts (please see acknowledgments) added more authenticity to the relationship between Nancy and Lars.

From watching video clips of Stockholm between 1970 and 1979 to researching what people wore, how they decorated their homes, and what devices and brands were present during the various decades reflected in this work, writing this book was a deeply profound journey of humility, learning, gratitude and understanding.

For this, I am extremely grateful I get to do what I love... Write stories which make people feel seen, heard and acknowledged.

ACKNOWLEDGMENTS

First and foremost, all thanks to God for His steadfastness and unceasing love. I am truly a living testament of divine grace.

To my incredible sisters Dami, Kay and Tope, my parents Remi and Femi, and my extended family for your unconditional love and support. For holding me during the dark times and celebrating me in the light. I love you beyond words and I am grateful we get to be family in this lifetime.

To my dear friends Lyota Swainson and Pär Johansson, thank you for always holding space for me. You are a grounding source of encouragement here in Sweden.

To all my friends—old and new—especially Nyamusi Nyamok, Gerry Bjällerstedt, Angela Harris, Germaine Thomas, Anja Mutic, Andrea Pippins, Emily Joof, Yomi Abiola, Kristin Lohse, Pamela MacNaughtan, Leigh Shulman, Steph Darvill and Meryem Aichi. To my sisterhood from our #dothewritethingretreat—Rafaela Stålbalk Klose, Kimberly Golden Malmgren, Hana Al-Khamri, Juliet Atto, Palmira Koukkari Mbenga and Aurelia Dey. To my sisterhood of 6Cs, Rasheka Scott, Katja Presnal and Candice Brathwaite. To the incredible Mathapelo Mzizi, Isatou Aysha Jones, Gertrude Chilufya Westrin, Esther Babasasa and Chisom Udeze for being inspirational champions of our collective voices here in the Nordics—thank you all for your grace and friendship!

To dear Amy Egerbladh (@glammmbyamy), Sweden's best makeup artist for all skin tones—so proud to call you friend. Thank you for all the elevated and pure conversations we have about standing in your power and reclaiming your peace, while you make me shine on the outside.

To my incredible agent Jessica Craig, editors Asanté Simons, Kimberley Atkins, Sophie Whitehead and Tessa James, and my entire publishing family at both William Morrow and Head of Zeus, thank you for yet another beautiful journey together.

To Tom Söderlund for pushing me through writer's block to meet my deadline, and to Otis the Sphynx (@otistheesphynx), the real-life inspiration behind Leo the Sphynx.

To Ida Sonko, Emily Joof, William John Joof and Alpha O Jallow for helping me verify and check all my Mandinka phrases in the book, and to my wonderful beta readers for additional cultural references, Yassin Sallah Sowe and Mariama Jobe, I am grateful for every single one of you.

And most importantly, my two beautiful kids. All I do, I do for you so you can thrive and fully self-actualize in this crazy world of ours. No one gets to define who you are and who you should be. I love you with every fiber of my being.

Thank you for my life's purpose. My gratitude knows no bounds.

READING GROUP QUESTIONS

1. In the opening scenes of the book, we meet Tina. What do you think of her – physically, mentally and emotionally?
2. In the heated restaurant scene, where Tina and Tobias confront their mother for lying, what was the most powerful moment and/or takeaway for you?
3. What do you think of Malik as a character, and his relationship with Nancy?
4. Why do you think Nancy warmed up to Lars? What did she find appealing in him?
5. We see Tina fumbling and making questionable decisions throughout. Do you think she should have taken the gamble on stage at Eurovision? What does this say about Tina as a person in her early twenties?
6. Do you think Lars is a narcissist? What behaviors does he display that might lead you to this belief?
7. Throughout the book, the author references Nancy's indifference toward her daughter Tina. Why do you think Nancy acts this way?
8. What do you think of Tina's relationship with Jonas Jonsson? What do you think the author was trying to convey by pairing Swedes of similar mixed heritage?

9. Even after all he did to Nancy, Lars wouldn't divorce his wife to be with Nancy. What do you think the author was trying to convey through Lars's character and his decision?

10. What do you think about the relationship between Tina and Sebastian? Is it a healthy pairing for both? Why?

11. Tobias plays a supporting role in this book and has historically dated only white women. When he makes the comment about wanting Black women during an argument with Tina, what point do you think the author is trying to make? Is there something about Tobias which deters the kind of woman he seeks?

12. What do you think about Leif as a character, and his relationship with both Nancy and his brother?

13. What do you think of the final scene between Nancy and Frida?

14. Who are your favorite characters in the book and why?

15. Overall, what were some of your favorite moments in the book?

ABOUT THE AUTHOR

One of *Condé Nast Traveler*'s "Most Powerful Women in Travel," Lọlá Ákínmádé is an NAACP-nominated international bestselling author, keynote speaker and award-winning travel photographer. Her work has appeared in *National Geographic*, BBC, CNN, the *Guardian*, the *Sunday Times*, the *New York Times*, and *Lonely Planet*, among others. She is the author of award-winning non-fiction book *Due North*, international bestselling *LAGOM: the Swedish Secret of Living Well*, and highly acclaimed novels *In Every Mirror She's Black* and *Everything Is Not Enough*. Her honours include: Hasselblad Heroine, Travel Photographer of the Year Bill Muster Award, Newsweek Future of Travel Storytelling and MIPAD 100 (Most Influential People of African Descent).